EXPECTING MIRACLES

Expecting Miracles

by
Linda U. Howard

G. P. Putnam's Sons
New York

The author wishes to express appreciation for permission to quote from "My Blue Heaven," words by George Whiting, music by Walter Donaldson. Copyright © 1925, 1927, renewed 1953, 1955, Leo Feist, Inc. All rights reserved. Reprinted by permission

Library of Congress Cataloging in Publication Data

Howard, Linda.
  Expecting miracles.

  I. Title.
PZ4.H8523Ex   [PS3558.08822]   813'.54   79-28571
ISBN 0-399-12496-9

PRINTED IN THE UNITED STATES OF AMERICA

To Pearle and Duke, the loving grandparents.
To Owen, the noted obstetrician.
And, most of all, to Tucker, the proud papa.
This book is affectionately dedicated.

Contents

1 Seeds

"Mommy, where do babies come from?"

"Well, God puts a seed in the mother's belly button and it grows inside her stomach and becomes a baby."

Interesting story. But was it true? Nelly checked her news sources even then. She asked her grandmother.

"Nana, where do babies come from?"

"God puts a seed in your navel and it grows inside your stomach and becomes a baby."

It must be true then. Nelly was a little confused about the details. Her mother said belly button and her grandmother said navel. In a child's way of imposing logic on illogic, she pictured navel oranges in her mind. Navel oranges and mothers' stomachs became synonymous. The fact that this didn't make sense didn't bother her in the slightest. In those days, at that age, nothing made complete sense. She checked out six or seven navel oranges from the fruit basket, looking for signs of pregnancy. Each navel orange had a belly button, but no baby.

Her grandmother was old and undoubtedly not clear on the specifics. She went back to the belly-button version offered by her mother. Seeds in belly buttons. First Nelly tried a grapefruit seed. It seemed the most likely. It was small and white and slightly rounded in the middle. It fit perfectly in her oblong-shaped belly button. For over a week during her nap time, she lay with the grapefruit seed in her navel. Nothing happened. Next she tried a watermelon seed. Finally a prune pit. Nothing grew except the number of seeds in and under her bed.

There was another news break the summer she was four. Billy Thomas from next door gave her this totally unsubstantiated but highly quotable version: The man puts his wee-wee into the lady's pee-pee and then tinkles. The tinkle gets hard inside the lady's stomach, swells up, and turns into a baby which comes out two years later. Out of where? Billy didn't know.

Nelly found this last a far more intriguing theory than the seed story. "Let's try it," Nelly said. But Billy, with all his pulling and stretching, couldn't even get his wee-wee close to Nelly, let alone in.

Nelly's fact gathering on the whole subject coincidentally came at about the same time her own mother's stomach began to assume magnificent proportions. Nelly never put her mother's wonderful, magical mound and the coming of a baby together until later. They say children have a way of knowing. She had no way of knowing that her mother's smooth beach-ball stomach would soon become her sister Sarah.

It was, therefore, quite a shock one day when she gave her mother a friendly, inquisitive punch in the stomach.

"Stop that, you'll hurt the baby," her mother screamed.

Nelly gasped, taking a giant step backward.

"What baby?"

"The baby. In my stomach."

Nelly turned white. There was a baby in there! A live baby, underneath her mother's red-flowered smock. How could it breathe? How could it see? How could it eat? Why couldn't she hear it crying?

"Why don't you let him out?" she asked, feeling alarmed and slightly queasy.

"Because it's not time yet."

Not time yet? How long could a kid survive in there? What was it, some sort of weird punishment? No, it couldn't be. There was no baby there. Her mother was kidding. It was another joke. Like the belly-button hoax. But her mother never kidded. And good as her word, she disappeared one day carrying her beautiful stomach far out in front of her and came back a week later with a red, wrinkled, skinned-rat-looking creature whom they called Sarah. Nelly would stare at baby Sarah for hours and think how amazing it was—all those soft-curled toes and eensy-teensy fingernails and that mewing little mouth, that whole wonderful thing, all from one small grapefruit seed.

Thirty-one years later, Nelly was finding that the where-do-babies-come-from question was considerably more complicated than it used to be. She was working on a news special, tentatively entitled, "Making Babies: Or, Changing Our Conceptions." She filmed an interview with Marge and Joe Lapinski from Speonk, Long Island. After fifteen years of marriage they were childless and still trying. They had been told there was no hope, and then the test-tube baby was born. Now they were planning to fly to England to meet with the famous doctor. He had already refused to take their case and refused to meet with them, but they were not to be dissuaded.

"Listen," said Joe, a fortyish man with a red face and a huge beer belly that made it look as though he himself were six months pregnant, "as soon as the doctor gets a look at Marge here and sees what a natural mother-type she is, he'll take us on. I'll betcha anything."

Lapinski had already bet almost everything. He had sold his TV repair business and mortgaged his house to cover the expenses of a prolonged stay in England.

Marge Lapinski, a thin, frail woman in her thirties who wore her white-blonde hair piled on top of her head in elaborate curlicues, said very little. She looked tired.

At the end of the interview, Marge took Nelly on a tour of the house. She stopped at the doorway of a small white room. Pastel giraffes and elephants gamboled across the walls. The curtains were circus-striped. In the corner was a new crib piled high with small soft animals.

"This is the baby's room," Marge said.

"Aren't you being a little premature? You don't even know if the doctor will take you on," Nelly said.

"Oh, we've had this room since we were first married," Marge said. "That's how much we wanted a baby."

Marge's eyes misted over. Nelly had a hard time keeping the tears out of her voice as she closed that segment of the story:

"This is Nelly Diamond, WABC news, at the Lapinski home, Speonk, New York."

Her heart went out to the Lapinskis. It seemed so unfair. Here was a couple that had given up everything to have the one thing most people took for granted.

Nelly felt for all the people she had interviewed for her story, even the Johnsons, who had had a baby by artificial insemination. Mr. Johnson was suing the clinic for a million and a half dollars. He claimed that the sperm used wasn't his but, in fact, some stranger's. Some redheaded stranger.

"Look at my hair," Johnson said. "See any red, even a touch? No. Look at her hair," he said, pointing to his sobbing wife. "No red. There hasn't been a redhead in either one of our families, ever. They told me they were using my sperm. They lied and I'm gonna make them pay. I've suffered mental anguish. I feel cuckolded and my wife here feels like a whore. Dontcha, honey?" Mrs. Johnson nodded her head, tears streaming down her cheeks.

They planned to keep the baby and to raise it, according to Johnson, "as their own." But they were going to make the clinic pay, by God.

The only truly happy part of the whole special was the surrogate-mother couple, the Marches. They were having a baby à trois. Sally March had had a hysterectomy years before. Luckily, with the help and womb of their dearest friend, Valerie Jilka, they were about to be the proud parents of a new little baby.

Two-hundred-pound Valerie explained: "I have all the equipment and none of the mother instincts. Sally and Mike here are my dearest friends. I know how much they want this kid. I am happy to be able to do what I can. It's no big deal. I don't plan on getting that involved with raising it. We all live together, so I'll be available for baby-sitting. But as far as I'm concerned, the baby belongs to them. I just sort of rented them a womb."

Babies from belly buttons. Life had been so simple then. Now, thirty-one years later, babies came from test tubes and sperm banks and other people's stomachs. Nelly had yet another variation to add to the list: babies also came from too much champagne and not enough diaphragm. At least that was what had obviously happened in her particular case.

It had been her first one-night stand in almost fifteen years—the night of the network affiliates annual sales meeting. The very attractive station manager from KWRZ, Albuquerque. It was funny, Nelly could remember the call letters of his station, but she could not, for the life of her, remember his name. It wasn't as if she had needed random sex. Her love life was full and complete. She had three lovers who occupied her time without occupying her mind. It was just that he, KWRZ, had been so very attractive, the evening so very boring, and the champagne so very dry.

She felt a little guilty. Here were all these couples who were trying desperately to conceive, and here was Nelly Diamond, knocked up without even trying. Already, by her calculations, almost two months gone. Aside from the "why me/why not them?" pangs of guilt, she also experienced a vague kind of gladness. She was glad to know she could get pregnant. Glad to know all her parts were in working order. It was, after all, the first time it had ever happened to her. There had been times, over the years, when she had wondered if, indeed, it was possible. Now she knew.

She also knew that she had to get rid of it. Because if you were pregnant and hadn't planned for it and didn't have one steady man in your life or a full-time housekeeper or an extra bedroom or a job that you could take off from without somebody else stepping right into your shoes, then you had one choice: an abortion.

Sure, you could have second thoughts. But first, you had the abortion. There was plenty of time for second thoughts later. There was even time for a baby later. Not too much later. But certainly not right now.

Nelly made a promise to herself: as soon as she had the abortion and everything was back to normal, she would start thinking seriously about having the baby she had always planned on having. Someday.

2 The Abortion

The abortion business was pretty confusing. There were twenty different abortion services advertising in the New York *Post* that day. The prices varied according to the type of anesthesia preferred (general was higher than local), according to the length of time you were pregnant, and according to the individual clinic.

One clinic was running a special on early pregnancies (only $75). Another promised a "hospital-quality facility" for a slightly higher price. And yet another ad stated that if your last period was less than six weeks ago, an abortion may not even be required. Nelly wondered what method they used in lieu of abortion. Telekinesis? Voodoo? Or just benign neglect?

She just couldn't decide. Should she opt for the costlier general anesthetic on a twenty-four-week abortion which could run her $500, or should she economize with the 50-percent-less-for-early-pregnancy termination?

She needed an expert opinion on this. Paisley would know. She had had three abortions during her back-to-nature period, when she had given up all birth control. It wasn't that she had believed in having babies. She had just viewed birth control, whether it be the pill, a diaphragm, or an iud, as some sort of additive that a woman shouldn't take into her body.

After the last abortion Paisley had gone on the pill, although she still didn't use sugar or salt on her food.

"Hi Paisley, Nelly. Just a quick question: where do you get your abortions?" There was silence and then:

"Is this for your own personal information or are you doing a special on me for the ten o'clock news?"

"For my own information. We've already got enough sports coverage as it is."

"Ha, ha," Paisley said, unamused. "Why do you want to know?"

"Why do you think I want to know? I'm pregnant."

"Oh."

"I've been looking in the paper and there are so many different places and different prices I really can't tell which is the best clinic to go to."

"Clinic! My *chère* Nelly, this is no time for your bargain-basement mentality. Forget clinics. They're strictly for poverty cases and runaway teenagers. Go to your own gynecologist."

"I can't. He retired two months ago."

"Then go to mine. He's wonderful. He's done all my abortions. He's supremely competent and very attractive, in an anesthetic sort of way."

"Oh, good. He washes his hands. Is he expensive?"

"Of course he's expensive. I assume he's at least the most expensive in the city. His name's Hoffman. Eric Hoffman. On Park Avenue and Eightieth Street. Call him. And don't worry. He's really very good."

"Who said I was worried?"

"Well, aren't you?"

"Of course I'm worried. I don't have an abortion every day of the week."

"Well, contrary to popular opinion, neither do I," Paisley snapped.

Nelly selected a sweet little Albert Nippon dress to wear to the doctor's office. It was a tiny print of green roses against a white background, with long puffed sleeves and a high gathered waist. She didn't want the doctor blaming her pregnancy on the way she dressed.

Nelly checked her TV image in the gold-framed mirror in her bedroom. Overall color: perfect. A smooth complexion of peach and rose tones topped by a shiny cap of delicately streaked honey-blonde hair. Eyes: pale denim blue. Nose: straight and simple. Mouth: sensuous, soft and smiling. She stepped back. The verticals and horizontals of her five-foot-seven-inch frame were more than well-tuned.

At thirty-five it was a nice feeling to look in the mirror and like what looked back at you. Nelly hadn't been born a beauty. It had taken a lot of hard work. When she was a little girl and believed in luck, magic, and miracles, she would sneak glances in the mirror hoping that just once she'd be pleasantly surprised by some major change for the better. But she was never surprised by that bespectacled, round-faced, large-nosed, tooth-braced face that stared back at her.

By the time she was twenty-one, she had given up on magic and miracles. She knew there was no fairy godmother. And, if there was a God, he was capable of error, particularly in the area of faces and figures.

That was when she took things into her own hands. She had her nose fixed. Losing two ounces of cartilage inspired her to more. She worked her way down from 165 pounds (perhaps the youngest woman in the world to have developed cellulite on the front of her legs as well as the back) to a well-toned 120. She got contact lenses. The doctor had told her that her eyes were too sensitive ever to get used to them, but she was wearing them comfortably within two months. She even worked to get her nails the same exact perfect length, an incredible accomplishment for a former nail-biter and hangnail chewer.

Nelly was living up to what a sixth-grade teacher had once written in her report card: "Nelly isn't afraid of hard work and responds well to challenge."

Years later, having achieved the state of physical loveliness that she had always longed for but never dreamed possible, she turned her efforts inward. Nobody had more dreams during analysis, more confrontations in group therapy, screamed louder or longer in Primal, had better attendance in a consciousness-raising group, stayed awake longer in est, or hurt more in rolfing.

Hard work was what propelled her from being a receptionist to researcher to writer to reporter to a $75,000-a-year newscaster on the WABC "Evening News." Hard work was what convinced her producer that she could do a lot more than just cover fashion and food. She could handle murders, muggings, and city politics with the best of them.

She sat in Dr. Hoffman's waiting room. It was your standard Park Avenue doctor's waiting room. There were the required original oils by some unknown artist: inoffensive florals and tranquil turquoise seascapes. There was the modern, but not too modern, furniture. And, of course, the waiting. Two other women were there before her. No one spoke. No one even glanced up. There was a great deal of surreptitious studying of everyone else's shoes. Nelly wondered why people never talked in doctors' waiting rooms. She was sure there was much to be learned. What are you having done? How much does he charge you for that? How long did it take before it cleared up? What do you do for cramps?

She was nervous. She couldn't remember ever being so nervous. She opened her bag and took out her cigarettes. She put one to her lips just as her eyes met the Thank You for Not Smoking, The American Cancer Society sign on the opposite wall. She snatched the cigarette from her mouth. The woman in the burgundy Gucci pumps stared at her as if the mere contemplation of a cigarette could cause cancer in others.

She turned her attention to the thick stack of magazines on the Danish-modern coffee table next to her. There was *Modern Medicine, Modern Gynecology* (the branch keeping up with the field), *Today's Mother,* and *Baby Talk.* They were all back issues. Not a *Time* magazine or a *People* among them.

Without thinking, Nelly reached for a cigarette again. The woman in the burgundy Guccis cleared her throat loudly. Nelly looked at the cigarette in her hand, murmured an apology, and put it back in her purse, where it promptly broke in half.

She wondered if he would do it today. Would she be able to walk out? Would it hurt? Ah, now she was getting down to it. Of course it would hurt, she told herself. She remembered that her secretary Lisa, after her abortion, had been in bed for four days with cramps. "The worst cramps I've ever had in my entire life," Lisa had moaned.

On the other hand, Paisley hadn't had any cramps at all after her last abortion. She just went on a crying jag for a week.

"It's not psychological," Paisley had sobbed, "it's hormonal. Just your standard postnatal depression."

"But how can you have a postnatal depression without the natal?" Nelly had asked.

"Your hormones do not have a mind of their own," Paisley said, blowing her nose. "All they know is one minute we're pregnant and the next minute we're not. So they jump to the conclusion of birth."

Oh, Nelly was scared all right. With her luck she would probably have the cramps and the postnatal depression to boot. Not to mention extensive and dangerous hemorrhaging. She tried to calm herself. There was nothing to worry about. Wasn't everyone having abortions these days? It couldn't be all that bad. Or maybe it was, and the women were sworn to secrecy.

Why was the idea, the very word, *abortion,* frightening to her? She supposed it was a holdover from the prelegalized abortion days. But certainly they had improved techniques since then. She could still remember the horror stories. The coat hangers, the hot-water douches, the quinine pills. The quinine pills didn't work. Neither did the hot-water douches. The coat hanger was, unfortunately, pretty sure-fire. There were also the foreign and highly suspect doctors in murky-sounding places like San Juan and Montreal. In those days it was so much harder to get an abortion and yet so much easier to get pregnant.

Nelly had spent so much time considering the mechanics of this abortion that she hadn't really thought of herself as pregnant. The idea of a fetus growing inside her was not something she wanted to dwell upon at this particular moment.

She looked at her watch. She had been waiting for forty-five minutes. When she first arrived, the nurse had asked for a urine specimen and had taken some blood. Since then there had been no activity. From where she sat she could see the three nurses huddled around the desk in the anteroom. She wondered what they were doing. Maybe their nails. Maybe a crossword puzzle. Maybe they were snickering over the patients' charts.

She looked around the waiting room. The two other women had disappeared. She hadn't even seen them go. Her turn had to be soon. Maybe she

16

should just leave. Come back another day when they weren't so busy.

"Mrs. Diamond," one of the nurses called.

She got up, and as she did so, her purse dropped to the floor. The entire contents spilled out, including five ounces of loose tobacco. She tried to vacuum it up with her fingers.

"That's all right, the cleaning lady will take care of that," the nurse said.

Nelly's legs were shaking as she followed the nurse down the long hallway. The nurse handed Nelly a little orange-and-yellow-flowered Dixie cup.

"Could you please empty your bladder and save me a urine specimen?"

"But I already gave urine," Nelly protested.

"Oh, that was for the pregnancy test. This is for something else."

Jesus, Nelly thought to herself as she locked the bathroom door, these people are insatiable.

She sat on the toilet holding the little Dixie cup under her. Nothing happened. She was so tense she couldn't pee. And then, suddenly, she couldn't stop peeing. The cup overflowed and still Nelly couldn't stop. She was peeing on her own hand but she couldn't let the cup go. It was the only one she had.

Nelly washed her hands, dried them, and picked up the cup carefully. It was filled to the brim. She slowly unlocked the door. She was concentrating so hard on not spilling that she had walked into one of the nurses. Half the urine splattered out, leaving a little buttercup pattern all over the bodice of the nurse's white uniform.

"Oh, I'm so sorry," Nelly said, wiping away at the nurse's starched front.

"No problem," the nurse answered through semiclenched teeth. She carefully extricated the half-empty cup from Nelly's damp hand.

"Just go into the examining room," she said, indicating an open door, "and disrobe from the waist down."

Terrific, thought Nelly as the nurse closed the door, how do you disrobe from the waist down when you're wearing a dress? Should she roll the dress up above her waist? That would wrinkle the light cotton terribly. Should she just rip it off at the waist and have the doctor suture it back on later after the abortion? Or should she just take the whole thing off and thereby risk being branded an exhibitionist? She looked around for a robe. There was no robe, naturally. There was a piece of folded paper at the end of the examining table. She opened it up, tearing it slightly as she did, and held it in front of her. It was a 3 x 5 sheet of one-ply paper, large enough to cover one side of her. She took off her dress and her panties and then, feeling ridiculous with just a bra, took that off too. The nurse popped her head into the room.

"The doctor will be with you in a minute."

Nelly knew what that meant. That was the same thing she had been told when she walked into the office almost an hour ago. She looked around for someplace to sit. There was only the cold, stainless-steel examining table. She hoisted herself up on the edge of it, trying to keep the paper covering in place. The paper was so light that the slightest movement caused it to float gently upward.

She wished she had brought something to read. Even *Modern Gynecology* would do at this point. Maybe she should lie down. She lay down. If the doctor came in he might think she was sick or dead. She sat up again. She crossed her legs. The paper covering started to tear and so she uncrossed them. There was nothing to lean against. Nothing to do but wait.

A long white cabinet occupied one entire wall. It had hundreds of small, appealing drawers in it. She thought about rummaging through them but it occurred to her that they might check for fingerprints. She couldn't relax. She felt like pacing, but the room wasn't big enough. The minutes passed. Finally she lowered herself off the table. There was a microscope on the cabinet with several slides next to it. She pulled out one of her hairs, placed it on a slide and inserted the slide under the microscope.

She was standing there bent over, peering into the microscope, the paper sheet clutched to her front, her naked back facing the door, when Dr. Hoffman walked in.

"Up on the examining table, please," he said, not looking at her.

She whirled around. The paper flew in the opposite direction. Paisley was right. He was attractive, in an anesthetic sort of way. He was very tall, quite lean, and looked as though he scrubbed his scalp as frequently as his hands. He wore his nickle-gray hair so closely cropped that you could see the pink skin of his scalp shining through. She got back up on the table and lay down; her face was red with embarrassment.

"Feet in the stirrups, please."

Nelly bent her legs and inserted her feet at oblique angles, a position that a normal person, without double-jointed ankles, could hold only for a minute before cramps began to set in.

Dr. Hoffman pulled out a stool from underneath the examining table, sat down, and switched on his head lamp. His head disappeared from view. She knew what he was going to say next.

"This will feel a little cold at first," he said.

Gynecologists were masters of understatement, Nelly thought to herself as what felt like the long arm of the Abominable Snowman was thrust suddenly into her womb. "This will feel a little cold" was in the same category as "This won't hurt. This will just pinch a bit," which was followed, of course, by a wrenching, stabbing pain deep inside the wall of the uterus. Pap smears always "pinched a bit" and insertions of any kind of instrument, large or small, always "felt a little cold."

Dr. Hoffman's head popped up. He switched off his head lamp, removed his see-through plastic gloves, and tossed them expertly into the metal trash basket.

"Well, doctor, what do you think?" Nelly asked, knowing what his response would be. Another standard:

"We'll talk about it in my office," he said.

There is a cardinal rule for gynecologists. It clearly states: never discuss anything with the patient while she is in the examining room. Nelly figured there were probably several good reasons for this: (1) talking to a half-naked woman is, at best, a precarious undertaking; (2) discussions in the examining room did away with the necessity for the twenty-by-twenty-foot wood-paneled office, which put an extra 30 percent on the monthly overhead; (3) if a gynecologist spends more than two minutes in any one examining room, then rumors start flying among the nurses; and (4) (this last was Nelly's own personal choice) a delay in any discussion was necessary because the news was so bad, so very bad, the doctor needed time to compose himself before breaking it to the patient.

"Take your time getting dressed," he said to her with a smile as he quietly exited.

Another rote statement. This meant the doctor could squeeze in five or six more examinations while you were taking your time getting dressed. After all, how long could it take for a semidisrobed woman to reattire herself?

Nelly was convinced that if one were to do a survey, they would find that the total average waiting time in a gynecologist's office would be at least five times the national medical average, second only to that of a dentist's office. Gynecologists could get away with it. If you were an internist, you couldn't keep a heart patient waiting around forever; his blood pressure would go way up. A dermatologist couldn't keep a rash in his waiting room for too long; they spread so quickly. An eye/ear/nose and throat man would have people postnasal dripping all over his office furniture if he kept them there for any length of time.

Nelly walked down the hallway and past the nurses' desk.

"Just have a seat outside," the nurse said. "Doctor will . . ."

"Don't tell me; I know. He'll be with me in a minute."

Back in the waiting room, there were two new women, one in rather elegant suede sandals, the other wearing tennis sneakers. Nelly picked up *Today's Mother* and stared at the cover blankly. There was a picture of a perfectly pudgy little baby chewing on her fist as she stared serenely at the camera. Cute, thought Nelly. Probably the offspring of some woman whose abortionist told her he'd be with her in just a minute.

The woman in the tennis shoes lit up a cigarette. Nelly stared at her admiringly. Then she realized that the woman was sitting underneath the Thank You for Not Smoking sign. She inhaled deeply, blissful in her ignorance. Nelly waited for someone to say something to her, but no one did.

"Mrs. Diamond, the doctor will see you now. Excuse me, Miss," the nurse said, turning to the woman who was smoking, "but there's no smoking."

"Oh, I'm not smoking," the woman replied as she stubbed her cigarette in the potted philodendron next to her, "I'm just putting out." Nelly thought the woman was wonderful. She would have gladly done anything for a cigarette at that moment. Even given more urine.

She entered the doctor's inner sanctum. Sure enough, the walls were wood paneled and there was a four-by-three-foot desk of pure, polished mahogany. On the desk was a small marble statuette of a woman holding a baby high above her head like a watermelon. Not a good sign for an abortionist, Nelly thought.

She sat down at the desk. Hoffman was writing notes in what she presumed was her chart. Or maybe he was catching up on a chart from six patients before. He did not look up at her.

"So," she said after a few minutes of silence, "when will you do it?"

"Do what?" he asked, not looking up.

"The abortion."

"You don't need an abortion."

"What?"

"You're not pregnant."

"I'm not?"

"No, not at all. The reason your period has been delayed is that you've got a pretty severe case of PID."

"PID?" she asked, feeling like his straight man.

"Pelvic inflammatory disease." At the word *pelvic* he finally looked up. He could, it seemed, make eye contact when the vocabulary merited it.

"PID is an umbrella term. The inflammation is a result of large cysts on both ovaries, which have created the condition." He took out a prescription pad and resumed writing.

"I'm giving you massive doses of antibiotics. You'll be taking 500 milligrams four times a day for the next two weeks." He handed her the prescription.

"I want you to refrain from sex and any strenuous activity. Also, keep track of your temperature. If you start to run a fever, call me immediately. Otherwise I'll see you in two weeks' time."

Nelly wanted to ask if running a temperature wasn't a strenuous activity, just to lighten things up, but she decided against it.

Leaving Dr. Hoffman's office, she felt confused and disoriented. No pregnancy. No abortion. All she had was a massive pelvic inflammation. She had gotten off easy, hadn't she? Why should she feel so strange? She tried to zero in on her feelings. First of all, she felt disappointed. Disappointed about not having an abortion? That was crazy.

No, she wasn't disappointed about the abortion; she was upset about the pelvic inflammation, that was it. She hated the idea of being sick. Especially when it was something mysterious and unseen, something she couldn't touch and, in fact, couldn't even feel. She only had Dr. Hoffman's word for what was wrong with her. She herself had no way of gauging the extent of her malady and consequently her recovery from it.

But there was another feeling that was beyond even Nelly's analytical eye. She knew it was there (practiced as she was in the art of defining her emotions), but she didn't know what it was. It felt like a loss of some sort. But what had she lost? A couple of monthly periods. Some time while researching the abortion clinics. Some peace of mind in worrying about the abortion itself. No, it was more than that. It was the same kind of funny, foggy feeling she had once had when she left her billfold in a taxicab. She hadn't realized it was missing till half the day had gone by, and the fog had lifted.

She took the prescription to be filled at her corner Walgreen's. As she waited for it, she became immersed in the counter in front of her. The entire area was taken up by the Trojan Family Planning Center. She hadn't realized condoms were making such a comeback. Each package was illustrated with photographs of young, loving couples leaning close to each other, in a field of flowers in some cases, or wheat in others. The selection was endless. There were ribbed Trojans, lubricated Trojans, and plain Trojans. There were also Trojans Plus, "naturally shaped, specially lubricated for sensitivity and ribbed for confidence."

"You the one with the gargantuan infection?" the pharmacist bellowed across the condom display. Nelly dropped the package of Trojans Plus. "Or do you have a sick horse at home?" he asked.

"No, that's for me," Nelly said, grabbing the bottle of huge green and yellow pills from him.

She walked out of the drugstore feeling better already. All she had to do was take her pills and avoid any sex and strenuous activity for the next couple of weeks. Oh, Christ, she suddenly remembered that she had a date with Clark that evening. A date with Clark meant both sex *and* strenuous activity. She would have to cancel. It wasn't as if they could go to a movie or the theater or anything. Theirs was what is commonly termed a purely physical relationship. Nelly liked it that way. Engaging in any kind of pastime with Clark other than sex was always a downer. Sex was the only thing he ever got excited, or rather, undepressed about. It wasn't just the doing of it, either. It was the talking about it before, during, and after. And the planning, the setting up, all those little details that involved him so. It was the ideal hobby for someone who was simply not the hobby type. He often said that sex was the only thing that kept him sane. And this was from a man who was in and out of Payne Whitney on the average of eight times a year, so he should know.

Clark was forever coming up with new positions, new devices, and new variations to try. She enjoyed his general sexual enthusiasm although she couldn't always go along with some of the specifics. One night he had shown up with a rather hefty looking young woman dressed in a parachutist's costume.

21

"This is Shirley," he said. "She's going to beat us."

"At what?" Nelly had asked.

"It's not *at* what, it's *with* what," Clark clarified.

"You better count me out on this one," Nelly had said, slamming the door in both their faces.

An hour later he came back alone.

"I didn't know you were into that kind of thing," Nelly had said.

"I'm not. But it's something I've never tried and how do you know whether you're going to like it unless you try it?"

Once home, she let herself into her apartment and tried to call Clark to cancel their date. All she got was his message machine.

"This is a warning," his voice intoned menacingly. "I am not at home. My guard dog, a 120-pound Doberman Pinscher, is patrolling the area. He has been trained to lunge on sight. There are sophisticated electronic burglar devices on all the windows and doors. They are designed to go off with the slightest tampering, at the nearby Twentieth Precinct. The men of the Twentieth will not hesitate to use their considerable brute force in detaining any intruder. So, I warn you: keep away from my property. It does not belong to you. If you care to leave a message, please wait for the beep."

Clark never got any messages. Nobody had the patience to sit through his entire recorded threat. Besides, there was no room left on the tape to leave a message. She had tried to tell him this, but he refused to listen to her.

The irony was that Clark was robbed at least once every six months. People were forever climbing in and out of his back window, without, obviously, telephoning first.

"At least," he said, "I feel safe in the certainty of knowing I will be robbed twice a year. It's the not knowing that kills me. And they have yet to touch my comic-book collection. I can always buy another TV or stereo."

At eight o'clock the doorbell rang. It was Clark, right on time as usual. He was holding a huge book under his arm.

"Hi, Clark. Bad news. Can't have sex tonight. Have a little something wrong in the female department," she said coyly at the doorway.

"Well, listen, that's perfectly okay," he said, pushing his way past her. "I have this new thing," he said, showing her a book.

The cover of the book featured a couple—it seemed to be a man and a woman (although it was difficult to tell)—involved in a rather intricate position of lovemaking. It looked as though they were having sex in a pool of safflower oil.

"It's pretty complicated," he explained, "so it requires some reading up on. We can do the book work tonight and then be all ready for the next time."

"What exactly is it?" she asked warily.

"It's called tantric sex," he said, making himself comfortable in her Eames chair. "It's very oriental. Very mystical. You don't go for the orgasm. You go for the nonorgasm."

As Clark's voice droned on late into the night, Nelly lay quietly on the couch, her hands resting lightly on her tummy. She could almost feel the PID quietly raging on somewhere deep inside her, and she didn't like the feeling one bit. Odd, she thought, from pregnant this morning to inflamed pelvis tonight. She was having a hard time making the transition. Both seemed mysterious and out of her control. But there was a big difference. Now, with this pelvic thing, she felt like she had something wrong with her. Whereas, when she had thought she was pregnant, she had felt like she had something right. Not so right that she hadn't considered abortion. But right, nonetheless.

3 Scars

Three weeks had passed and Nelly was back on her back in the examining room with Dr. Hoffman hidden from view like a turn-of-the-century portrait photographer.

"Hmmmmmmmm-mmmmmmmmm," he intoned.

"Hmmmmmmmmm?" Nelly asked, lifting up her head to get a glimpse of him.

"Hmmmmmmmmm," he answered, noncommittally.

"We'll talk about it in your office," Nelly offered.

"We'll talk about it in my office," the doctor said, ignoring her. "Take your time getting dressed."

It must have been an off day for him. Nelly had only had to wait a half-hour before being summoned into his den.

"Well, the inflammation looks like it's clearing up nicely. We'll continue with the antibiotics for a couple of weeks as a safeguard, but I think we have everything under control."

"Does that mean I can resume my sexual and strenuous activities?" Nelly asked demurely.

"By all means," he answered with more enthusiasm than Nelly had thought he was capable of.

Nelly got up to go.

"Oh, one more thing."

"Yes?" she said, turning at the open door.

"Are you planning on having any children?"

"Not right at the moment. Why do you ask?"

"Well, if you were planning on having children, I would say you have a problem."

"How's that?"

"The type of pelvic inflammation you have, though it's easily cleared up, can leave adhesions on the fallopian tubes."

"Adhesions?"

"Scars. And scarring can make it difficult, sometimes impossible, for the egg to pass through the tubes, thereby preventing conception."

"And I have these scars?"

"Yes. How extensive they are or how much damage they have done to the tubes, I really couldn't say. But as long as you're not planning any children, there's no problem."

"And if I were planning children, there would, in your opinion, be a problem?"

"Yes. Most definitely."

Nelly had a lunch date with Abby at the Palm Room of the Plaza Hotel at one P.M. It was almost twenty of. She hailed a taxi at the corner of Park and Eightieth.

"The Plaza Hotel, please."

"Which way do you want to go?" the driver asked.

Oh, Jesus, not another democratic taxi driver. Nelly hated them. They always wanted you to take part in the decision-making process. The whole reason she took taxis in the first place was so she wouldn't have to think about the logistics of getting around New York.

"You decide, you know best," she said.

For some reason this put most taxi drivers on edge.

"Well," the driver explained, turning around to make his point, "there are different ways to get to different places and everybody's got their favorite route."

"Not me. I don't have any favorites. I promise."

"Okay, it's your money." He began to mull over his alternatives out loud. "Let's see now, I could take Fifth all the way down to Sixty-first, but traffic could be all backed up because it's lunchtime. Or I could take the park at Seventy-ninth down to Fifty-seventh and Sixth and make a left up Central Park South. But they're doing subway construction and that could be a problem."

Nelly refused to get involved. Finally, having reached a decision, the driver put the taxi in gear. The meter, by this time, was already up to $1.05.

She leaned back and stared out the window. He had opted for the park. Nelly was glad. It was much the longer, more circuitous route.

Babies. She really hadn't thought about having a baby since Jordan had mentioned it as something they might think about doing. That had been toward the end of their marriage, when he was constantly coming up with all sorts of desperate schemes in an effort to save their flagging relationship.

He had, for instance, once dragged her to a video therapist. They were taped for two hours discussing how they did the grocery shopping, why Nelly always insisted on sleeping on the right-hand side of any bed (something that apparently had bothered Jordan for years), and why Jordan never consulted Nelly before investing in stocks. It was two hours of the worst television Nelly had ever had the misfortune to view. As therapy, it hadn't really worked. Particularly because Nelly, being a professional, always played to the camera.

The baby discussion had taken place when they were returning from a romantic weekend on Montauk Point. (It had been romantic in the visual sense only. It was the middle of February, the beach was totally deserted, and the huge waves were spectacular.) They hadn't said a word to each other the entire time. Jordan was sulking and Nelly was reading *The Godfather*. Then, going through the Midtown Tunnel, Jordan turned to her and said:

"Maybe we should think about having children."

"Why?" she had asked, putting down her book. She had twenty pages to go.

"Well, I think it would be good for us and for the marriage. It would bring us closer together. Besides, I think having a child is kind of a neat idea."

If there was one thing that doomed their marriage even from the beginning, it was Jordan's overuse of the word *neat*.

"Having and raising a child is not exactly a casual undertaking," Nelly had pointed out. "You say it as though you're suggesting we go away for the weekend or something."

"We did go away for the weekend. It didn't work."

"Well, I really don't think, at this point in our relationship, that staying home and having a child instead of going away to the Hamptons is really a solution."

Jordan didn't pursue the subject.

Children simply had not figured into her life. Which was not to say she had ever planned on having children. She had always assumed she would someday. Which day was never clear.

Now it seemed the decision had been taken out of her hands. She would have trouble conceiving, the doctor had said. Well, that was that. A woman without children. A childless woman. Other words popped into her head: Barren. Sterile. Infertile.

She remembered her Aunt Madge. She wasn't really her aunt but a very close friend of her mother's. She had been Nelly's favorite adult when she was a little girl. She was incredibly nice, infinitely patient, and forever thoughtful. She was the one that always remembered Nelly's love of horses and white chocolate. Even better, she would sit down and talk with Nelly. Just Nelly and no one else. She seemed to care genuinely about her.

Nelly once asked her mother why Aunt Madge didn't have any children. She was certainly every kid's dream of the ideal mother as far as Nelly was concerned. It seemed a shame to waste her.

"Well, she's not able to have babies of her own," her mother had said.

"Why not?"

"She's infertile."

"What does infertile mean?"

"It means she can't make eggs. So she can't have babies."

Nelly was amazed. Aunt Madge seemed so smart. Even her father, who had difficulty opening a can of soup without having to pry the top off, could make eggs. They were runny and icky, but he could make them.

Ultimately, Aunt Madge and her husband adopted two children. But Nelly always felt sorry for her. People who couldn't make eggs were fated to spend the rest of their lives being nicer to children than any regular mother would ever dream of being.

Nelly had always taken for granted her ability to reproduce. It was like her right to vote. Now, suddenly, it had been taken from her before she had ever had an opportunity to exercise it.

Having babies was something almost every woman could do. Even her mother had managed to bring it off. Not that her mother was a bumbling idiot. But, as she herself had said so many times: "I'm not the world's best mother material . . ." Her mind was always elsewhere. Nonetheless, she had managed to conceive two children without any problem. Giving birth and raising them had apparently been slightly more difficult.

She had refused to go to the hospital when she was in labor with Nelly. She was waiting for a new couch to be delivered and didn't want to miss it. She had been waiting, in fact, for over two months. She was afraid they would take it back to the warehouse. The delivery men were appalled at the sight of a woman nine months pregnant sprawled in an overstuffed chair, with water running down her legs.

"Over there in front of the bay window," her mother had moaned. Nelly had just narrowly missed being born at home on top of the new plastic-covered couch.

At the age of five her sister Sarah had her crossed eyes operated on. Shortly after being released from the hospital and while she was still wearing bandages over her eyes, her mother took her to the eye doctor for a postoperative checkup.

They had arrived early. With a little time to kill, she took Sarah to a nearby duck pond to feed the ducks, which Sarah always loved doing. As Sarah threw two-day-old Wonder bread in the general direction of the ducks, she slipped and fell into the water. She couldn't see a thing. She couldn't swim, either. Her mother, realizing the danger of the situation, immediately fainted dead away, leaving Sarah thrashing about in the small pond scattering hysterical ducks every which way. Luckily a man was passing by at that moment and pulled Sarah out, still clutching a soggy fragment of Wonder bread in her white, tight, little fist. Her mother came to shortly afterward.

"I'm such a terrible mother. A terrible mother," she had cried. And she carried on that way for days after the incident. Her father, a calm man except when it came to opening soup cans, had tried to reassure her:

"You're not a terrible mother, Agnes. It's just that you don't always think."

Well, Nelly could think. It was, therefore, inconceivable that she couldn't conceive. She felt cheated. And sad. Very sad. She couldn't believe how sad she felt.

Maybe I'm just getting my period, she thought to herself. My period! Now what was the sense of all those menstrual cycles when she couldn't have children? She did some quick mental arithmetic. She had, to date, suffered through 264 monthly periods—1,320 days or 3½ straight years of bleeding. She had endured many hours of cramps and gone through approximately 7,920 Tampaxes since puberty, and what was the sense of it all? The whole point to having a period is to have children.

The taxi pulled up to the Plaza. Nelly got out.

"Hey, lady, didn't you forget something?" the driver yelled after her.

Nelly returned to the taxi and looked in the back seat.

"No, I don't think so," she said to the driver.

"You forgot to pay me."

"Oh," Nelly said, taking out her billfold. Odd. She had never done that before.

Abby was already seated at a table in the Palm Room, becomingly framed by palm fronds. She was a petite brunette with an oversized bosom, huge brown eyes, and deep dimples. People invariably described her as darling or adorable. She played it up and hated it at the same time.

Smiling brightly, she waved gaily at Nelly. Nelly could tell even from that distance that Abby was depressed. She was one of those women who was raised to put on a happy face regardless of whatever misery she might be feeling at the time. And with her face it was very easy.

"How did your audition go?" Nelly asked, sitting down.

"I don't think it went too well. It was for a Wisk spot. I was supposed to register dismay and despair upon discovering my husband had ring around the collar. It's an incredibly difficult role playing to a dirty shirt without having any lines to say. It would've been a great job if I got it. Once you get yourself into detergent commercials the sky's the limit. Oh Nelly, I'm so depressed," she grinned.

"About the job?"

"No, about my life."

"What's the trouble?"

28

"Well, first of all I think I may be pregnant."

"Abby, how wonderful."

"It's not wonderful at all. Jill and Jane are all the children I need. But Jeff has his heart set on a boy. And he won't give up until he gets one. I told him the odds are against him, genetically speaking, but he's adamant. Besides, I don't want to have another baby. I want to have an affair. Do you realize, I've been married over ten years and I've never had an affair?"

"Abby, for Christ's sake, it's not some sort of a mandatory thing, like visiting the top of the Empire State Building."

"Well, I think it is. I think it's important to a marriage to be able to experience someone other than the person you're married to."

"So have an affair."

"I can't."

"Why not?"

"Come with me. I'll show you."

Just as they got up from the table, the waiter came by to take their order. He was somewhat mystified by their premature departure.

"We're just going to the ladies' room," Abby explained. "We'll be right back."

Abby was forever explaining herself to waiters.

The ladies' room was a green-and-white-striped affair designed to coordinate with the Palm Room. In the corner a ladies' room attendant, dressed like a nurse, sat on a small stool reading *Love's Daring Dream*. Next to her was a glass plate filled with quarters.

"Look," Abby said, opening her blazer and unzipping her Calvin Klein slacks.

Nelly bent over and looked closely at Abby's exposed abdomen.

"What is it?" she asked, seeing nothing.

"Stretch marks. I have awful stretch marks. Can't you see them? Who would want to have an affair with someone who has stretch marks?"

"First of all," Nelly said, straightening up, "you have to find someone who appeals to you, then find out how he feels about stretch marks. Maybe you'll be lucky enough to meet a man who has a thing for flaws."

The ladies' room attendant put down her book and walked over. Her square red face was lit up with interest.

"Stretch marks! Honey, you ain't seen nothing," the attendant said competitively. "Look at this," she lifted the skirt of her white uniform and pulled down her girdle to reveal a twelve-inch scar running across her belly.

"Wow," said Abby, obviously impressed, "a cesarean."

"Not just any old cesarean, I don't mind telling you. Twins—one seven and a half pounds, the other over eight. I almost died. The babies, too," she added proudly.

"Gee, fifteen-and-a-half-pound twins. What a job!"

"You're not kidding. I was in labor for thirty-six hours before they decided to cut."

"Why didn't they just go ahead and do the cesarean so you wouldn't have to go through all that labor?"

"Don't ask me. You know those doctors."

Nelly stood watching the two women compare combat scars.

"Listen, Abby, I don't think I can stay for lunch, after all."

"Why not? Where are you going?"

"I've got a doctor's appointment I forgot all about."

Damn them, Nelly thought to herself as she stalked through the Palm Room. I'll show them. No one was going to tell her she couldn't have a baby. No way. She could have a cesarean and stretch marks with the best of them. After all, wasn't she the one they said would never make it through college because her college boards were so bad? Not so bad that she didn't graduate *summa cum laude*. Wasn't she the one who was told she'd never get a decent job without typing and shorthand? And hadn't her total ignorance of office skills propelled her out of the office and onto the airwaves? Hadn't everyone assured her that nobody, but nobody, could get an interview with Greta Garbo? And who had gotten almost thirty minutes on film of an intimate, in-depth interview with none other than the great Miss G? Of course, later Miss Garbo had changed her mind and refused to let the piece be aired. She had also instituted a suit against the station for invasion of privacy. But Nelly had, indeed, gotten the interview.

Nobody could tell Nelly Diamond something was impossible. Show her a mountain, she'd climb it. Lead her to a chasm, she'd clear it in one graceful leap. Tell her a Broadway show was sold out for months, she'd get tickets to it. And they'd be orchestra seats, too. Give her ovaries, a womb, and tubes—scarred or not—and she would, by God, deliver.

Storming out of the Plaza, she waved aside the doorman and got into a waiting taxi.

"Park Avenue and Eightieth Street," she said.

"Which way do you want to go?"

"Take Madison up to Seventy-ninth, hang a right and drop me on the northwest corner of Eightieth Street," she commanded.

This time she managed to get away from the curb while the meter was still at ninety cents.

4 The Workup

As the taxi pulled up, Nelly saw Dr. Hoffman leaving his office. He was wearing tennis clothes and carrying a tennis racket stuck jauntily inside a Gucci tennis bag. He strode quickly across the street toward a double-parked Mercedes Benz sedan. Nelly ran to catch up with him.

"Dr. Hoffman. Dr. Hoffman."

He whirled around. The look on his face was that of a man about to be mugged.

"Oh, Mrs. Diamond. I'm sorry, the office closes early on Wednesday. You can call me tomorrow if you want." He continued walking.

"I just have a few quick questions. Won't take but a minute," she said, following him.

"Listen, I'm late. My wife here is double-parked. Call tomorrow and the nurse will be happy to arrange an appointment."

He got into the car. There was an attractive woman in her late forties at the wheel. She had the same well-washed look as her husband. The doctor dismissed Nelly with a smile and closed the car door. He bent over his wife, nudging her cheek with his lips. She, in turn, kissed the air in front of her. Nelly was not about to be put off. She was thirty five and getting older every minute. His tennis game could wait. His wife could wait. Her baby could not.

Using the same skill, charm, and perseverance she had used on Greta Garbo and countless others, she opened the back door and got in. Mrs. Hoffman turned around in surprise. Her precisely lipsticked mouth was slightly ajar.

"Mrs. Hoffman, terribly sorry to take up your time, but I have a few questions for your husband." It was as if she held an invisible microphone in her hand and the cameras were rolling. The doctor and his wife were trapped.

Nelly got right to the point. "Dr. Hoffman, I want to have a baby. And I want to know exactly what the problems and possibilities are." She turned to Mrs. Hoffman, who was staring at her with amazement through the rearview mirror.

"I'm sure you'll understand, Mrs. Hoffman. I'm thirty-five years old and I've never had any children. Do you have any children?"

Mrs. Hoffman nodded. "We have three."

"Well, then you certainly can understand," Nelly said, throwing the woman one of her winning smiles. She leaned forward on the seat, speaking intimately but not exclusively to the doctor, who was staring straight ahead, biting his upper lip.

"Now, Dr. Hoffman, you said my tubes were scarred and that could be a problem in getting pregnant. I have to know exactly how much of a problem and what can be done to overcome it. I want to get pregnant immediately."

"Mrs. Diamond, this isn't the time or place to discuss these things," the doctor said, looking at his wife.

"Oh, I'm sure Mrs. Hoffman is used to gynecological problems after all these years."

"Of course I am. Go on, dear," she said to her husband, "don't mind me."

The doctor was surrounded. He turned in his seat and spoke with great earnestness:

"First of all, I said there was a strong chance you would have a problem. How badly your tubes are scarred or how much the scarring might interfere with pregnancy I can't say. What is involved here is something called an infertility workup. It's a whole battery of tests that checks out the entire reproductive mechanism. It's a scientific process, you see. A matter of deduction. And in the process itself a patient can and does oftimes get pregnant. Many of the tests are therapeutic in nature."

"But you said it was my tubes. Why not just concentrate on them?"

"Because, as you said, you have never been pregnant. If we just focus on the tubes, we may be overlooking something else. We then would have to backtrack and look at all the other factors. Believe me, Mrs. Diamond, this is the standard procedure."

"An infertility workup, huh? Okay, what's the first test?" Nelly asked, as though the first test were a question to which she, of course, had the correct answer.

"Call me tomorrow and we can start setting the tests up."

"I can't wait till tomorrow. I want to get started right now."

"Mrs. Diamond, you're being unreasonable."

"Go on, Eric, I can wait," said Mrs. Hoffman.

"Very well," he sighed, "but let's make this quick."

Nelly followed him into the office. She glanced into the waiting room half-expecting to see women still waiting. Dr. Hoffman led her into his office and sat down behind the desk. He looked strangely out of place dressed in his tennis clothes. The whites were all right. It was the legs that bothered her.

"I won't go into great detail on all the tests now. There are six different areas we look into. There is an average of about one test a month. The first is to have your husband's sperm checked." He took out a small plastic jar, the kind Nelly carried cold cream in when she traveled, and handed it to her.

"Have your husband ejaculate into this container and then drop it off at the office within two hours."

For some reason Nelly didn't correct him about the husband. She was embarrassed by his mistake. She imagined that he was of the old school that believed people didn't plan children unless they were safely married, and that only men who were husbands could ejaculate into small jars. She was not about to tell him that she wasn't married. She was afraid he would lose interest in her case or drop it altogether, just because she didn't fit into his picture of the potential mother.

"Why is the sperm the first test?"

"Because if your husband's sperm count is low or nonexistent, then you would have difficulty getting pregnant regardless of what's going on with you. We have to be assured that the sperm is of good quality." He took out a sheet of paper and handed it to her. "Now, for the next three months I want you to take your temperature every morning upon waking and before you get out of bed. This will tell us if and when you are ovulating. Use an oral thermometer and mark down on the graph when you have intercourse and when you start your next period."

Nelly took the temperature graph. It seemed simple enough.

"So," the doctor said, rising, "you're all set. After we do the sperm count, we'll set up the next test." He escorted her toward the door.

"I feel much better now. It's nice to have something constructive to do. Thank you so much," she said, smiling up at him.

"Don't mention it."

Nelly followed him back to his car.

"Wish me luck," she said to Mrs. Hoffman.

"I do. All the luck in the world," said Mrs. Hoffman.

Nelly turned and walked briskly down the street.

"Strange woman," Dr. Hoffman said, shaking his head.

"Oh, I don't think she's so strange at all," his wife answered, putting the Mercedes into gear.

5   Counting

Whom she returned to the office, there was a blue interoffice envelope on her desk. It was marked "Personal and Urgent." She opened it.

> This is to inform you that as a direct result of remarks made during your story of March 5 on David Rockefeller and the Chase Manhattan Bank, the network is being sued by the Rockefeller family for two million dollars. Please contact me immediately regarding our course of action.
>
> Signed,
> B. W. Goodstein, Network Counsel

Nelly grabbed the memo and took the elevator to the tenth floor, where the legal offices were located. Goodstein's door was closed. She entered his office, quietly closing the door behind her.

Brian Goodstein was deeply immersed in a thick pile of legal briefs and didn't hear her come in. He was a big, burly bear of a man in his late thirties. He had the kind of thick, curly hair you had trouble getting your hands through and thick, curly eyebrows to match. He moved his lips as he read.

Nelly lifted her leg and laid it gently across his desk and onto the brief he was reading. He didn't look up.

"Now, about the Rockefeller case," she said softly, turning her foot in a sexy, semicircular motion. Goodstein stared at her toes, mesmerized. After a

few moments he removed Nelly's Charles Jourdan sandal and bit down gently
on her big toe.

"Counselor, please. What would the Rockefellers say?"

"The Rockefellers will have to wait their turn. Fuck me."

"Right on your briefs?"

"I'll take my briefs off."

"You're very funny, for a lawyer. And you do think up the sexiest
subpoenas."

"Listen, I have an even sexier idea: marry me."

"I feel it my duty to point out to you, as I have done on previous occasions,
the fact that you are already married," Nelly said, indicating the three-part
picture frame on his desk. On the right was a picture of a dark-eyed woman in
a white wedding gown. In the middle and left sides were pictures of his three
children, ages three, five, and seven. A girl and two boys. The boys had his
curly hair. Her dark eyes.

"But I want to be married to you," he said, looking up at her.

"Brian, we've been through this a million times before. We're having such a
nice extramarital affair. Why do you want to go and spoil it? Why do you insist
on robbing our relationship of all the joys of adultery?"

"I love you, you know."

"I know you do, Brian. That's because we have the perfect relationship. I'm
telling you, marriage would ruin everything."

"Can't you be serious for a second?"

"Don't give me that earnest Jewish routine, it won't work."

"All you have to do is give me the word and I'll ask Miriam for a divorce."

"If you're so unhappy with your marriage, you could get a divorce without
me. But you won't do that. Know why?"

"Why?"

"Because you're not the divorce type. You're the marrying type."

"I know; I just picked the wrong woman, that's all."

"I really can't conceive of someone as methodical as you making such an
error. You must have loved her once."

"We got married because we had to get married."

"She was pregnant?"

This was the first time they had talked about his marriage. Nelly always
avoided the subject. She was surprised. So Brian's was an old-fashioned
American love story. Nelly picked up the picture frame and studied it closely.

"So your wife never had any trouble getting pregnant."

"She had trouble not getting pregnant. All I had to do was look at her and
zap, she was pregnant. She's had two abortions, besides having the kids."

Nelly looked at Brian with a new fondness. He was perfect. Married.
Responsible. And the proven, potent father of three children. All she had to do
was figure out how to get him to fill the sample jar with his sperm. She

couldn't tell him what it was for. He was, after all, a little gun-shy about getting people pregnant.

Nelly had begun to tire of their affair. It had been going on for almost two years. For two years Brian had been begging her to give him the word so he could leave his wife and three children and make an honest woman of her. Being a lawyer, he tended to approach life in terms of honest and dishonest.

"Are we on for dinner tonight?" Nelly asked, changing the subject.

"Not only are we on for dinner, but I can spend the night."

"That's stretching the working-late story a bit far, isn't it?"

"It's okay. Miriam and the kids are at her parents."

"Okay. Where do you want to meet?"

"Let's meet at the restaurant. I heard about a new place on Columbus and Seventy-first Street. It's supposed to be terrific."

Terrific meant it was sufficiently out of the way so there wouldn't be a chance in a million that Brian would ever run into anyone he knew. For a man who didn't give a damn about his marriage, he took very few chances getting caught at his affair.

The name of the place was La Meat Hook. It was small and dark and had sawdust on the floor. The maitre d' met them at the door.

"Yes sir, back room or front room?" he asked Brian. Then he noticed Nelly. "I guess you'll want the front room." Throughout the meal tall, handsome men walked through the restaurant and into the back room.

The waiter wore shiny vinyl running shorts and nothing on top. He was young and incredibly handsome.

"I guess a steak would be good," Brian said. There was no menu.

"No steak. Only seafood, sir," the gorgeous waiter replied.

"I don't understand. The name of the place is the meat hook, and you have no meat?"

"It's a play on words," the waiter explained patiently.

Nelly ordered the scallops and Brian the swordfish.

Nelly's scallops came garnished with rose petals. Brian's swordfish was actually skewered on a small sword, and flambéed.

They were sipping their espresso when Nelly broached the subject. "Brian, I'm involved in a fund-raising drive for a very worthy cause."

"Oh, what do you want, a check?"

"Well, it's not really money they need. I know this sounds weird, but they are desperately in need of good sperm."

"What?"

Nelly rushed on. "It's an organization called the National Artificial Insemination League. They operate a free sperm bank for women whose husbands are impotent. And they need volunteers. You see, many donors are

36

drug addicts and welfare bums who do it just for the money. And they can't always be sure of the quality of the donation. What they want are men who have already fathered healthy, intelligent, and attractive children. Like you, for instance."

"Why don't you just get involved with something simple, like MS?"

"Listen Brian, this is important. I would really like to see you do your part."

"Okay, okay. You want my sperm—it's yours."

"It's not for me, it's for the foundation," Nelly put in quickly.

"You want it now?" he said, leering across the table.

"Not now, silly. Tomorrow morning's soon enough."

Brian seemed amused. It was much easier than Nelly had thought it would be. Everything went well until, back at her apartment, Nelly refused to have sex with him.

"I think you should save up for tomorrow," she said.

"Aw, come on," Brian protested. "There's plenty enough to go around."

"Okay, okay, but you better come through tomorrow."

"I never knew you were such a little philanthropist."

"All done?" Nelly called from outside the bathroom the next morning.

"Jesus, Nelly, give me a chance." He had already been in there for fifteen minutes. Nelly waited patiently at the door.

"Can I help?" she asked after a few minutes of silence.

"Believe me, I can do it myself," he said angrily. "I have to come in this dumb little jar, is that right?"

"Right."

"Okay. Just give me a minute." More minutes passed.

"Want me to get you a magazine or something?"

"A magazine?"

"I don't have *Penthouse*, but I have a copy of *Viva* somewhere. Maybe that'll help." No answer.

"Or I can say things to you." No answer.

"Let's give it a try. Can't hurt." She thought for a minute and then rattled off a few words:

"Fuck. Come. Vagina. Bosoms. Breasts. Pubic hair. Does that do anything for you?"

"Nothing. Absolutely nothing."

"How's this: Faye Dunaway. Jacqueline Bisset. Jeanne Moreau."

"Too old."

"Come on, Brian," Nelly said impatiently, "it's almost ten."

"Oh, that's it. Say numbers."

"Numbers? Ten, eleven, twelve, thirteen, fourteen, fifteen . . ."

"Faster."

"Sixteen, seventeen, eighteen, nineteen, twenty, twenty-one, twenty-two, twenty-three, twenty-four, twenty-five, twenty-six, twenty-seven . . ."

"Bingo!" he yelled.

She and Brian took separate taxis. Nelly told him she was going out on a story.

The nurse that Nelly had spilled urine on was seated at the desk, typing out bills.

"I have something for the doctor," Nelly said, clutching the opaque plastic jar in her hand.

"Fine, Mrs. Diamond, I'll make sure the doctor gets it," the nurse said, snatching the jar from Nelly's hands.

"Oh no you don't." Nelly tried to pry the jar out of the nurse's clenched fist. "We went to a lot of trouble to get this and I want to give it to the doctor myself."

"Really, Mrs. Diamond, I'll take good care of it," the nurse said, trying to loosen Nelly's fingers from hers. At that moment Dr. Hoffman opened his office door.

"Oh, Mrs. Diamond. Back so soon?"

"Here's the sperm, Dr. Hoffman. It's fresh."

"Well, good," he said, taking the jar. "We'll put it through the tests immediately."

"Can't I watch?" Nelly asked.

"There's really nothing to see."

"Please?"

"Very well," he said, knowing better than to argue with her, "come with me."

Nelly broadcast a bright, triumphant smile at the nurse and marched down the hallway behind Dr. Hoffman.

Dr. Hoffman took a glass slide, put a drop of clear solution on it, removed an eyedropper of sperm from the jar, and placed the slide under a microscope.

"Aren't you going to use all of it?" Nelly asked.

"No, it isn't necessary," the doctor said, peering into the microscope. "There are about 700 million sperm per fluid ounce. Looks good to me. Good number. Good mobility. But we'll send it to the lab to get a complete count. Here," he said, stepping back from the microscope, "take a look for yourself."

She saw hundreds of minuscule, tadpole-shaped creatures swimming around, blindly bumping into each other. None of them bore much resemblance to Brian. She felt a great surge of pride looking at the wiggly school of tiny sperm.

"Looks good to me, too," she said smugly.

"Now I want you to call me when you get your next period so we can set up a postcoital test."

"What's that?"

"You have intercourse with your husband in the morning and then come in within two hours and we'll check the cervix to see how far the sperm has gotten. The test will take place during mid-cycle when you're most likely to be ovulating. We get a clear picture of how hospitable the cervical mucus is to your husband's sperm."

(There he was again, the phantom husband. Who else would one have intercourse with?)

"But if the sperm count is good, there shouldn't be any problem, right?"

"Do you have any idea what these sperm have to go through?" Dr. Hoffman asked.

Nelly shook her head.

"Have you ever seen Alaskan red salmon?"

"Only in a can."

"A man's sperm, you see, is very much akin to the Alaskan red salmon." The doctor got a faraway look in his eyes.

"It has to survive almost insurmountable odds. It's upstream all the way for them. Going against the current, through the sometimes-hostile environment of thick mucus. Only the strongest swimmers survive. Many die en route. Some, at the very beginning of their journey. Some are washed up onshore along the way. It is a long, hard road to hoe."

Roads to hoe? Rivers to swim? Nelly was getting mixed up with the doctor's metaphors.

"The purpose of the postcoital test is to make sure that the sperm get through the cervix, that they don't get headed off at the pass. It just takes one, but we have to make sure that one gets there. One little tiny swimmer to achieve its goal."

Dr. Hoffman took a deep breath, the first since he had started his soliloquy on sperm. His eyes were shining. He was greatly moved. So was Nelly. She would never again take a can of Alaskan red salmon for granted.

6 Paisley

The phone rang at ten P.M. that evening. Nelly was into the fourth chapter of *Healthy Mother, Healthy Baby*. It was one of six books she had picked up at Doubleday's on her way home from covering the mayor's press conference.

"How was it?" It was Paisley. There was the sound of soft piano music in the background.

"How was what?"

"Your abortion. How'd it go?"

"Oh, that. I didn't have it," Nelly said, yawning.

"Nelly, that's crazy."

"It's not crazy at all. I decided I'm going to have a baby."

"I want you to get in a taxi right now and meet me at Peartree's."

"What for?"

"I want to talk to you, Nelly."

"But Paisley, I'm in bed."

"I don't care where you are. I have to talk to you. Now."

It was far easier obliging Paisley than having to deal with her ire later, so Nelly went.

Paisley was sitting by herself at a corner table in the front room of Peartree's, a dark, slick-looking East Side bar. She was not one of those people you have to search for in a crowd. Paisley had red hair. Not bright red or carrot red, but a deep, dark burnished red. Redheads run in two distinct categories—beautiful and not beautiful at all. Paisley was gorgeous: long, tall bones and deep cobalt blue eyes with—what else?—alabaster white skin.

"How many months along are you?" Paisley asked, eyeing Nelly's stomach critically.

Nelly sat down. "Well, it turns out I'm not pregnant after all."

"*Merci à Dieu!*" Paisley breathed a sigh of relief. "Why didn't you tell me that on the phone?" she asked, narrowing her eyes.

"Because I've decided I want to get pregnant. I want to have a baby."

"Are you taking weird drugs, or are you by any chance having a small nervous breakdown which you have neglected to mention to your friends?"

"Nope. I just think it's time I took my thirty-five years of experience, intelligence, and humanity and devoted it to being someone's mama."

"Why, in heaven's name?"

"I've never had a baby before."

"You've never had tuberculosis before, either."

"Paisley, pregnancy isn't a disease. Motherhood is not an illness."

"The next thing you're going to tell me is that it's nature's way, that it's our divine destiny, that if God hadn't meant for women to bear children, He wouldn't have given them elastic waistbands."

"I'm not going to discuss it with you. Clearly we're of two different minds on the subject."

Paisley was angry. "Most women these days are trying to break out of centuries of vassaldom and martyrdom and motherdom and you sit there, an educated, intelligent, liberated woman, and tell me that you just want to lie back and get yourself impregnated so you can be a mother?"

"Haven't you ever wanted a child?"

"You mean have I ever wanted to walk around with a big belly and get stretch marks and sick in the morning and give birth to a creature whose primary aim is to suck the life from me?"

"They usually just suck milk."

"Don't try and get technical with me, Nelly."

A man separated himself from a group at the bar and began weaving his way through the tables and chairs to their table. He looked as though he had just accepted a dare. The other men at the bar giggled among themselves as they watched him make his way. They were obviously from out of town. They wore expensive leisure suits, white shoes, and had short razor-cut hair—not straight razor but electric.

"Can I buy you two lovely ladies a drink?" he asked, addressing himself exclusively to Paisley's cleavage. Paisley had cleavage where others just had sternums.

Nelly turned away, ignoring the man. Paisley opened her little beaded disco bag, took out a small white card, and handed it to the man.

"Call anytime, day or night," she said, smiling.

The man took the card, squinted at it, nodded his head, and weaved back to the bar.

"What was that?" Nelly asked.

"I just gave him a number to call," Paisley replied nonchalantly.

"Your number?"

"No, of course not."

"Whose number?"

"I can't tell you."

"Why can't you tell me?"

"It's a secret."

"You have a secret with a strange drunk man and you won't even tell me, your dearest friend?"

"*One* of my dearest friends."

Paisley never liked to be pinned down to a monogamous anything. Nelly was always one of her *two* best friends. Her other best friend was Abby. Abby and Paisley were not that close, but Paisley needed her to make up the second of her best friends. It was something that stemmed from her childhood. She always had two of everything: two mothers (one step and one real), two fathers, two homes (one country and one city), two horses (one hunter, the other four-gaited), and two boats (one motor and one sail).

"All right," said Paisley after a moment's consideration, "I'll tell you, but you have to swear to keep it to yourself."

"I swear," said Nelly.

"I'm involved in an underground movement." Paisley was always involved in movements. She was, in her own way, very political. Not very consistent, but very political.

Paisley leaned across the table, dropping her voice and her eyelids. "As you know, I was very active with the National Organization for Women."

"I know that, right."

"Well, I finally realized they're a bunch of pussies. They just saw women's liberation as a matter of women gaining equal rights. That is not the point."

"What is the point?"

"Men have to pay. They have to be taught a lesson. *Jamais encore. Jamais encore.* Don't you see that the minute women turn their backs, men will try to fuck them? Women's liberation is not a political, intellectual, or economic issue. It is purely a physical one."

"What are you into, raping men?"

"Hardly." Her voice got even lower here. "I am part of a new splinter group called the GTWIH."

"The GTWIH? Catchy name. What does it mean?"

"It stands for Get Them Where It Hurts. And that's exactly what we do."

"What exactly do you do?"

"We work as prostitutes. High-class call girls."

"For some reason, Paisley, that doesn't sound terribly liberated to me."

"Let me finish. The card I gave that man has the number of our madam on it. She screens all calls, making sure the men are legitimate. We charge two hundred dollars an hour, so the price discourages anything but the most established businessmen. The madam sets up the tricks, the time, the place, etcetera."

"Then what?"

"The usual. Man comes over to my apartment. I take his money. We take off our clothes. I pour him a drink, chat him up, ask him what he wants, how he wants it, all in a nice, high-class-hooker sort of way. He tells me and then I give it to him."

"You give it to him."

"Right. First, they get the tape-recorded message. A loud, motherly voice is heard through every speaker in the apartment." Paisley's voice took on a stern, maternal tone: "'You are a bad, bad boy. You wanted to stick your weenie into that girl. That isn't nice. You know better than that, you naughty, naughty boy.' The message goes on for twelve hours, over and over again."

"And they sit still for that?"

"Of course not. We have to physically detain them. There's a backup squad of three women. We lock him in the bedroom. There's the twelve-hour deprogramming with tape recordings, charts, slides, a whole audiovisual presentation in a sensory-deprived environment. We render their erections into plowshares . . . After we get done the male chauvinism has been exorcised out of them, and their consciousness has been raised on a real sexual level. Their two hundred dollars goes to a rehabilitation program for prostitutes."

"Paisley, that's the craziest scheme I've ever heard," Nelly said.

"Look who's talking about crazy, Mother Hubbard," Paisley said disdainfully.

"So how many men have you done this to?" Nelly asked.

"Well, not any yet. I just joined the group. I hope he'll be my first trick," she said, indicating the man in the leisure suit who was, at that moment, showing her number around to his pals at the bar.

Nelly thought about Paisley all the way home in the taxi. How had they gotten to be such strangers, this woman who was supposed to be one of her dearest friends? Paisley had always been radical. Going off the deep end had been part of her charm. Nelly realized now that she had never taken that seriously Paisley's grape boycotting or her Save The Whooping Crane or her Ban The B-1 Bomber involvements. Or rather, she had taken seriously the cause but never the effect it seemed to have on Paisley. Paisley possessed a general, undefined fury, and the various movements were acceptable areas in which she could vent her wrath.

It had been that awesome, almost overwhelming anger that had first attracted Nelly to Paisley. It was an emotion that Nelly had a great deal of difficulty experiencing, let alone expressing. Paisley had taught her the art of anger. She had shown her that it was okay to snap and seethe and even shout on occasion.

They had met in a consciousness-raising group seven years before. There had been six of them. Paisley, with three marriages under her belt. Nelly with her one marriage going on the rocks. One self-described happily married housewife who didn't open her mouth for the first month and then didn't shut up after that. (That was Abby.) One very young, very sexually liberated law student who wasn't going to lie down and "let some man walk all over me." One widowed grandmother who was in the group because she had been too shy to join the senior singles club that her daughter kept pushing. And one very overweight woman in her middle thirties who had said she was seriously thinking of taking a female lover but hadn't yet met anyone who appealed to her.

Six different women with six different stories, which began to sound very much the same after a while. Six different women with supposedly vastly different needs, which ultimately boiled down to the same needs: to live, to love, to be loved, and, as the song goes, to laugh and be happy.

Each of them had gone into the group thinking of women as fillers. As people you saw in between dates or marriages or mealtimes. Women made good friends while you were waiting for your lover to call, your husband to get home, your children to grow up, or your share of happiness to come knocking at your door.

And then came the joyous discovery. It was as if they had uncovered a whole lost race. Women. They were fine, wonderful, strong, smart, sensitive, really terrific people. They understood anger and remembered birthdays and never forgot a face that had ever shared a pillow.

Hey, where had women been all their lives? If they were so terrific, how come nobody had ever said so? The men must have known all along, those bastards. But they had kept it to themselves. If women were so wonderful, then it somehow followed that men must be selfish, self-involved, self-congratulatory, self-assured, no-good bums.

There emerged a period of the most incredible anger at the injustices, insensitivities, and injuries inflicted by men. But their fury didn't last. In discovering and celebrating and appreciating themselves as women, the group soon came to forgive and forget.

Men, they began to realize, were human beings too. And Nelly had come to understand that the anger was just another way of avoiding that not-so-welcome responsibility of having to handle her own life.

It was clear now that Paisley had never gone through that stage. Why hadn't

Nelly seen it? She, who had valued her female friends so much, had let the relationship go like a bad marriage.

The phone was ringing as she let herself into her apartment. It was Paisley again.

"You know, Nelly, I worry about you."

"I worry about you too," Nelly said.

"I don't think you realize a child is a major responsibility."

"Funny, I was going to say the same thing about brainwashing."

"I don't want to argue with you, Nelly. Just promise me you'll think it over before rushing into anything."

"I have thought it over. And I'm still thinking it over. I appreciate what you're saying. But I'm not having the baby tomorrow. It takes at least nine months and I'm not even pregnant yet."

"And who is going to be the proud producer of this little Diamond production?"

"I guess that's one of the things I'm going to have to think about," Nelly answered.

"I suppose it will have to be some man."

"As things stand now, yes, I think you're right," Nelly said and laughed.

7 Tyler

Paisley had raised an interesting question. Who was going to be the father of her child? Luckily she had a choice. There were three men in her life. There was Clark. There was Brian. And there was Tyler.

Tall, gangling, blue-eyed Tyler. Nelly had met him the year before. He was having a major show at the Whitney Museum of American Art, and she was assigned to cover it. The show was composed of various parts of Tyler's body, done up on a monumental scale in polyurethane and plaster. The Whitney had never seen anything like it. The show, entitled "Me, Myself and Me," was a huge success.

Nelly had a preliminary meeting with him before the show to get some background for a news story. He was 100 percent Texas, from his beautiful hand-tooled cowboy boots to his authentically faded and perfectly fitted Levi's. He looked more like some horse's dream of the perfect wrangler than New York's hottest young artist.

"When did you first get involved with this Self Art, Mr. Hanks?"

"Whale, ma'am, Ah've always been involved with mahself from the time Ah was old enough to count my toes. The art part just came along later."

He had a way of speaking that expanded short, simple words into a time slot ordinarily occupied by entire sentences. The word *and* passing through his perfect mouth came out slowly, softly, and in three distinct syllables.

"See, mah art is just an excuse for me to noodle around with bodies. Ah think the human body is God's greatest creation. Ah love mah body. Ah love your body. Ah love everybody's body. Ay-ann-dah, every single part of everybody's body."

Nelly was still trying to translate what he was saying when he gently picked up her arm.

"Look, take your ar-um, for instance." His big brown forefinger traced a line along the inside of her arm. "Look at the way the upper arum curves into the elbow. And how the whole thing can fold up so nice and neat. And how the muscle there lies so quiet until you give it a little squoosh. Now if that ain't beautiful Ah don't know what is."

Nelly stared at her arm. She had certainly never thought of it as particularly beautiful. Definitely not one of her better features. Just a device to hook a hand onto. He continued lightly caressing the skin of her arm with his finger. An obscure tingle fluttered up her spine.

"Look at the little gold hairs," he said, turning her arm over. "See, each one has a little home of its own that it grows out of. And then the hairs all grow and bend together like a field of baby wheat. Ah could do a beautiful thing on your arm."

"I bet you could," Nelly said, trying to pull away.

He kept hold of her arm and lowered his head, touching his tongue to the vein on the inside of her elbow.

"Why, it even tastes good," he said, looking up at her, his Redford-blue eyes shuttered by thick, dark blonde lashes.

Nelly quickly jerked her arm away. She thought he was slightly crazed, this Texas arm-eater. Or, at the very least, strongly on the make. He smiled at her. A long, lazy grin that slowly revealed each of his flawless front teeth. His blue eyes were so translucent you could almost see through them to the other side of his sun-blonde head. He was one of the most beautiful men Nelly had ever seen. Definitely not her type. She never totally trusted a man that good-looking.

He called her the next morning and asked her out. She had even more trouble understanding him on the phone than she did in person. She said yes. She had decided that just because he was big and gorgeous didn't mean she had to discriminate against him. Maybe, underneath that flawless exterior, he was just an ordinary mortal. Maybe, she thought hopefully, he had hammer toes or some endearing defect like that.

They were supposed to go to the Lone Star Café that night to hear a friend of his who played authentic south Texas mouth-harp blues. They never got there.

As Nelly remembered it, when Tyler arrived, he had expressed an interest in "jest sorta gittin' a feel of yore place." He wandered slowly through her apartment, stopping here and there to admire a painting, caress the fabric on a chair, or gently finger the leaves of a plant. At one point he picked up one of her embroidered throw pillows, held it to his face, and inhaled it with pleasure. Nelly followed him around, fascinated as much with his sensual investigations as she was with the way his Levi's hugged his buttocks and the backs of his clearly muscled thighs. His eyes lit up when he saw the apricot silk down-filled comforter on her bed.

"Ah hope y'all won't mayund," he said, "but Ah jest have to feel that for mahself."

"Oh no, go right ahead," Nelly replied. She assumed he was going to run his fingers over it like he had everything else. Instead, he pulled off his boots and removed his jeans and shirt. He wasn't wearing any underwear. He took a deep breath, closed his eyes and fell backward on the puffy comforter. A long, sweet sigh escaped from between his soft, half-parted lips as he lay spread-eagled on the bed.

What could she do? She certainly couldn't leave the poor man all alone and unclothed in the middle of a stranger's silk comforter. She didn't want him to feel embarrassed by drawing attention to his odd behavior, so she took off her own clothes and joined him. Later, they folded back the comforter. After all, silk was silk. And he was the most wonderful lover. He knew how to make love in all the ways she liked, which was all the ways there were.

A week later, as he was cooking what he called the only bona fide chili in the world, which involved using almost every pot in her kitchen ("I thought chili was supposed to be one of the original one-pot meals." "Not Texas chili, honey-bunch."), he turned to her and said:

"I told him about us."

"Who?" Nelly asked, bending down to pick chopped onions off the floor.

"Alex."

"Who's Alex?"

"Alex is my lover."

"Your what?" she asked, standing up to look at him.

"My lover."

"Let me get this straight," Nelly said, dropping the onions into the sink. "Alex is a he or a she?"

"He's a he."

"You have a man who is a lover. I mean, you have a lover who is a man?"

"Yep."

She was shocked. She had never been to bed with a homosexual before. Naturally, most homosexuals she knew didn't go around going to bed with and making incredible love to women.

"Listen, I don't want to screw up anything for you," Nelly said, wishing it weren't her apartment so she could make a graceful exit.

"Oh, he understands. That's the great part about Alex. He knows Ah have to work this out for mahself."

"Well, you can just count me out of this working out business," Nelly said angrily. "I certainly don't want to be the one to come between you and your Alex."

"It can't be helped," Tyler said, running his hand up the back of her neck and through her hair. "It seems Ah have a thing for women. Or at least Ah have a thing for you."

He leaned over and lightly ran his tongue across her collarbone.

"They can't hang a man for having a hankerin' for a woman, can they?" he breathed.

"Not last I heard," Nelly moaned.

He was the most loving man Nelly had ever met. It was very simple as far as Tyler was concerned. He loved people, both men and women. Why rule out an entire gender from his sex life?

Their affair continued. While Tyler was satisfying his hankering for women, Nelly was satisfying her hankering for Tyler. It was one of those trial basis relationships that, by virtue of its sheer temporality, seemed like it could probably go on forever. They made no demands on each other, no promises. Their affair lacked all those elements Nelly had once considered basic to a relationship: possessiveness, jealousy, and insecurity.

So who would be the father of her child? Clark or Brian or Tyler? She really ought to narrow it down, she thought. And in all fairness to the baby, she should really disqualify Clark. He was genetically unsound. He had once told her that insanity ran in his family like color blindness.

"We've had an average of one suicide every generation for the past 150 years. When we have family reunions, the women don't swap recipes and baby pictures, they exchange medications and names of psychiatrists."

That left Tyler and Brian. Brian or Tyler? She couldn't possibly choose between the two. Both would make good father material. Brian's dependability, intelligence, sense of humor, and thick, curly hair. Or Tyler's creativity, good nature, love of life, and beautiful blue eyes. The ideal would be a mix-and-match affair, a double-decker fertilization. Their two sperms fertilizing her one egg and combining the best of all qualities from both of them. They could produce an incredibly handsome blonde-haired, blue-eyed Jewish lawyer with a flair for color, or a down-to-earth, extremely dependable, wildly creative artist with a Jewish nose. Was it possible? It was certainly an egg's ultimate sexual fantasy, wasn't it?

Nelly envisioned the whole seduction scene: two sperm—one from Brian, the other from Tyler—swimming rapidly up the narrows of her cervix, neck to neck, tail to tail. They fight the rapids upstream through the uterus, struggling to keep abreast of each other. Finally they arrive simultaneously at her egg, which lies waiting, pretty and passive, at the foot of the fallopian tubes. Her egg beams, emanating sensuousness, voluptuousness, and sheer desirability. The sperm look at the egg and then turn and face each other for the first time since they began their arduous journey. They are both breathing heavily from exertion and anticipation. Brian's sperm is feeling awkward and sort of shuffles in place. Tyler's long, wiry sperm stands still and relaxed, waiting to see what the other sperm will do. Brian's sperm makes a joke. Tyler's sperm doesn't laugh. It is a Jewish joke. But they seem to like each other even though they have nothing in common except the act at hand. They take Nelly's egg together like two old friends playing one-on-one with a giant basketball.

Or maybe there would be trouble: Brian's sperm doesn't like the looks of Tyler's sperm. It is too flamboyant. Too gentile. It is wearing cowboy boots.

"Who wears cowboy boots to a fertilization?" Brian's sperm demands, outraged.

Tyler's sperm thinks Brian's is square and uptight. Tyler takes the offensive and becomes insulting in his slow, drawling way:

"Y'all couldn't impregnate the backside of a barn."

"Sez who?" Brian retorts.

"Ah sez."

"Oh yeah?"

"Yayuh."

"Well, put 'em up," says Brian, squaring off.

There is a fight. A battle to the death right in the middle of Nelly's uterus. They batter each other mercilessly and ultimately kill each other off. And Nelly's egg, now all alone, weeps quietly at their passing.

Nelly snapped herself out of her reverie and made a decision. She would use Tyler for the postcoital test. Whereas Brian's sperm was probably ideal for counting, she knew that Tyler's would survive the trip up the uterus better. Nobody fucked longer or harder or deeper than Tyler did, which would seem to give his sperm a head start. He had tremendous stamina. Nelly assumed his sperm would, too. Tyler was about as Alaskan red salmon as they come. Even more important, she could see Tyler just about anytime she wanted to. And she couldn't always count on seeing Brian. Since Dr. Hoffman had said the postcoital test must take place during ovulation, timing was of the essence. Brian couldn't be expected to schedule his marriage around her cycle. So Tyler was it. The only trouble would be getting sex out of him in the morning. He usually didn't get up until two in the afternoon. But she could handle that.

All she really had to worry about was setting things straight with Clark. She couldn't possibly take any chances by sleeping with him from here on in. What if one of his crazy sperm sneaked in?

Nelly looked at her watch. She had been sitting at the kitchen table for a half-hour. She had a press conference to cover with Senator Scarborough late that morning. There was still plenty of time. She got dressed, gathered up her

50

Scarborough notes, put them into her Hunting World canvas bag, and left the apartment.

Maybe a combination fertilization was possible after all, she thought to herself.

Lika a pizza with both sausage and mushrooms.

8   Healthy Mother, Healthy Baby

It was a beautiful April day. Nelly decided to walk to the senator's office instead of taking a taxi. She took up a brisk, steady pace. After a few blocks she heard someone following her. Someone right behind her, breathing heavily. She began walking faster. The breathing grew even heavier. She stopped. The sound continued. It was coming from her. It was her breathing.

Oh my God, she said to herself, I am in terrible shape! Two packs of cigarettes a day probably didn't help her respiration much. She had always planned to give up smoking. She just didn't want to be one of those people who were forever quitting, announcing it to friends, only to take it up again later. She had decided that she would only quit when she knew she could stay quit. In the past she had made slight adjustments in her smoking habits—from Marlboros to Virginia Slims to True Blue 100s. Now she smoked Vantages with aqua filters. Naturally she smoked three times as much. She would definitely have to quit. There were no two ways about it. She knew babies could be affected by their mothers' addictions, even in the womb. She had visions of giving birth to a nicotine-and-tar-covered baby whose first reach would not be for the breast but a cigarette. She took her cigarettes out of her bag and dropped them into a trash basket.

Today she would start a whole new health regime. Healthy food, healthy exercise, healthy mother, healthy baby. She was really going to start taking good care of herself.

*   *   *

The story on Senator Scarborough was a real bore. She had decided to spend as little time with him as possible. She was in a rush to get to the nearest health-food store.

The senator had hooked onto what seemed to be a winning strategy for the next election. Six months before, when public opinion was running at its lowest for the three-term senator, he came out with a startling disclosure. He held a press conference to reveal the fact that he was a confirmed alcoholic. The day after his dramatic confession, the polls showed a 30 percent rise in his favor. Now the elections were drawing nearer. People no longer cared that he was a recovered alcoholic. His opposition was a fresh face. They were tired of the same old senator. The public wanted someone new with a whole new set of vices. Senator Scarborough called a second press conference. Nelly was there with her crew.

"A few months ago when I disclosed my problems with drinking, I wasn't altogether honest. In fact, I covered up something that was actually the cause of my drinking and the problems I was having at home. I have had long talks with my wife, my children, and my psychiatrist, Dr. Richard Brace. I feel, and they agree with me, that in fairness to the voters they must have all the facts at their disposal before the election so that they can decide for themselves. This is a very difficult thing for me to do."

Standing to the left of the senator was Mrs. Scarborough, who looked at him, eyes filled with love and mouth concealed by a crumpled white hanky.

"I won't mince words. I am a homosexual. I have been a homosexual for many years. My children, my wife, and my lover, Dr. Richard Brace (a slight, mustachioed man stepped forward as his name was mentioned), are all behind me and support me in this. Now, let the voters make their choice. Thank you."

A short question period followed. Nelly had no questions. She also had no doubt that the senator had managed to clinch the next election with this latest confession. The public loved admissions of guilt.

Nelly made a beeline to the largest health-food store on the East Side. For a one-a-day person, the array of bottles and names and letters of the alphabet was overwhelming. There were at least seven hundred different kinds of vitamins and minerals.

A young woman dressed in a floor-length burlap jumper came over. She wore her heavy brown hair in a single braid that ran well past the middle of her back. Her eyes were a watery green behind bottle-thick glasses. She was wearing a rather odd fragrance that seemed to be composed of a blend of brewer's yeast and lilacs.

"Can I help you?"

"Oh, please. I really don't know where to begin. I want some vitamins. A nice healthy assortment. I'm going to have a baby and I want to make sure I'm getting all the proper nutrients."

"What are you taking now?"

"Well, not much of anything really. One-A-Days and a couple of vitamin Cs now and then."

"You feel listless and tired and your bowel movements are probably soft and colorless, is that right?"

"No, I feel fine. And my bowel movements are beautiful," Nelly said defensively.

"Well, I think what we can put you on is a general vitamin maintenance program, then. Nothing complicated, just your basic requirements." She started removing bottles from the shelf.

"We'll start you out with 2,000 milligrams of C a day. Take them four times a day, as the body burns them up within five hours. You'll eventually build up to 5,000 milligrams. Now the E. Take 1,000 IUs. Be sure not to take them without eating. They need food in order to be absorbed into the system. I personally recommend a combination of wheat germ and brewer's yeast as the best vehicle for vitamin E." She handed Nelly another bottle and a larger jar.

"Vitamin D: 1,000 units. Be sure never to take more than the prescribed dose, as you can o.d. on them. Same holds true for vitamin A. The niacin will cause a flush and a general rash over your body within thirty seconds of taking it," she said, handing Nelly yet another bottle. "But don't worry, that's to be expected. Now, let's move on to the Bs."

The Bs took up one entire wall of the store. "Starting with B_1 for the eyes . . ." By the time she had finished with the B_{12}, Nelly had a shopping cart filled with brown bottles.

"And now the minerals," the woman said, leading Nelly over to another side of the shop.

"Don't you think I have enough here already?"

"It's not the quantity, it's the correct balance we're striving for. It does absolutely no good to take, for instance, a B_{12} without offsetting it with calcium and iron. You could really screw yourself up. You can't let one vitamin or mineral dominate. It can cause liver damage, hair loss, all sorts of things." Twenty minutes and twenty more bottles later, she turned to Nelly once more.

"Now, you'll want to do your food, I imagine."

"I don't see how I'll have room left to eat," Nelly said.

She chose to ignore Nelly's attempt at levity. "Vitamins, you understand, are merely a supplement. What you eat determines how well they work."

"Well, to tell you the truth, I really don't like health food," Nelly said looking around the store. "I mean, I absolutely get sick at the idea of sprouts of any kind."

"Are you eating for yourself or for your baby?" the woman snapped.

Nelly left the health-food store laden with packages, the last words of advice from the saleswoman still ringing in her ears: "Absolutely no coffee, no sugar, no salt, no alcohol, no additives of any kind, and need I say, no tobacco. They are all poisons. And whereas you might be able, by some stroke of luck, to survive ingesting them, your baby will not. Every grain of salt you put on your food contributes to future heart failure in your infant."

Clark was waiting for her in the lobby of her building.

She wasn't ready for him. She had had no time to prepare a speech. But she knew from experience that this was probably the best way. In her premarriage, pretherapy, preliberated dating days, guilt governed many of her relationships with men. At that time she gave all too much thought to how to say no to a man. Her refusals, whether for a date, a little sexual intercourse, or a long-term affair, were so elaborate, so couched in explanations and excuses, that the men, rather than taking no for an answer, always assumed a maybe. While wanting to get rid of someone forever, Nelly would invariably find herself making arrangements for the next date. She could never understand why these men continued to call her. Couldn't they add up all the excuses she made, flimsy and otherwise, and see that it was quite clear she wasn't interested? Only when she realized that a maybe was a chickenshit way of saying no and that it came very close to sounding like a yes and had nothing to do with saving feelings, but in fact made matters worse, only then could she begin to shake her head. Only when she really understood that she wasn't saying no because she couldn't say no, because a no was the one thing she herself always feared, only then could she be honest and direct. But still it was never easy.

"What's all that?" Clark asked, indicating her packages. He was sopping wet, breathing heavily, and wearing jogging shorts.

Nelly explained she was going on a health regime.

"That's insane," said the man who would know. "Throw out all that junk. If you really want to get in shape, then run."

"Run? Where?"

"Just run."

"I didn't know you ran."

"I just started. My shrink suggested it as a nonchemical cure for depression."

"Is it working?" asked Nelly, unlocking the door of her apartment.

"Not yet. I told you I just started," Clark said, collapsing onto the couch.

"How do you feel?"

"Tired, sore, and depressed. But I really think it might work. I think that the more tired and sore you get, the less chance you have to feel down. Fatigue and muscle strain are real, physical things. I'm trying to get out of my mind and into my body. You should really try it. The doctor tells me that after you pass the six-mile point, you start to experience a real high. It certainly would cure what ails you."

"What's that?"

"Your decreasing sexual drive," he said accusingly.

"I want to talk to you about that, Clark. My sexual drive isn't really decreasing. It's just that I don't feel that way about you anymore."

"You have no sexual desires for me?" he asked incredulously. "I don't believe that."

"It's true. I'm sorry, but it is."

"But you always loved having sex with me."

"I know. But things change. Women change."

"Jesus Christ, Nelly," he groaned, clutching his head. "What kind of thing is that to say to a guy . . . especially a manic-depressive? That's exactly the kind of thing that could throw me right over the line."

"I know; I'm sorry. I don't know what to do about it."

"Luckily you're catching me in a semidepressed period. I think I might be able to handle this," he said, straightening up on the couch. "So you want to stop seeing me?"

"No, actually, Clark, I don't want to stop seeing you. I just thought maybe we could eliminate the sexual intercourse from our relationship."

"You realize, of course, we have nothing else in common."

"I know, but we could always find something. I'm very interested in your head, for instance."

"You want to be friends, is that it?"

"Yes, I really would like that."

"I see." He seemed strangely pleased, not upset at all. "All right, we'll try it. But don't count on it being a raving success. I'm not known for my terrific friendships."

"I'm willing to take a chance."

"Luckily, even though I don't have that many friends, I do have a lot of people to go to bed with."

"I'm glad. I really am."

"So let's shake on it," he said, holding up his hand. She walked over to the couch and took his hand. He pulled her down on top of him.

"Come on, Clark. I mean it," she said, pulling out of his arms.

"I was just horsing around with my new pal," he said, grinning up at her.

56

9 The First Month

Nelly entered into a period of high energy, high spirits, and high activity. She was sleeping right, eating right, and thinking positively. She took her temperature religiously every morning, followed by handfuls of vitamins washed down with orange juice, wheat germ, and brewer's yeast.

She tried jogging but soon gave it up as it seemed too jarring, not conducive to the delicate process of fertilization or to an egg getting a handhold on her uterus. Instead she joined the Nickolaus Exercise Studio. The exercises were quieter and more inner-muscle oriented. There was a lot of lying on your back, tensing and relaxing the stomach muscles. It seemed to Nelly that it was good groundwork for pregnancy and delivery. She called Dr. Hoffman when she got her period to schedule a postcoital test during her next mid-cycle.

The phone rang one Saturday morning as she was taking her temperature. She answered it without taking the thermometer out of her mouth. ("It's important to get a reading directly upon waking," Dr. Hoffman had told her.)

"Hlow."

"Sweetheart!" It was her father.

"Nellikins!" And her mother.

They always got on the phone together. She couldn't ever remember talking to one of them at a time. They spoke simultaneously and usually about two different things.

"Well?" her father said after a moment's silence.

"Weh whab?" Nelly asked.

"What's new?"

"Nuffing."

"What's the matter, dear? Your voice sounds funny," her mother asked. Her mother always picked up on subtleties.

"I'b gob a themememter in my mouf."

"Are you sick?"

"Uh, just a libble colb, I thnk." Nelly looked at her watch. The three minutes were up and she removed the thermometer, studied it. It read 98.0°. She didn't know if that was good or bad. But it did seem low. She marked it down on her graph.

"You should take better care of yourself," her mother was saying. "If you would wear bedroom slippers you wouldn't catch colds." Her mother had been trying unsuccessfully to get her to wear bedroom slippers for thirty-five years.

"You know, I just can't communicate with her," her father said out of nowhere.

"With who, Dad?"

"Sarah. She just won't listen to reason. I wish you would talk to her."

"Dad, Sarah and I don't communicate any better than you do. In fact, she stopped talking to me twelve years ago. What's going on with her?"

"Vitamin C is supposed to be good. I know it helps get rid of a cold. But I really don't think it's as good as people say. Dorothy Lee's been in bed with a cold for two weeks. And she always takes vitamin C. But she also goes barefoot everywhere, so she's paying the price," her mother said.

Dorothy Lee was her mother's best friend. She was always paying the price for some kind of behavior that her mother disapproved of and had advised against.

". . . she almost cut off her arm. Had to have twelve stitches and cracked her tibula." It was her father again, on Sarah.

"How'd that happen?" Nelly asked, expecting her mother to say, "No bedroom slippers."

"She slammed the car door on her arm." Nelly knew better than to ask for details. Only her sister Sarah could figure out a way to slam a car door without removing her arm from inside the car. She was incredibly accident prone. Luckily or unluckily, she still lived at home, so there was always someone there to rush her off to the hospital. She had had her own apartment for about a year. But a severe case of Asian flu had brought her back to the homestead and she had been there ever since. Her parents were happy with the arrangement. Sarah was, after all, their baby. Sarah always talked of leaving but could never seem to bring it off. Just when she seemed to be standing on her own two feet, she would break one of them, or a leg, or get mononucleosis. Most of the ailments she seemed to suffer from were childhood diseases. She had had the measles the year before, and before that the mumps. Nelly had all but given up hope for her.

58

"Do you remember Sally Jackson?" her mother asked.

"No, I can't say that I do."

"Well, she and Bob are getting a divorce. You remember Bob? Can you imagine, after all those years?"

"They didn't put her arm in a cast. But she has to keep it immobile for six weeks. She has a sort of sling affair. I have to cut her meat for her."

Nelly could remember her father still cutting Sarah's meat for her when Sarah was twelve years old.

"Is Sarah still working at that place?" Nelly asked, not remembering which place it was.

"Oh no, she quit that job weeks ago," her father said. "They were taking terrible advantage of her. And they wouldn't give her a raise. She's looking around for another job. I told her she should take her time, make sure she gets something she's going to be happy with. No sense rushing into a new job if it's not right for you."

Sarah was not exactly the type to rush into new jobs. Over the past five years she had spent approximately fifty percent of her time standing in line for unemployment.

"Dad, don't you think she's a little old to be supported?"

"I'm not supporting her. I'm just helping her out until she gets relocated. You know, I'd do the same for you."

"I know, Dad. How's your arthritis, Mom?"

"Oh, I've had a pretty easy time of it this winter. Doctor's got me on a new medication, and of course I never go barefoot around the house. Do you remember Ethel Eagrims?"

"No."

"She was the mother of Sally Kornblum, you remember, the copper-enamel artist?"

"No, Mom, I can't place either one of them."

(Did her mother make up these names or was Nelly just losing her memory?)

"Well, anyway, she died last week. All of a sudden. One minute she was making cheese puffs and the next minute she was dead. Just like that. Cerebral hemorrhage."

"I'm sorry."

"I never liked her. She was the cause of a lot of grief around the neighborhood here, I can tell you that."

"Sarah says to tell you hello and to thank you for the blouse. You know how she hates to get on the phone."

Nelly couldn't exactly blame her sister. A conversation between the three of them was bad enough. They concluded their various subjects and said goodbye. She had almost wanted to tell her parents about the baby. She thought they would be thrilled. But wait until she was pregnant. She thought that if they could just be grandparents, they might retire from parenthood and leave Sarah to grow up on her own.

Nelly got out of bed and dressed. She was driving out to Great Neck to spend the day with Abby. Abby had wanted to meet her in the city, but Nelly said she was dying to get out in the country for a while.

"I don't exactly think of Great Neck as the country," Abby said.

"It's got trees and grass, doesn't it?"

"So does Central Park."

"Yeah, but I don't think there's as much chance of me getting mugged in your backyard."

"Where are the girls?" Nelly said when Abby greeted her.

"They're out with Jeff throwing footballs or something."

Jeff was a shortstop for the New York Mets.

"Isn't he supposed to be in spring training?"

"He's on the disabled list. He's torn the cartilage in his knee. Nothing serious; he just has to take it easy for a couple of weeks." Abby was wearing an old sweat shirt. Her hair was straight and lank. She kept picking at a loose piece of skin on her lower lip.

"What's the matter, Abby? You look awful."

"Nothing. Just a passing depression. I'll be okay in about twenty years." For once she didn't smile.

"Oh, come on, Abby, what could be that bad?"

"For one, as of yesterday it was too late to get an abortion."

"Why would you even consider an abortion?"

"Because I really don't want to go through the whole thing again. I've done it. I've had the wonderful experience of giving birth to and raising two babies. I love them both dearly. But I don't want any more. I don't think I've had a minute to myself for the last eight years. Look at my nails. I don't have time to file them. I have to clip them. Look at my head. It's empty. I literally haven't read a book since Dr. Spock, and believe me, his plots leave a lot to be desired. Now just because my husband doesn't consider a family complete without a boy, I have to keep turning them out until I get it right." Tears welled up in her eyes. "I'm too old for batting practice."

"You're the same age I am."

Abby looked stunned. "I am? You could've fooled me. Listen," she sighed, "I'm pregnant and that's all there is to it. Feeling sorry for myself is not going to help, especially when it looks as though I'm not getting much sympathy from you. You hungry?"

"I could eat."

Abby made thick turkey and cranberry sandwiches on fresh home-baked bread. She put them both on a plate and set the plate in front of Nelly.

"I can't eat all this," Nelly said. "Where's yours?"

"Oh, I'm not eating," Abby said, staring wistfully at the sandwiches.

"How can you be on a diet while you're pregnant?"

"I'm not on a diet. I'm just watching my weight. The eating for two thing is a myth," Abby explained. "It's just an excuse for women to get fat while they're pregnant. Doctors don't like you to gain any weight. They allow five pounds over the baby's weight, that's about it. I'm not starving my unborn fetus, if that's what you're worried about. She's getting plenty."

"You think it's going to be another girl?"

"What else?"

Nelly finished the first sandwich and started in on the second. "How does it feel?"

"How does what feel?" Abby took a piece of turkey off Nelly's plate and popped it into her mouth.

"How does it feel to be pregnant? Physically, I mean."

"Well, your boobs get bigger almost immediately. And you feel tired all the time. And you have to go to the bathroom constantly. In fact, that's how you first know you're pregnant. You're running to pee every five minutes."

"Don't you get morning sickness?"

"I never had it. There are certain things that give me indigestion, but that's about it. Why all this sudden interest?"

"Promise not to laugh?"

"I won't laugh."

"I'm planning on having a baby."

"Oh no! You're not pregnant?"

"Not yet. But I plan to be as soon as it is physically possible."

"I'm still not laughing," Abby said. "Also, I'm not comprehending either. You've got everything I want: a terrific career, a great figure, a wonderful love life, all the freedom in the world, and no stretch marks. What in the world do you want to tie yourself down with a kid for?"

"Obviously you thought kids were important enough to have."

"It's different in my case. I married young. I just never had as many choices as you have."

"Having a baby is one of my many choices. It's something that I don't plan to miss out on. You've already had two kids. But I've never even been pregnant."

"How come you never had any children with Jordan?"

"I don't know. I guess it never seemed like the right time or the right marriage."

"But you're not married now. How can you even begin to think about it?"

"That's one of the excuses I've always used—waiting for the right man and all that. But it's just an excuse. I realize now if I really want a baby, I can have it. And I really do want a baby."

"What are you going to do once you have it? There's the raising part, you know."

"I'm getting about as much enthusiasm from you as I did from Paisley."

"What did Paisley say?"

"She said I was crazy."

"Ditto," said Abby, taking the half-finished sandwich off Nelly's plate. She stared at it as though looking for bugs and then bit into it with vigor.

"Listen, why don't you just wait? If my next one's a girl, I'll make a gift of her to you."

"I almost think you're serious."

"It's not a half-bad idea, you know. I'll have her. You can raise her. That way I don't have to take time off from my career."

"What career?"

"That is exactly my point. How the hell am I ever going to get anywhere if every time there's an audition I can't go because I'm having a baby?" Abby said angrily.

"Listen, I appreciate your offer," Nelly said, "but I think I'd rather have my own baby."

"Don't say I never offered." Abby took the empty sandwich plate, got up from the table, and walked over to the kitchen sink. She turned on the tap, then stood for a moment staring out the window.

"Nelly, about you having a baby," she said, still looking out the window.

"Yes?"

"It's not that I don't understand. It's just that I don't understand. Do you know what I mean?"

Nelly smiled. "Strangely enough, I do."

10 The Second Month

According to the engraved invitation, the party was to begin at 10 P.M. At Studio 54 that meant 1 A.M., which is when they arrived. It was a party in honor of one of Tyler's biggest patrons, Dewey Morton III. He had the largest private collection of unclassified art in the world. If it was expensive, Morton collected it. A high price was the only prerequisite.

Even with the engraved invitation they still had to wait to be allowed entrance. It was humiliating, insulting, and incredibly effective. People loved the feeling of exclusivity that emanated from Studio 54 even if the exclusiveness extended to them. Luckily she and Tyler didn't have to wait long before they were passed through.

Three hours and six hundred songs later they were still dancing. The multimedia show was already on its third repeat and Nelly was tired. She had told Tyler she wanted to get home early. His idea of early was while it was still dark, which could mean seven A.M. in the wintertime. She was scheduled for the postcoital test at eleven that morning. That meant that they had to have sex by nine or ten at the latest. Tyler, of course, knew nothing of this. Just as she hadn't told Brian, she also felt that Tyler shouldn't or wouldn't want to know about her push to get pregnant. She didn't want to confuse the whole issue with men and their fears or desires regarding fatherhood.

Tyler liked sex in the afternoon or early evening. He was practically comatose until three P.M. Having been raised on a ranch and getting up at the crack of dawn for most of his childhood had instilled within him a great love of sleeping late.

"Tyler honey, let's go," Nelly said as he twirled her in on one arm and then let her out on the other.

"Sweetpea, it's early."

"I told you, I've really got to get up in the morning. Please?"

"Okay, boss lady."

Tyler stayed up another two hours humming old Roy Rogers songs to himself as he made sketches for new pieces on a roll of paper towels. When he finally slipped under the covers, it was almost eight A.M. He fell asleep immediately. Half an hour later, Nelly began licking his ear. No response. No movement. She ran her tongue lightly down the side of his neck. Still no response. She moved to his penis, licking and sucking and licking and sucking. After fifteen minutes, her mouth was dry and she couldn't go on. She got out of bed, got herself a glass of orange juice, washed her face, brushed her teeth, and went back to her ministrations. She gently caressed his penis and balls with the tips of her fingers. Still he didn't wake. Finally she took his entire penis in her mouth and she proceeded to hum his favorite: "Ghost Riders in the Sky." Suddenly his cock rose to the occasion. His eyes fluttered open and he smiled.

"And all at once he listened as he heard this mournful cry . . ." Tyler sang.

Before she left she kissed him on the eyebrow. He had fallen asleep again, his long brown arm hanging off the side of the bed.

Everything was on schedule. She was, according to her temperature graph, ovulating. There had been a sharp drop the day before, which signaled the start of the migration of the egg. She was excited as she made the mark on the graph. Something was happening. She had released an egg and it was making its slow, lazy way down her fallopian tube. And now, thanks to Tyler, there was going to be a welcoming committee of strong, healthy sperm. Who knows, she might at this very minute be getting pregnant. She hoped the postcoital test wouldn't interfere with the whole fertilization process. She would have to ask Dr. Hoffman about that.

She walked gingerly, as though too strong a step might disturb the inner aquatics of sperm and egg.

The actual test only took a minute. In and out and under the microscope.

"How'd I do?"

"Mrs. Diamond, the way we conduct these tests is to go through the entire infertility workup before giving a diagnosis. It can be misleading to evaluate each individual test."

"Oh come on, Dr. Hoffman, you can tell me. I can handle being informed, truly."

"Well, so far everything looks good. Your cervical mucus appears to be hospitable to sperm during ovulation."

"That's good, right?"

"It's neither good nor bad; it's just another test."

"But I passed, didn't I?" Nelly pressed.

"Yes, you passed."

"Hooray."

"I have to caution you again, Mrs. Diamond, this is just one test. There are others."

"I know. I know. But so far, so good."

"I just don't want you to get your hopes up until all the data is in."

"I won't. I won't. I happen to be a very rational, realistic, don't-jump-to-conclusions kind of person," she assured him, her spirits soaring.

It was only about two weeks later when Nelly first noticed that her breasts seemed to be getting larger. She felt them gingerly. They were definitely bigger and felt slightly sore. At the same time she was aware of feeling a little tired. And, in looking back over the day, she remembered peeing with much greater frequency. She tried to be cool and objective about all the symptoms. She ran through them all in her head. It just seemed like she was urinating more often because she was watching for it. Her breasts just seemed to be larger because she was constantly checking them. (She had probably massaged them into a bigger cup size.) She was feeling tired just because she had been working hard. As soon as she successfully eliminated each of the hypothetical symptoms, she went back to her original assumption: she was pregnant. She knew the postcoital test was an even greater success than Dr. Hoffman had supposed. True, she had no morning sickness, but then Abby had said it wasn't mandatory. Her stomach even seemed larger. There was already a slight swelling. Could that be possible? She didn't want to ask Dr. Hoffman any more questions at this point. He would only tell her she was jumping the gun. But boy did she have a surprise for him. Wait till all the data were in. Ha!

For two days she went around with a silly little secret smile on her face. She ran her hand over her stomach at every available opportunity. She felt wonderful. A little tired. But wonderful.

When she saw the bloodstains on her panties, she panicked. Her first thought was: miscarriage. And then it hit her.

The swollen tummy and breasts, the feelings of fatigue—it was nothing more than her monthly period. Her same old every-monthly period.

She had always suffered through a little menstrual depression every month. Nothing more than a minor shortness of temper, a slight reduction in good spirits. But it was nothing compared to the deep down, dark, heavy depression she then experienced. She couldn't get over the feeling that having her period was no longer just having her period; it was like having a dead baby. Maybe that was what her mother had meant when she called it the curse. It was the curse of the unborn child.

65

When Nelly was ten, her mother had very calmly and very clinically explained it all to her: as a mature woman, she could expect bleeding once a month. It was nothing to be alarmed about. It was natural. It was beautiful. And it was called: the curse. Somehow the term was not in keeping with the whole celebratory woman's function thing.

How could she have let herself get carried away like that? Dr. Hoffman was right. She was jumping to conclusions. She was being too impatient. Give it time, she said to herself. After all, she was just a beginner at this pregnancy thing. She couldn't expect it to happen the first month.

But then again, she had been ovulating; at least she thought she was. She had seen it there in black and white on the temperature graph. And she had had intercourse during ovulation with a healthy male. Wasn't that the standard procedure? Her cervical mucus had been warm and welcoming. Dr. Hoffman had said so himself. What could have gone wrong?

There would be other months, other chances, she thought to herself. She had cramps. Terrible, clutching cramps. It was as if her body were willing her period away, rejecting the whole concept of it. So what? It was just another period. Nothing to get upset about. Better luck next time, she told herself.

She opened up a new box of Tampax, hoping it would be her last.

11 The Third Month

Nelly entered into the third month of tests vowing to keep cool. It wasn't that she wouldn't think about getting pregnant. She was just determined not to get as involved or carried away as she had previously. She would go about the business of her life and just let nature take its course.

For the first time in years, she remembered the superstition that had governed so much of her childhood: it is unlucky to want something too much. To hope for and wait for something to happen was a very good way to insure that it never would. Your best bet was not to even think about it and then be pleasantly surprised when whatever it was transpired. It was the kind of passive approach to life that Nelly had long since rejected. She had learned that if you want something you have to go out and get it, or at least go out and try for it. But this baby thing seemed slightly out of her control, slightly out of reach of even her best trying. She decided to put it as much out of her mind as possible.

She was having coffee one morning at the studio cafeteria with Joe Williams, another newscaster, when Ben Simon, their executive producer, came over.

"The only way I can think of to be fair about this is either by flipping a coin or arm-wrestling. Arm-wrestling is out because Nelly would probably win," he said.

"What is it?" Joe asked.

"We got permission to do an exclusive up at Hyannisport. It involves a couple of weekends with the family, probably a little sailing, a little touch football, a little lobster. You know, the usual Cape Cod routine. And, of course, the undivided attention of our possible next Prez."

"Okay, Nelly, best two out of three," said Joe, putting his elbow on the table.

"Joe can have it," Nelly said to Ben. "I'm working on something else."

"Wait a second. You're not giving in that easily," Joe said suspiciously. "What something else?"

"I'm doing research on a natural-childbirth story."

"Nelly, that ain't exactly news. And no news ain't exactly down your alley. What's the matter, competition getting too tough for you?" asked Joe.

"Listen, if Teddy Kennedy had anything important to say, don't you think he'd call and tell me?" Nelly joked.

"I don't get it, Nelly. There was a time when you would've fought tooth and nail for this assignment," Ben said.

"Well, let's just say I'm letting my nails grow," Nelly answered, smiling sweetly at both of them.

"What is your angle on the natural childbirth thing? Joe's right. It's not exactly new," Ben said.

"I'm doing a comparison of natural childbirth versus cesarian to see how the babies are affected in their first months. There is some new research which shows how these two totally different methods of delivery create two totally different personality types."

"But you just finished the 'New Conceptions' thing. I don't understand this sudden preoccupation with motherhood," Ben said.

"You may not be aware of it, Ben, but we are entering into a whole new psycho-sociological era. It's a return to traditions, to the old values. What I'm saying is, this goes beyond the back-to-nature kick. Statistics indicate that births are on the rise again. Motherhood is back by popular demand. Child rearing has taken on tremendous importance. People want to do it and do it right this time. Once a week with 'The Waltons' just isn't enough to assuage the old family feeling. Trust me; I know what I'm talking about. Natural childbirth isn't news. But the way people are dealing with it is."

"Okay, okay. Sounds interesting. Go ahead with it."

It did sound interesting. Nelly had just made it up on the spur of the moment. But she had needed Ben's approval.

She had tried to enroll in a Lamaze natural childbirth class the day before, but the coach wouldn't take her, on the grounds that it was much too early.

"We like mothers to come in six weeks before delivery. That seems to be the most effective. And you certainly aren't that far along."

"Well," Nelly had said, "actually I'm not pregnant. I'm a newscaster for WABC News and I wanted to take the course for background on a story I'm doing."

68

"It really isn't necessary for you to take the whole course. I can give you all the information you need in a book we put out. And, if you like, you can observe a couple of classes.

"I'd really like to have the total experience," Nelly had said.

The woman had finally agreed. But she insisted on getting a letter of clearance from the station. Now Nelly would have no problem getting Ben to write it.

She worried for a moment that she was getting obsessive again. No, she argued with herself, she was just getting a head start. It was like getting into condition. The longer you did the exercises, the better the birth. And it was a good way to get her mind off fertilization and pregnancy. It certainly seemed a healthy enough interest for someone who could be pregnant any minute now.

"Did your wife have natural childbirth?" she asked Brian one night over drinks.

"I guess so."

"What do you mean, you guess so? Don't you know? Weren't you there at the delivery?"

"To tell you the truth, I wasn't."

"Why not?"

"Well, they wouldn't let me in."

"I don't understand. That's part of the whole natural childbirth thing. Why wouldn't they let you in?"

"I guess it was because I was unconscious."

"Oh, you passed out in the delivery room?"

"Actually, I passed out before. When they handed me the mask, that's when I keeled over. It happened all three times."

"What was it, the idea of seeing all that blood?"

"Oh, no, it wasn't that at all. It was the damned mask. I'm claustrophobic. I couldn't breathe."

"Was your wife disappointed?"

"I don't think so. She always had the Lamaze teacher standing by. The two of them handled it together. She said they were wonderful births. So I guess it really didn't matter that I wasn't there."

Abby had had both her children *au naturel.* Her husband was a firm believer in the Lamaze method. He had color Polaroids and cassette tapes of every second of each birth. Nelly asked to hear the tapes.

"You mean Jeff never played these for you before?" Abby asked, amazed.

"Well, I think he did try once. I just wasn't interested at the time. But I'd love to hear them now."

"They go on for hours. I'll just play selected highlights."

Nelly could hear the sound of someone breathing. Short, quick outakes of breaths. "Whooo. Whooo. Whooo."

"This is about five minutes before Jill came out," Abby interjected.

The breathing got quicker and louder. "Whoo. Whoo. Whoo."

"That's beautiful," Nelly said, her eyes misting.

"That's not me you're hearing, that's Jeff breathing. I couldn't breathe. My teeth were gritted."

"Whooo. Whooo. Whooo."

"In a minute or two you'll hear me. I'm the one screaming out for painkillers. On second thought, I think we'll skip that part," Abby said, switching off the tape recorder. "Jeff is very big on Lamaze. I think you should probably talk to him. He had wonderful deliveries. Me, I hurt like hell. And they wouldn't give me a damn thing. Not even an aspirin."

"But that's against the whole principle of natural childbirth."

"It's not against my principle: avoid pain at all costs. I suppose it is a wonderful thing. Jeff certainly got a high from it."

Nelly's next scheduled test was the hysterosalpingography.

She was a little nervous about it. Especially when Hoffman had difficulty pronouncing it. She had to go to a radiologist for this one, as Dr. Hoffman didn't have all the fancy X-ray equipment needed for the job.

The radiologist's nurse explained the test: it was simply an X-ray examination of the inside of her uterus and her fallopian tubes.

"A liquid dye is injected through the vagina into the uterus and we take pictures. The doctor can watch the progress of the fluid on that screen over there," she said, pointing to what looked like a TV monitor. "So if it slows up or stops at any point, he can actually pinpoint the blockage. It'll only take a few minutes and will probably give you cramps . . . very similar to bad period cramps . . . but just for a second."

It was a relief to have a woman explain exactly what was going to happen and exactly how it would feel. The radiologist came in. He looked as if he were ready to go on the "Today Show." He was all smiles, flourishes, and nonstop chatter. So unlike Dr. Hoffman. Nelly figured he was probably excited about doing something other than X-rays of femurs or tibulas. Getting to do a hysterosalpinograph was probably a nice break in routine for these guys.

"Look over there," he said, pointing to the TV screen.

Nelly was having cramps and didn't want to look at anything.

"Look, you're on TV. Live," he said.

Nelly grunted and looked up at the screen. Sure enough, she could see a thin line of white opaque fluid making its way into the fallopian tubes.

"It's going through," she cried. "It's going through. That means my tubes aren't blocked?"

"That's right," the doctor nodded. "Of course, this is not the definitive tubal test. Because it's liquid, it passes through very easily, even through the narrowest openings. It's a kind of one-dimensional picture, but not a bad picture at that, if I do say so myself," he said, staring proudly at the screen.

Nelly agreed. She had never felt as pleased with a television performance as she felt at that moment.

12   Testing, Testing

Nelly got into the rhythm of the tests. She now looked at the workup as a series of steps that she had to go through before she got pregnant. Each individual test was like a prerequisite that had to be fulfilled. She knew that when the tests were all completed and the data in, and it was scientifically proven beyond a shadow of a doubt that she could get pregnant, then she would, indeed, get pregnant. She viewed the whole process as a sort of trial by microscope that was necessary not just to prove her physical capability but to establish the seriousness of her purpose. In other words, she felt she had to make up for all the years of never wanting or never thinking about having a baby. In order to prove herself a worthy candidate for motherhood, she had to pay her dues. The longer it took, the more it cost, the more painful it was, the closer she felt to achieving her goal.

There was the endometrial biopsy, or egg test.

"The endometrial biopsy not only determines whether or not ovulation has occurred, but it also tests for the quality of the ovum, or egg," Dr. Hoffman explained.

"You mean there's such a thing as good eggs and bad eggs?" Nelly asked.

"Yes, indeed."

"How can you tell the difference between a good egg and a bad one?"

Hoffman, who had been so eloquent on the subject of sperm, was much more clinical when it came to eggs.

"A good egg, as you call it, is one that is surrounded by a mass of follicular nutrient cells. These cells help the microscopic hairs in the tube get a firmer hold on it so the egg can be passed along to the uterus. Moreover, eggs of good quality create good hormonal production, that is, succulent glands in the womb which provide the best possible nesting place for a fertilized egg. Now, if it's a bad egg, there is mediocre hormonal production and the lining of the womb shows poorly developed glands and, consequently, poorer chances of supporting the life of a fertilized egg."

"I wonder if that's where the expression He's a good egg comes from?"

"I really wouldn't know."

"Are some women better egg producers than others?"

"Sometimes. But the point is that eggs are at a premium. A rabbit ovulates every time she copulates, but a woman only produces one egg a month. That's about four hundred eggs during her lifetime, or period of fertility. Now, fifteen percent of these are completely unfertilizable. Twenty-five percent, if fertilized, never make it. That leaves no more than sixty percent for making babies."

"But sixty percent of 400 eggs is, let's see . . ." Nelly made some quick calculations on a pad she always carried with her to these conferences, "that's 240 eggs."

"That's the total maximum a normal woman produces. Which is not to say that every egg is of good quality, or if it is of good quality that it will be fertilized, or if it is fertilized that it will survive to term. And if pregnancy does occur, the woman stops producing eggs for nine months. So there aren't really as many possibilities as you might think."

"In other words, don't count your eggs before they're hatched."

"Exactly. Now, the egg test involves taking tissue from the lining of the uterus a week after ovulation should have started. Then we examine it under a microscope to see whether the succulent glands associated with progesterone production are present. So we know two things: first of all, that ovulation has occurred, and second, that a good egg has been produced."

It all sounded terrific to Nelly. So methodical and logical. Unfortunately, the egg test hurt like hell—sharp, unexpected pain that exploded in some deep, tender, never-before-touched area of her womb. The fern test, the spinbarkeit and the estrogen index, all tests for hormones, were painless. Then came the Rubin test. To Nelly it was just another test. To Dr. Hoffman it was crucial.

"We pass carbon dioxide through the tubes from the cervix," he explained. "It is passed through very slowly, with measured pressure."

"Pass away," Nelly said, staring up at the ceiling. Whereas her mind had welcomed all the facts and details and explanations about each individual test, her body resisted the reality of being invaded by foreign objects, probing fingers, and the roving eye of Dr. Hoffman's head lamp. She had begun to feel that the passage between her legs had become a long hallway down which modern medicine and all its machinery marched.

She heard the hiss of gas. It seemed miles away. She focused on a tiny hairline crack in the ceiling. She followed the crack with her eyes from the corner of the room to where it ended at the round, white, light fixture. It looked like the Colorado River. No, it didn't curve enough. It was more like the Mississippi. She wondered how often the doctor had his offices painted. Did he have to pay for it or was it in his lease? Her apartment was due for a painting. She thought of doing it in eggplant with white trim. Which would mean she would have to have all her furniture recovered. How many coats would she need? A designer friend of hers had told her that eggplant went with everything. Was that possible? She didn't even like the color. She just liked the idea of having eggplant walls.

"Okay. You can sit up now," Dr. Hoffman said.

Nelly sat up, swinging her legs off the side of the examining table; she clutched the paper covering to her chest.

"Any pain?" Dr. Hoffman asked, studying her face closely.

"No, none at all. I feel fine."

"Let's wait a few seconds to see if any pain does occur."

That was odd, Nelly thought. He was usually out the door by this time. Instead he stood there looking at Nelly and waiting. They both waited without speaking. It was almost as if he were listening for something. Minutes passed, and he asked again.

"Pain?"

"No."

It occurred to her that she was, perhaps, not understanding this particular test.

"Am I supposed to have pain?" she asked finally.

"Pain in one or both of the shoulders indicates that the gas has passed through."

"All the way to my shoulders?"

"That's a result of the gas pushing up at the diaphragm, which means that it has gotten through the tubes."

"So if I have no pain that means that the gas hasn't gotten through which means that it's been blocked in my tubes."

"That's right."

"I don't understand. When I had my X-ray, the dye passed through my tubes. I saw it myself."

"That's an entirely different matter. The dye is a liquid and therefore passes through more easily. But you must remember, that the Rubin is a therapeutic test. In other words, the pressure of pushing the gas through can open up blocked tubes, especially when we increase the pressure, which we'll do next time."

"There's no danger of explosion, is there?" Nelly asked worriedly.

"No, none at all," Dr. Hoffman said, smiling.

He did the Rubin test three more times. Each time he asked her if there was any pain in her shoulders, and each time she replied no. There was, however, the unpleasant sensation of having gas pumped into her as if she were a balloon being prepared for ascent. The repetition of the Rubin test worried her a little. She felt as if she had flunked something and was required to repeat the course. She asked the doctor about it. He was, as usual, totally noncommittal. It was just another test.

Her concern over the Rubin test was offset by her temperature graphs. Now after taking her temperature every morning for three months, she could see a pattern. She checked it with a chart she had found in a gynecological textbook. In all three months there was a definite drop during her mid-cycle. There were two curves in the graph. She was, as far as she could tell, duplicating the fertile graph in the book. She was a bonafide egg producer.

She stopped asking questions and stopped reading books. She felt that she had done her homework and that everything was in Dr. Hoffman's capable hands. She had had enough of science for the time being. She looked forward to the magic and miracle of conception.

In order to get her mind off the various tests and her forthcoming pregnancy, she decided to throw Abby a shower. She discussed it with Paisley.

"I really don't think Abby wants a shower," Paisley said. "I mean, it's not as if this were her first blessed event."

"All the more reason why she would appreciate a shower," Nelly argued.

"I suppose what you have in mind is one of those suburban gatherings where sixty women devour multilayer pimento, cream cheese, and tuna sandwiches followed by large pieces of pineapple upside-down cake while they sit and chatter over gifts of diaper pails and bottle warmers."

"Paisley, you surprise me. I never thought you'd been to a shower before."

"I never have. Those are my worst fears of what one must be like. I have a much better idea. Why don't we just take her out to lunch at Lutece or someplace comparable?"

"You think she would prefer that?"

"I do. I really do."

"All right. But let's make it a surprise."

"How can we make it a surprise? We have to tell her about it, otherwise she won't know to get a baby-sitter."

"You sure know how to take the fun out of everything."

"Really, Nelly, a surprise party! How *mal élevée* can you get?"

Lutece was one of the few four-star restaurants in New York. Those people who were not discouraged by their outlandish prices were invariably intimidated by their haughty demeanor. Paisley had been a regular of Lutece for years and so merited the ultimate privilege of one of the front banquettes. Paisley and Abby were the first to arrive. Henri, the maitre d', gave them his maximum bow—a slight lowering of his sleek head—and led them to their table. A waiter came and took their drink order. Paisley had a Lillet and Abby a dry martini.

"I suppose you know all about her master plan," Paisley said, lighting up a thin black cigar.

"You mean Nelly's baby? Oh yes, we've discussed it several times now," Abby said.

"I take it you've had no more luck than I have talking her out of it."

"Has anybody ever talked Nelly out of anything?"

"But this is really too much. I've always thought of Nelly as the level-headed one. The whole idea is absurd."

"It's funny—she's gotten into the habit of calling me practically every day."

"To talk about her baby?"

"No. To find out how I'm feeling. It's as if she's going through my pregnancy with me. Or maybe it's because I'm the only mother she knows."

The waiter hovered above them, mustache quivering, pencil poised.

"*Oui, mesdames, vous voulez faites votre selection?*"

"No, we're still waiting for someone," Paisley answered. "Oh, here she is now. My God," she gasped, "what in the world has she got with her?"

Nelly was carrying a large, bright yellow, plastic laundry basket filled to the brim with small, colorfully wrapped packages. Her eyes and cheeks were glowing. She sat down at the banquette, placing the basket on the table, and flashed Paisley and Abby a huge smile.

"What in the world is that?" Paisley asked, not capable of pointing at the basket.

"Surprise," Nelly said grinning.

"Oh Jesus, Nelly, not at Lutece," Paisley hissed. She quickly glanced over at Henri, who stood at the doorway looking at them, his thin lips curled in disgust. He met Paisley's eyes and then looked the other way. With the exception of Henri, there was not one person in the entire restaurant who wasn't looking at them.

"They're going to revoke my banquette forever," Paisley moaned, pressing down her eyelids with forefinger and thumb.

Abby's mouth was open. It had been open since Nelly placed the yellow basket in the center of the white damask tablecloth.

"What is it?" Abby said, barely breathing.

"Shower gifts, what else? Go on, open them," Nelly said brightly.

"Oh, Nelly, I couldn't. Not here," Abby whispered.

"Why not here? Don't you think these people have ever seen baby gifts before? Come on, Abby."

Abby cautiously reached forward and took the top package from the basket. She held it in her hands, staring at it as if it were some foreign, vaguely obscene object. The wrapping paper was covered with pink and yellow baby ducks sitting on a baby-blue background.

"Go on, open it," Nelly urged.

Abby carefully peeled off the baby duck wrapping. Not knowing whether to laugh or cry, her mouth was scrunched up somewhere in between.

"It won't stop here," Paisley mumbled to herself. "Henri will call the maitre d' at La Caravelle, and they'll ban me there too. I'll end up having to eat at Schrafft's."

Abby unfolded a small, round piece of fabric with little ties on it. "What is it?" she asked, trying to focus in.

"It's a bib. Isn't it adorable?" Nelly chirped. She took the bib from Abby's limp hands and held it up for everyone, including the maitre d', who was now looking their way again, to see. "It's hand embroidered from Finland. Go on, do the rest," she coaxed.

"I just couldn't," Abby pleaded.

"Don't be silly. There're so many darling things. Just look." Nelly began opening the baby-blue packages. She held up the contents, identifying each item and extolling its individual virtues.

"Look, a mobile from Creative Playthings." She read from the tag which was connected to the multicolored floating fish mobile, "'Helps the infant make eye contact in the first months.' Next a set of six dinosaur diaper pins. A cashmere layette for size one to three months. You can exchange it for pink if it's a girl. A baby-food warmup tray with rechargable batteries. The saleslady told me they're terrific. You can keep the food warm no matter how slow an eater the baby is. A scrapbook for baby's first six months. See, it's got a page for the first tooth, first words, first steps, and a place to keep weights and measurements. Little sockettes with flowers. And little sockettes with rabbits. A sun hat. And a rain hat. A stuffed turtle. Hypoallergenic. A fish rattle. It goes with the mobile. A teething bagel. Isn't that hysterical? A baby muffets sleeping bag. Nonflammable. And look: a jogging outfit with little booties that look like running shoes. I never had so much fun shopping in my life," she said, surveying the gift- and wrapping-strewn table. She turned to Abby. "What's the matter, don't you like them?"

Abby took a deep breath. "Oh, I do. I'm just overwhelmed, that's all," she said, trying to stuff the loose paper back into the basket. "Everything's wonderful, Nelly, really."

"I could move to San Francisco. Or maybe Sao Paolo," Paisley was muttering. "They have restaurants there. They may not be all that good, but they have them."

"What are you doing after lunch?" Nelly asked Abby.

"Nothing. Why?"

"Why don't we go shopping?"

"Not more baby gifts! You bought everything any baby would ever need."

"Or want," Paisley added.

"I was thinking you might like to go shopping for maternity clothes," Nelly said, eyeing Abby's one and only presentable maternity dress, which had all the style and much the same color of a pup tent.

"I really have all the maternity clothes I need," Abby said.

"Or want," Paisley piped in again.

"Oh, come on," Nelly said, ignoring Paisley. "It'll do you good."

"Stop it!" Paisley snarled.

Nelly turned to face her, her eyes wide with surprise. "Stop what?"

"Stop this baby-buying, maternity-shopping, shower-throwing lunacy. I can't stand it anymore. Leave poor Abby alone. Let her carry on her pregnancy in her own quiet little way. If you want to buy out Bloomingdale's baby department or drive some saleslady crazy at Lady Madonna, you go right ahead. If you want to get pregnant, then get pregnant. But you leave Abby and me and Lutece out of it, do you hear?"

Nelly's eyebrows shot up. The color flooded into her face. "I don't understand you. Either of you. All I wanted to do was have a little celebration for what I consider to be a major joyous event in Abby's life . . . in all our lives. It's gotten so that nobody is allowed to feel good about anything anymore without someone saying they're getting carried away. If both of your lives are so filled with happiness and cheer that you can't possibly handle anymore excitement, then fuck it, fuck you. And fuck Lutece!"

Paisley's eyes rolled heavenward in exasperation.

Abby reached across the table and grabbed Nelly's hand. "I'm sorry, Nel. Really. I do love everything. And the baby will, too. And I am happy you're so happy about the baby. Please let's not argue. Let's just have a nice lunch, okay?"

"I doubt seriously if they'll take our order at this point," Paisley said tonelessly. "But I'll give it a try." She started to signal for the waiter but he was at their table before she could lift a finger.

When Nelly stopped by the station later that afternoon, there was a message for her to call Dr. Hoffman's office.

"Dr. Hoffman, please. Nelly Diamond calling."

"Oh, Mrs. Diamond." It was the nice nurse. "Dr. Hoffman just wants to set up a conference with you. When would be convenient?"

"Not a test?" Nelly asked.

"No, no. He just wants to have a talk with you."

"Well," she said glancing at her schedule, "I could come in tomorrow just about anytime."

"Shall we make it about two?"

"Two would be fine."

Nelly wondered if she should go back and review any of the material she had read. Then she realized that this was probably the all-the-data-is-in-so-I-can-give-you-my-prognosis conference.

She slept very little that night. She plotted the temperature graphs in her mind's eye, ran through the various tests in her head, and tried to think if there was anything he or she had overlooked, any corners left unturned, any areas yet unprobed. Finally, around four A.M., she came to the conclusion that he would tell her everything was A-okay and that it was all right for her to go ahead and get pregnant. The medical data, charts, and instruments were mentally set aside, and in their place emerged the picture of a baby nestling inside her tummy, thumb in mouth, eyes squeezed shut, toes tightly turned up. Her baby. Her soon-to-be baby. Her baby, baby little baby. Sleeping. Sleeping. Curled and quiet. With that picture firmly in place, she fell asleep, her mouth lifted in a smile.

"There is one more test to do. It's called a culdoscopy. It involves an overnight hospital stay and a local anesthetic," Dr. Hoffman said.

"The hospital! I don't understand. What exactly is this test?" Nelly asked, alarmed.

"It's a direct visualization of the pelvic organs—the ovaries, uterus, and most important, the tubes."

"But I had that beautiful X-ray done."

"As I said, this is a direct look. We transmit a blue dye through the tubes, so we can tell exactly what's going on there. As in the Rubin test, the culdoscopy can also be therapeutic; by virtue of the pressure exerted, it can result in an opening of the tubes, in the event of any closures."

"You're saying that there's still a problem with my tubes," Nelly said warily.

"I'm saying that I can't make a complete diagnosis until I get a direct look, which the culdoscopy will provide me."

"If this culdoscopy is such a definitive test, why didn't we just do it first, instead of all this pussy-footing around, if you'll forgive the expression?"

"Because there is a proper procedure, as I've told you many times . . ."

"Okay, okay. Just tell me, how exactly do you get this panoramic view of my inner organs? Do you cut me open?"

"No. There is a similar procedure called a laparoscopy, whereby a small incision is made through the belly button and . . ."

"Don't tell me. I like the sound of the culdoscopy much better. There's no cutting, right?"

"That is right. It's completely painless."

"Completely painless," Nelly repeated, as if saying would make it so.

"Here, let me show you." Dr. Hoffman opened the top drawer of his desk and took out an object of pink, molded plaster.

"What's that?"

"This is a model of the female reproductive system." It resembled nothing Nelly had ever seen before. There were winding canals outlined in red, and large, vague cavities outlined in blue. She studied it for several minutes, trying to get her bearings.

The model was made out of the same materials that were used to illustrate human organs in her high-school biology class. Except those models all looked like they were supposed to look—the eye looked like an eye, the brain like a brain, the heart exactly as one would expect a heart to look. But this, this was like a Chinese puzzle. No hint of pubic hair, not even the slight delineation of an ass to help clarify the form.

"I think you have it upside down," Nelly finally said.

The doctor looked down at the model, studied it for a minute, and then shook his head.

"Which is the front?" Nelly asked.

He picked up a silver Mark Cross pencil and pointed to the front.

"And the back?"

He pointed to the back. Nelly felt stupid. She gave up trying to figure it out. Whatever it was, it had nothing to do with her body.

"Now then, we go in through here," he said, indicating one of the myriad passages with his pencil, "and move up through here." He moved the pencil up. "And stop about here." He tapped the model with the pencil point.

"Aren't you worried about lead poisoning?" Nelly asked, indicating the Mark Cross pencil.

"No, no. We use a culdoscope. It's a very delicate instrument with a system of prisms at the end that allows us a clear view of everything that's going on."

"Ah, I see. Thus, the name: culdoscopy."

"Correct," said Dr. Hoffman. He smiled as though he had finally gotten through to a remedial student.

The culdoscope sounded suspiciously like a periscope to Nelly, but she had to trust the doctor. When he said delicate instrument, he meant delicate instrument.

"So," she sighed, "when do we operate?"

"As I said before, this isn't an operation. It is an exploratory, nonsurgical procedure."

"Excuse me. When do I go into the hospital?"

"Can you make it the day after tomorrow?"

"So soon?" Nelly gasped.

"Lenox Hill has a free bed. It just so happens one of my patients canceled out."

Canceled out or chickened out, Nelly asked herself.

Nelly wished she hadn't read *Coma*. She tried to erase the opening chapter from her mind: girl checks into hospital for a simple D and C. D and C turns out to be slightly more complicated. Girl dies a horrible, bloody death. Nelly had a terrible fear of hospitals. It had nothing to do with her only other previous stay in a hospital, which was a tonsillectomy when she was a girl. She remembered that as a pleasant, partylike experience with lots of Jell-o and ice cream. Her fear was based on the belief that once you entered a hospital there was every likelihood that you would never leave alive. It had certainly happened to enough people. Two complete sets of grandparents, her father's sister, General Eisenhower, and countless others.

For some reason Nelly felt a tremendous need to call her parents now. She didn't want to worry them, on one hand. On the other hand, she felt the need for some worry, for the kind of hysterical concern that only parents could provide. She felt frightened and vulnerable. She wanted a little attention, sympathy, and coddling. She wanted her Mommy and Daddy. Because you never really knew about hospitals.

Their phone was picked up in the middle of the first ring.

"Hellow?" Her mother.

"Helloo?" Her father.

Nelly pictured each of them posted by their separate extensions, just in case the phone might ring. She suspected that the main reason her father had retired was to be home so he wouldn't miss a call.

"Hi, it's Nelly."

"Hi, sweetheart," her father said.

"We were just talking about you," her mother said.

There was no doubt in Nelly's mind that they, indeed, were just talking about her. Carrying on a conversation from one part of the house to the other.

"Linton, I just called to tell you I was going into the hospital for a day."

"What's wrong?" her mother said, alarmed.

"Nothing's wrong. I'm, uh, having my nose fixed."

"But you already had it fixed," her father said, still remembering, undoubtedly, the bill from almost twenty years before.

"I just need a little prop job."

"A what?" her father asked.

"They're just moving the cartilage around a little. I have a deviated septum." Nelly couldn't remember where she had heard about deviated septums before, it just popped into her head. "Anyway, it's very minor."

"Are you sure you're telling us the truth?" her mother said.

"Why would I lie?" Nelly said, wondering why she was lying. She still didn't want her parents to know about the fertility workup until it all worked out. Wait until the tests were in and the baby was on her way.

"We'll fly in," her mother said.

Her mother always made a big deal about hospitalization. She had the same fears Nelly did, which, of course, was the reason Nelly had called in the first place.

"That really isn't necessary, Mom," Nelly said. "I'm only going in for a day."

"You're sure?" her father asked.

"Of course." Nelly knew they were just making the gesture. They didn't dare leave Sarah alone. But she liked the offer, nonetheless. She knew they would worry now. And that was all she had wanted. In addition to letting them know which hospital she would be in in case they had to claim the body. Just in case.

"Anyway, I'll be in Lenox Hill Hospital," she said. They would probably send flowers. She would like flowers.

13 The Hospital

Dr. Hoffman had told her to be at Lenox Hill at one o'clock. She was there on the dot. The woman at the desk asked her name and directed her to a large waiting room around the corner. She took a seat. There were about twenty people waiting. Old men, young men, middle-aged women, young women, people of every age, size, and shape. Everyone had a suitcase. They were all the small, weekender size. Optimistic, Nelly thought to herself. It looked as though they were all at the airport waiting for their flight to Miami to begin boarding.

After thirty minutes Nelly's name was called. She went back to the desk, gave her Blue Cross/Blue Shield number to the woman and received a "Welcome to Lenox Hill" brochure.

"Someone will be with you in a moment to show you to your room," the woman said.

A very old, very black woman dressed in a green smock with a white nameplate which read Volunteer shuffled up to the desk. The woman at the desk handed the volunteer Nelly's hospital form. "Room 813B," the woman at the desk said to the volunteer.

Nelly followed the old woman down the hall to room 813B. It was a small, semiprivate room. The other bed was concealed by a green curtain which divided the room in half. Nelly could smell flowers. The old volunteer placed Nelly's bag on a chair and left. She passed a nurse on her way out.

"Did you bring your own nighty or do you want a hospital gown?" the nurse asked.

"I brought my own nighty," Nelly said.

"Well, you can change into that now."

"Can't I stay dressed?"

"Oh, no. That's against the rules."

Nelly changed into her champagne-colored John Kloss nightgown and robe. She heard someone moaning softly from the other side of the curtain. She decided to go for a walk. She walked up and down the hallway looking, but not wanting to look, into each of the rooms. There were only women on the floor. Women asleep with their mouths open. Women curled up on their sides, their backs to the door. Women walking slowly and carefully down the corridor, wheeling ivs along with them like shopping carts. Women sitting and smoking in the solarium at the end of the hallway. In a corner room was a very, very old woman propped up in a wheelchair. She was connected to an iv. Her head was thrown back, her jaw slack. She looked dead and long forgotten. Next to her room, at the end of the corridor, was a closed door. Nelly tried it. It was locked.

"What's through there?" Nelly asked a passing nurse.

"That's 8A, the maternity ward," the nurse said.

"Can I walk through?"

"Oh that door's always locked."

For the first time Nelly realized there was a very definite separation in this one branch of medicine. On one side of the same floor was OB and on the other was GYN. And yet both wings had the same doctors. She could envision them splitting their time between the two wards, running back and forth: pull out a baby here, take out a cyst there, tie an umbilical cord there, tie the tubes here. She felt segregated and discriminated against. She couldn't wait for the day when she would qualify for 8A.

She walked back to her room. The curtain was still pulled and now there was the sound of crying. She turned to leave again just as a youngish man with a two-day growth of beard, dressed in a white rumpled suit and white bucks, walked into the room. He was carrying a clipboard. Nelly assumed he was an intern.

"Mrs. Diamond?" he asked.

"That's right," she said, sitting on the edge of the bed.

"Just want to get some information. Your doctor is Dr. Hoffman?"

"Yes."

"Your age?"

"Thirty-five."

"Do you have any allergies?"

"I'm allergic to penicillin." She wasn't really allergic to penicillin, but she had heard people died from an allergy to it, and you never knew when you might develop an allergy. Besides, there were all sorts of terrific new antibiotics they could use instead. Why take the chance?

"Any history of heart disorder?"

"No."

"And what are you having done?"

My God! Didn't they know? Nelly thought to herself. "I'm having a . . ." She suddenly went blank. What was it called? Jesus, she had better get it right, otherwise they might do something that she hadn't signed up for. "It's a . . . a . . . they're looking at my tubes with a telescope."

"A culdoscopy?"

"That's it," Nelly said with relief. She was glad to know it was a recognizable medical term. The intern left and only a few minutes passed before another nurse came in. She also carried a clipboard.

"Mrs. Diamond?"

"Yes."

"Are you allergic to anything?"

"Penicillin."

"And have you any history of heart disorder?"

"No."

"And what are you having done?"

"A culdoscopy," Nelly said, rolling the word off her tongue with authority.

"And you're Dr. Stein's patient?"

"No. Dr. Hoffman's."

The nurse nodded and left. Why didn't they get organized, Nelly thought to herself. Where was all this information going? Maybe there were separate departments that never talked to each other. Or maybe they compared notes later to make sure all her answers were correct and that she didn't contradict herself.

Nelly sat back on the bed. She thumbed through the "Welcome to Lenox Hill" brochure. There were all sorts of special services available in addition to just the regular cutting open and sewing up facilities. There was a gift shop, a cafeteria for visitors, a beauty shop, a book cart, a chapel and a chaplain, a social worker, an arts and crafts coordinator. Everything but a funeral director. Or maybe he just wasn't listed.

A man in a green uniform walked into the room carrying yet another clipboard.

"I'm allergic to penicillin, I have no history of heart disorder, and Dr. Hoffman is performing a culdoscopy on me," Nelly said.

The man looked at her strangely. "Do you want the television?" he asked after a moment.

"Is that part of the culdoscopy?"

"Listen, I do televisions. I don't know nothing about anything else. You want it or not?" he said, indicating the small-screen television in the corner.

"Oh, sure. TV. Thanks."

The afternoon wore on. Nelly tried reading, but she couldn't concentrate.

She turned on the TV and watched it without sound. She didn't want to disturb the woman in the next bed who was now quiet and probably sleeping.

At five o'clock dinner was served. Chicken, mashed potatoes, pale green beans and Jell-o with a peach. Nelly couldn't eat. Her stomach was clenched tight with tension. She was afraid. Afraid of the culdoscopy. Afraid of the nurses. Afraid of the woman in the next bed. She had no control over the situation. She was sorry she hadn't told Paisley or Abby she was going into the hospital. She could have used a couple of visitors.

At seven o'clock a thin, bald man dressed in a tweed sports jacket and white hospital pants came in and took the chair at the end of her bed. He was carrying a Louis Vuitton appointment book. He opened it and read from it without looking up at Nelly.

"Mrs. Diamond?"

"Yes."

"I'm Dr. Bromberg, your anesthesiologist. Your billing address is 300 Central Park West?"

"Yes, that's where I live."

"And you have Blue Cross/Blue Shield?"

"Yes."

"And does your insurance policy cover anesthesiology?"

"I really don't know. I assume so."

"It doesn't matter. I bill you directly, anyway. You will receive an invoice within ten days from the time of the operation. See you tomorrow."

Maybe he wanted a little something on deposit, Nelly thought to herself after he had gone.

Visiting hours were over at 8:00. At 8:05 a Puerto Rican woman carrying a metal washbasin and towels entered. She pulled the sheet off Nelly and laid it over the end of the bed.

"Leeft," the woman said.

"What?"

"Leeft," she repeated, indicating Nelly's hips. Nelly lifted them and the woman placed a rubber sheet and towel underneath Nelly's buttocks.

"Sprad."

"What?"

"Sprad," she said, indicating Nelly's bent knees.

"Why?"

"For the chaving," the woman explained, holding up a razor.

"Oh no, do I have to?" Nelly said cringing.

"Oh, yas. Everytheeng chaved."

Nelly turned bright red. The woman pulled up her nightgown, pulled open her legs and proceeded to lather her pubic hair with soap and warm water. At that moment Nelly made an attempt to leave her body, to walk down the hall for a cigarette, to wait until the woman had finished her job. But she couldn't shut off the woman's voice as she stroked the razor over her crotch.

"Tik hair. You vairy hairy lady," the woman said.

During the summer Nelly went to Elizabeth Arden every six weeks to have what they called a bikini wax. There a silent lady in a pink smock painfully pulled off any wayward hairs that might show in a bathing suit. It was done with pink towels discreetly covering her crotch and always followed by the luxurious application of emollient creams, delicately scented astringents and sweet-smelling powders. It was a beauty ritual done in the most modest and ladylike manner. Not like this.

"All feenished," the woman said, flipping Nelly's nightgown over her. Nelly lay there for a moment letting the color drain from her face. She started to swing her legs off the bed when yet another orderly or nurse walked in with another rubber sheet, set of towels and a rubber bag and tubing.

"On your side," the woman said.

"What now?" Nelly groaned.

"Enema," she said, lifting Nelly's nightgown up. "Bring your knees up to your chest."

Nelly did as she was told, gritting her teeth at the rude entrance of the enema nozzle.

"Okay. Now breathe through your mouth."

She felt the warm water move up her intestine. Up and up it flowed until it pushed against the wall of her stomach. She moaned. A dull cramp turned into a sharp, almost unbearable pain. She felt as if she were bursting inside.

"Hold it there for as long as you can," the woman said, rolling up the tubing.

"I can't," Nelly groaned.

"If you don't wait, it won't work," the woman warned.

"I can't," Nelly said through clenched teeth. The pressure kept building. She felt like a dam about to burst.

"Come on, you can certainly wait a few more minutes."

What did this woman know about waiting, Nelly thought. She wasn't sure she could even make it to the bathroom. She lowered herself slowly off the bed and bent over double, stumbled into the bathroom. There was an explosion of water. And then nothing. She waited but nothing more happened. She crept back into the room. The woman was still there, gripping the enema tubing in her hand.

"Well?" the woman said.

"It was just water," Nelly said.

"I told you. You have to wait. Can't expect miracles in a minute. Come on, back up in bed. We'll have to do it again."

After the third enema, Nelly lied.

"Well, we did it," Nelly smiled to the woman triumphantly, closing the bathroom door.

The orderly looked at her suspiciously.

"You sure?"

"Of course I'm sure," Nelly said, indignantly.

As soon as the woman left, Nelly began to worry. What would happen to her? Could filled bowels cause some kind of complication in the operating room? Would she lose control on the table? She would have to take her chances. She just couldn't go through another enema.

At nine o'clock a huge nurse wearing a man's letter sweater over her uniform stood in the doorway.

"Mrs. Diamond?"

"Yes."

"Come with me, please."

Oh Jesus, Nelly thought to herself, they know I lied about the enema. They're going to bring me up on charges. Or they're going to employ a more drastic method to get it all out of me. She got out of bed, put on her robe and followed the nurse to the end of the hall. There, sitting in the solarium, were six women, all in robes and slippers. They looked as if they had been roused from a sound sleep. No one spoke. Nelly took a seat on the couch next to a thin, frail-looking woman who was tearing a tissue into tiny shreds. The nurse took a seat and began speaking. She referred every now and then to her clipboard.

"This is a preoperative conference. My name is Johnson. The purpose of this meeting is to clear up any questions you have regarding what will take place tomorrow, when you are all scheduled for surgery." (Surgery! Nelly screamed to herself.)

"Someone will come and give you a light sedative about an hour before you're scheduled for the OR. Then you will be taken on a gurney to the OR. You will be administered your various anesthetics and have your various procedures. Afterward, you will be taken from the OR to the RR." (It must be a hospital rule, Nelly thought to herself: never give the full name when you can use initials.)

"You will stay in the recovery room for a minimum of one hour, or longer if necessary. After that you will be wheeled back to your rooms, where you will be given an iv, which will contain either glucose, antibiotics, or painkillers, again depending on the individual need. When you wake up, you will feel nauseous, or dizzy, or have pain, or all of the above—again, depending upon the extensiveness of the surgery. Mrs. Diamond, Mrs. Hall, and Mrs. Citron, you are all scheduled for morning surgery. Mrs. Halinski, Mrs. Willis, and Mrs. Hogan, you won't go in till after lunch. Although, of course, no lunch will be served to you.

"All right, ladies," said Johnson, "come with me. We're due at X-ray and EKG."

They all stood and silently followed her down the hall to the elevators. They got off at the fourth floor, and she led them through dim gray corridors to the X-ray department.

She handed her clipboard to a young Puerto Rican X-ray technician.

"Six for X-ray, José."

He took the clipboard and eyed each of the women.

"Hokay, who wants to be the first to have José take their peectures?" he said.

No one answered.

"I take de bast peectures in de whole department."

No one laughed.

"Hi got me a shy bonch," he said to the nurse. "Who wants to be de peenup? I theenk you," he said, pointing to Nelly. "Come wis me, sweethairt, I make you beeyoutiful beyond your fandest dreams."

Nelly dutifully followed him into the dark room.

"You stand hair, and push against thees machine," he said, pushing her up against the cold X-ray machine with his body.

"Now, leeft your arms and take ha deep brath and hold eet, hokay?" Nelly took a deep breath. José was still leaning his body against hers.

"Hokay," he said finally and walked out of the room.

"Now hold eet and smile," he called from outside. She held it. She heard a faint whirr and then he stepped back into the room.

"That's eet. Naxt."

When they had all completed their X-rays, they followed Johnson to EKG, where they were individually greased, hooked up to little suction cups, monitored and graphed, and told to wait until everyone was finished. Johnson led them briskly back to their ward. Nelly looked at the women as they walked. They looked as scared and tense as she was. And suddenly she felt far less lonely. Each of the women had given their insurance numbers, names, and addresses, and the same answers over and over again to the same stupid questions. Each had been shorn and enemaed, X-rayed and EKGed. Each had experienced the same humiliations and inhumanities as Nelly had. They were all in this together. Just as they had all had cramps and periods, had worn belts or pads or pulled strings on Tampaxes, had endured breast probes and pap smears, had suffered through infections and inflammations and erosions of the cervix and cysts and tumors and God knows what else. Nelly felt like a member of a brave, uncomplaining army as they marched back to their rooms.

"What are you having done?" one of the women whispered to Nelly. Before she could answer, Johnson whirled around and said:

"No talking in the hallways, please. People are trying to sleep."

Nelly couldn't believe her ears. No talking in the hallways! They were part of an army, all right. A captured one. No one said a word after that. All these women, Nelly thought, with their secret sufferings, their insides and most private parts open to public scrutiny, their pussies unceremoniously shaved by strangers. She was struck and moved by their bravery. Were they braver than men? Maybe not, Nelly thought. But their courage was on a much quieter level. She supposed it was about even. Men had their sports injuries and war wounds and women had their wombs and internal skirmishes. Unfortunately, they didn't give medals or award prizes for having periods that lasted twenty days, ovarian cysts or yeast infections or fibroids or any of that.

When she got back to her room, the dividing curtain was pulled open. In the next bed sat a pretty blonde woman who looked to be about Nelly's age. She was very pale, and there were fine new pain lines etched around her mouth. Her hands lay quietly on her stomach, and connected to her arm was the thin tube of an iv. Her hair looked as though she hadn't washed it in weeks. She smiled at Nelly.

"Hi, bet you were wondering if I was dead or alive."

"How are you feeling?" Nelly asked.

"Oh, much better, thanks It only hurts when I breathe."

"What did you have done?"

"Oh, sort of a general housecleaning."

"A D and C?"

"A little more radical. I had a hysterectomy."

"Oh, I'm sorry," Nelly said.

"Nothing to be sorry about. I'm actually very lucky. They caught it in time." Nelly didn't want to ask what "it" was. She knew.

"You know, I never took those pap smears seriously. You're supposed to have one every six months. And I went for years and years without it. I always thought it was a way for doctors to make extra money. It seemed to me if you had cancer, you'd certainly know it. It was really ironic. I was getting fitted for a new diaphragm anyway, so I had my pap smear and here I am."

"Wow," Nelly breathed. She didn't know what to say.

"I'll tell you, it's a good kind of cancer to have. See, it's pretty much self-contained. So if they get it in time, chances are they got it all. I just have to take a few radiation treatments, and that's it. I was a little depressed for a while afterward. But I guess that's to be expected. Besides, I've had all the kids I plan to have, so what do I need a uterus for?" Nelly shuddered.

"How many children do you have?" Nelly asked, glad to change the subject.

"I've got three. How many have you got?"

"Me? Oh, I don't have any. Not yet. That's what I'm in the hospital for. It's a special procedure they do to make sure my tubes and everything are okay."

"Have you had problems getting pregnant?"

"Well, I can't say I've really tried that hard up until now. As a matter of fact, I haven't tried at all."

"You're starting sort of late, aren't you?"

"I guess."

"Me, I had my kids right away—one, two, three. I just couldn't wait. Now I'm glad I didn't. It's funny, you never know what's going to happen. Listen, I'm sure everything's going to turn out okay for you. They really do amazing things now. My sister-in-law couldn't get pregnant for the longest time and they put her on one of those fertility drugs and wouldn't you know, she's got twins. Maybe you should ask your doctor about fertility drugs."

"He doesn't seem to think that's the problem," Nelly said. She was beginning to feel slightly uneasy. Was it being in the same room with a woman who had cancer? No, it wasn't that. The woman felt sorry for her. You could see it all over her face. There she was with her insides newly ripped out and she was feeling sorry for Nelly. Nelly felt silly and insignificant. She was in the hospital to have something minor, something constructive done, something that would enable her to have yet one more thing that she had decided she needed to make her life even more fulfilling, more rewarding, more challenging. And here was this woman talking about good cancers and bad cancers and thank God for pap smears and only a few radiation treatments.

A nurse came in and gave the woman a hypodermic. The woman smiled at Nelly. She looked embarrassed. "Morphine," she said. "They give it to me every night. The Demerol didn't work."

"Is the pain very bad?"

"Not so bad. I don't know if I'm getting used to it or it's going away. Anyway, I'll let you get some sleep. You've got a big day tomorrow." She reached up slowly and turned off her light. Nelly turned off her light too.

"It's funny," the woman said dreamily.

"What's that?"

"I'll never have my period again. Isn't that wild? The weirdest thing is, I think I'll sort of miss it."

Nelly didn't answer. She lay awake for a long time listening to the woman in the next bed breathing. She couldn't sleep.

They came to get her for surgery. They put her on a table and wheeled her down a long hallway and into the operating room. She knew it was the operating room because there were huge white lights in a circle above her. A doctor stood at her feet. She couldn't tell if it was Dr. Hoffman or not because a mask covered his face.

"All ready?" he asked. It was Dr. Hoffman's voice.

"Wait a minute," Nelly said, "you haven't given me anything. Aren't you going to give me an anesthetic?"

"Has she had her anesthetic?" the doctor asked.

"Of course she has," a voice answered from behind her head.

"But I haven't. I swear. I haven't had anything."

"We can't give her too much," the voice from behind her head said. "It isn't safe."

"Don't worry," said Dr. Hoffman, "it won't hurt."

He pried her knees apart. She could feel him prying them apart. She could feel his fingers digging into the flesh. It hurt.

"Come on now, Nelly, relax. If you don't help, it'll hurt even more. Just breathe deeply. It'll be over in a second. Before you know it, it'll all seem just like a bad dream."

"But you've got to give me something," Nelly said. "I don't like pain."

"Junkie," hissed the other voice.

"Come on, Nelly," Dr. Hoffman said. "It's not as if you had a football injury or something. You're not the first woman to have a hysterectomy."

"Hysterectomy! I'm not supposed to have a hysterectomy," Nelly shouted. "You've made a mistake."

"No, my dear, you're the one who made a mistake. You lied about the penicillin. And you know what happens to people who lie about penicillin . . ."

"Oh no," Nelly screamed.

"It's okay, Mrs. Diamond, time for your shot." A smiling black face looked down at her. It was a nurse.

Before she was fully awake she was given a hypodermic and immediately she became stoned. The next face she saw was that of an orderly wearing a green operating uniform with a matching green cap that covered his hair.

"Time to go," he said. She felt herself being lifted gently onto a gurney and wheeled out of the room. She felt terrific. And she felt terrific that she felt terrific. She was doing just fine. Sensational. They wheeled her into the operating room. There was Dr. Hoffman, looking very doctorlike, and there was the anesthesiologist and three busy, professional-looking nurses doing busy and professional-looking things. It was like a small, important party.

"Okay, Mrs. Diamond," Dr. Hoffman said. "I want you to get onto the operating table on your stomach."

"On my stomach?"

"Yes, we go in through the back."

"Wait a minute," Nelly giggled, "are you sure you've got that right?"

"That's right," the doctor said patiently, helping her onto the table. "We get a better view that way."

"Oh."

She lay on her stomach on the table and they raised her buttocks with some sort of pillow. Her hands lay on either side of her head. It was the same position Nelly had slept in as a little girl. It felt cozy and comfortable. She wanted to put her thumb in her mouth. She was still giggling.

"I think you guys are just perverts," she said, laughing delightedly.

"We're giving you the anesthetic now," said the anesthesiologist, whose name she couldn't remember. "You won't feel a thing."

"*Quel dommage*," said Nelly, giggling. And she didn't feel a thing and she had a wonderful time and all she was aware of was their quiet murmuring behind her. Hope they're having as much fun as I am, she thought to herself. Time had no measure. She couldn't remember if she'd been there for five minutes or an hour. She was utterly and completely high when they wheeled her out.

Back in her own room, she was attached to an iv. She had always thought they hurt. It didn't hurt at all. It just dripped silently into her arm. She felt proud. She had an iv just like everyone else. There was no pain, no nausea, not even any soreness. Just a slight light-headedness. She had survived. She felt giddy and happy and hungry. That wasn't so bad, she said to herself. Not so bad at all. She vowed never to be frightened of hospitals again.

Dr. Hoffman came in just as Nelly was finishing her lunch.

"How are you feeling?" he asked. He was still wearing his OR getup.

"I feel terrific," she bragged. "No pain. No nausea. Nothing. You did a sensational job," she said, thinking that she shouldn't claim all the credit herself for feeling so good.

"And how are you feeling, Mrs. Costanza?" he said to the woman in the next bed.

"Much better, Dr. Hoffman."

Nelly was impressed. He really got around, this doctor. From Paisley's abortions, to Mrs. Costanza's hysterectomy, to paving the way for Nelly's pregnancy.

"Care to take a little walk?" he asked Nelly.

"Love it," Nelly said.

What a nice man, she thought. What a sweet way to see how I feel. They walked to the solarium. He sat down.

"Have a seat," he said, indicating the chair next to his. It suddenly occurred to her that something was up. He must have a court booked, or at least several hundred patients waiting for him in his waiting room. He seemed to be stalling for time.

"What is it?" she asked, no longer smiling.

"It's bad news, I'm afraid. Not that I didn't expect it. But, as I told you before, the culdoscopy is the most definitive test. And you never know until you really get in there and look."

"What is it?" she said again.

"The scarring on your tubes was much more extensive than I thought."

"What does that mean?"

"It means your chances of ever getting pregnant are about ninety-nine to one."

"Can't you fix the scars?"

"There is such a thing as tubal reparation, but in your case it isn't advisable. There are small scars up and down your tubes caused by the pelvic inflammation. So there is no particular area that one can operate on. It's a generalized condition. Surgery would be a waste of time and money, in my opinion."

"But how can that be? Everything was going along so well."

"It's true, everything else checks out fine. I even had hopes during part of the procedure today. When the dye passed through the tubes, I was sure they were open. But, you see, when I got a direct look, I could see the scarring. Lots of tiny scars, the kind that would probably prevent an egg from passing through. I'm sorry, Mrs. Diamond."

Nelly was stunned. "I don't understand. All those tests. All those mornings taking my temperature. The sperm count. Everything. And all this time my tubes are sitting there scarred and beyond repair. How could you lead me along like this?"

"It wasn't a matter of leading you along. I told you in the beginning that it was a series of tests and I cautioned you against jumping to conclusions before all the data were in. As a matter of fact, I've told you that several times."

"But you said in the beginning, in the very beginning, that there was trouble in the tubes. Why didn't you do this test first instead of last?"

"Because that isn't the procedure. I told you that." He was beginning to get angry. Not nearly as angry as Nelly.

"Fuck your procedures. It doesn't make sense. If someone came to me with a foot cut off I wouldn't give them a general physical to see what was wrong. How could you do this to me? How could you have me thinking that I could be pregnant any minute?"

"I'm sorry, Mrs. Diamond. I know news like this can be very upsetting. I know you're disappointed. And I am sorry. I don't know what else to say. There is an off chance that the culdoscopy itself may have opened some of the scar tissue. But I have to be honest. It is a chance in a million."

"I thought you said it was one in a hundred," she snarled. "You can't even keep your lousy, goddamn odds straight. All you know how to do is perform abortions and take out wombs and do workups. You know nothing about having babies. Nothing at all. It's all just data and procedures and microscopes and cold instruments and . . ."

Nelly fell back into the chair and covered her eyes with her hands. The tears poured out, wetting her palms and seeping between her fingers. And still they kept coming. Dr. Hoffman patted her back awkwardly. The sounds of her sobbing filled the solarium and people standing around outside moved gingerly to the other end of the corridor.

94

14 Another Chance

Nelly's tears sizzled away in the heat of her anger. Anger had always been a tricky thing for her. She had spent years learning how to handle it, where to put it, and what it was all about. Basically she believed there were two kinds of anger: a good or healthy one, i.e., external and appropriate, aimed at obstinate people or impossible situations. And there was a bad or neurotic anger, i.e., aimed at herself for things she couldn't help. She had learned that it was perfectly okay to be angry at foes, even friends, as long as you expressed that anger in a rational, reasonable, nonviolent way. It was the other anger she had to watch out for. That was the kind that started out as simple rage and ended up as depression with a capital D.

She wanted to turn her anger outward, to find a reasonable outlet for it. She wanted to be angry at Dr. Hoffman, but she knew she was really angry at herself. At her body. At its inability to work the way she wanted it to work. To do what she wanted it to do. That was simple enough. That clear, perceptive observation should have made her feel better, but all the understanding in the world was of no use to her now. She was on the verge of what could only be described at a Primal Tizzy.

The anger she was feeling was of the refrigerator-kicking, fist-pounding, hair-tearing kind. The kind that hurts. She looked down at her hands. They were clenched into tight fists. She realized now what she was about to do. She was about to punch herself in the stomach, to punish her body for its failure. Oh, no. She just couldn't afford that kind of tantrum now.

She made a quantum leap back to Dr. Hoffman. If anyone deserved her anger, it was he. Hadn't he led her along? Hadn't he raised her hopes? Hadn't he taken her through his step-by-step fertility workup, content with the fact that he was following dictated procedures? Whether or not she actually became pregnant was probably the least of his concerns. He was so wrapped up in his own stupid tests, what did he really care about babies?

Well, she would show him. She would show them all. She had an ace up her sleeve that hadn't even occurred to the good doctor. It hadn't occurred to him because he probably hadn't read a medical journal in over twenty years. There were miracles being performed that he didn't even have a clue about. Test-tube babies were being born at this very minute. There had been the one in England, one in India, and then one in Scotland and God knew how many more. And she—she was the perfect candidate, was she not? She couldn't wait to show that bastard.

She checked out of the hospital and went directly to her office. She pulled out her file with notes from the "Conceptions" special that had been filmed months before. She jotted down the name of the leading fertility expert in New York. She hadn't interviewed him for the program but had some background on him, nonetheless: Dr. William Reagen. He had been working on test-tube babies for years. Recently his progress had been slowed up by lack of funds and grants from the government. She dialed his office number.

"I'd like to make an appointment with Dr. Reagen," she said.

"For what purpose?" the woman on the other end asked.

"I'm interested in having a test-tube baby." Jesus, it sounded so casual.

"I'm sorry, Dr. Reagen isn't seeing any new patients. His research takes up all his time."

"But I want to be a research subject."

"There are a lot of women who want the same thing. Unfortunately, as a result of all the recent publicity, we get hundreds of calls every day. As I said before, the doctor is not taking any patients. And he has all the subjects he can handle."

Nelly dialed the doctor's number again. This time she disguised her voice by lowering it several octaves. It was her broadcast voice. It usually worked wonders.

"Dr. Reagen, please. This is Nelly Diamond of WABC News calling."

"What is this in reference to?" the woman asked politely.

"I have some questions for the doctor regarding the progress of his research and the need he may have for funding from the government. You see, the network feels that the government is taking too passive a position on this whole issue. We feel that a special report of some sort might get them moving on awarding grants for the work that Dr. Reagen and so many other dedicated men are doing. I'd like to set up an appointment with him. A half-hour of his time at the most."

That did it. Nelly got an appointment for the very next day.

Dr. Reagen's office was located on York Avenue and Eighty-third Street. It was a small, four-story, white brick building. On the front of it was a plaque which read: World Wide Fertility Research Institute.

Dr. Reagen, a tall, slender man in his early forties, met her at the door. He was an attractive man with pale blond hair and a slightly darker mustache. He wore aviator glasses modishly perched back on top of his head. The sleeves of his white lab coat and the muted gray shirt he wore underneath were casually rolled up on his arms in the best Ralph Lauren fashion.

"Miss Diamond, I presume," he said, smiling charmingly. "I'm Bill Reagen." He held her hand for a moment, squeezing it lightly as he stared into her eyes. Nelly recognized the stare immediately. There was nothing sexual or provocative about it. It was one of those I-am-totally-focused-in-the-now-so-we-both can-share-the-reality-of-the-moment looks that was so characteristic of veterans of the human-potential movement. Nelly herself had had that look for about two weeks after a self-actualization course. She dropped it when she realized that an unwavering focus on other people's eyes tended to make them feel incredibly awkward and ill at ease. Dr. Reagen looked behind her.

"You didn't bring a cameraman. I'm glad. It gives us a chance to talk. What show are you with?"

"I'm with the news. WABC Evening News," Nelly answered.

"Oh, yes, of course. I recognize you now. This will be something in the way of a documentary or news feature, then?" he asked as he led her through the reception area and up the stairs to the second floor.

"Yes, more or less," Nelly said, not liking the direction their interview was taking.

"Well, let me show you around first and share what my experience of this work is. Then you can share with me any questions you might have. This is the lab," he said, indicating with a huge sweep of his arm a room that looked like a laboratory.

"We started out here doing research on rats—implantation, artificial insemination, and so on. Up until a few years ago, the government, specifically HEW, had given me the space to get into invitro research."

At first Nelly thought he meant by space that the government had donated the lab itself, then she realized he meant something else. *Space* meant "freedom" or "support," like *share* meant "tell."

"Recently they have held back on approval for any additional funds, just when we need it the most. By the way, how long do you think the show will be?"

"Well, I'm not sure at this point."

97

"See," Dr. Reagen said, again fixing her with his brown-eyed earnestness, "I don't think it can be done in just thirty minutes. I'm very clear on the fact that what we need is at least an hour, preferably two hours to really share what we're doing here."

"You're involved in test-tube babies, aren't you?" Nelly asked, beginning to fear that this man was not, in fact, a doctor but some sort of independent television packager.

"We prefer the term invitro. But yes, we are very close, very close indeed to America's first test-tube baby. I have six patients I am dealing with presently. We expect success at any moment.

"Now, I'll want to share with you the step-by-step procedures. But first, I want us to get very clear on the intent and overall tone of the show. You see, I'm very clear on how I want it not to be. Do you get that I'm not being negative but just defining my parameters?"

"I got it," Nelly said dutifully, wondering how she was going to get this man off his "show" and onto her baby.

"Good," said the doctor, squeezing her arm. "I have written a rough scenario for the program. You see, I shared my idea with one of the other networks last year. But I got that they weren't ready for it or for me," he said with a coy touch of self-deprecation. "Look, let me give you an idea of what I have in mind." The doctor took Nelly by the arm and led her over to a corner of the lab. With his two hands he formed a TV screen and held it up so they both could see.

"We'll open up there at the lab table. The camera will pan by my two assistants and then move in for a close-up on me peering through a microscope. We'll hold on that for the credits. By the way, I have a good title. I think you'll like it. Get this: 'William Reagen: Taking Life into His Own Hands.'" He carefully laid out each of the words of the title in the air in front of them.

Nelly took a deep breath and plunged in. "Well, actually the network has a proposal they'd like to make to you."

"Oh?"

"They would like to supply their own candidate, in addition to those patients who are already involved in your program."

"I already have a full load."

"We know that. But this would be an interesting human-interest angle. We could pick a subject from the public at large. A woman who cannot have children and has all but given up hope on her ability to ever have them. You see, this would add a note of immediacy, of nowness that the television audience could share."

Dr. Reagen pondered this for a moment. "It's not a bad concept. Not bad at all," he said. Nelly could see he was weighing the idea's promotional value.

"And," Nelly continued, "it could even be a known person, a public figure of sorts, someone the audience already knows and could identify with."

"Even better," the doctor enthused. "Who could we get?"

"Well, to tell you the truth, the network has already found someone. Subject to your approval, of course."

"Oh, who is it?"

"Me."

"You!"

"Yes, me." She rushed on. "Let me explain. I have scarring of the tubes. The doctor just finished a culdoscopy on me and he says I'm not surgically repairable, I do ovulate, my eggs are okay, my hormones are okay, I have a good sperm count at my disposal, and I am a known name at least in local television circles."

"It's not possible," the doctor said. "Not only isn't it possible, it could be disastrous."

"What do you mean? It would make a terrific show. A whole series of shows," she said, appealing to his entertainment instincts.

"How old are you, Mrs. Diamond?"

"I'm thirty-five; why?"

"I can't take anyone over thirty. As you know, chances of pregnancy and frequency and quality of ovulation decrease steadily with age."

"But I told you—I am ovulating. I have temperature graphs to prove it."

"It's not that you can't ovulate and it's not that it isn't possible. It's the odds."

"What odds?"

"The odds for success. The elements all have to be in my favor. Age happens to be one of the important elements. I want you to get that I totally support your desire to have a baby. But I couldn't possibly take you on as a candidate. You have to be clear that what is at stake here is not your baby but millions of women's babies. If I took your case on and failed, it would be a failure for all, not just for you. The government is not about to fund a failure. Do you get that?"

Nelly shook her head.

"In simple terms, you are too old," the doctor said gently, putting his hand on her shoulder. "Now then, that is not to say that I don't think it is an interesting media concept. The idea of using a public personality to participate in my invitro fertilization is not only interesting but has a tremendous high-Nielsen potential attached to it. Which ultimately could mean real government support. How about this? Let's put together a list of possible people. We already know the prerequisites. It has to be a young woman with tubal problems, who has no other children and is a known name."

Nelly nodded her head. Her eyes panned past Dr. Reagen's intent face to

99

the door. She inched her body camera right until she had her hand on the knob.

"Right, yes. Well, I'll set that up and then get back to you with a meeting date," she said vaguely.

"Let's not let it wait too long. We're very much on the brink of something here, and if your network doesn't get on the stick with this . . . well, there *are* other networks, not to mention public broadcasting, if you follow my drift."

"I got it," Nelly said, making a quick exit.

She spent the next few days trying to call every doctor in the country who was connected with tubal-implantation work. In most cases she couldn't get through to them at all. When she did, she would put it to them point blank:

"I am a twenty-nine-year-old woman whose tubes are scarred. I am ovulating, have normal hormonal makeup, of sound mind and body, and willing to pay anything."

"Of course you would; so would thousands of others. We have a waiting list that goes on for years. I'm sorry, we are unable to take any new names at this time."

She hung up the phone and stared out the window. Minutes later she looked down at her hands. They were almost white with clenching. Slowly, painfully, she uncurled her fingers.

15 Flunking

A test-tube baby. It had seemed made to order for her. Life had found yet another way to serve her purposes, to support her ambitions, to make her dreams come true. It had to be more than just a happy coincidence. Just when she was confronted with the inability of her tubes to pass along an egg, medical science had come up with a way to bypass her tubes. It had been her best and last shot at having a baby. And she couldn't even make the list of prospective candidates. She was too old, too late, and too one of many. She was totally without hope. Worse, she was even without anger.

Because now it was no longer a failure of the system, of ambitious doctors who weren't interested in taking chances, of money-hungry, opportunistic fertility clinics, of narrow government spending policies and thinking. No, it was her failure. If her tubes hadn't been messed up in the first place, then she wouldn't have had to rely on the miracle workings and good graces of fertility experts.

Until this baby thing Nelly had thought of herself as pretty much of a success. She had spent many years working at being one. Professionally, emotionally, physically, and socially her progress over the past ten years had been duly noted. There were accomplishments to be savored and relished, though never taken for granted. She took pleasure in feats both large and small, as only a person who has grown up with a deep regard for failure can. It had been years and years since she had thought of herself as a failure. And now that old flunking feeling came back to her in a flash.

101

In the seventh grade her algebra teacher had handed out slips of paper a month before the end of the semester. They were failure notices, warnings that you were, if you continued along the same path, going to flunk the course and have to repeat it.

Nelly got a failure notice. It was to be taken home, signed by one or both parents, and then returned to the teacher. She didn't understand the need for a notice. She knew by virtue of her test scores that she was flunking. Her parents knew she was flunking. They had seen her sweat and scream over her homework. The teacher knew she was flunking; she had to be the first to know. So why the slip of paper? She thought perhaps it was some sort of ritual or penance that, if followed to the letter, would allow her to pass the course. It wasn't. Even with the paper duly signed by both parents and returned to the teacher, she still flunked algebra and had to take it again.

She could list her past failures by the thousands. They had all seemed monumental at the time, but seen from the point of view of a successful adult, they became funny and insignificant.

Unfortunately, the successful adult normally in residence had left for parts unknown, leaving the failed algebra student to walk down memory lane alone.

She had been the only girl in the girl-scout troop who had failed to sell her quota of girl-scout cookies. She just couldn't bring herself to approach complete strangers and ask them to buy something. Consequently the family was left with, and had to pay for, seventy-five boxes of assorted butter cremes and chocolate mints. She had been the only camper at Camp Wilderness Falls who had failed to learn how to end a lanyard properly. And as the arts and crafts counselor had pointed out, a lanyard that didn't close wasn't much of a lanyard at all.

You were given all the elements with which to make a success, and if you weren't able to do that, then it was a failure. Your failure. You were given numbers by the math teacher. All you had to do was memorize them and repeat them back. You were given girl scout cookies by the Girl Scout Association. You had at your disposal the entire girl-scout-cookie-consuming American population. All you had to do was sell. You were given long strips of plastic and a method of lanyard braiding by the arts and crafts counselor; all you had to do was end it properly. You were given a uterus, tubes, and egg-laying ovaries, and just about any man at your disposal. All you had to do was conceive.

A failure when one started out even, with a fair allotment of the proper equipment and materials necessary, was a failure of the most fundamental nature. To flunk algebra was to be a failure at math. Not to turn over one box of cookies was to be a failed girl scout. No lanyard to show at the end of the summer pretty much meant your parents could save their money on next year's camp. Not to be able to produce a child . . . that must make her—what else but a failure as a woman.

Oh no. That was too easy, too self-pitying a trap to fall into, Nelly told herself as she fell headlong into it.

But wait. Wasn't it this supposed failure as a woman that had driven her into therapy years before? That's how she had thought of it at the time. If you didn't have an orgasm, then you were a failure sexually, and since her sex happened to be female, then it followed that she was a female failure.

After two years of marriage, two years of Jordan asking, "Did you come yet?" she took herself to Dr. Ira Abrams for the purpose of eradicating her problem of frigidity. Naturally, at that time she couldn't talk about her frigidity. She spoke of vague feelings of unrest, feelings of inferiority, mild attacks of anxiety. She told him her dreams, traced her childhood, and outlined her fantasies, or at least those fantasies of a nonsexual nature. It was interesting. Dr. Abrams certainly seemed interested. To keep his interest became one of the main goals of each session. After a while she began to talk about sex. Not sex specifically, but sex in general. The principles of it. The Freudian aspects of it. The changing nature of it. It takes time to feel at home with someone. With Dr. Abrams it took her about six months.

When finally she got up her nerve to talk about it (for she was always quite aware of what she wasn't talking about), it turned out to be colossally anticlimactic.

"I don't think I've been completely open with you," she said into her coffee cup.

"Oh, how so?" Dr. Abrams asked.

"Well, there is something that I haven't been able to talk about at all."

"And what might that be?"

"I'm frigid."

"Frigid? You don't like sex?"

"No, actually I do like it. It's just that I, uh, don't have orgasms."

"Oh, Christ! Not another one. Another woman in search of the mythical multiple or spectacular singular orgasm."

"I really don't care whether they're multiple or spectacular or anything. I'd just like to have one."

"You'd like rockets to go off and bells to ring and the earth to open up?"

"No. I'd just like to have an ordinary orgasm, that's all," Nelly said, miffed at his response to her most deeply hidden problem.

"Well, I can't help you out there."

"I don't mean you. I mean my husband."

"I know what you mean. Let me ask you this: You enjoy sex with your husband, is that correct?"

"Yes."

"Okay. Do me a favor, do yourself a favor. Forget about the orgasm business. The most important thing, the only thing about sex that you need to know, is that it occurs between two people and that they both should enjoy it."

"But isn't an orgasm proof of enjoyment?"

"So is heavy breathing. The sooner you forget about orgasms, the better off you'll be and ultimately the better off your orgasms will be. If God had meant women to have orgasms all the time, He would have put the clitoris in the palms of their hands so they could get their rocks off while they were washing dishes."

Naturally Nelly didn't believe a word Dr. Abrams said. Orgasms had recently been introduced and everyone was having them. Lots of them.

She knew what the problem was even if Dr. Abrams didn't. Not having an orgasm was her punishment for years of pretending she had. The lie had started with her first time. It was when her 17th Century English Poetry professor posed the question that would be asked by countless others:

"Did you come?"

Nelly didn't know what to say. What was the proper response? What was the question? It really didn't matter because before she could answer, he happened to notice that she was hemorrhaging all over his bed.

"I'm really sorry," Nelly said, tears of embarrassment welling up in her eyes. "It'll come out in cold water." She pulled the sheet off the bed and took it into the bathroom. She was almost thankful for having bled all over the place. It gave her something to do so she didn't have to worry about the correct answer to the question: Did I come or didn't I come?

Later, with other lovers, she was ready with a variety of responses:

"Did you come?"

"Did I ever!"

"Was it good?"

"Was it ever!"

"Did you come?"

"What do you think." This said with a knowing smile. Sometimes the knowing smile was sufficient in itself. Then a lot of men never asked. But by that time Nelly's simulated orgasms were so good there was no reason for them to. Jordan, however, asked almost all the time.

"Did you come?" "How was that?" "Was that good for you?" "How good was it?" His questions began to annoy her. Rather than being just points of information, they seemed like criticism of her performance. But when he didn't ask, she would ask herself: Did I come? Will I come? Can I come? How come I never come?

Interestingly enough, the first time she actually came was the first time she forgot all about coming. She even forgot to pretend she came. It was while she was still married to Jordan and still seeing Dr. Abrams. She was just lying in bed minding her own business as Jordan made love to her. She was thinking about a Calvin Klein coat sale at Bloomingdale's. Calvin Klein coats on sale. Calvin Klein. She didn't really need a new coat, but who could pass up a Calvin Klein? She had seen a rich mulberry red coat with a huge collar, made of the softest, warmest wool, with no buttons, just a thick, loosely tied belt of the same warm red fabric, and suddenly there was a tightening in her vagina, a tremendous building of the most excruciatingly exquisite pressure, and then it let loose with spasm after surprising spasm of quick waves of pleasure from her cunt to her toes back up her legs to her cunt again then up her spine and down again and on and on, ripple after ripple. She heard someone moaning. And it was her. It was frightening: her body going on like that without her. And it was fabulous. And from that moment she never passed up an opportunity at an orgasm. Ironically, Jordan appeared not to even notice the difference between the real thing and the "let's pretend" orgasms of before.

So when it came to sex, to having orgasms, she was definitely not a failed woman. She had had plenty. More than her share? Maybe that was the problem. Maybe there were women somewhere who were not getting their share of orgasms because Nelly was being a hog. In her mind there was a finite number of things in the world. Like money. If you had more, someone else somewhere was living on food stamps because of it. This she would readily admit was not a rational concept.

To Nelly counting your blessings always seemed to involved enumerating others' misfortunes. It was a system of checks and balances that existed no matter how strong her feelings of entitlement. This attitude emerged only during times of crisis and stress. It was part of the same system of beliefs that had good things arriving in threes, followed shortly thereafter by a series of three bad things. It was a totally unenlightened approach to life and its workings. Nelly knew it and tried to reject it as such. But she never completely succeeded.

That's why she now made the connection of having orgasms and having babies. She could have orgasms. Easily, plentifully, exquisitely. But she couldn't have babies. It must be some sort of trade-off, some kind of penalty paid for having enjoyed too much sex with too many people. The moment this thought entered her head she dismissed it as any rational, well-adjusted, guilt-free, liberated woman should. Still, she had thought the thought.

She was definitely not thinking clearly. She knew it was the result of feeling that everything was working against her in this baby business. She had to find some rationale for the whole thing, even if it was a crazy one. It wasn't enough to say, I can't have a baby because I can't have a baby. There had to be something bigger operating. If she had learned one thing in analysis, it was that there were no accidents. Dr. Abrams might have said that she couldn't have a baby because she didn't really want a baby. But she knew that wasn't true. He might have said her subconscious was working against her. But she knew her subconscious had nothing to do with this tremendous need to create a child.

Analysis. She had completed five years of it almost five years before. Dr. Abrams had pronounced her cured, another triumph for therapy.

"Now you are ready to take your part in the human-potential movement of life," he said. "You are an effective person, a beautiful woman, a credit to my genius and your own perseverance. Now get out there and live."

The reason Nelly had liked him so much was because he was so up to date and open to what else was going on in the world. With Freud as a springboard, he dove headlong into the newer disciplines such as est, actualization, TM, mind control, and hot tubs. According to Dr. Abrams, if it makes you feel better, it works. For a shrink he was refreshingly antiintellectual. And for a New York shrink he was very West Coast. He grew impatient with long, drawn-out interpretations of what were basically stupid actions. If what you did was dumb, you shouldn't have done it. And try not to do it again. Case closed.

Nelly often wondered where he had gone to school. He refused to hang up his diplomas. She sometimes suspected he was self-taught.

At her last session he had pronounced her *al dente* and told her, "If you ever want to call, feel free. But I really don't want to see your face in here again. We both have better things to do."

She dialed Dr. Abrams's number. She didn't even have to look it up.

"Hi, Dr. Abrams. It's one of your old therapeutic triumphs, Nelly Diamond."

"Hi Nelly. What's up?"

"I just wanted to make a little appointment with you."

"There's no such thing as a little appointment. My fees are now up to $75 an hour, and cheap at that."

"Fine. I'll take one."

"Tuesday at 3 P.M. sharp."

"What's the problem?" Dr. Abrams always got right to the point.

"Why do you think it's a problem? Maybe I'm coming to chat about old times."

"Cut the crap. Like I said, it's now $75 an hour and your forty minutes are running out fast."

"This is a whole new you."

"I've taken assertiveness training. Do you like it?"

"I'm not sure."

"Wait; it grows on you. So what's your problem?"

"I can't have a baby."

"I didn't know you wanted a baby."

"I do and I can't and there's nothing that can be done about it. My tubes are beyond repair. I can't get a tubal implantation and I can't have a baby."

"Neither can I."

106

"That's not funny."

"It's not meant to be funny. I had a vasectomy."

"That was by choice."

"That's right. But the truth remains: I can't have a baby."

"But I want to have a baby."

"But you can't. And you're depressed and upset because having a baby is something you really and truly want."

"That's right."

"You feel frustrated and unfulfilled and pretty much like a failure."

"That's right."

"That's good."

"What do you mean, that's good?"

"I'd say your feelings are quite appropriate. It is a big deal for a woman to find out she can't have children. It's upsetting and depressing. You're upset and depressed and, therefore, your emotional responses are right in line with the facts at hand. I don't know what else to tell you except that you've lived this long without any children in your life and you've done pretty well so far. You're a happy, attractive, successful woman. I don't see why not having children should change what is, in reality, a very good life. Unless, of course, you want your life to change. Unless you want to go around feeling like a failure, sulking about not being able to do something."

"I wouldn't exactly call it sulking."

"Sorry. But I must remind you that we spent a few good years, you and I, getting you to realize that there were a lot of things you could do and, in fact, have done. We didn't spend all that much time in helping you learn how to deal with failure because you were already much too well versed in that area. I'm not about to indulge you in this failure. If, as you say, you have pursued all the areas and you can't have a baby, well then, that's that. Let's get on with it."

"With what?" Nelly asked, knowing what he would say.

"With life, my dear girl. With life. Now we have about ten minutes left. Let's talk about me."

Nelly felt better after seeing Dr. Abrams—not totally better, but he made her feel less hopeless. Her life was not going to end just because she couldn't have a baby. She was going to make a supreme effort to put the whole idea out of her mind and, as Dr. Abrams said, get on with it.

16   Bad Jokes

It turned out not to be quite as easy as all that. In an effort to put motherhood behind her, she seemed to run headlong into the subject of babies everywhere she turned.

Joe, the newscaster she worked with, handed her a cigar one afternoon. His wife had just given birth to their first baby. He had gone through all twelve hours of labor and the delivery with her.

"It was the most beautiful experience of my life," he beamed. "I never realized how lucky women are to be able to give birth to a baby. It's got to be the single most creative thing a person can do. Oh, have one, Nelly, have a baby. Everybody should have a baby," he said as he floated on by.

Nelly stood there staring down at the Henri Wintermans Half Corona that lay in the palm of her hand. Suddenly she broke the cigar in two and then hurriedly hid it in the pocket of her blazer.

Easy, easy, she said to herself.

"Did you hear the joke about the ninety-two-year-old couple who went to see a lawyer about getting a divorce?" Brian asked over dinner that night.

"I heard it," Nelly said. Brian ignored her.

"And the lawyer said: 'Ninety-two years old! How come you waited this long to get a divorce?' And the man answered: 'We were waiting for the kids to die.'"

"That's not funny," Nelly said, drinking the last of her martini. Why was she still seeing this man? she wondered.

"I know it's not. But it's true," Brian said, signaling the waiter for another round of drinks. "Except for those kids, my marriage is a total farce. We don't talk. We don't have sex. We can't even have a decent argument. But I love those kids. With the possible exception of you, they mean more to me than anything else in the world."

"You know, if you really left your wife, your kids would survive."

"I know they would. But I'm not so sure about me."

He took her hand in his. "How come life doesn't work out the way we want it to? How come you're not the mother of my children?"

"Because I'm not," Nelly snapped, pulling her hand out of his and knocking her new drink off the table. The evening ended badly. But Nelly didn't have the energy to end the relationship.

And then Paisley called.

"I have to talk to you."

"Okay. Talk to me."

"Not on the phone. This is serious. I'm coming over."

Twenty minutes later Paisley swept in. She was wearing a frothy Mary McFadden chiffon dress with a fox boa casually flung around her neck. Her hair was flying, her face was flushed, and the whites of her eyes were a pale red. She collapsed onto the couch, threw her head back, and uttered a long, deep moan.

"Paisley, what on earth is the matter?"

"I don't think I can talk about it."

"Jesus, Paisley, it's twelve-thirty at night. I didn't call this emergency conference, you did. Now talk."

Paisley lifted her graceful white hand to her forehead. Shiny little rivulets of tears ran down her ivory cheeks.

"Oh, Paisley, honey, what's the matter? Please don't cry," Nelly said, sitting down on the couch next to her. "Tell me what's wrong. It can't be that bad."

Paisley looked up at her. "It depends on what you consider bad. For me it's the end of an era, the end of the world, the end of life as I know it."

"Jesus," Nelly breathed. "Did someone die?"

"No. I'm in love."

Nelly hadn't spoken to Paisley in weeks. But all the time in the world could not account for this drastic change. Nelly asked the impossible: "Is it a man?"

"Of course it's a man. If it were something else would I be this upset?"

"How did it happen?"

"You know the organization I was involved with?"

"The GT Whatever thing?"

"GTWIH. Get Them Where It Hurts. Well, he got me before I could get him."

"I don't understand. What did he do?"

"He arrested me. He was my first trick and he turned out to be a detective for the vice squad. He thought we were running a high-class call-girl operation."

"I can understand that."

"Anyway, I had taken his money and taken off my clothes, and that's when he read me my rights. Unfortunately, my backup squad had fled by the service elevator."

"Did you have to go to jail?"

"No, I explained the whole purpose of what we were doing to him. How we were trying to raise men's consciousness and so on."

"And?"

"He laughed. He wouldn't stop laughing. Then he said: 'You must have a screw loose, lady.' His exact words. He said I didn't deserve the face and figure God had given me. He told me that if I spent more time making love and less time messing around with men's minds, I wouldn't be so frustrated. He's uneducated, uninformed, unenlightened, and I'm crazy about him."

"But Paisley, what's wrong with that? I think it's wonderful."

"Well, first of all, none of the sisters is talking to me. They think I've sold out, and I guess they're right. But you haven't heard the worst part," Paisley said, dabbing her eyes with an antique lace hanky.

"Go on."

"He wants us to get married. He wants me to have his baby. In fact, he's insisting on it."

"His baby? He has a baby?"

"No, no. He wants us to have a baby together."

"Oh."

"Nobody ever asked me to have a baby before. Not one of my husbands or any of my assorted lovers."

"You mean to tell me the only reason you got all those abortions was because nobody asked you to have a baby?"

"Well, it is nice to be asked. Besides, I probably wasn't ready to be a mother."

"And now suddenly you're ready? It really doesn't sound to me like you're thinking very clearly, Paisley."

"You're right. I'm not. My head feels like mousse à chocolate. That's why I wanted to talk to you. I really don't know if I want to or I want to because he wants me to, or what. It's a big decision."

"You're certainly not planning on making it tonight, are you?"

"No, I just want to discuss the options. I know you've really looked into the whole thing. I can't believe that only a few months ago I thought you were crazy to want a baby. Now I'm not so sure. What do you think? Do you think if I don't go ahead with this, I'll regret it years from now?"

"I think you're being impulsive. I think you should go home and get a good night's sleep. You don't know what the hell you're doing. And I just don't want to debate the whole question right now."

Nelly was sure Paisley hadn't heard a word she had said. She had a dumb, dreamy look on her face. Nelly had never hated anyone as much as she did Paisley at that moment. The fact that she had the choice, that she would or she wouldn't, all depending on what she decided she wanted to do. It wasn't fair. Paisley didn't give two hoots about having a baby, let alone being someone's mother. The vice detective was right: she must have a screw loose. From self-appointed male avenger to potential mother figure. It was crazy. Like another bad joke.

The bad jokes kept coming. She met Abby at the Plaza for lunch. Abby looked beautiful. She was five months pregnant and Nelly tried her best to keep her eyes off her stomach.

"I hope you won't be too upset by what I have to tell you," Abby said, unfolding her napkin and placing it on top of her belly, where it immediately slipped off onto the floor.

"What is it?" Nelly asked, picking up the napkin and handing it back to Abby.

"Clark's involved with another woman."

Abby had known Clark even longer than Nelly. In fact, she had introduced him to Nelly. They had gone to drama school together. Abby had introduced them because she thought Nelly would get a kick out of meeting a certified lunatic.

"Why would I be upset? First of all, I don't own Clark. Second, we're just friends now. We stopped being lovers some time ago."

"I know."

"So why would I be upset? I'm glad he's involved with someone else. Who is it?"

"Me."

"You! You never even liked him."

"I like him now."

"But you're pregnant."

"You're the one who told me to find a man who didn't mind stretch marks. Clark loves my stretch marks. He even loves my big belly."

"But what about the baby?" Nelly asked with alarm.

"What baby?"

"The baby inside you."

"Oh, I can have sex until the beginning of the ninth month. It doesn't hurt the baby. And besides, Clark is very gentle."

Clark gentle, Nelly thought to herself. What an astonishing concept.

"I've never been so happy or felt so alive," Abby said, smiling. "And I really have you to thank."

"Me? How?"

"If there's one thing I've learned from you, it's that a woman can get everything she wants from life. It's okay to have your cake and eat it too. It's okay for me to be a wife and a mother and have an affair and even a career. In fact, Clark says he can get a part for me in his new screenplay."

"As a pregnant adultress?" Nelly asked.

"No, silly," Abby answered, immune to Nelly's sarcasm. "It's a really good small part. I play a waitress. They probably won't start shooting until next spring. The baby will already be born by then. Oh Nelly, aren't you happy for me?"

Happy was not the word to describe what Nelly was feeling at that moment.

Bad things weren't limiting themselves to three. She had an unexpected visit from Clark that same evening.

"Abby told you about us."

"Yes."

"And you think it's sick, right?"

"Right."

"Do you want to talk about it?"

"Why should I want to talk about it? I think it's sick. Abby has no business running around having affairs. She should stay at home and be pregnant."

"Maybe if I explain."

"I'm not interested in your explanations. I'm not even interested in your affairs."

Clark was not to be put off. "You know, I've never felt like this. She's beautiful. She's so filled with life. Literally. Do you know what it's like making love to a pregnant woman?"

"Let me guess. Awkward?"

"No, it's like communing with nature. I feel like that baby inside her is a part of me. When we make love, it's like making love to the baby."

"Baby-fucking! That really is perverted. You know it's not your baby. It's Jeff's."

"I know. It doesn't matter. I feel it belongs to all of us."

Babies. Babies. Babies. What was going on? Was she going crazy? Was there a plot against her? Why was everyone suddenly talking about babies? She stopped at a newstand to pick up something light to read to get her mind off the whole thing. *Cosmopolitan* featured an article by Nora Ephron on the joys of motherhood. The cover story in *Redbook* was by Erica Jong. It was entitled "Fear of Crying. How to deal with baby's tears." The cover of the *National Inquirer* was a picture of Farrah Fawcett with the headline: "I want to have a baby to make me feel more like a woman." There it was in black and white: Farrah Fawcett needed a baby to make her feel more like a woman. Nelly could just picture Farrah pregnant. A gorgeous belly perched somewhere between her flawless breasts and her still seductively slim hips.

112

What was this, some sort of goddamn baby boom? Hadn't babies gone out with the birth control pill? What happened to zero population growth? It was all a very bad joke. Even the front page of the *Times* carried the story: "Births on the rise." She knew she was still thinking about it too much. It just seemed like everyone was having or talking about babies. She knew it was all part of that perfectly appropriate depression that Dr. Abrams had described, but knowing didn't make it any easier.

Tyler was the last straw. But then she probably needed a last straw anyway.

One night before turning out the light, Tyler turned to her and said, "Ah think Alex and Ah are, as they say, headed for the last roundup."

"Oh, what happened? Did you have a fight?"

"No, it's just that our relationship ain't goin' nowhere. Ah guess Ah got a yearnin' for other things from life."

"Like what?"

"Oh, like children," he said, looking at her meaningfully.

"Well, don't look at me," Nelly screamed. "I can't help you out there, pardner." She threw back the covers, jumped out of bed and ran into the bathroom. She yanked one of the apple green towels off the rack and held it to her face. Then she cried and cried until her throat hurt with the sobbing.

The crying made her feel a hell of a lot better. But what really worked was the soft-shell crabs. The next evening she was feeling moody and mean and not fit company for anyone, so she took herself to a lovely little seafood restaurant a few blocks from her apartment. She wasn't really hungry. She couldn't think what she wanted to eat. The waiter came to take her order.

"The specialty for tonight is striped bass stuffed with clams. We're out of soft-shell crabs."

Soft-shell crabs. Of course. That was exactly what she wanted. Not wanted—craved, hungered for. That was why she had come to this restaurant in the first place. They were famous for their soft-shell crabs.

"Are you sure you're out of them? Can't you check with the kitchen?"

"I'm sure. We just served our last order," he said, indicating a large gentleman eating in the corner.

Nelly had visions of throwing herself at the man and wrestling him for the last of the soft-shell crabs. If only she had come half an hour earlier. If only she had called first and reserved them. She looked around the restaurant. Everyone was eating soft-shell crabs but her. She was sure of it.

"I highly recommend the bass," the waiter said. "It's really very good."

"I don't want the bass," Nelly snapped. "I want the soft-shell crabs."

"As I said, we're out of soft-shell crabs," the waiter said nicely, his pencil still poised.

"When will you get the next ones in?" Nelly asked, thinking perhaps they made night deliveries.

"Oh, it's hard to say. They're shipped in from Florida. Sometimes we get them, sometimes we don't. We also have some very good bluefish," he added hopefully.

"I don't want bluefish. And I don't want bass. In fact, I don't want anything," Nelly hissed. She tore her coat off the chair and stormed out of the restaurant.

It hit her while she was waiting for the light to change at the corner. She didn't like soft-shell crabs. She didn't even like hard-shell crabs. She hated shellfish of all kinds. She preferred food that looked like food: simple, harmless shapes that in no way reminded her of a previous life. What in the world had possessed her to throw that scene? Wasn't it because the waiter had told her she coldn't have soft-shell crabs that she, in fact, wanted them so desperately? Hadn't that been a major theme through most of her life? Hadn't she always wanted what she couldn't have? Like cheekbones. Like the men in her life. Didn't Tyler and Brian have special appeal because they were slightly out of her reach? Hadn't the baby become a big deal because Dr. Hoffman had told her she couldn't have one? Until that point she had rarely thought about children. If having a baby had been so vital to her, why hadn't she had one with Jordan? Why had she waited so long? Why had she even considered abortion when she first thought she was pregnant?

She took a long, deep breath. She was beginning to understand the source of her unhappiness, the disappointment and frustration involved in not being able to get something that seemed so much within everyone else's grasp. She just wasn't used to not getting what she wanted. And she was not used to wanting something in quite the same way that she wanted this baby. She had turned a frustrated desire into a major tragedy and it wasn't a tragedy at all. It was unfortunate. It was sad. And it would make for a good tear-jerking movie. But she had to be honest with herself. If she wanted soft-shell crabs so badly, she could pack up and move to Florida. And if having a baby had been so all-important to her, she should have realized it years before and done something about it—like get pregnant before her tubes decided to close down for business.

She felt lighter for the first time in months. She just wasn't cut out to be the tragic queen of the East. She was not about to break down every time someone mentioned the word *baby*. She was not about to go through life feeling like a failure. She was going to pull herself together or her name wasn't Nelly Diamond.

First thing tomorrow she would make a list of all the rich and famous people who either could not or simply chose not to have children. And she would propose a news feature to the network on the joys of not having children and let that asshole Reagen eat his heart out.

17 Bad News

That night the phone woke her from a not-so-sound sleep. Her eyelids sprang open between the first and second ring. She glanced at the clock radio. It was 3:30 A.M. Not the best time slot for a newsbreak. Someone must have died. It must be her father. Or her mother. Or, God forbid, both. She hestitated before picking up the receiver.

"Hello? Nelly?" It was her father.

"Nellikins." And her mother. The telephone twins, alive and well

"Oh God," her father said, his voice breaking.

"Oh Nelly," her mother sobbed.

"The baby's gone," her father choked.

"The baby? What baby? Whose baby?"

"Sarah. Sarah's gone," her mother said. Nelly gasped.

"Dead! Dear God!" Of course, she thought, from accident prone to permanently prone, the story of Sarah's life. "What happened?" she asked.

Her father took a deep breath: "She's not dead. She's gone."

"She might as well be dead," her mother said.

"I don't understand. What happened?"

"She eloped. She ran away with her physical therapist. The one who's been working on her arm," her father said.

"They went to live in Germany. Someplace called Duffeldorf," her mother added.

"Dusseldorf," her father corrected.

"I didn't know she was even seeing someone," Nelly said with great relief.

"Just her physical therapist," her father said. "Three times a week. To work out the muscles on her arm. I thought three times a week was a lot," he added as an afterthought.

"Well, that doesn't sound like the end of the world to me," Nelly chided. "A physical therapist can't be all that bad. Did you meet him? Is he a nice guy?"

"He's not a guy. He's a woman," her father moaned.

"A German woman," her mother cried.

"Oh, I see," Nelly said. "I guess I see why you're so upset." For someone who had never gotten out of the house much, Sarah had certainly made a worldly leap.

"Oh Nelly," her mother sobbed, "please come home."

Nelly hadn't been home in five years. Not since her divorce from Jordan. It was no longer, in fact, home to her. The only time she saw her parents was when they came to New York. She preferred seeing them on her own turf. Well, she owed them a visit, certainly. Apparently Sarah's running off was a real family tragedy to them. She arranged to take some time off and caught a plane out that weekend.

Sarah a lesbian? Maybe that's why her relationships with men had always been short and disastrous. Nelly hoped she would be happy. A physical therapist, regardless of sex, sounded ideal to her. Someone who could take care of Sarah and patch her up when she fell down and broke something.

Nelly wondered why she wasn't more upset. It wasn't every day that one's only sister ran away with a woman to faroff Germany. She realized that she had said good-bye to Sarah a long time ago. They had never really communicated that well, and in recent years Sarah had simply stopped talking to her.

Well, at least Sarah had managed finally to get out of the house.

Her parents showed her the note Sarah had left pinned to her pillow.

Dear Mommy and Daddy,

I am going off with Schottzie to live in Dusseldorf, Germany. She has a house there. I love her very much and she does me. Schottzie's the only woman I've ever loved. Not counting you, Mommy. And you too, Daddy. I hope you'll understand. Write soon.

Love and kisses,
Sarah

Next to her signature was one of those round circles with little dotted eyes and a great big girl-scout smile.

"We'll never see her again," her father sighed.

"We've lost our baby," her mother whimpered. "You're all we have left."

"You can always visit her," Nelly said helpfully. "It's not that far away."

"No, she's gone from us forever." Her parents were adamant.

"I knew three times a week was a lot," her father said, shaking his head.

They went around mourning for Sarah as if she had died. As if she had slammed her head in the car door instead of just an arm.

Her father took her upstairs and showed her the apartment he had made for Sarah by knocking down the wall between her old bedroom and Nelly's.

"I tried to make things nice for her," her father explained.

He had built everything himself. There were hanging bookcases and shelves for records and a stereo. The closet was totally custom-made, with shelves for shoes and drawers for sweaters and lingerie. There was a platform bed with storage drawers set into the platform. The bed was neatly made and covered with the same dolls and stuffed animals Sarah had had as a child. They were arranged in precision formation according to size. For a person whose life was one messy mishap after another, Sarah had always liked to keep her things very neat.

"I was building her a desk," her father said, his eyes filling with tears. "I got some beautiful old walnut. Do you need a desk? It wouldn't take long to finish up. It's just a simple writing desk with a drawer."

Nelly longed to tell her father she would love a desk or a platform bed or something, but she couldn't.

"Oh, Daddy, thank you, but I already have a desk."

"What about something smaller? Like a coffee table? I bet you could use a nice coffee table for your apartment. It's just a matter of cutting down the legs."

Before Nelly could answer, he was off to cut the legs on Sarah's desk. Her mother, in the meantime, was off in another world. She wouldn't even talk about Sarah. She was busy with a flurry of cooking and cleaning and constant motherly reminders. Nelly felt like she was five years old again.

"Sweetheart, put your slippers on. You'll catch cold walking around in your bare feet." How someone could catch cold walking barefoot in a house with wall-to-wall carpeting was beyond Nelly's comprehension.

"I didn't bring my slippers," Nelly finally said after the third or fourth time. She didn't want to admit the worst to her mother: that she didn't own a pair of slippers. Particularly since her mother had sent her a pair of slippers for her birthday every year for the past twelve years.

"Honey, don't snack now; you won't be hungry at dinner."

It got worse. At dinner, while her father reached over to help her cut her meat, her mother said: "Nelly, finish your brussels sprouts or no dessert."

Brussels sprouts were the only vegetable her mother ever served. She thought of them as a good, compact, all-around, all-purpose vegetable, like a one-a-day vitamin.

At 10:30 P.M.: "Nelly, don't you think it's about your bedtime? You need your sleep."

In the morning: "Coffee! That's all you're having? That's no way to start the day. Have some cereal. Did you take your vitamins?"

"No, I had a couple of brussels sprouts instead," Nelly said and was immediately sorry she did.

"You shouldn't eat old brussels sprouts, they lose their vitamins after the first day."

"Then why do you save them?" Her mother kept a gallon-size Tupperware container filled with leftover brussels sprouts on the bottom shelf of the refrigerator.

"For my brussels bread," her mother said. Her mother had an answer and a use for everything.

Nelly had planned to spend a week with them to help them through their mourning period, but she was ready to go through the roof. She had to get out of the house. She grabbed her coat to take a walk.

"Nelly, wear something on your head. It's chilly out."

Nelly exploded: "Mother, I'm not a child anymore."

"That may be, but I'm still your mother," she said with triumphant logic.

But she wasn't really. Just as her father wasn't her father. Not in the way they wanted to be. Not in the way they had been for Sarah. For the first time Nelly saw her parents as roleless. They had not only lost a daughter, they had lost their function in life. Sarah was gone, and with their baby went their justification for playing Mom and Dad in perpetuity. Their Ozzie and Harriet contracts had just been terminated.

Nelly understood how they had gotten stuck in their roles. It wasn't just Sarah and her endless need to be babied. It was also the fact that her mother had always thought of herself as falling short of her concept of the perfect parent. Weren't Sarah's constant misfortunes evidence of that? Wasn't the fact that Nelly never wore slippers proof in itself? Her mother must have decided some thirty years before that she was going to keep working at it until she got it right. Until every last brussels sprout disappeared from the face of the earth. Her father, being the ideal helpmate, had joined right in with her. And, in truth, they hadn't been bad parents at all. The trouble was that they didn't have a clue about how to deal with offspring over the age of ten.

If only they had grandchildren. If only they had someone to take the place of the baby daughters they had lost. Nelly caught herself. She had come too far, gone through too much; she was not about to fall for that.

She had saved herself from her own anger, had overcome her feelings of failure, had lived through the fact that everybody in the world seemed to be having or planning to have a baby, had analyzed and come to terms with her frustration at her inability to deliver. She had made it through; she was not going to start falling apart all over again.

It was a sad fact of life. She could never have a child. Her parents would never know the joys of grandparenthood, nothing could bring the old Sarah back, and nothing could make Nelly take her place. And that was that. She blew her nose, took a deep breath, and walked back to the house.

Her mother was in the kitchen cooking.

"What are you making?" Nelly asked, sitting down at the kitchen table.

"Tuna Surprise," her mother said, turning her back in such a way that made it impossible for Nelly to see what she was doing. That's what made her Tuna Surprise a surprise. You never knew what you were going to find in it. She had a need to infuse her dishes with an element of the unexpected in order to make up for how predictably bad they always turned out.

She didn't just make meat loaf, it was Surprise Meat Loaf. Stew was Surprise Stew. Ham hocks and lima beans were incomprehensibly Ham Hocks and Lima Bean Surprise. There was no such thing as plain eggs. They were Surprise Eggs, which were made by cutting a hole in a thick slice of bread, hiding the egg, and then frying the bread. Sometimes Surprise Eggs were made without the egg, which made them, of course, even more of a surprise. There was also Surprise Dessert, which could be almost anything topped with Cool Whip. Surprise Chicken was her specialty. Basically this was a simple roast chicken with an unexpected stuffing—like ham hocks and lima beans. Her mother was famous for her Fortune Chicken, which was Surprise Chicken with a stuffing made of bread crumbs, celery, chopped giblets, and little slips of paper with famous sayings written on them in indelible ink (one famous saying per individual helping of dressing).

Her mother was a truly terrible, if not inventive, cook. Which was odd, because Nana, her mother's mother, had been such a fine one. Her roast chicken was a study in simplicity. To stuff a bird with anything was, her grandmother believed, a sacrilege.

"Never stuff a bird," Nana had explained, "because it leaves no room for the soul."

Nelly remembered it as if it were yesterday. "The Sermon on the Chicken." It had been in this very kitchen. She had been six years old. Nana held the chicken in both hands like a little baby.

"When a chicken dies, its soul doesn't go to heaven right away like ours does. It stays inside the chicken to watch over it. Because a chicken's life isn't really over until it gets to the dinner table."

"Let me see," Nelly asked, peering into the hole between the chicken's legs. She didn't know what a soul looked like. She half-expected to see a small yellow chick. Instead there was nothing but dark red walls and the faint outline of the inside of the ribs.

"You can't see a chicken's soul," Nana said, "you can only taste it. The inside of the chicken is like the soul's altar, so first we have to clean it and make it pure."

She took a clean white rag, dampened it, and rubbed it inside the cavity. "A chicken," she explained, "leads a very good life. Simple and clean. That's why it has a soul in the first place. A chicken is one of God's purest animals. Now we make an anointment."

She took butter in her hand and rubbed it gently, lovingly all over the chicken.

"Just salt and pepper," she said, sprinkling the chicken, "to bring out the true spirit. That's it."

All this from the same woman who had substantiated the story that babies come from seeds placed in mothers' navels. No wonder Nelly had believed. Her grandmother's chicken was as good as her words: crisp, golden skin that crackled when you bit into it and moist, delicate meat that fell away from the bone. Nelly had never since tasted a chicken as fine as those anointed by Nana. Her mouth watered with the memory of it.

As if she had been reading Nelly's mind, her mother said: "Remember Nana?"

"Of course I remember her. She was my grandmother."

"Remember how she used to scrub the kitchen before she started cooking?"

"I remember."

"Remember how she would spread papers over everything after she cleaned? She used to say it was to keep the germs busy reading so they wouldn't get into the food."

"I remember."

Her mother went on and on. So many familiar stories. Nelly wasn't sure if she, in fact, remembered the actual event or was just remembering the memories her mother had shared with her so many times before. She knew some of the stories probably took place before she was born. But still they had a reality to her that was so strong she could picture them clearly in her mind.

Her grandmother's lifelong fight with the local butcher, her claiming he was a sadist who didn't know the first thing about how to cut meat. Her grandmother putting blueing on her white hair to take out the yellow and ending up with sky-blue hair. Her grandmother having all her teeth pulled because she couldn't bear the idea of having one cavity.

"If they're starting to go bad, let's get rid of them all now."

It was funny how they were both remembering Nana instead of Sarah, who had just flown the coop. It was probably still too soon for Sarah's life to be molded into memories.

She watched her mother as she secreted special surprise ingredients into her tuna casserole. Suddenly she thought her eyes were playing tricks on her. Her mother looked like a replica of her grandmother standing there at the kitchen counter. The only thing that was missing was the newspapers. She realized for the first time how old her mother was. Nana must have been around her mother's age when she died.

She felt an overwhelming surge of love for her mother, a love for her as she was now and as Nelly would remember her years later. It was all connected to the love she felt for her grandmother and for the memories of her that her mother carried with her and kept alive. Nelly was aware of the fact that she

120

was, at that moment, already forming memories of things that hadn't yet been forgotten. She was filing pictures away in her mind like recipes in a box, a reference file for the future.

It hit her. It wasn't just embroidered pillow cases and souvenir silver spoons and old faded snapshots that got handed down from one generation to the next. It was the memories. That was what a family was about. That was how they all survived. And she thought: but who will I hand my memories to? Who will remember my memories of my mother or her memories of Nana? And who will remember me? Nana was dead. Sarah was gone far away. Her mother and father would be gone before long. And one day she would die. Then there would be no one. And that would be that. Yet another sad fact of life.

She knew at that moment that she had to have a child. It was clear to her now in a way that it hadn't been before. She knew that her desire for a baby was not just a frustrated longing for something she couldn't have. It was not just a need to cast her parents in new roles as grandparents. No.

She wanted a child so that sometime someone would remember that coffee tables can be created by cutting down the legs from desks, that you can make bread from leftover brussels sprouts, that you shouldn't slam a car door without removing your arm first, that walking barefoot around the house won't necessarily give you a cold, and that chickens have souls which stay around for the roasting.

She understood now that just because she couldn't conceive didn't mean she couldn't be a mother. Just because she couldn't give birth didn't mean she had nothing at all to give. She had a lot to give. She had the love, the desire, the need, and the know-how—and a great recipe for Surprise Eggs. She wondered why she hadn't thought of it before. It was so simple: she would adopt a child.

18 Immediate Delivery

When you have a baby of your own, a certain amount of genetic guesswork is, of course, removed. The baby will undoubtedly look like someone, probably someone you know quite well. The beauty of adoption, Nelly felt, was that there were no givens, no need to place any limitations on either your expectations or your imagination. And after being bogged down for so long by the scientific realities of human infertility, it was a pleasure to set her head adrift with thoughts of the perfect baby to come.

As any other expectant mother, Nelly was forming a picture of her baby in her mind. But, in her case, she wasn't limiting herself to one image. Rather, she conjured up a whole photo album of different baby pictures and created stories to go along with each:

1. The Kansas-in-August Story

The story is shot entirely in brilliant blue and gold in a field near a small town somewhere in central Kansas. Blue is the color of the sky and the girl's eyes, gold the color of the wheat and her hair. She, a beautiful sixteen-year-old girl, has just graduated from high school with straight As. (And that's with all her extracurricular activities too: head cheerleader, lead in the school play, soloist in the school dance recital. Plus helping her mother out every day after school.) She has a sunny disposition, a keen mind, and a cavity-free mouth. He, captain of the football team and president of the senior class, also gets straight As, has perfect teeth, and writes poetry which his English teacher says shows great sensitivity. Neither he nor she smoke or drink; they wouldn't touch marijuana even if it were growing free and wild on the back forty.

They are deeply in love and have been for years. She wears his blue and gold letter sweater. He wears her high school ring on a chain around his strong, handsome neck. They plan to get married after they finish college. Both have full scholarships. Unlike many of the other kids in their class, they have both agreed to save themselves until their wedding night.

But, on this one hot summer day while swimming in their secret place in the cool creek that runs through the back fields, love and clean-cut sexual desire overcome them. She surrenders herself underneath the gold Kansas sun and they make rapturous love for the very first time. They aren't sorry. They aren't guilty. They are just glad to be in love and alive. A gentle breeze ripples across the wheat and caresses their sun- and sex-warmed skin. They kiss and part, making plans to meet later that evening for the Saturday Night Square Dance. It is the happiest day of her life. It turns out to be the last day of his.

Walking home, his head filled with thoughts of her, her name singing on his lips, the young man trips and falls in a tall field of wheat, hitting his golden head (he too has blonde hair and blue eyes) on a large stone. He is knocked unconscious and so doesn't hear the harvester thrashing its way through the fields toward him.

His death is sudden, painless, and requires a closed casket. He leaves behind a large family with five brothers who will comfort each other and eventually get over his tragic death. And, of course, he leaves behind his young, beautiful and just-that-day pregnant girl friend who, even in her grief, knows that she must go on living and will, for his sake, someday find happiness after she graduates from college.

When she discovers she is pregnant, she makes a vow to have the baby as a final commemoration of her lost love. She knows she cannot keep the child. She knows he would have wanted her to go on and become a nuclear physicist just as they had always planned. So she will have the baby and then give it up for adoption, because in that way she will be able to make a gift of his child to the world. No, not to the world. But to some one deserving person. Some woman who cannot have children of her own. Who also has blonde hair and blue eyes to serve the baby as a constant reminder of the Kansas wheat fields where the conception took place. Her beautiful baby will have a perfect mother and a beautiful home. Preferably in New York City, where there are more career opportunities.

She gives birth to a beautiful, golden-haired, blue-eyed girl who now lies cute and cuddly in a sunny little nursery somewhere in Manhattan, just waiting for someone to come and adopt her. Someone just like Nelly.

2. *The Silver-Cloud Story*
The *New York Times* called it "the most perfect match since the Kelly-

Rainier marriage"—she from the *crème de la crème*, the toast of the town-house set; he, the son of the son of the man who founded one of New York's biggest banks. The couple with everything: money, looks, brains, and aristocratic chromosomes. Both the last of their noble family lines. She, the only surviving daughter, and he, the only surviving son, are the proud parents of a month-old baby who luckily survives without a scratch the fatal crash of their Rolls-Royce Silver Cloud.

Nelly and her remote crew are the first on the scene. They were on their way to cover another news story when they saw the flames bursting out of the once-elegant automobile.

"No one could have survived that," her cameraman says, shaking his head.

"Shhhh," Nelly says, "I hear someone crying."

They are quiet. Sure enough, there is a small, plaintive cry coming from the bushes several yards away. Nelly goes over to investigate. There, lying in the soft grass, is a tiny baby, wrapped in a 100 percent English cashmere baby blanket. Nelly picks up the baby and it stops crying immediately. The infant looks up into Nelly's face and the most perfect little smile forms on her rosebud lips. The cameraman informs Nelly of an obscure New York State adoption law which is applicable only to the sole survivor of incredibly wealthy families killed in tragic automobile accidents. It allows Nelly to adopt the baby, who has dark curly hair, dimples, and sweeping black eyelashes. Nelly donates the baby's inheritance to charity and receives an Adoptive Mother of the Year Award.

3. *The Tahitian-Princess Story*

The youngest and most beautiful daughter of the chief of the tribe is pregnant. This is good. She is supposed to be pregnant. Her baby, fathered by the biggest, strongest, bravest, and most intelligent of the warriors, assures the natives of good rainfall (not too much, not too little) and consequently good coconut crops for that year. But that's not all.

It's the custom of this particular tribe to sacrifice the youngest princess's first baby to the sea shortly after her birth. This guarantees good fishing, good boating, and no sharks or sea urchins for seven years. The baby is born. She is beautiful. The tribe rejoices. According to the ancient custom, the small infant is placed gently in a hollowed-out tree trunk and set adrift on the ocean. The young mother waves good-bye as she watches the little craft disappear into the sunset. She is not sad. She knows she has done well by her people. One good year of coconuts and seven years without sharks or sea urchins is truly a blessing from the gods.

As luck would have it, a passing yacht spots the floating tree trunk and saves the beautiful, honey-skinned baby girl. The people who own the yacht are from the New York Yacht Club. They take the baby back to the city with them. They love the baby girl very much, but since they have plenty of children already, they put her up for adoption. They specify that the baby must be adopted by a woman who cannot have children of her own, one who is preferably involved in the broadcast news profession, because they think it will make an interesting story.

And that is how Nelly gets to be the mother of the Tahitian princess's beautiful baby girl. A baby girl who possesses a native intelligence that practically guarantees she will be a success at anything she undertakes. She will grow up and be a credit to the royal blood that flows through her veins. In ten years or so Nelly will take her back for a visit to the beautiful island on which she was born. Nelly will caution her about walking in the shallow water without shoes because of the many sea urchins hidden in the sand.

Those were her favorite adopted-baby fantasies. It was good she had them. The realities were to come soon enough.

She cleared her desk of all other materials and set to work on the "Nelly Adopts the Perfect Baby" story. She got out the Yellow Pages, opened it to the As and looked for Adoption. Her eye hit upon the New York Council on Adoption. She had seen their commercials on television. ("Find room in your heart, make room in your home . . . adopt a child.") She dialed the number. It was busy. She waited a minute and then dialed it again. Still busy. The third time, it rang.

"Thank you for calling the New York Council on Adoption," a recorded voice intoned. "Our social workers' lines are temporarily busy. Please hold and one of our volunteers will be with you shortly. This message will not be repeated. Thank you."

There followed a vocal rendition with tambourine and harmonica background of "My Blue Heaven": "Just Molly and me and baby makes three, we'll be so happy . . ." Nelly continued to thumb through the Yellow Pages while she waited. She turned to the Bs. Under Babies:

Baby accessories, Baby carriages and strollers, Baby crib rental. That seemed like a very good idea. After all, a baby didn't stay in a crib forever and what do you do with a crib after the baby's gotten too big for it? It's not exactly something you can make a planter out of.

At the bottom of the page was a large display ad for Ben's Baby Store. "We deliver when you deliver. Featuring Simmons, Lepine, Perego, Marmet, Sealy and others." Must be brand names for baby carriages or cribs. She jotted down Ben's number on a pad.

It occurred to her that immediate delivery was one of the major advantages of adoption. After waiting all these months to find out the results of her infertility workup, it was gratifying to know that she didn't have to wait another nine months to give birth to a baby. Adoption meant ready-made babies. No waiting. No worrying. No muss. No fuss. No stretch marks. No morning sickness. No maternity clothes. In fact, the money she saved on maternity clothes she could spend on a Lepine or Perego or whatever was at the top of the line in baby carriages. She wondered how long the whole adoption process would take. Certainly there must be some sort of paper work involved. But she was sure they must expedite things. After all, they wouldn't want little newborn babies sitting around getting old waiting to be adopted. That wouldn't make sense, would it?

"Hello. New York Council on Adoption, Mrs. Fehlinger speaking. Can I help you?"

Nelly snapped to attention. "Oh, yes. Thank you. I'm interested in adopting a baby."

"Fine. Name?"

"Nelly Diamond."

"Single or married?"

"Single."

"Address?"

"300 Central Park West, New York City, 10023."

"Good, I'll put all the information you need in the mail today. You should be getting it tomorrow or the next day at the latest."

This was even easier than Nelly had imagined.

"Is that all you need to know?" Nelly asked. "Don't you want to know what kind of baby I'm interested in?"

"Oh, no. Let me explain. You see, we are not an adoption agency. What we are is a nonprofit organization, a group of adoptive parents who coordinate things for people interested in adoption. Our purpose is to make it easier for people to adopt. What I'll be sending you is all the information you need, a list of the New York adoption agencies to call, and so forth. Now, the standard procedure is for you to first locate an agency. They, in turn, help you locate a child. Each of the agencies has its own individual requirements and its own list of children that are under its care. When you find an agency that you feel is right for you and vice versa, then you arrange with them to have a home study done."

"When you say 'home,' do you mean apartment or house?"

"Oh, they don't care what it is as long as there are adequate living arrangements. The home study really means they come to your home to study you."

"Oh, I see."

"Now, once the home study is complete, they locate the right baby for you. They give you the child's background, history, et cetera. You can even take him for a couple of weekends to see if you feel right together, sort of a trial period. If that goes well, you finalize the adoption with your lawyer and that's it."

"It sounds so easy."

126

"Well, that's our job. To make it sound easy. Too often now you hear how difficult it is to adopt—how there's a shortage of healthy babies, a lot of paper work, and an endless waiting period. But I'm sure you've heard all that."

"No, actually I haven't. But then I haven't been paying much attention."

"Well, we here at the council believe adoption is possible. If they can put a man on the moon, then you can adopt a baby."

Nelly didn't understand the connection. "So the first thing I do is choose an adoption agency?"

"That's right. Now if any one of them gives you a hard time about requirements or long waiting periods, just call another one. There are over two hundred adoption agencies in the New York area alone. In addition to those, there are adoption exchanges that handle children from foreign countries. There is one other way to go about it. That is to come down to our office and look at the photo listings of available adoptable children in the New York area. We have books of listings of all the children. Pick a child, and then contact the adoption agency that handles that child. But of course that's a more inverted approach and your chances of getting that one particular child are greatly reduced."

"You're an adoptive parent?"

"Well, I'm a prospective adoptive parent. We're expecting to finalize it any day now."

Nelly looked up. Ben, her producer, stood in the doorway.

"I've been trying to call you. Your line's been busy all morning."

"Busy phone, busy fingers, busy brain. I'm just earning my keep."

"How's that thing you were working on?"

"What thing?"

"The natural childbirth story."

"Oh, that. I dropped that. Turns out you were right. There wasn't much in the way of anything new. But I'm glad you asked. I've just started working on something else extremely topical and very exciting."

"What's that?"

"Adoption."

"Adoption? What's your angle?"

"Well, I haven't zeroed in on a particular angle yet. There's a very big trend going on now. More and more people are adopting. Fewer and fewer people are having children of their own."

"You've got figures on this, I assume?"

"Oh, yes."

"But no angle. No black-market scandal or anything like that?"

"Oh, you mean something sensational?"

"Well, I guess what I'm aiming at is something that smacks of a news story."

"Don't worry, Ben, I'll have a story that will have people sitting on the edge of their ottomans."

"Nelly, is there something else going on with you?"

"What do you mean?"

"Well, first it was the infertility thing, then natural childbirth, and now adoption. It seems to me that you're going through some kind of motherhood phase."

"Oh Ben, this has nothing to do with me." Nelly laughed. "Motherhood and having babies is just what's happening in the world. Don't you read the papers?"

"Well, that's the thing. You see, I do read the papers, strange as that may seem. And the big news seems to have to do with energy shortages, crime, inflation, and presidential politics. Unless, that is, you are way ahead of your time and are reading something between the lines that I, narrow-sighted news producer that I am, have somehow missed."

"I am way ahead of my time. I've also got my finger on the pulse!"

"That's good. It just seems to me a little ironic that you're turning into the one thing you never wanted to be labeled as: a woman's newscaster. There was a time when you wanted to slug it out on the streets, or at city hall, or wherever hard news was happening. You would've turned your nose up at the whole idea of motherhood and babies. You would've called it soft, sexist news. It just surprises me to see you turn around like that."

"Listen, Ben, if you don't want me to come up with new story ideas, just say so."

"Now you're trying to bully me."

"No, I'm not. Can't you even tell the difference between bullying and a little manipulation?"

"Oh, it's just manipulation." He made an exaggerated sigh of relief. "You had me worried there for a second. Listen, as long as you don't fuck up your regular assignments, I don't care what stories you want to pursue. I just hate to see you wasting a lot of time and energy on stuff we may never use, that's all."

"And you're telling me you'll never use a story on adoption?"

"It depends on what it is, you know that. It just seems to me to be low priority as far as the news. Like a women's-page thing."

"You know, men adopt children too."

"Men also rob banks, swindle investors, run for major office, and play in the World Series."

"Now who's being sexist?"

"I can't win."

"Didn't you know this isn't the century for men to win? You guys won in the last century."

"You're right," he said, bowing low, "I totally forgot."

Nelly spent the rest of the day poring over her most recent purchase from the baby section at Barnes and Noble. The book was entitled *Name Your Baby*. It was a paperback by Lareina Rule. Over 100,000 copies in print.

"The name you give your child will be one of your most important gifts to him. It is, therefore, necessary to give your baby a pleasant sounding name . . . persons with unusual or freakish names have more difficulty as youngsters getting along with other children . . . Check name combinations for the initials they form, discarding names that may form the initial letters of words that might prove embarrassing to your child." (Sarah Ann Diamond would spell S.A.D. That would look terrible on a monogrammed bag. Same was true for Melanie Agnes Diamond. Betty Eleanor Diamond, or B.E.D., might be troublesome for a girl, but could prove to be a real conversation piece for a boy.)

Marquis Diamond, Kimberly Diamond, Hope Diamond, Burton-Taylor Diamond. No, plays on her last name were out. They sounded so contrived. Probably because they were. Maybe she could name the baby. Little Nelly, Nellyette, or Nel, if it was a girl. Nelly Junior or Nelly II, if it was a boy. Nelly on a boy sounded like a baseball player's name. Or Nelson. That was a nice, strong-sounding name. Nelson Diamond. Nelson Diamond II. Vice-President Nelson Diamond. President Nelson Diamond.

She thumbed through the book. There were all sorts of wonderful names. Names she had never heard of. Oriana meant "golden one." Alanna meant "bright, fair and beautiful." You could hardly beat that. Cliantha meant "glory flower." It was such a pretty name, Cliantha. It sounded so soft and sweet and lacey. She noticed that she was only studying the girls' section of names. It occurred to her that if, indeed, she had her choice, she would opt for a girl. Not that it really mattered all that much and not that a little boy wouldn't be wonderful, but still, she leaned toward girls. It was probably because she felt she would understand a girl better. What do boys really like? What do they really want? How would you explain a penis to a little boy? A girl was someone she could be pals with, go shopping with, try on makeup with. She could help a little girl with her hair, with her boy problems, with her first period. She would take the cue from her mother and do just the opposite. She wondered if she should specify girl only to the adoption agency she picked. No. It didn't really matter. A baby was a baby. If it turned out to be a baby boy, then she'd just learn more about boys, that's all.

David Diamond. That had a nice ring to it. But David wasn't appropriate for a girl. There were those boys' names that were great on girls. Like Stacy,

Brook, Wallace, Sidney. They sounded so competent and classy. Of course Sidney wasn't all that terrific on a boy. Kiley was a nice neutral name. Kiley Diamond. But wasn't that too faggy for a boy? She tended toward boys' names that sounded solid, albeit boring. Names like Sam, Joe, Gus, Jack, Charlie.

And speaking of names, what would the baby call her? Certainly not Nelly. She hated it when kids called their parents by their first names. It seemed so smart-assy. What about Mother? No, Mother was too formal, too unfriendly sounding. It had to be some derivation of Mother. Ma sounded rude. Mama sounded rude and retarded. Mom was too common. Momala, too foreign. Mumsy too affected. Ditto with Mater. Nobody called anybody Mater except in the movies. The old movies. She sort of liked Mammy but she supposed that it was one of those terms that belonged exclusively to black people, the kind that white people were always using in order to appear cool. Like sister, brother, and nigger.

That left her with Mommy. Mommy it had to be. Mommy sounded warm, affectionate, and went well with Diamond. Mommy, in fact, was what she had called her mother as a child. Eventually Mommy had become Mom, and then finally Mother. She wondered if that was a measure of the distance that existed between her and the woman who had given birth to her. She supposed it was. She hadn't called her mother Mommy in almost twenty-five years. Maybe she should start again, especially since she was going to be a mommy too. Baby, this is Mommy's Mommy. You can call her Grandmommy. And this is Mommy's Daddy. You can call him Grandpoppy. She wondered when she should tell the baby she wasn't her real mommy. She didn't want to worry about that now.

Brian had yet another great restaurant for them to try that night. It was called Woks Off. It was supposed to be the new "in" Szechuan place in SoHo.

"I'll have the Moo Shoo Pork," Brian told the waiter, who was wearing black pants, a rumpled white shirt, and a black satin *yarmulke.*

"No pork. No shellfish. No uncovered heads," he said, handing Brian a *yarmulke.* "This is a kosher restaurant."

"A kosher Szechuan restaurant?" Brian asked.

"An orthodox kosher Szechuan restaurant. We used to require women to sit in a separate area from the men but the city threatened to revoke our license. Here, cover your head, too," he said to Nelly, handing her what could only be described as a *schmata,* or a rag.

"Let's go," said Nelly, eyeing the ragged kerchief with distaste.

"No, let's stay," said Brian, placing the *yarmulke* on his head. "It's supposed to be terrific."

Instead of egg noodles, the waiter placed a wooden bowl of deep-fried matzo pieces on the table in front of them. The menu was in Hebrew with Chinese translations. It took them awhile to order.

130

"Brian, I want you to be my lawyer," Nelly said, helping herself to a second helping of the Moo Shoo Brisket of Beef. Brian had chosen the Emperor Tung Chicken with Farfel.

"But of course. I'll be your lawyer, I'll be your lover, I'll be the cream in your coffee," he said, singing this last.

"What I mean is, I want you to do something legal for me."

"Well, knowing you, Nelly girl, I can't think of anyting legal I could do for you that would really turn you on."

"Brian," Nelly warned, gripping her chopsticks like a dagger.

"Okay, okay. What do you want me to do?" He smiled, amused at himself.

"Well, it's nothing that immediate, but I am going to need you to finalize my adoption."

"You never told me you were adopted," Brian said, surprised. "Why didn't your parents take care of that years ago? That's really very foolish."

"It's not my adoption. I'm adopting someone."

"You're what?"

"*I'm* adopting a baby."

"Why in God's name do you want to do something like that?"

Nelly realized that Brian knew nothing of what she had been through these past months. When it came right down to it, she didn't want him to know. She still felt ashamed and embarrassed about the fact that she couldn't have children of her own. Once she was firmly established as somebody else's mommy, it wouldn't matter. But at this moment she was still very much a woman in search of a child. How could she make him understand about adoption?

"I just want to be a mother," she said after deliberating for a moment.

"Why don't you have one of your own? I could help you out there."

"I don't have the time or temperament to be pregnant. Besides, I've always wanted to adopt a baby."

"What is it with you? First it's fund raising for a sperm bank, now this. Are you becoming socially responsible in your old age?"

Nelly had forgotten about Brian's sperm "donation." "No, it's not that at all. I just want to have a child. To raise it, take care of it, be its mommy."

"I never thought of you as mommy material," he said, looking at her closely. "But now that you mention it, I think you would make a terrific mother. Let's you and me make a baby."

"I told you," Nelly snapped, "I don't want to be pregnant. I don't need to experience the whole childbirth thing in order to fulfill myself as a woman. Besides, there are too many people having too many kids already," she said, looking at him accusingly.

"You know, kids are a big responsibility," Brian said. "They take up a lot of time. Like about eighteen years."

"I know."

"And it's not easy to get good sitters or housekeepers these days."

"I know."

"What happens if we want to go away for the weekend?"

"But Brian, we've never gone away for the weekend before."

"Well, what happens if we want to go out for dinner? Like tonight?"

"I'm sure something can be arranged. People with children do go out to dinner."

"Well, how are you going to explain me to the kid?"

That was it. He was already worried about this new person in her life.

"I'll just say that you're the lawyer who was kind enough to finalize the adoption and make the whole thing possible without even charging a cent for his legal fees."

"Is it going to be a boy or a girl?"

"I don't know. I don't care. As long as it's a healthy baby."

"It may not be as easy as you think."

"Well, that's why I have you. You're the brilliant lawyer."

"No, I don't mean the legal part. I mean the healthy baby part."

"Oh, Brian, come on," she said, shrugging it off. "I liked you better when you were talking about ways to turn me on."

"You know I'll do anything to help you get what you want. And if adopting a baby is what you really want, then you can count on me. I just want you to understand what you're getting into."

"I know."

"Another thing. Raising a child by yourself isn't all that easy. I want you to count on me there, too. I'll help you raise it."

"You've got enough problems of your own without worrying about being the father of my child."

"I happen to be a very good father."

"I know you are," Nelly assured him.

"Now that we've taken care of the legal matters, let me run through a few of the things I can do for you in the illegal area," he said. "See if anything strikes your fancy." He reached for her hand, dipped her index finger into the duck sauce, then placed it in his mouth and sucked it off. She laughed delightedly.

19 Selecting an Agency

Nelly received her Adoption Kit in the morning mail. It contained *Proud Parents,* a monthly newsletter put out by the council; several brochures on the care and raising of adopted children; and a big white book entitled *A Complete Guide to Adoption.* It covered adoption in the New York area, adoption outside the New York area, and adoption in foreign countries. The first page outlined a step-by-step procedure to follow in obtaining a child. Nelly was perfectly willing to put aside her grievances with step-by-step procedures. Just because that approach hadn't been successful for having a baby didn't mean it wouldn't work for adopting one.

As Mrs. Fehlinger had explained on the phone, there were five simple steps: (1) select an agency; (2) make arrangements for a home study; (3) undergo the home study; (4) locate the child; and (5) finalizing the adoption.

It was a snap. No urine specimens were required, no X-rays, no sperm counts, no hospital stay. The only part of her body that was needed for the whole procedure was her index finger to dial the phone. She studied the little white book carefully to prepare herself for step number one.

She narrowed the list of agencies down to those that had "good" addresses. Since neighborhood meant everything in New York, it stood to reason that the better addresses would have the better babies. Nelly wasn't sure what a better baby was; she just felt that she should be as discriminating as possible. Finally she automatically eliminated some agencies because of their names. For instance, the New York Area Adoption Exchange sounded a little shady to her.

133

The whole idea of exchanging a baby if you weren't satisfied with it didn't strike Nelly as a legitimate way to operate an adoption agency. Similarly, she crossed off the New York Foundling Home because it reminded her of frostbitten babies left on doorsteps in dirty blankets.

When she had cut the list of prospective agencies down to ten, she began her calls. The first was the Little Angel Child Care Association.

"I'm interested in adopting a baby."

"Fine. Your name?"

"Nelly Diamond."

"Address?"

"300 Central Park West, New York CIty, 10023."

"Age?"

"Thirty-five."

"Religion?"

"Nonsectarian."

"Race?"

"White."

"Single or married?"

"Single."

"Good. I'll put your name on our waiting list."

"How long a wait is there?"

"For a single woman waiting for a baby, I would say about eight, maybe ten years."

"Forget the waiting list," she said and hung up.

The second place she called was Bubbling Brook Child Care.

"Do you have waiting lists for single people adopting babies?" she asked right off.

"Oh no, there's no waiting list."

"That's terrific because I'm interested in adopting a baby."

"You don't understand. We have no waiting list because we have no babies. No babies at all. So we aren't taking any names at this time."

At the Booker T. Washington Foster Home and Adoption Service:

"I'm interested in adopting a baby."

"Do you want a white baby or a black one?"

"Well, I was thinking of white, preferably."

"I'm sorry, all we have is black children. That's all anybody has."

Nelly gave that some thought. How did she feel about a black baby? A baby was a baby. And Nelly was nobody's fool. She called the Alex Haley Adoption Agency.

"I'm interested in adopting a black baby."

"Are you a black person?"

"Not really."

"Sorry. We only place black with black."

134

There were more calls and more requirements that had not been mentioned in the little white book:

"Are you single?"

"Yes."

"Sorry, you have to be married."

"Are you Jewish?"

"I could be, easily."

"Sorry, we deal with people of Arab extraction only."

"Are you deaf?"

"No, not at all."

"Sorry, we only place our deaf children with people who have the same handicap."

It was only after she hung up that she realized that had she, in fact, been deaf, she wouldn't have heard the woman's question.

Nelly decided to take a more practical approach. She would lie.

She began calling every agency listed in the little book, regardless of name, or address. She got a different answer each time. But basically the answers all boiled down to a simple no. No single parents. Nobody over the age of thirty. No waiting list. In many cases, simply no answer. They just never picked up the phone.

Step number one in the adoption procedure was turning out to be all bullshit. She wasn't selecting an agency; they were selecting her. Or, more correctly, they were not selecting her. They would not even take her name for their waiting lists. Or the waiting lists were all too long. While she had been wasting her time with her infertility workup, people had been rushing to get in line.

Nelly pictured a line of people stretching from one end of Manhattan to the other, waiting patiently from one year to the next just for the chance to adopt a baby.

Worse than the lines, there were the no babies. No white babies. No black babies. No Jewish babies. No Catholic babies. No healthy babies. No babies to be had anywhere. Where had all the babies gone?

Nelly went straight to her adoption handbook. She turned to the listings for Foreign Adoptions. Her hopes lifted. Foreign adoptions literally opened up a whole new world to her. The book was organized by country.

Nelly narrowed down the nationalities in her mind. Color of skin really didn't make that much difference to her. The only skin color she drew the line at was no skin color at all. She would have great difficulty accepting an albino child.

Her first choice was an oriental baby. She thought orientals were the most beautiful people in the world. Nelly focused on the Far and Middle East. There were no adoptions taking place in China. There were no babies available from Japan. There were, occasionally, older Japanese children available but only to Japanese families. Nelly moved on to Vietnam. Isn't that what people were adopting these days? Wasn't it, in fact, the ethically American thing to do? After killing their mothers and fathers and tearing up their backyards, it made sense to offer an American home and an American life as some sort of partial reparation. She had marched against the war, but that hadn't done a hell of a lot of good. This was something concrete. She wondered how a Vietnamese baby would feel about moving to America. Would it still harbor ill feelings about the war? She would just have to deal with those problems as best she could. She checked each of the listings under Vietnam. They were not accepting applications except for children over seven. Or they were not accepting applications, period. Or there were no singles accepted. One agency explained that the Vietnam baby lift had all but stopped adoptions of Vietnamese children. Another agency was more hopeful but stated that the waiting period could be as long as five years. All agencies were still in operation and accepting donations despite the baby shortage.

Korea: according to the reference material, the Wayne Adoption Program in Topeka, Kansas, was the one agency to deal with when adopting babies from Korea. Nelly called them long distance.

"I'm sorry, but we aren't taking any applications," the man from Wayne said. "The Korean government has reduced the number of children available for adoption to only three per month."

"That's okay," Nelly said, "I'm only looking for one to start with."

"But you're not on our waiting list."

"No, but I'd like to put my name on it."

"Well, we've closed our waiting list to only those people who have been waiting a minimum of three years."

"You mean I have to wait three years before I can qualify for your waiting list?"

"That's correct. However, I'll be happy to take your name for our mailing list and if our waiting list opens up we'll contact you."

"Okay, fine, put my name on your mailing list."

"Let me just explain first that there's a standby list waiting to go on our mailing list. You see, at the present time our mailing list is full. Because of limited funds and the cost of postage, we have to limit our mailings. But our standbys get on the regular mailing list pretty quickly. As people move on to the waiting list, they are dropped from the mailing list . . . You should be able to get your first mailing within, say, ten months."

Nelly decided to look elsewhere. She was not prepared for what she found in India.

"The babies," the report stated,

> by virtue of being born in India, have a special set of problems. They suffer from a variety of diseases. If they survive birth, these children

136

are likely to have contracted any or all of the following: malnourish-
ment; intestinal parasites—of the long-incubating, hard-to-detect
variety which can surface many years later. (Don't be satisfied with
one stool specimen)—worms; lice; scabies; boils; upper respiratory,
ear, and neurological infections [infections of the nerves?]; rickets;
poor or no teeth; enlarged livers; malaria; paralyzed or missing one or
both limbs; and positive tuberculosis.

Nelly wondered if positive meant good or bad.

In addition, there are undetected or undiagnosed, due to poor medical
facilities, the following: hearing loss, rare and common blood
diseases, and slight to major brain damage.

Following this checklist was a long section on emotional problems which
Nelly skipped over, or more literally, closed her eyes to. She couldn't bear to
read another word.

But there was more on India. One agency had what only could be called a
special offer: children of parents who were afflicted with leprosy.

This is not an inheritable disease. The children need to be placed
for adoption due to the poor living conditions of the leper colonies.
Although the parents have seen that it is in the best interests of their
babies to give them up, they also want, and should be given, the
opportunity to keep in touch with their children through letters and
pictures.

Nelly could understand the letters. But pictures too?

And what about these long-incubating, hard-to-detect intestinal parasites?
Nelly, like her mother before her, had *always* been satisfied with one stool
specimen. As long as it was one a day. She made up her mind to stick with her
own country. Adoption was proving to be difficult enough without taking on a
whole new set of long-incubating problems.

The infertility workup had been a snap compared to this. No wonder people
had children of their own. There was no paper work, or visas, or question-
naires involved in getting pregnant. You just did it. You didn't have to be
white, black, under or over thirty, single or married, deaf or deceitful, you
didn't have to travel halfway around the world, you didn't have to worry about
getting horrible post cards from leprous parents. Nelly now saw the ability to
give birth in a new light: it was not just a matter of fulfilling yourself as a
woman or continuing your family line, it was simply the most direct way
around adoption.

She met Abby for coffee in an Italian pastry shop.

"Do you think I look fat?" Abby asked. She was sitting a foot away from the edge of the small wrought-iron table. That was as close as her mountainous belly would allow her. She reached over for her cappuccino and brought the cup slowly to her mouth. The coffee left a dribbly path on the table and over the pass to her lips. She repeated her question.

"Well, do you? Do you think I look fat?"

Nelly stared at Abby's coffee-spattered belly. It took her a second to speak. "Abby, you're eight months pregnant. How do you expect to look?"

"I don't mean that," she said, indicating her belly with disdain, "I mean my face. Do you think my face looks fat? Do you think it looks bloated or puffy?"

Nelly studied Abby's face. She couldn't believe she was having this conversation with a woman who was so big she probably wouldn't even recognize her own two feet, it had been so long since she'd seen them.

"No, I don't think you look fat," Nelly lied.

"I've really been trying to watch my weight. But it's so hard. I get on the scale and first I have to add for the baby and I'm not sure how much that is. Then I have to subtract for me. It's never accurate. And you know, a few pounds on me, being as short as I am, can really show. The only way I can tell if I've gained any of my own weight is by my face. I'm thinking of going on a fast for a few days."

"Abby, you can't do that. You're pregnant," Nelly said with alarm.

"I don't know that I can't. I'll ask my doctor. I'd love to get my hair cut, but I'm afraid it'll make my face look even fatter. What do you think?" she asked, holding her hair away from her face.

"I think you look terrific. Absolutely radiant."

"That's what Clark says. Jeff, too. Maybe everybody's right and I'm wrong," she said, smiling contentedly. "Maybe I'll have a canoli."

"What's the favor?" Nelly asked.

"What favor?"

"You told me on the phone you had a big favor to ask me."

"Did I say that? That was clever of me. Helps pave the way."

"So what's the favor?"

"It's a hard favor to ask because it's the kind of favor you could easily say no to. And then I'd be sorry I asked. On the other hand, as a friend, you could just as easily say yes. It's the kind of thing I won't really know unless I put it to you. Of course, I'd feel terrible if you said no. It's really a true test of our friendship. For me to be able to ask the favor and for you to be able to give me your honest answer."

Nelly was wondering if the fluid from Abby's belly had gone to her brain. "If it's so difficult to ask, why don't you just spit it out?" Nelly coaxed.

"I guess I'm trying to think what I'd say in your place. I guess I might say no. But then," she said, thinking a minute, "maybe I wouldn't. I guess it all

138

depends. No, as a matter of fact, I think I would say yes. Knowing what I know now, I would definitely say yes."

"Abby, I'm going to walk away and leave you here to get up from the table all by yourself if you don't get to the point," Nelly threatened.

"Okay, I want you to invite me to come stay with you for the weekend."

"Well, that's easy enough. But why in the world do you want to spend the weekend with me?"

"I don't. I want to spend the weekend with Clark, but I want to be able to tell Jeff I'm spending it with you."

"Oh, I've got it. You want me to be a front for you and Clark. You want me to lie to Jeff."

"No, you don't have to lie to Jeff. If he calls, you can just tell him I'm out, which will be true."

"You're taking a terrible chance. Why don't you wait for your clandestine weekend until after the baby is born?"

"Because this is my last chance to get away. Once the baby is born, I'll be tied down for months. And besides, I've never spent the night with Clark. And besides, he wants to be with my belly one last time. I told you how much he loves my belly."

"Yes, you told me."

"You're the only reasonable excuse I can use to get away for the weekend. I'll tell Jeff I want to stay in the city so we can go shopping together."

"What happens if he calls late at night? Do I tell him you're waiting outside Bloomingdale's to get an early start?"

"Say I'm asleep."

"Listen, I don't like this. I don't like being put in the middle one little bit."

"I knew you wouldn't. I told Clark you'd never go for it."

"Whose idea was this, his or yours?" Nelly asked angrily.

"What difference does it make?"

"I'd just like to know who dreamed up this really tacky scheme."

"Well, it was Jeff's idea."

"Jeff came up with the idea of you and Clark spending the weekend together and then using me as a cover?" Nelly asked with amazement.

"No. He and I talked about going away for the weekend before the baby's born."

"Then why don't you go away with Jeff? It would be so much simpler, all the way around."

"Nelly, silly, I'm not having an affair with Jeff. I can spend a weekend with him anytime. I just want to have one measly weekend with Clark. I'll never ask you again."

"You can't possibly expect me to believe that."

"Please, Nelly. Will you do it?" Abby pleaded.

"I'll do it. But I hate it. I think it stinks."

"Tell you what. You can ask me a favor. Anything, and I'll do it. Please ask me a favor. It'll make me feel better. Anything."

"Anything?"

"Just ask."

"Okay. Let me adopt your new baby."

"Are you still going through that baby thing? I thought for sure it would pass by now."

Nelly took a deep breath and blurted it out. "I found out I can't have any children. I had tests and everything. My tubes aren't working. I spent months trying to get pregnant, and then when I found out I couldn't, I thought I'd be able to forget about it. But I couldn't. I really want a child. I want to be a mother. Adoption is the only way. But it's so hard. So many people are waiting for babies. They've been waiting for years. And I just started. I can't tell you how frustrating it is."

"I'm sorry," Abby said, reaching out to take Nelly's hand. "I didn't know."

"How could you be sorry?" Nelly seethed. "You don't even know what it means. You just take having babies for granted. You don't even begin to appreciate the miracle of it."

"You're right. I never thought of it as a miracle."

"How would you feel if someone told you you couldn't have children?"

"I don't know, really. But I don't think I'd feel all that bad. Maybe that's because I've had them."

"That's right. You've had them. And now you're having another one and you don't even want it. It's not fair." Nelly was very close to tears. She knew her eyes were filling up and she hated herself for it. She saw that Abby was now looking at her with pity, and she wanted to kill her.

"Maybe it's not such a bad idea. It could very well be a brilliant idea, in fact."

"What?" Nelly said, touching a napkin to her eyes.

"You adopting the baby. It's not like we wouldn't ever see her again. It's not like you're a complete stranger."

"Oh, come on, Abby. It's a ridiculous idea and you know it."

"No, listen, it could work. You be the baby's mother and I'll be the aunt and we'll get together every Mother's Day and all holidays."

"Abby, cut it out. What in the hell do you think Jeff would say?"

"Well, he probably wouldn't react too well at first. But I could explain it to him. In fact, he could still be the father if that's all right with you. Like you got divorced and he had visiting rights."

"Do you seriously think Jeff would ever go for it?" Nelly asked sarcastically.

Abby thought a minute. "Probably not."

"So let's drop the whole subject. I'm sorry I brought it up."

Abby was still thinking. "You know, Jeff is very fond of you. He might just see his way clear to going along with it. Especially if it's another girl. He's sick to death of playing baseball with two kids who can't catch. I know for sure if it's a boy it's out of the question. But a girl . . . now that's another thing."

"I don't want any of your leftover girls, thanks all the same. I'll get my own baby. Please, let's drop the subject."

"Okay, consider it dropped. How's this weekend?"

"This weekend? For what?"

"For me coming to stay with you."

"What do you want to come and stay with me for?"

"Nelly, we're having a lot of trouble communicating here. Maybe we should start all over at the beginning."

Nelly wasn't listening anymore. She was looking around the pastry shop for a phone. She had remembered what Mrs. Fehlinger from the New York Council on Adoption had said. If she had any problems she should call. It was the council's job to make it easier for people to adopt. Why hadn't she thought of calling her before?

20 Anjelica

The offices of the New York Council on Adoption were not really offices but rather one large room with two desks surrounded by stacks and stacks of cardboard file boxes. There were children's Crayola drawings taped to the walls. At one of the desks a middle-aged woman with steel-wool hair and green-tinted glasses was talking on the phone. Nelly approached the desk.

Mrs. Fehlinger?" The woman looked up, smiling. She motioned to Nelly to take the chair opposite the desk. Nelly sat down and waited.

"Just be patient," Mrs. Fehlinger was saying on the phone, "don't be discouraged. These things take time. Listen, if I had the patience, then so can you. You'll get your baby. I know it. And call me anytime you start feeling frustrated." She hung up the receiver and beamed at Nelly. "What can I do for you?"

"My name's Nelly Diamond. I talked to you a few weeks ago."

Mrs. Fehlinger began riffling through a stack of index cards on her desk. "Nelly Diamond. Nelly Diamond. Oh, here you are," she said, extracting one card from the pile. "You're a single woman looking to adopt a baby. I remember you. How's it going?"

"Not too well. I can't even find an agency that'll take me, let alone a baby to adopt. How did you adopt yours?"

"Well, as I may have told you on the phone, the adoption hasn't been finalized yet. It takes about six months. But we've got our baby."

"How did you get him?"

"Oh, we had him first in foster care. It's what they call preadoptive placement. Sort of like renting with an option to buy. Want to see his picture?"

"I'd love to."

Mrs. Fehlinger took out her billfold, extracted a 3 × 5 photograph, and handed it across the desk to Nelly. Nelly thought she had taken out the wrong picture. The snapshot was of a smiling, cross-eyed boy who looked to be about twelve.

"But this isn't a baby. This is a full-grown boy."

"That's our baby. See, the good thing about preadoptive placement is that you can get a child right away. The only bad thing is that there's always the off chance that the natural mother will want him back. But in our case, I'm not worried. His mother was a drug addict and prostitute. Poor thing just had her hands full; that's why she had to give up the boy. I can't say I'm sorry; he's the best thing that ever happened to us. Of course, that's just one way to get a child. The thing to do is look at the baby books and see if anything strikes your fancy."

"Then there are babies?"

"Well, we call them baby books. They're photo listings of all the available adoptable children. They're actually all ages. But you must realize that the younger the child, the more problems there are."

"I don't mind diapers at all."

"I don't mean those kinds of problems."

"But you said on the phone that the photo listings were a more difficult way to adopt. You said I should contact an agency first."

"Well, if you can get through to an agency, all the better. But as you said, you've had your problems. Agencies aren't always as cooperative as they should be. You see, they have to keep the best interests of the child in mind, and of course there's the stipend."

"Stipend?"

"Well, they do get about $12,000 a year for each child in their care."

"Are you trying to tell me that these adoption agencies hold onto the children just because they make a lot of money on them?"

"I never said that. I wouldn't say that. I have to work with these people, after all. I'm just saying they're very careful about placing them. Now, let me show you about the baby books. I think that's the smartest way for you to go about getting your child."

Mrs. Fehlinger showed Nelly to a small room across the hall. There were several people sitting in straight-back chairs, thumbing through large, three-ring notebooks.

"The way it works is you find a child you're interested in and then tell me. I put you in touch with the particular agency that handles that child. So already you know you're dealing with an available child. You contact the agency, and they are more or less obligated to do a home study on you to see if you'd make a fit parent for that child. Here," she said, handing Nelly one of the big notebooks, "this is a book of our most recent listings. These children have just come up for adoption."

Nelly felt like she was in a Hamptons real estate office looking for a summer rental. She thumbed through the book. Each page had a picture and a short biography of the child. The book read like an anthology of horror stories:

Juan is fifteen years old. He is very outgoing. He likes flowers, music, and going to school. Currently he is attending a special school for the handicapped where he has quickly picked up braille. His deafness makes it difficult for him to communicate, but his teachers are very optimistic. Juan is anxious to be adopted and would like to be with a couple who either share or have had experiences with his type of handicap.

Mary Jane is a beautiful little girl. At age four she already shows a keen interest in life around her. She is warm and affectionate, which is typical of children afflicted with brain damage. Her psychologist's evaluation indicates that she has moderate to severe retardation, but is teachable. According to her foster family, she is able to sit quietly for hours watching TV and is very little trouble to take care of.

Peter is a clever boy according to his teachers, his psychologists, and his parole officer. He understands more fully now that crime and violence do not pay. The trouble he got into a few years ago when he was twelve shows no indication of being repeated. Currently he is enrolled in a vocational program that teaches him auto mechanics. This has helped channel his interest in cars into more socially acceptable behavior.

Nelly picked up the book and went back into the office.

"But Mrs. Fehlinger, these children are all older and all have terrible problems of one sort or another."

"Well, we all have problems, don't we?"

"But where are the babies?"

"You don't want to see the babies."

"Yes, I do. I had my heart set on a baby."

"This is the infant baby book," she said, holding out a thinner three-ring notebook. "As I told you, usually the younger the child, the more problems there are."

Nelly was staring at the first picture in the book. It was an adorable six-month-old baby girl who had a sweet, wistful smile on her face.

"Now here's a baby. A perfectly darling baby. What's the matter with her? The only thing they mention here is something called Down's syndrome. What's that?"

"Oh, that. A lot of people are adopting babies with Down's syndrome these days. It's a genetic defect."

"That doesn't sound so bad. And she looks perfectly all right."

"Well, they don't know what causes Down's syndrome and they don't have any cure for it. It comes out in a lot of different physical and mental ways. Tongue thrust. Slanted eyes. Zero intellectual development after six months. Let me put it this way—Down's syndrome is another name for mongolism."

"Oh," said Nelly, closing the book. There were tears in her eyes. "But when I first called, you made adopting a baby sound so easy."

"That's my job. My job is to get you interested in adoption, not to discourage you. Lord knows there are enough children, healthy or otherwise, who need good homes. But it's also my job to make sure you know the realities."

"And Down's Syndrome is one of the realities?"

"If you're a single woman looking for a baby, I'm afraid so. Now if you set your sights a little lower—or a little older, I should say—you'll see that there are thousands of children who have problems that aren't all that bad. You know, physical handicaps can be anything from a cleft palate which is surgically operable to asthma which can be controlled.

"Many of these children have some sort of emotional problems. Those too are treatable. They're also completely understandable, considering that many kids have gone from foster home to foster home, feeling rejected and unwanted. Many have spent their entire lives in the care of the state. So my advice to you is that if you're really interested in adopting, better face the fact that it won't be a baby. And if you don't feel you can handle an older child or one with a physical or mental handicap, then admit it to yourself now. It's no crime. No one says you have to adopt a child. So think it over. Think about what you yourself can handle. If you're still interested, come in and look at the rest of the photo listings."

Nelly thought about what Mrs. Fehlinger said. She stayed up all night trying to define what she wanted in a child. She came to a few conclusions:

As wonderful a person as she had always considered herself to be, she didn't feel she had the qualities, the saintly goodness to deal with a child who was severely retarded. She knew she wasn't in this adoption thing for altruistic reasons. She was not interested in doing charitable work. She just wanted a child, someone she could raise and watch grow and talk to and play games with and send to a good school. That seemed to eliminate a severely mentally retarded child. Physically handicapped was another problem. There were some physical handicaps she thought she could handle. Others she couldn't.

Who the hell did she think she was, she asked herself at one point toward

145

morning, picking and choosing among handicaps. Blind, no; deaf, yes. Polio, maybe, as long as it wasn't a crippling case. If she had had her own child and it had been stricken with something terrible, would she have thrown it out? No. But adoption was a choice. A conscious, serious step that could be made only after careful deliberation. And, because this child was to be chosen, Nelly had to be honest with herself. Painfully honest.

Anything that was surgically repairable was no problem—cleft palates, hair lips, club feet were all okay. After all, hadn't she gone through major surgery on her nose? Similarly, she felt emotional problems were manageable. She totally believed in therapy, the earlier the better. She was sorry she hadn't seen someone when she was a kid. She would find the best children's shrink in the city. The mind, Nelly felt, was eminently repairable. In checking off the list of possibles and impossibles, Nelly totally forgot what had been her primary need in adopting a child: someone to kiss and hold and cuddle and coo over. She was dealing with real problems and real children now, and she realized she felt differently about adoption. The desire to adopt was much more immediate. Because now there was some unknown child somewhere who needed her. Needed her desperately. By the time the sun came up, she wasn't even aware of the fact that she had made the big transition from fantasy baby to potential problem child.

Mrs. Fehlinger didn't seem surprised to see her the next morning.

"Here are the most recent photo listings," she said, handing Nelly the book she had seen yesterday. "Oh, wait a second. Here, I've got to add this listing." She took the book from Nelly, inserted a page at the back of the book, and handed it back to her.

Nelly turned to the page Mrs. Fehlinger had just included, and there was Anjelica.

She wasn't a baby. She wasn't beautiful. She was eight years old, wore glasses, and had a nose that overpowered the rest of her small face. She had a brilliant, wide, bucktoothed smile that practically jumped off the page. Her hair was parted in the middle and pulled back in two lopsided bunches. Nelly fell in love on the spot.

She read the description below the picture.

"Anjelica is eight years old. Clearly she is not what you would call a pretty child, but according to her social worker, she is affectionate, outgoing, and extremely verbal. Her psychologist says she tests well above average and could be an excellent student, given the proper encouragement. At present she is doing poorly. She daydreams in school and seems to be living in a fantasy world much of the time. She has been in four foster homes in the last three years and has all but given up hope of anyone ever adopting her. She likes painting.

Nelly couldn't believe it. She thought she was looking at a picture of herself. Or a picture she had in her mind of what she had looked like at eight years old. Big nose, big teeth, big glasses, big complex, big dreams. Nelly's thoughts raced ahead. First thing we do is call the orthodontist. Contacts can wait. Too tricky for a little girl to handle, and besides, your eyes keep changing up until you're eighteen. The nose, that beautiful hooked affair that shadowed her upper lip—now that was a nose Nelly could love. They could always have it fixed, but Nelly loved it. Eight years old with a nose like that. Amazing. Nelly wondered what grade she was in. What size clothes did she wear? What kinds of things did she like to do? She liked to paint, the bio said. That was nice. Nelly would buy her an easel. Oh, they were going to have a wonderful, wonderful time together. A wonderful life. How dare they pass her from one home to the next! How dare they treat the world's most perfect child that way! Nelly would make it up to her.

She ripped Anjelica out of the book.

"I found her! I found her! Here she is!" Nelly said, waving the page at Mrs. Fehlinger. "She's beautiful. She's perfect. Oh, I have to have her. Call up right now and get her out of that terrible home, wherever she is."

"Calm down, Ms. Diamond. Let me see." Mrs. Fehlinger studied the page. "Let's see what her reference number is. That will tell us what agency is handling her." She jotted down a number on her pad. "That's Hearts and Flowers Agency. We'll call them first thing tomorrow and set up an appointment for a home study."

"Oh, now, please. Call now."

"I can't. They're closed today."

"You promise you'll call first thing tomorrow?"

"I promise." Mrs. Fehlinger smiled. "I'm glad you found someone you liked."

"I didn't find her. She's been waiting for me all along."

Anjelica Diamond. Now that's what I call a classy name, Nelly thought to herself. She wondered how she could have ever wanted a baby. Anjelica was a person. A person with a past and now a beautiful, wonderful future. Anjelica. My little angel. My little girl. Not that little, but certainly still lap size, still small enough for hugs and kisses and cuddles.

She stopped by the manager's office in her apartment building.

"Hi, Mr. Mansfield. What are the chances of my getting a bigger apartment in the building?"

"Oh, not bad at all. The Fergusons on the twentieth floor are moving out next month. You could probably get their apartment."

"How big is it?"

"Two bedrooms, a dining room."

"Does it overlook the park?"

"Sure. Now I have some people on a waiting list, but they aren't residents. I'll be glad to give you preference."

"Thanks a lot. I appreciate that."

She had a weird invitation that afternoon from Paisley. "Come to dinner tonight?"

"Where?"

"My place."

"Are you having a caterer or what?"

"No, silly. I'm cooking dinner. Just the four of us."

"What four?"

"Joe, me, you and your date."

"My date? Is it anyone I know?"

"It's anyone you want to bring. But bring someone nice. It'll just be a quiet evening *chez moi*. Come about six. Joe likes to eat early."

She called Tyler up and invited him. She felt the need to forewarn him, but about what she didn't know. Maybe it was the fact that Paisley, to her knowledge, had never cooked dinner in her life. Or lunch. Or instant coffee. Or anything that required touching a stove. She always ate out or ordered in from the few four-star restaurants that deigned to deliver. And she had always made fun of couples getting together for boring little foursomes. Also there was Joe, whom neither she nor Tyler had met. Joe, she assumed, was the love of Paisley's life. The vice-squad cop.

They arrived at Paisley's apartment at six sharp and rang the bell. There was no answer. They waited a few minutes and then rang again. From behind the door there came the sounds of giggling and running barefeet. Finally, the door opened and there stood a tall, ruggedly handsome, familiar-looking man in a purple velour knee-length bathrobe which was open to the waist revealing a well-muscled chest garnished with fine curly hair.

"James Caan," Nelly gasped under her breath.

"Joe McGorey," James Caan said, shoving his hand out to Tyler. He scrutinized Tyler as if he had seen him somewhere before.

"Tyler Hanks, pleased to meet y'all. This here's Nelly Diamond."

"Oh sure, Nelly Diamond and the News," James/Joe said, giving Nelly the dazzling Caan smile.

"James Caan," Nelly said again, looking at him closely.

"That's what Paisley's always telling me," he chuckled, "I don't see it myself. Come on in. Sorry, we're running a little late. I think Paisley's messin' around in the kitchen if you want to stick your head in," he said to Nelly. It was not James Caan after all.

"You sure look familiar to me," Joe said to Tyler as he steered him into the living room. "I think we musta met somewhere."

148

Nelly was not even sure where the kitchen was. Paisley's apartment was one of those enormous Fifth Avenue co-ops. She wandered down the long hallway following her nose. Something smelled like it was burning. After five minutes, she found the kitchen and Paisley.

Paisley was wearing an identical velour bathrobe. She was hovering over a large pot on the stove and there was a slight sheen to her unmade-up face. Nelly watched her for a few minutes, fascinated. Finally, she cleared her throat and Paisley jumped, knocking the large pot onto the floor.

"Oh, look what you made me do," she groaned. "You scared me."

"You scared *me*. I wasn't sure if that was you," Nelly said.

Paisley began scooping what looked to be stew back into the pot. Nelly grabbed a sponge and leaned down to help her.

"Looks interesting. What is it?"

"I think it's beef stew. It's Joe's favorite."

"When did you learn how to cook?"

"One doesn't learn how to cook. You either have a flair for it or you don't. Like French. Do you think I should wash this off?" she asked, indicating the stew in the pot.

"No, I'd just leave it be. The germs'll cook right out of it. Listen, if we're too early, we can leave and come back later."

"Oh, no. I just got a little way laid," she said coyly. "Joe was in the kitchen watching me peel potatoes and he got turned on and the next thing I knew. . . ."

"Don't tell me. He grabbed the peeler from you and started doing the potatoes himself," Nelly said.

"Oh, Nelly," Paisley giggled.

"What can I do to help? Make a salad? Set the table? Order out?"

"Tell me what you think of him."

"Who?"

"Him. Joe. Do you like him? Do you think he's cute?"

"Paisley, I just met him. He's certainly attractive enough."

"Do you think we're right for each other?"

"Now, how do you expect me to answer that? I haven't even seen the two of you in the same room yet."

"Don't you think he has a funny sense of humor?"

"All he did was open the door. He was pretty serious about the way he handled that, considering the bathrobe. I don't think he's said anything really funny yet."

"Oh, he will. Give him a chance. He has to get warmed up. He's really quite funny," Paisley said, chuckling to herself as though remembering some hilarious anecdote from another time. "I do think a good sense of humor indicates a high degree of intelligence, don't you?"

"Absolutely," Nelly said, watching Paisley pick out a piece of meat from the stew and rinse it under the faucet. She took a French linen dish towel, carefully wiped the meat and put it back in the pot.

"He's not like any man I've ever met before. I've been limited my whole life to nothing but millionaires. Spoiled, boring, custom-tailored twits . . . just because they weren't after me for my money. Well, I'm through with all that. I don't care about the money. All I care about is love," she said, closing her eyes and squeezing a head of Bibb lettuce to her chest where it left a damp mark on the purple velour. She opened her eyes again and looked at Nelly.

"Do I look like I'm in love?" she asked.

"Well, let me ask you this: are you happy?"

"I don't know. How can I tell?" She sighed dreamily. "It's all so strange, love is."

"It's probably just like French. You either have a flair for it or you don't," Nelly offered.

"I do want you to like Joe. After all, you're one of my two closest friends in the world and your opinion does matter," Paisley said, trying to cut a tomato with a pair of poultry shears.

"Here, let me do that," Nelly said, rescuing the tomato from Paisley. "My opinion never mattered to you that much before."

Paisley looked surprised. "It didn't? Well, I guess that shows how important this relationship is to me. Who'd you bring by the way?"

"You mean, my 'date'? Tyler."

"Oh, Nelly, how could you? Couldn't you have brought someone straighter?"

"Tyler is perfectly straight enough, thank you. He's not going to rape Joe, if that's what you're worried about. Just because he's bisexual doesn't mean he can't behave himself in mixed company."

While Paisley and Nelly were having their heart-to-heart in the kitchen, Tyler and Joe were having a tête-à-tête in the living room.

"I'm trying to figure out where the hell I know you from," Joe said. He was standing over Tyler, who was slouched comfortably in a chair sipping a beer. "You from the Bronx?"

"No, Ah'm from Texas, originally."

"You go to hockey games?"

"Nope."

"Knicks games?"

"Nope."

"I wonder where it is we coulda met?" Joe said, scratching his head.

"Whale, Ah don't think we actually met, formally speakin' Ah mean. Y'all did arrest me once."

"I did? What for?"

"Indecent exposure. Ah was havin' a show in SoHo and . . ."

150

"Oh yeah. Now I remember. You were the turkey who stood around all day without a stitch on. Tried to con us into thinkin' it was art," Joe laughed, uproariously.

"It was art. Ah got off. The charges were dropped."

"No kidding? Well, I'm glad to hear that. 'Course I never did understand art that well. No hard feelin's then?" Joe said, extending his hand.

"No, not at all," Tyler smiled, taking Joe's hand. "I never did understand hockey that well either."

"Dinner," Paisley sang from the dining room.

"Good stew," Tyler said, helping himself to a third plateful.

"The potatoes are *parfait*," Nelly added.

They were struggling to make conversation. But neither Joe nor Paisley was paying any attention. They hadn't said a word for fifteen minutes. Joe was running the tip of his finger back and forth across Paisley's wrist. Paisley stared at him, dewy-eyed. Her lips were parted. Her breathing had become noticeably heavier. Joe's eyes were half shut. He looked more like James Caan than ever.

"Oooooh Joe," Paisley moaned. Nelly had never heard of it before, but she could swear Paisley was having a wrist orgasm.

"We're going to make a baby," Joe said, not taking his eyes off Paisley.

"Y'all want me to clear the table?" Tyler asked, chuckling.

"Why don't you adopt a child?" Nelly burst in.

Paisley and Joe turned and looked at her.

"Why should we adopt one when we can have one of our own?" Paisley said.

"Well, you could do both. There are a lot of children who desperately need good homes. You've certainly got the room and can well afford it," Nelly rushed on. "It just so happens that I'm adopting a child. A beautiful little girl."

"You're pullin mah leg," Tyler said with surprise.

"You are?" Paisley said, astonished. "Are you really?"

"No kidding?" Joe said.

"Yes, I am. Her name is Anjelica. She's eight years old."

"Well, I think that's just *merveilleux*, if that's really what you want to do," Paisley said stiffly.

"I think it's terrific," said Joe.

"Whale Ah'll be," Tyler grinned.

Later, as Nelly was helping Paisley stack the dishes for the maid, Paisley turned to her and said:

"Don't you think it's a little risky, adopting a child like that, without knowing the family and all?"

"What do you know about Joe's family?" Nelly said, angrily.

151

"I'm not adopting Joe."

"No. But you're talking about having a child with him and he's not even your type."

"Type! You're talking about the man I love. The man I'm going to marry."

"You're suddenly very positive about him."

"I always was."

"No you weren't. Only a few hours ago you were asking me if I thought he was cute, for God's sake. Just because I said I don't think he's your type, you take the opposite position. If I said I thought he was perfect for you, you'd probably be throwing him out. I swear, Paisley, some day your perverseness is going to get you in a lot of trouble."

"Don't you get so superior with me," Paisley raged, "just because you can't have a baby of your own, doesn't mean you have to take it out on me."

"Who said I couldn't have a baby of my own?" Nelly gasped.

"Well, Abby just happened to mention it to me. She was concerned about you and . . ."

"Nobody has to be concerned about me," Nelly shouted. "I can take care of myself. And Anjelica. You just stick to your stews and mind your own business."

The first thing Nelly wanted when she got home was a long, hot bath to soothe her frazzled nerves. Tyler had the same idea. Only he got to the tub first. So she just lay down on top of him and let him lather her up.

"Ah think that's terrific, you adoptin' a child," he said, moving the soap from one breast to the other.

"Do you really?" she sighed.

"Shore Ah do. In fact, Ah envy the little heifer. You'll make a terrific mamma."

Mrs. Fehlinger called to tell her someone from Hearts and Flowers would be contacting her within a few days. Nelly could hardly contain herself. And she certainly couldn't contain her mouth. She found herself telling all her friends about the impending adoption. This was odd, because she had told almost no one about her previous efforts to have a child. Nobody asked her why she was adopting. Somehow, adoption was the socially acceptable thing to do. More than just socially acceptable, it carried with it a kind of moral clout which Nelly hadn't anticipated. People reacted as though she were doing something wonderfully virtuous rather than just fulfilling her own singular, selfish need to be a mother. Nelly found this newly bestowed nobility a little difficult to bear. The more she denied her altruistic purposes, the more people seemed to admire her and what they thought of as her humble goodness.

152

Clark was an exception. He thought the whole idea was disgusting. "You and Sally Struthers," he said with contempt.

"What's this got to do with Sally Struthers?"

"You know, all those obnoxious ads with Sally Struthers and her child."

"That's just a fund-raising device to get money for impoverished children."

"Oh yeah? Well, who says those kids ever see a penny? And Mia Farrow, she's another one. Every time you turn around she's adopting another adorable orphan. It makes me puke. You'll get bored with the whole thing within two weeks. It's like those people who buy puppies, and when they aren't cute and puppylike anymore, they leave them in Central Park for the squirrels to eat."

"Why are you so angry?"

"Do-gooders make me sick."

"I'm not trying to do good. I just want a kid. I want to be a mother."

"Then why don't you get a puppy like other people? They understand rejection, abuse, and indifference. It's bred into them."

"Jesus, Clark, you're really being irrational about this whole thing."

"Well," he pouted, "nobody ever adopted me."

"I didn't know you were an orphan."

"I might as well have been. My parents were totally inoperative. I tried to hang around with the family next door, but they called the cops on me. The only reason my parents didn't give me up for adoption was because they needed somebody around to ignore. I don't believe in parenting, adopted or otherwise. They should put kids in a big bin and raise them by committee."

"According to Abby, you're awfully enamored of her belly for someone who's against parenthood."

"That's different. Abby's belly is a sex object. Abby is a mother figure to me. She represents everything my mother never was."

"You mean kind and loving?"

"No, that's not what I mean at all. You've been in analysis; you should understand. My mother never went to bed with me."

"Oh, come on, Clark. That's all too Oedipal."

"Nothing is *too* Oedipal," Clark retorted.

She met Brian for dinner a few nights later. He was standing outside the restaurant when she got there. He had a bewildered look on his face.

"What's the matter?" she asked.

"It's closed."

"Closed?"

"Closed by the Board of Health," he said, indicating a notice on the door.

"Brian, I don't believe it. You said this was your favorite health-food restaurant. How could a health-food restaurant be closed by the Board of Health?"

"Rat feces," he said, reading off the notice. "I'm not that hungry. Let's take a walk."

"You're going to let a few rat feces bother you?" Nelly asked, taking his arm.

"It's not that. I'm depressed. Depression always ruins my appetite."

"Okay, I'll bite. Why are you depressed?"

He stopped and looked at her. "I slept with my wife last night."

"Oh, Brian, you don't have to tell me every time you sleep with your wife," she smiled.

"That's the first time I've slept with her in over six months . . . and it's going to be the last."

"Brian, I really don't want to hear about it," Nelly warned.

"It was awful," he said, ignoring her. "It's funny, I've been dreading sleeping with her. I always have excuses all made up. Then I noticed she never asked. That's when I decided to do it, just out of spite. Turns out she didn't want to have sex with me any more than I did with her."

"I've got something very exciting to tell you," Nelly said, changing the subject.

"You can tell me in bed. Depression always increases my sex drive," he said, pulling her arm.

"I found her. I found my baby. The little girl I'm going to adopt."

"That's terrific, Nel. Congratulations," he said, giving her a big hug.

"All I have to do is have the home study done and then we can file for adoption. Are you sure you know how to do that?"

"Don't worry. I can look it up. I have a big book in my office that explains how to do things legally. I'm sure I can figure it out. And if I have any problems, I'll just ask one of my smart lawyer friends."

"I'm glad I have a smart lawyer friend like you," she said, kissing him. "Oh, wait till you see her. Her name's Anjelica. She's smart enough to be a lawyer herself. Brian, do you know anything about schools?"

"Law schools?"

"No, private schools. I have to start thinking where to send her."

"Well, you've got time. School doesn't start till September. Tell you what: let's go home, get under the covers, and we'll discuss it at greater length," he said, hailing a passing taxi.

Nelly decided to take the day off and pay a visit to some of the better private schools in the city. She was just on her way out the door when the phone rang.

"Come and get her." It was Abby.

"Who?"

"Your baby. Eight pounds, nine ounces. She's all yours."

"Oh Abby, you had your baby! How wonderful. Isn't she early?"

"Does eight pounds, nine ounces sound premature to you? Stupid doctor," Abby grumbled. "Ruined my weekend."

"How do you feel?"

"Like I gave birth to a bulldozer. Jeff, however, feels on top of the world. He's going through his usual misty-eyed, catch-in-the-throat, postnatal high. Ugh. Never again. Come and see me. I'm so depressed."

"What are the visiting hours?"

"Oh, please. They don't have any visiting hours here. They let visitors come and go any old time they want. It's like Grand Central Station."

Abby was propped up in bed reading *Adrienne Arpel's 3-Week Crash Makeover/Shapeover Beauty Program.*

"I never saw you in glasses before," Nelly said, laying a bunch of fresh cut flowers on Abby's lap.

"Oh, just another little side effect of motherhood. My eyes are going."

"Where's the baby?"

"I made them take her away. They have this new theory that the mother should be with the baby every waking minute. This will probably be my only chance to have a few minutes alone for the next ten years."

"Was Jeff disappointed about it being a girl?"

"Disappointed, hah. He could care less if it's a girl, boy, or bunny rabbit. That was a ruse on his part to get me to have a baby. To him it's just another bundle of joy. I really wish they'd figure out a way for men to give birth. You should have heard him in the delivery room, panting like a fool. If he could've gotten down on the table next to me he would have. There just wasn't enough room."

"What's her name?"

"Her name? I don't know. I'm sure Jeff will come up with something cute, something that starts with a J, of course. Like Julie or Jack Rabbit or Jonquil. I told him about our discussion. About you adopting the baby. Needless to say, he didn't go for it."

"That's okay. I've found a baby to adopt. Well, she's not exactly a baby. It's a little girl, eight years old."

"Eight years old *is* pretty big for a baby."

"I gave up on the baby idea. It's so difficult to get one. And besides, I like the idea that she's already got her own personality, she's already a little person."

"Eight years old. That's the same age as Jill. Oh yes, they have their own personalities."

"She and Jill can play together."

"Jill's not into playing this year. She's focusing on television exclusively."

"Her name's Anjelica. Isn't that beautiful? She likes painting and she's very smart in school." Nelly was really beginning to feel like a mother. She was already exchanging kiddy news with another mother.

"Have you met her yet?"

"Not yet. I just saw her picture and read a little biography they had on her."

"What happens if you don't like her or she doesn't like you? What happens if you don't get along?"

"I can't imagine that. Of course we'll get along."

"Well, don't be so sure. One good thing, you don't have to go through the diaper stage. All you have to go through is the thumb-sucking, tantrum-throwing, question-asking, back-talking stage. If I had known you were interested in an older child, I think I could've talked Jeff into giving you Jill. *He* can't even stand her at this point."

The nurse came in carrying a small white bundle.

"Oh, great. Here comes the mouth eternal," Abby sighed.

The nurse smiled and placed the baby in the crook of Abby's arm. Abby opened her nightgown and the little pink face attached itself immediately to her nipple.

"That's amazing," Nelly breathed. "How she knows to do that."

"There's a sucker born every minute, as they say."

"That's just beautiful," Nelly sighed.

Her own breast throbbed as she watched the baby nursing. She wanted to ask Abby if she could try it for a second. But she had no milk. She wondered if the sucking created the milk or did the milk cause the sucking? What did it feel like? Did it feel the same as when a man put his mouth to your breast?

"Ouch," Abby said, frowning. "She feels like she's got teeth already. Easy, kid," she said. Nelly shook her head in wonderment. Abby's body was actually producing food for this little being. It was an amazing, miraculous fast-food phenomenon. That was one thing—you couldn't breast-feed an eight-year-old. It was something Nelly would never know. Her eyes filled up with tears. Abby looked at her sternly.

"Now don't you start in with that stuff," she said.

"It really is a beautiful picture," Nelly sniffed, dabbing at her eyes.

"You don't understand. It may look beautiful to you. But do you realize that I am connected, literally tied, to this little creature by a part of my body? Jeff would turn me in to the La Leche League if I tried to put her on a bottle. It's just another little chore that he can't help out with. Oh Lord," she said, lifting her eyes heavenward, "when will I be free? And Clark is even worse than Jeff."

"Clark was here?"

"Oh, sure. He and Jeff practically bumped into each other. Clark sat here for an hour watching me nurse the baby. He wanted to hook up to the other breast. I think that's why men like to see women with babies. They get to relive their infancy vicariously."

"Abby," Nelly said, "you talk tough, but I know you're a good mother."

"Of course I'm a good mother. That's my job, isn't it? It would be pretty sad if I screwed up the only real full-time profession I've ever had. I'll feed her and raise her and do the best I can, but I don't have to like it, do I?"

Nelly had never seen Abby in such a low state. She was glad she had her Anjelica. Otherwise she would have been greatly tempted to grab Abby's little baby, run out of the hospital, and never come back. Thank God for Anjelica, she thought.

21 The Home Study

Mrs. Jensen, head of child services at Hearts and Flowers, called Nelly to tell her that Wednesday at three o'clock the first of the home-study appointments would take place. A Ms. Glass would be her social worker and would conduct the study. It would be her recommendation that would determine Nelly's suitability as a parent for Anjelica. Nelly took Wednesday off to prepare.

The maid had been there the day before and the apartment was spotless. But not spotless enough. She went over everything a second time. A second application of Lemon Pledge. A second Windexing. A second Lysoling of the bathroom and kitchen, in areas where germs can cause odor. She took all her R-rated books and put them on the top shelf of the bookcase.

At one o'clock she took her second shower of the day. She ran through her closet in her mind. She had nothing really maternal in her wardrobe. The little printed Albert Nippon shirtwaist would be perfect. But it was the same dress she had worn to her expected abortion, so that was out. Maybe a simple skirt and blouse? All her blouses were silk. Did mothers wear silk blouses? Or what about a sort of ready-to-play-in-the-park outfit? Jeans, a T-shirt, and jogging shoes, possibly with an apron. She remembered she didn't own an apron.

Just as she stepped out of the shower, the downstairs buzzer sounded. Now who in the hell could that be, she wondered.

"Yeah?" she yelled into the intercom.

"A Ms. Glass to see you," the doorman said.

Ms. Glass! The social worker. It was only one-fifteen. Wasn't the appointment for three? She couldn't keep the woman waiting. That would look bad.

"Send her up, John," Nelly said, and then ran for the bedroom.

She was sopping wet. Her hair was dripping into her eyes. She grabbed a Diane von Furstenberg wrap-around dress and wrapped it around her damp body. It stuck to her like second skin. Her hair dribbled down, the water rain-spotting the shoulders of the dress.

Shit, shit, shit, she hissed. She grabbed a pair of pantyhose and put them on with such violence that her foot went right through the toe. She threw them into the wastebasket and took out a second pair. The doorbell rang just as she had one leg in and one leg out. She lunged for the door, trying to pull the pantyhose on at the same time. She lost her balance and fell, hitting her head on the edge of her platform bed. There was a white flash of pain and for a moment she couldn't see. She got up, shook her head clear, pulled on the pantyhose the rest of the way, and ran for the door.

As she was unlocking the door, she took a quick glance in the hallway mirror. There was a thin stream of blood running from the end of her eyebrow down the side of her face to her chin.

Oh fuck, she whispered. She ran to the kitchen for a paper towel to blot up the blood, then ran back to the door and opened it.

There, standing in the doorway, holding a huge man's briefcase, was the woman from the health-food store who had sold her hundreds of dollars' worth of vitamins. Her thick braid was wrapped back and forth across the crown of her head. In place of the burlap jumper, she was wearing what appeared to be a Rumanian foot soldier's jacket over a Czechoslovakian folk dress.

"Ms. Diamond, I'm Gretel Glass from Hearts and Flowers."

"Oh yes, come in," Nelly said. "I'm sorry, I thought you weren't coming until three."

"Well, I got out of my other appointment earlier than I thought. Haven't we met before?"

"Well, as a matter of fact, we did meet. In a vitamin shop on Madison Avenue a few months ago."

"Oh, I remember now. I was working there while I was waiting for my certification. I put you on a high vitamin B potency regimen. You were pregnant at the time."

"Yes, well, no, actually. I thought I was pregnant. But it turned out I wasn't. I'm still taking my vitamins," Nelly assured her.

"If that's true, then why are you bleeding?" Gretel Glass asked, eyeing her suspiciously.

"Oh, that. I bumped my head on the bed." She was sorry the minute she said it.

"Do you have any vitamin E in the house?"

"Vitamin E?" Nelly racked her brains. She had a whole shelf full of vitamins. She had stopped taking them months before. They gave her indigestion.

"Get me a vitamin E and a razor blade," Gretel Glass commanded.

Nelly did as she was told. She rummaged through the vitamins, found the vitamin Es, found a razor blade, and delivered them both to Ms. Glass.

Glass took the capsule and cut it open with the razor blade. Then she squeezed the oil onto Nelly's still-bleeding cut. The oil ran down her eyebrow and into her eye, fogging her vision. She rubbed her eye to clear it, which made it fog up even more.

"Vitamin E prevents scar tissue from forming. Of course if you're taking your Bs and everything else, your body will supply the tissue with its own antiscarring nutrients. This is just an extra safeguard."

"Yes, well thank you," Nelly said, still trying to wipe the oil and blood out of her eye with the wadded-up paper towel.

"Shall we sit down?" Gretel Glass said, sitting down on the Eames chair. "I'll sit here and you sit over there," she said, indicating the footstool.

"Can I get you something? Some coffee?"

"Coffee? Coffee?" Gretel Glass made a horrible face. It was as if Nelly had just offered her a glass of horse pee.

Nelly tried to remedy her error. "Perhaps some tea? I have some nice tea."

"Tea!" Glass exploded. "Do you know that the caffeine content of tea is almost equivalent to that in coffee? And then there's the tannic acid. God in heaven, the tannic acid! Do you have any spring water?"

"I have tap water but it goes through a water purifier."

"Never mind. What about lemons? Do you have any lemons, at least?"

"Oh sure," Nelly said, much relieved. "Would you like lemonade?"

"No, I'll just have a lemon, sliced in two please."

Nelly brought her the lemon sliced in half on a small plate. Then she sat on the edge of the footstool and watched in amazement as Glass ate the entire lemon, one half at a time, without even the slightest pucker.

"Now, do you know what the purpose of the home study is?" she asked as she opened up the bulging briefcase and took out a yellow pad and pencil.

"I think so, yes," Nelly said.

"The purpose of the home study," recited Glass, "is to study your attitudes, your reasons for wanting to adopt, your motivations, your qualifications, your potential as a good parent. Now, the most important thing is that we be relaxed and honest with each other. I am not here to judge you, only to appraise your suitability as a parent to Anjelica. Anjelica is a very special child."

"Yes, I know," Nelly smiled.

"How could you know?" Glass snapped. "You haven't been working with her for months like I have. You haven't had to pull her out of one foster home after another."

"Why did she have to change foster homes so much?" Nelly asked.

"We're here to find out about you, not her. If you must know, the foster parents did not measure up," she said, giving Nelly a meaningful look. "Now, the questions I will ask you are not in any way meant to put you on the defensive. The areas that I probe are areas that are important in helping me make my recommendation. If, for any reason, you feel a question or an area is one which you would rather not get into, feel free to say so. So," she said, sitting back, crossing one laced combat boot over the other and fixing Nelly with her steel-framed gaze, "do you often black out?"

"Black out? What do you mean?"

"You said you hit your head on the bed. I have to assume that it was because you blacked out."

"Oh no, I didn't black out. I've never blacked out. Never even fainted. It was just that I hadn't expected you till three, and when you came early, I was rushing around to get ready and I was in such a hurry that I tripped over my pantyhose and hit my head on the bed." Nelly laughed.

"I see," said Ms. Glass, writing something down on her pad.

"I'm not usually so clumsy," Nelly rushed on. "I mean I have been known to be clumsy at times, but not that clumsy. And I never fall down, I mean, unless I'm skiing or something and then I fall down a lot." Nelly was trying her best to be charming. Admitting to human frailties like a little clumsiness had, in her experience, helped endear her to people who, for some reason, had not taken an instant liking to her.

"Do you enjoy skiing?" Gretel Glass asked, looking genuinely interested.

"Oh, I love it! I just took it up a few years ago and I was terrible at first, but then I took lessons and got over my fear of speed and also my fear of falling and now I really enjoy it."

"Do you go often?"

"Oh, whenever I can." She stopped, sensing a trap here. "Well, actually not that often, and of course I would never go without Anjelica. I know she'd love it. We'll take lessons together. It's so much better to take skiing up as a child." Nelly was nervous. She was talking a mile a minute, as though some unseen director had given her the hurry-and-wrap-it-up signal. "I mean, it's hard enough just skiing but there's always this fear of breaking your leg. I don't know why, but it's the one thing I've always dreaded, breaking a bone. I guess that's because I never have broken anything, so I still have this fear. I'm sure it would've been a lot better if I had broken my arm or something like all kids do, but I never did. I have very strong bones, which is odd, because my teeth aren't all that good. It has something to do with calcium, but you would know more about that than I do," Nelly said, catching her breath. Dear God, she prayed, please make me stop talking. Ms. Glass just stared at Nelly, waiting for her to go on. Nelly bit down on the inside of her cheek to prevent herself from saying another word.

Suddenly she remembered who she was. She was a professional interviewer. She wasn't going to let this monster dressed in mishmash peasant garb get the best of her. She knew the rules of the game. She would ask the questions. She would be on the offensive for once.

"Tell me," Nelly said, clasping a knee with both hands and leaning back on the footstool nonchalantly, "how long have you been doing home studies?"

Glass was obviously familiar with the same rules of play that Nelly was. She didn't even answer Nelly's question. Instead, she said the worst possible thing you can say to a nervous person:

"Ms. Diamond, why don't you try and relax?" It put Nelly instantly on edge.

"Or why don't you pour yourself a good, stiff drink?" Gretel Glass said sweetly.

"Oh, I don't drink," Nelly said, knowing what was coming next.

"You certainly have a rather lavish liquor supply for someone who doesn't drink," the social worker said, motioning to the three-tier liquor cabinet in the corner.

"That's for my company. You know, friends who might drop in. Although most of my friends don't drink all that much. And they never just drop in unannounced." Nelly was trying to cover every base.

Ms. Glass jotted down something in her pad.

"I wonder if I might use your ladies' room?" she asked.

"Oh, of course," Nelly said, standing up as Glass got up. Nelly remained standing at attention. She was eyeing the yellow pad Glass had left on the sofa. The social worker picked up the yellow pad, opened her briefcase, took out a large red enema bag, and left the room.

She was in the bathroom for half an hour. Nelly wondered what she was doing. One thing she knew for sure, she had plenty of time to search the medicine cabinet for any telltale addictions. Finally Nelly heard the toilet flush, and Ms. Glass came back into the room. She carefully rolled up the enema bag and placed it back inside the briefcase.

Nelly decided to beat her to the punch. "About the Valium," she said, "I had the occasion to take it when I was first promoted to the spot I have now. I was going through a lot of tension. As you may have noticed on the label, the prescription's dated at least four years ago and there are still half a dozen pills left. I really haven't taken a tranquilizer for three, maybe four years."

Glass looked at her without saying anything.

"I mean, I just don't believe in taking chemicals into your system, particularly tranquilizers or any of the other restricted drugs. Or any drugs, for that matter."

"I notice you keep your vitamins in your medicine chest," Glass said.

"Yes," Nelly said, happy that they were now talking openly.

"I assume you know that this completely depletes their potency. With the exception of vitamin E, which should be kept at room temperature, everything else must go in the refrigerator."

"Oh, no, I didn't know. I'll put them there now," she said, starting to get up.

"It's too late. They've already been ruined."

"Oh," Nelly said, sitting back down again.

"It's a waste of good vitamins and good money, but then I guess you aren't too concerned with money, what with the salary you earn. How much is it that you earn?" Glass asked with a social worker's sheer hatred of the upper-income percentile literally gleaming in her eyes.

"Oh, oh, say, well, you mean before or after taxes?" Nelly asked, torn between telling her how much money she made so as to impress upon the social worker her ability to care for a child financially and her instinct to underplay the amount, because she sensed Glass would never forgive her for earning six times what she did.

"Before taxes? Oh about, mmm, let's say about seventy-five."

"That's seventy-five thousand a year?" Glass said, spitting out the figures.

"That's before taxes," Nelly explained quickly. "And the taxes they take out are, believe you me, monumental. It's more than fifty percent. See, the federal government takes out the maximum, which is fifty, but then there's the city and the state. So it comes out to be more like sixty-five percent." She started to say that when she got her actual paycheck, it was probably not much more than Glass's, but she bit down on her lower lip instead.

"You obviously have enough to live on," Glass said, surveying the apartment.

"Oh yes, more than enough. I'm just not rich, that's all," Nelly said, wanting to clarify her position come the revolution.

"There's no reason to hedge. I want you to be completely candid with me."

"Yes, I'm sorry, I will."

"All right then, let me ask you this: Do you find me attractive?"

Nelly stared at the round-faced, thin-lipped, squinty-eyed, squat-bodied Ms. Glass. What kind of question was this now? Was Gretel Glass coming on to her? Was it a test of her honesty? Or was she, underneath that cold, military exterior, just another insecure woman, desperately in need of some reassurance? And what did all this have to do with Anjelica?

"How do you mean?" Nelly asked, stalling for time.

"I mean, do you think of me as a physically appealing person?"

163

"Well, I think you're very interesting looking. You have beautiful hair and you dress in a very original, imaginative way."

"Thank you," the social worker said, giving her a measly little smile. Nelly had obviously lucked upon the right response. She took a deep breath and began to relax. That was a mistake.

"Of course, what you think of me has absolutely nothing to do with Anjelica or whether or not you would be the proper parent for her," Gretel Glass said menacingly. "Just as my personal feelings about you have no place in my report. For example, I think you wear too much makeup. (Nelly had none on, having just come from the shower.) Your dress has spots all over it (the vitamin E, mixed with blood and water), your fingernails are too long. You could easily scratch a small child. And you have the beginnings of a rather unattractive scar above your right eyebrow."

Nelly touched the cut. The vitamin E obviously wasn't working.

"But what I think about you or the way you dress or your political views has nothing whatsoever to do with whether or not you'd make a good parent for Anjelica. My job is to be objective. If I went around operating on my personal likes and dislikes, what kind of social worker would I be? Besides, you can always cut your nails, can't you?"

"Oh sure," Nelly said, looking dazedly at her hands, "no problem."

"Well, I think we've covered enough ground for one day," Glass said, glancing at her pocket watch. "Why don't we set up the next appointment now? When would be convenient for you?"

"Oh, anytime at all. I can make myself available for whenever you say."

"Today is Wednesday; shall we say a week from today? In the evening?"

"Next Wednesday evening. That would be fine."

"How's about seven o'clock."

"Just fine."

"Wednesday evening at seven; see you then. Thanks for the lemon."

She was no sooner out the door than Nelly was on the phone to Hearts and Flowers Home for Children. She asked for Mrs. Jensen, the woman in charge of child placement.

"Mrs. Jensen, this is Nelly Diamond."

"Oh yes, you're going through the home study for little Anjelica."

"That's right. Mrs. Jensen, I just had my first appointment with your Ms. Glass and I was wondering if it was possible for me to change social workers?"

"Change? Whatever for?"

"Well, I don't think we hit it off. I really don't think Ms. Glass likes me. In fact, I think she might even hate me. I don't want to accuse her of being prejudicial or anything; it's just one of those personality things. And I really think it would be better if I had another social worker assigned to my case."

"Oh, Ms. Diamond," Mrs. Jensen said, laughing good-humoredly, "this happens all the time, I assure you."

"People change social workers?" Nelly asked hopefully.

"No, no. Prospective parents are always very concerned about their social workers liking them. Many times they jump to the same conclusion you did: that the social worker has taken a dislike to them for some reason. Let me tell you, that just isn't the case. Our workers are trained to be objective. Gretel Glass, new as she is, is still a professional. What you mistook for dislike or even hostility is purely imagined. Believe me, everyone goes through this. Try to relax, Ms. Diamond."

"Well, let's just say she really, truly didn't like me and that we really didn't get along. Those things happen, too. I mean, let's say I punched her in the nose or something. Aren't those circumstances that would indicate a change of social worker?"

"That happens very rarely. It really is to your benefit to work things out with Ms. Glass. Let me put it this way: if you change social workers for any reason, it does go on your record. And that wouldn't look very good, would it?"

Nelly hadn't realized that they had already started a record on her.

"Stick with Gretel," Mrs. Jensen said. "Her only purpose is to find a good home and the best possible parents for the child. She certainly isn't out to get you. Will you try and remember that?"

"All right. I'll try."

"And, between you and me, I think it would be best to forget we even had this little talk, don't you?"

"Yes. Yes, thank you very much, Mrs. Jensen."

Mrs. Jensen was right. She was overreacting. Glass was her social worker, not her friend. She was just doing her job. And her job had nothing to do with them becoming great pals. Gretel Glass wasn't about to move in with her. Anjelica was.

Nelly was thankful Mrs. Jensen had said she wouldn't mention their phone conversation. She didn't want Glass finding out she had requested another social worker. Next appointment, Nelly was going to put her best foot forward. Let Glass put her through the wringer, the ropes, whatever she had up her sleeve. She welcomed it now. Anything was worth it to get Anjelica. She could hardly wait for Wednesday and the next interview.

As it turned out, she didn't have to wait until Wednesday. Six days later, on Tuesday night around 6:30, the doorbell rang. It was not an opportune time for visitors. It was particularly not an opportune time for a visit from Gretel Glass.

She and Tyler were taking a bath together. It was another of Tyler's special recipes: four capfuls of Sardo, four tablespoons of turtle oil, and four teaspoons of Dr. Castell's peppermint soap. Pour into one tub of hot water. And then soak two bodies for one hour.

She grabbed a bath towel and padded to the intercom.

"What is it, John?"

"It's Ms. Glass," the doorman answered. "She's on her way up."

"Oh Jesus, no! Oh, no! Oh, Christ!" For a moment Nelly just stood there, dripping water all over her off-white carpet. Then, as if a button had been pushed, she launched into a series of frenetic movements. She ran for the bathroom, ran back toward the door, and then ran for the bathroom again.

"Tyler, it's that social worker. She's a day early. What am I going to do?"

The doorbell sounded.

"Oh shit," she said. Tyler sat in the tub with his mouth open. She slammed the door shut on him and ran for the bedroom, looking for her terry-cloth robe. She remembered it was in the bathroom with Tyler. She found a silk caftan, threw it on, and ran for the door.

"Just a minute, I'm coming," she sang. She made a detour to the bathroom. "Lock the door. And don't splash around," she whispered. She closed the bathroom door and hurried to answer the bell. By now the caftan was sticking to her bath- and perspiration-wet body. She tried to pull it away as she opened the door.

"Ms. Glass. I thought you were coming tomorrow night."

"I said Wednesday night," Ms. Glass said tersely.

"But this is Tuesday."

"Is it?" she asked, "I could've sworn this was Wednesday," she said, pushing her way in. "I'm not disturbing you, am I?"

"Well, I was just taking a bath."

"Showers are better for you. When you take a bath, you're just sitting in your own germs and dead skin cells," she said, taking her usual seat on the Eames chair.

There was something different about the social worker tonight. Her dress was basically the same. Her hair was the same. But there was something different about her face. It was the mouth. Her mouth was turned up at the corners, almost at right angles. That was it. She was smiling. What was she smiling about, Nelly wondered. Was it a good sign? It must be.

"Can I get you a lemon?" Nelly asked pleasantly.

"Oh no, nothing, thank you," Ms. Glass said, still smiling strangely. She opened up her briefcase and removed her enema bag. "I'd just like to use your ladies' room, if you don't mind.

Nelly stared at the enema bag.

"Colonic irrigation," Ms. Glass explained. "I do it three times a day. The colon, you know, gets clogged up with mucus and uric acid from dairy products. When it's clogged, it becomes distorted, and when it's distorted, it cannot absorb nutrients properly. Worse, it can cause toxicosis." As she spoke, she made her way toward the bathroom.

"Oh, no, you can't," Nelly blurted out, catching her by the arm.

"Why not?" she said, slapping Nelly's hand off her arm.

"Well, it's broken. The toilet's broken. The super's supposed to come up and fix it but he hasn't been here yet. It's all stopped up. Been broken for days."

Gretel Glass grimaced. The look on her face told Nelly that she was picturing a toilet that had been stopped up for days and wanted no part of it. Anyone who thought taking a bath was unsanitary was not about to do her colonic irrigation over a broken toilet. She rolled up her enema bag and put it back in the briefcase. She took out her pad, then leaned back and stared at Nelly. She was still smiling. Nelly felt uneasy. The smile no longer looked like a good sign to her.

"So," she said after a few minutes, "I understand you tried to have me fired from the case."

"No! Who told you that?"

"Mrs. Jensen, of course."

Damn the woman, Nelly thought. "It wasn't that I was trying to get you fired. I just felt there was a bit of a personality conflict. I thought you didn't like me," Nelly said, playing for sympathy.

"Now why in the world wouldn't I like you?"

"I don't know. I just had that feeling."

"You were right. I don't like you. I am a very direct, forthright person, and many people don't like this quality in me. But I don't care. If there's anything I detest in others, it's dishonesty and deceit," she said, looking at Nelly accusingly. "Now, shall we continue with the study?"

"Please," Nelly gasped.

"As you know, single-parent adoptions are not uncommon these days. But in approving a single person, it is important for us to determine the relationships that exist with members of the opposite sex. Do you see anyone?"

"See anyone?"

"Do you date?"

"No, not really," Nelly lied.

"A beautiful woman like you and you never go out?"

"Oh, I go out occasionally."

"Of course. It wouldn't be normal if you didn't. Let's be frank with each other, Ms. Diamond. We're both adults. Besides, it's important that Anjelica's mother be a sexually well adjusted person. So let me ask again. Do you see anyone special?"

"Special?"

"Do you have one steady man in your life? Do you see someone on a regular basis?" Glass said, spelling it out as though to a dimwit.

"Well, I see a few people, but no one seriously," Nelly said, hitting upon what she thought was the best possible response.

"You have multisexual relationships, then," Glass said, writing that down on her pad.

"Wait a minute, what does multisexual mean?"

"It means you screw around a lot with a lot of different men."

"I don't," Nelly protested.

"Now, come on, Ms. Diamond. Are you trying to tell me you don't sleep with more than one person?"

"Not at a time," Nelly admitted.

"That's better," said the social worker. She continued making notes, speaking aloud as she wrote. "Sees different men on different nights. Of course, you know that this sets an extremely bad example for a young girl like Anjelica. You may be having one hell of a good time, but your child can be damaged for life. Not that I'm judging you on your promiscuity—I just wanted you to be aware of that."

"But I'm not promiscuous," Nelly said defensively.

"Have you ever been married?"

"Yes, for seven years."

"And what happened to your husband?"

"What do you mean, what happened?" Nelly was being very careful now.

"Did he leave you for someone else, or did you leave him in order to, as you put it, 'see a few people'?"

"No. We just ended the marriage by mutual agreement."

"It was a friendly divorce?"

"I guess you could call it that, yes."

"And how often do you see your ex-husband?"

"Well, actually not at all. He's remarried and lives in California."

"So the divorce couldn't have been all that friendly," Glass said accusingly.

"The divorce was perfectly amicable. It was the marriage that wasn't on good terms," Nelly snapped.

"Don't get upset, Ms. Diamond. I can see it's still a sore subject. So since your husband left you, there hasn't been one steady man in your life—is that correct?"

"I have some very good, very close, very steady male friends."

"Do you plan on getting married again in the near future?"

"No, not really."

"Then you plan on living alone for the rest of your life?"

"No, not alone. I hope to have Anjelica with me."

"But you don't ever see yourself living with a man again?"

"I really couldn't say. Right now my only concern is Anjelica."

"Well, I guess that about does it for today," Ms. Glass said, stuffing her notes into her briefcase. "But I must tell you, it's not looking too good."

"What isn't?" Nelly asked with alarm.

"Your social life leaves a lot to be desired as far as I'm concerned. There's no one steady male in your life; you yourself said so."

"But you said single adoptions are very common now. What difference does a steady man make?"

168

"Just because you're a single parent doesn't mean you don't have the obligation of giving your child the best possible environment in which to grow. The two-parent family, all experts agree, is still the ideal. It is necessary for the single person to approximate that as much as possible. I'm not telling you you have to get married. Obviously you tried marriage and failed miserably. But what I am saying is that it is important for you to be able to provide Anjelica with a dependable, loving male figure. Not a herd of studs. I think one more visit will finish us up. Get your toilet fixed, Ms. Diamond; that's a very unhealthy situation."

Nelly stood staring at the door in a state of semishock.

"How'd it go?" Tyler asked, wrapping a towel around himself.

"Not too well. I can't figure out what she's looking for. First she tells me it's okay if I'm single and that it's normal if I date. Then she tells me I date too much, then she says I have to have a man in my life. One steady male figure for Anjelica to relate to. I think I'm losing my mind," Nelly said, bursting into tears.

Tyler picked her up in his arms and carried her over to the couch.

"Well, anyway," Nelly said, snuffling, "one good thing came out of tonight."

"What's that, honeyplum?"

"I know exactly where I stand with her. She hates me. That's a comfort in itself. Oh, Tyler," she said, bursting into fresh tears, "I'm afraid I'm going to flunk the home study. And then I won't get Anjelica."

"How could you flunk? Anybody can see that you'd make a terrific mama."

"Anybody but Gretel Glass. You haven't met her."

"Maybe Ah should."

"What do you mean?"

"You said she thinks it's important to have a steady beau in your life. Why don't Ah be it? We can tell her we've decided to live together."

"But we haven't."

"Doesn't matter. All's you have to do is get the bitch's approval, right?"

"That's right. Oh, it just might work. Things can't get any worse. And if anybody could charm the pants off Ms. Glass's ass, it would be you."

"That happens to be mah specialty of the day," he said, reaching up under her caftan.

The next appointment for the home study was made for the following week. Amazingly, Ms. Glass showed up on the right day at the right time. Nelly was all ready for her. She had prepared a little luncheon: vegetarian cutlets, soybean soup, distilled spring water, honey cake, and a bowl of lemons to munch on. And, of course, Tyler, who was dressed in his Marlboro Man best.

"Ms. Glass, this is Tyler Hanks. We're going to be living together."

169

"Oh, I thought you said you weren't planning on getting married in the near future. You know we have done this home study strictly on the basis of you being single."

"We aren't getting married," Nelly assured her, "we're just going to live together. You know, for the steady male figure for Anjelica?"

"Is that a real Hungarian cavalry jacket, Ms. Glass?" Tyler asked, fondling her epaulet.

"Why yes, it is," Glass said, pleased.

Nelly just sat back and watched Tyler's charm go to work on Gretel Glass, softening her up like meat tenderizer.

"Did anyone ever tell y'all you have a beautiful aura?"

"Why no, no one ever did."

Tyler squinted his eyes as though taking in a new and beautiful work of art.

"Ah really get pure, clear pastels from you. Do you mind if Ah study your irises?"

"Oh, you know about iridology?"

"Well," Tyler said modestly, "just a smatter." He lifted off her glasses and peered closely into her eyes, his nose almost touching hers. "You must be into colonic irrigation. You've got just about the cleanest bowels Ah've ever seen."

Nelly wondered how he could tell that looking through her eyes.

"Perfect kidneys, perfect liver, and one hell of a fine gall bladder," Tyler was saying. He stepped back, shaking his head as if dazzled. "Tell me, Ms. Glass, do you meditate?"

"Yes, I do," she said. She had not replaced her glasses. She appeared mesmerized.

"I wonder, I hope Ah'm not bein' too presumptuous, but do you think you could find your way clear to meditate with me? Ya see, mah meditation hasn't been goin' well lately. Ah get this buzzin' that goes in and out and takes me a way from mah mantra. And I get such a powerful feelin' of centeredness from you, Ah would just love it if we could share some trance space together."

They were in the bedroom for a long time. Nelly's vegetable cutlets sat on the kitchen counter getting soggy. After an hour she heard a strange thumping sound coming from behind the closed door. First one thump, then silence, then another thump, then a series of thump, thump, thumps. Then quiet, followed by more thumping. He's thumping her, Nelly thought to herself, not quite sure what that meant. She wasn't jealous, just curious as to what exactly they were doing.

Finally, they emerged. Tyler looked tranquil. But then he always looked tranquil. The difference was with Gretel Glass. Her cheeks glowed pink and her braid had come undone. She was smiling broadly.

"I must say, I am very impressed with your choice of friends. He levitates," she said, casting Tyler a look of pure adulation.

"Levitates?" Nelly asked.

"Levitation is a higher form of meditation," Glass explained. "It can only be learned from Maharishi Mahesh Yogi. And Tyler tells me he never even took a lesson. It's truly amazing."

It was amazing, Nelly thought. As far as she knew, this was the first time Tyler had ever even meditated. Let alone levitated.

They sat down to lunch. Tyler and Glass chatted all the way through. They talked about vitamin equivalencies, liver manifestations, and mucous membranes. The social worker seemed to be having the time of her life. Nelly was delighted. It had been a brilliant inspiration, bringing in Tyler. Now she was sure that Glass would pass her on the home study.

Nelly focused back on the luncheon. Glass was getting ready to leave. Tyler had a long, lean hand on her elbow. He was looking down at her earnestly and giving her the full force of his lovely lone-star smile.

"Well, I really have to go now," Glass said, staring up at Tyler. "Thanks so much for the delightful lunch," she said to him.

"When are we going to have our next appointment?" Nelly asked.

The social worker turned to Nelly as though remembering for the first time that she was there. "We've concluded the study. You can call Hearts and Flowers first of the week for the results."

"Oh good!" Nelly smiled. "Thank you so much." She showed Glass to the door, fighting off the impulse to kiss her good-bye.

Nelly and Anjelica Diamond. Nellica and Angelica. Nelly and Jelly. She laughed out loud at this. Nelly and Jelly at the zoo. Nelly and Jelly on the slopes. Nelly and Jelly at the Museum of Modern Art. They'd bring Tyler along, too. He could explain the paintings. He was so good with people. Nelly gave him a big hug.

"You were sensational, absolutely sensational. How can I ever thank you?"

"How 'bout a little humpin' to counteract the thumpin' and work off that disgustin' lunch?"

Nelly called Hearts and Flowers on Monday.

"How'd I do?" she asked Mrs. Jensen.

"Oh, Ms. Diamond. I'm sorry, but Ms. Glass recommended against you in the home study."

"What? Why? What did I do wrong?"

"Well, it's nothing you did wrong. It's the requirement. Didn't Ms. Glass explain? You see, there are adoptions by married people or adoptions by single people. So you can be either single or married, but you cannot be living with someone. And according to her report, you are living with a Mr. Hanks."

"No, yes, I mean she told me that it would help to have a man around the house."

"Around the house. Not *in* the house. Not living together without the benefit of holy matrimony. The child-welfare board clearly states that a living-together relationship is one that is not considered permanent; it is not conducive to raising a young child. Too many people these days live together as a trial thing."

"We'll get married, then," Nelly said, trying to keep the panic out of her voice.

"Oh, that just wouldn't do. One does not go around changing marital status for the sake of a home study. That's exactly the kind of unreliable behavior that Ms. Glass referred to in her report. And frankly, I agree with her. You are not a suitable candidate for adoption. We're looking for stability, not someone who would rush into marriage willy-nilly."

"But that's not fair! I know I would make a good mother for Anjelica," Nelly cried.

"As far as Anjelica is concerned, you'll be happy to know that Ms. Glass has found a wonderful home for her. We're placing her with a young couple in Yonkers."

"Wait a minute! That's my baby. My child. How could you give her away? You have no right!"

"You're confused, Ms. Diamond. Of course we have the right. The state gives us that right."

"I want an appeal. I want a new home study done. And I want it done by someone else."

"There's no need to have another study done. You've already had yours."

"You mean that's it?" Nelly's voice trembled. "I don't even get a second chance?"

"Let me put it this way—the home study goes on your permanent record."

"And there's nothing I can do about it?" Nelly sobbed.

"The report is strictly confidential. Nobody ever has to see it. If you're not adopting a child, then there's no need to start dragging up bad reports, is there?"

"But I want to adopt a child. I have to adopt a child."

"Have you ever considered getting a dog?" Mrs. Jensen asked.

Nelly slammed the phone down on the receiver. Then picked it up again and banged it against the side of the coffee table several times before collapsing in tears.

"Mrs. Fehlinger, they've taken Anjelica away from me. They placed her with another couple."

"Well, you can come down and pick another child."

"And I flunked the home study," Nelly added, tearfully.

"Oh," Mrs. Fehlinger said after a long pause, "that's more serious, I'm afraid. Oh, I am sorry. I wish I could help you. But I've got problems of my own. They took our boy away."

"Took him away? How could they do that?"

172

"His natural mother—she changed her mind about the adoption. She wanted him back. There was nothing we could do," Mrs. Fehlinger said in a choking voice.

She had spent six months on the infertility workup and three months trying to adopt. A total of nine months, the time it takes any normal woman to have a baby. And Nelly had nothing to show for all her efforts. Nothing except a big, gaping, ever-growing emptiness deep inside her. The loss she felt was even greater than what she had experienced after the infertility workup. Before, she had felt she was losing a part of herself. But it was a vague, anonymous part, an unborn, unrealized thing. What she lost now was an identifiable substance with a name, a nose, a history, and a life that would go on without her. She had geared herself, primed herself totally for motherhood. Anjelica and the idea of Anjelica had awakened her maternal instincts completely. Now there was no putting them aside. She had become a mother without a child.

Never in her life had Nelly felt so alone or so much like she wanted to die.

22 The Suicide Study

When she had learned that her tubes were as blocked up as the Midtown Tunnel at rush hour, she had been enraged. Furious at Dr. Hoffman, angry at what seemed to be separate and uncooperative parts of her own body, incensed at fate or whatever it was that had dealt her such a low blow. But being a woman of action, she had acted, using her fury as fuel to sidestep depression and move her to the next logical step: adoption.

But now that same depression was there waiting for her, like an unpaid bill. It had no shape, no form, no end or beginning. There were no sharp edges to it, no ceiling, no depths. Just a dark, airless mass that closed in upon her and rendered her immobile, impotent, and worst of all, numb. Being a maker of plans, a doer of things, a woman of passion, she found this nonfeeling, noncaring state horrible. Yet she wasn't even able to experience the horror of it.

That was when the idea of suicide came to her. It wasn't much, but it was an idea, a thought to attach her befuddled brain to. And since she had nothing else to go on, plan for, or get excited about, she gave it her full attention.

She wasn't sure if she was serious or not. It didn't really matter. She had learned in analysis that it was a mistake to ignore an emotion no matter how unpleasant it might be. Neglected feelings had a habit of sneaking up on you and taking you by surprise. She was not about to have suicide take her by surprise. She felt it demanded her immediate attention, though not necessarily her immediate action. So she addressed herself to the subject as methodically and energetically as she could.

Suicide. People committed suicide every day of the week, with the numbers probably stacking up higher on Sundays and holidays. What made them choose one method over another? If, in fact, there was such a thing as a suicide type, then it followed that there were types of suicides that would appeal to some suicidals more than others. Clearly, personal likes and dislikes did enter into the choice. Not whether to, but how to, that was the question.

Nelly knew, of course, that most suicides were considered some form of hostility, an ultimate statement of protest. She didn't feel that this applied to her at all. And she didn't want other people to think so, either. That brought up the question of suicide notes. How to explain. Whether to explain at all. How to communicate the reasons without causing distress, pain, or, worse, pity in her family and friends. Was a note absolutely necessary? Her mother had always been very big on notes. Thank-you notes. Condolence notes. Congratulations notes. Bread-and-butter notes. Did this occasion require a note, too? No, better to leave nothing that would arouse suspicion or evoke pity. She could just remove herself from the vicinity. Just disappear. Of course, there was the possibility that people, in noticing that she was missing, would spend time looking for her. She didn't want that. She didn't want a lot of press and publicity, especially if she wasn't around to enjoy it.

Maybe the whole idea appealed to her because she knew that people would be upset, would mourn her. With no offspring, there would be no one around to mourn her passing in years to come. At least now she could be guaranteed a certain amount of bereavement on the part of surviving family and close friends. She set aside the problem of postmortems and turned her attention back to the question of methods.

She had read somewhere that the most relaxing and painless form of suicide was to cut your wrists in a nice warm tub of water. It had the added advantage of allowing you to keep your wits about you until the very end. She didn't remember where she had read this, nor did she question the writer's ability to describe with authority the elements of a successful suicide.

Nelly mentally inventoried the sharp instruments in her household. There were the French carbon-steel kitchen knives. No, too sharp. The idea of using them on her wrists sent chills up and down her spine. She knew they could cut through the cartilage of a chicken like butter. And whereas cutting her wrists hadn't bothered her, cutting her cartilage certainly did. She had just discovered in herself a real aversion to being cut and bleeding. Wrist-slashing was out.

How about an overdose of something? But an overdose of what? The only prescription drugs she owned were a half-dozen old Valiums and some leftover antibiotics she had had to take for the pelvic inflammation.

It seemed to her that the only things that were proven truly effective for overdosing were sleeping pills, barbiturates, and heroin. And she was not about to make mainlining heroin her last conscious act on earth. (NEWS-CASTER ODS ON SMACK.)

What about a dramatic leap from the top of a tall skyscraper? She walked back into the living room and stared out her window. Her windows didn't open. Just as well; with her luck she would most certainly have landed on an innocent bystander (NEWSCASTER SMACKS PEDESTRIAN.), and then she would never have been able to handle the guilt. What guilt? There is no guilt after death, is there? She didn't want to dwell on that one.

Off the top of the Empire State Building? No. She knew they were closed at night, and during the day there were too many tourists. Ditto for the Statue of Liberty (NEWSCASTER BESMIRCHES STATUE.). Besides, Nelly did have a fear of heights; a minor phobia, but it involved going up them as well as coming down.

Asphyxiation? She went into the kitchen and looked at her oven. It was a microwave. She could probably singe herself to death in an instant. No, wait. A microwave oven was supposed to cook things from the inside out. Even singeing to death sounded better than that.

Was it possible for her to electrocute herself? She used to think that had to be the easiest thing in the world to do. Far too easy. She had an absolutely irrational fear of light bulbs, electric outlets, plugs, even electricians' tape—anything that smacked of wattage. She traced this fear back to when her mother had warned her as a child not to put her finger in the empty light-bulb socket, and so she did. The shock she received was a mild one, but it had frightened her terribly. And it had hurt.

When it came right down to it, the last thing she wanted to do was hurt herself. She laughed out loud at this. Then what the hell was she doing, conjuring up ways to do herself irreparable hurt? What was she, crazy? No, she decided, not crazy, just suicidal and depressed. Somehow just saying that made it better. Maybe not even suicidal; just very, very depressed. It was a very bad case of despondency, with a little despair thrown in. And she had a cure for it without even realizing it. No one who had a sense of humor like Nelly's could seriously consider suicide. They might humorously consider it, but they could never pull it off with a straight face.

She reminded herself of the fact that she was a basically happy person. A basically happy person who was depressed. True, there was nothing she hated more than depression. But she was willing to suffer through it. It was a hell of a lot better than suffering through suicide. Suicide? What an idea. What a ridiculous waste. It had taken her thirty-five, almost thirty-six years to accumulate the brains, looks, charm, talent, and success that she presently enjoyed. And she wanted to throw it all away? Shame on her. Shame. Shame. Shame. What she needed was a good smack on the noggin, she said to herself, giving her head a light tap with the flat of her hand. No, she'd ride this through just like she had everything else. She didn't care how long it took.

As it turned out, it didn't take long. Because just then the phone rang.

"Well, she beat me to the punch." It was Brian.

"Who? What are you talking about?"

"Miriam. She left me. Me and the kids."

"You mean she left the kids too?"

"I should have left her years ago," Brian was saying.

"She left the kids?" Nelly repeated.

"Mr. Nice Guy, and I'm the one that gets left," Brian said.

"You've got the kids?" Nelly asked once again.

"That's right, I've got the kids, and if she thinks she's getting her mitts on them she's got another thing coming," he said angrily.

"You mean you can get custody?"

"Get custody? I've got custody. She's the one that left."

"But she'll want them back, won't she?"

"Who says? She wants a new life. Wants to start over. I don't see how starting over with the same old kids is going to fit into her plans. You know who she's using for a lawyer? Hal Rosen. I went to law school with him. He barely passed his boards."

"But how are the kids taking it?"

"The kids? They're fine. She had a nice long talk with them. Explained how just because Mommy and Daddy stop loving each other doesn't mean they stop loving their kids. They must have done divorce on 'Sesame Street' or something because they're taking it like real troopers."

"I don't understand why she left," Nelly said, not being able to comprehend how a woman could up and leave three perfectly fine children.

"I told you. She doesn't love me anymore."

"You didn't tell her about us, did you?"

"Sure, when she was leaving. I was pissed. Turns out she knew all along. Are you ready for this? She didn't give a damn. Jesus, all those years I've been lying and sneaking around just to protect her, and she never even cared. I compromised myself ethically just to spare her feelings. God. Well, anyway, I've got the kids and that's all I care about. I don't need her. I'm perfectly equipped to raise them by myself. The thing I can't get over is how incredibly inconsiderate she was. She knew I had to fly to California for a big litigation, and she picks this time to leave. Now I'll have to get somebody else to handle the case which I've been working on for six months. And what the hell am I supposed to tell them at the office? That my wife left me? That's terrific."

"Why don't you go anyway?" Nelly said.

"Nelly, I can't leave my kids at a time like this. They need me."

"But it's not as if you haven't had to travel before."

"You don't understand. It's not as if their mother has deserted them before."

"But I could stay with them."

"They don't even know you."

"Well, wouldn't this be a good time for them to get to know me?"

"Are you saying what I think you're saying?"

"What do you think I'm saying?"

"It sounds to me like you're saying that you'll marry me."

"You're so incredibly perceptive. I'd love to marry you."

"Well, what led you to this sudden turnaround? You've always vetoed the idea whenever I brought it up before."

"I think it may have something to do with the fact that a major obstacle has been removed, so to speak."

"You mean Miriam."

"I didn't want to name names, but yes."

"Well, that sheds a whole different light on this. But it still isn't a good idea for you to come and stay with the kids. First of all, they don't warm up to strangers. Second, until the divorce is final, it's not even advisable for us to be seen together. It's particularly not advisable for you to move into my house."

"But you won't even be there. You'll be in California. It really is a perfect time for me to get to know the kids. They don't have to know about you and me now. Just tell them I'm a new baby-sitter. Oh, Brian, I do want to meet them and I think the sooner the better," she said meaningfully.

Brian didn't say anything.

"I think it would be great if they knew I was there for them during a very crucial time in their lives. I don't want them to think of me as the wicked stepmother who just steps into the picture after all the dust has settled. The sooner we start building a relationship, the better. It would work out, I know it would."

It took another twenty minutes for Nelly to convince him.

"I'll take off a week from work," Nelly said.

"That's not necessary. They're in school until three. And the housekeeper's there till six. It's just having someone with them overnight."

"Then it would work out perfectly," Nelly said with controlled delirium.

"Maybe you're right. They might as well start getting to know you sooner rather than later. God knows how long this whole divorce thing will take."

Nelly hung up the phone exhausted and exhilarated. She couldn't believe that only an hour before she had been contemplating ending it all. Now she was on top of the world. Things did turn out for the best. Her failures at childbirth and adoption had left her free for this. For them. Three ready-made, ready-to-love children. She didn't have to worry about long-incubating parasites, leprous parents, or antagonistic social workers. She could hardly believe her good fortune. Three perfect children in one fell swoop.

She took a deep breath. She was not going to start fantasizing. She was not going to allow herself to be led astray by unrealistic expectations. She was not going to go off the deep end and fall into the trap that had put her into this most recent depression.

She reminded herself that there would be problems. What she had here was something real. Real children. Real problems. A real future. Nelly, for one, was ready for a little reality in her life.

She knew it would take time for them to get over the abandonment of their mother. It would take time for them to learn to accept her. The whole operation was going to take a great deal of time and a lot of patience. Time she had, and patience was a virtue she was going to do her level best to develop.

She thumbed through a recent issue of *Cue*. There was a weekend guide to children's entertainment in the city. She circled things that looked interesting. She was sure she could find activities that they would all enjoy. But she would not come on too strong. She wasn't going to try and pass herself off as an instant mother replacement. She was going to take it very easy. One little step at a time.

The first thing she did was arrange for a week's vacation.

23   The Courtship

"This is Brian Junior, or B.J.; this is Caroline; and this is Butch. Kids, this is Nelly. She's going to be staying with you while Daddy's in California."

"You're going to baby-sit us?" asked B.J. He was a small, compact version of Brian, with the same curly hair and thick eyebrows.

"I'm going to try," Nelly smiled.

"But I thought you worked on TV. How come you have to baby-sit?" B.J. asked, fixing her with a stern, brown-eyed gaze.

Neither one of them had figured on them having seen her on television.

"She's doing it as a favor," Brian said quickly. "She's a friend of the family," he added, carefully wording the alibi in the kids' heads.

B.J. looked like he didn't buy that one, but he didn't say anything. Caroline was sucking her thumb as she studied Nelly.

"Honey, don't do that," Brian said, gently extracting Caroline's thumb from her mouth. "You'll spoil your pretty mouth."

"I can always get braces," Caroline said, reinserting her thumb at the end of the sentence. She had long, straight, honey brown hair with bangs that ended just above her thick-lashed blue eyes.

"Are you going to be a good boy?" Brian asked Butch, who was yet a smaller version of B.J. They looked like twins born several years apart.

"I don't think so," Butch assured him. Brian wasn't listening.

"I want you all to be good and mind Nelly and do everything she says."

"Will you bring me a present, Daddy?" Caroline asked, mouthing the words somehow around her thumb. She removed it in order to make a precise request. "Some roller skates with big red wheels like Cher has?"

"We'll see," Brian said, caressing her cheek.

"She's a Jewish princess," B.J. said to no one in particular. Caroline beamed proudly as if her brother had just paid her the ultimate compliment.

"Okay, kids, I've got to go now." Brian gave each a hug and a kiss and then shot Nelly a look before he turned toward the door.

"Aren't you going to kiss Nelly good-bye?" Caroline asked.

"Do I usually kiss baby-sitters?" Brian asked, trying to laugh it off.

"We don't usually have baby-sitters like her," B.J. observed. "You can kiss her if you want. I don't care."

"I don't think that's appropriate," Brian said, flushing.

"Suit yourself," said the eight-year-old, taking out a pocket calculator and pushing the buttons quickly, as if he were keeping score on each situation that arose.

"B.J., you help Nelly out now. You're in charge while I'm gone."

"I'm too young to be in charge," B.J. said, "I don't even have a social security card."

Nelly walked Brian out to his car.

"They're great kids," she said.

"Well, sometimes they're a little too smart for their own good. Especially B.J. Don't let them take advantage of you."

"Oh, I won't. Don't worry," Nelly said, anxious for Brian to leave so she could be totally taken advantage of.

Nelly walked back up the long driveway toward the house. It was a huge six-bedroom Tudor affair situated on two acres of prime real estate in an older section of New Rochelle. She was nervous and excited. Three kids all to herself. She wondered what they'd like to do after dinner. Maybe they'd just spend a quiet evening at home. She would read to them. Nelly in the middle with the book. B.J. on one side and Butch on the other. Nelly warmly wedged in by the two sturdy little boy bodies, with soft cuddly Caroline on her lap. Or perhaps Butch should go on her lap since he was the baby? She didn't want to show any favoritism. Could she fit all three on her lap? She would read them their favorite story or stories—they undoubtedly had different literary tastes—and then tuck them into bed.

She let herself into the house. The children had disappeared.

"B.J., Caroline, Butch?" she called out. There was no answer.

"Kids?" she called, climbing up the stairs to where the bedrooms were. "Olly-olly-oxen-free," she yelled. The light at the top of the stairs was turned off. As she turned on the landing, she had to feel her way for the next step.

"Kids? Watcha doing?" One of the bedroom doors was slightly ajar. She tried to push it open. Something was in the way. She squeezed through the narrow opening, almost stepping on the body of four-year-old Butch. He lay on his back, his arms outstretched, his mouth wide open. There was a large, black-handled knife protruding from his small chest. The scream was halfway out of her throat when her eyes registered the fact that the knife was rubber. She quickly closed her mouth over the scream, stepped across the body and into the room. Caroline was lying half-on and half-off one of the twin beds. A three-foot rubber python was wrapped tightly around her neck like a Katharine Hepburn scarf. Her right hand clutched the tail. The snake's head was hidden from sight by her long hair. Nelly made "tching" noises. She went into the adjoining bathroom. B.J. was crumpled in the corner next to the bathtub. His head was lying in a pool of blood. Also rubber or plastic.

She loved these kids. They had a lot of imagination. They were a laugh a minute.

"Well," Nelly said, "that was the shortest baby-sitting job I've ever had. I don't know if I should call the police or make a quick getaway. I think I better make a quick getaway." She walked through the bedroom and flipped off the overhead light.

"No," Caroline shrieked. "We're not dead."

"We were just playing," Butch said, brandishing the rubber knife. It wobbled back and forth in his hand.

"Oh," said Nelly. "Well, if you're not dead, then maybe you're hungry. You want some dinner?"

Butch and Caroline nodded their heads and got up. Caroline had the tail end of the python stuffed in her mouth along with her thumb.

"B.J., are you hungry?" Nelly called out. There was no answer.

"Daddy says B.J. always carries things too far," Caroline explained.

"Well, okay," Nelly said in a voice loud enough for B.J. to hear, "we're all going downstairs and have a delicious meal."

"What do you want for dinner?" Nelly asked, opening up the refrigerator. It was well stocked. Brian had mentioned something about food in the freezer. She opened up the freezer compartment. It was filled with stacks of Tupperware containers. She took one out. The label on the side said: Italian casserole. Cook 350°, 45 minutes. She looked at the others. There was a French casserole (cook 350°, 1½ hours), a Mexican casserole (place in boiling water, 30 min.), an all-American summer casserole (let defrost slowly). The rest of the containers were brisket of beef. They were all labeled and dated. No wonder part of Brian's illicit life was the pursuit of exotic cuisine.

"So what do you kids want for dinner?" Nelly asked.

"Cookies," Butch said.

"Pancakes," said Caroline.

"Well, that doesn't sound like a very balanced dinner to me," Nelly observed, still studying the refrigerator.

"My mommy always cooks me pancakes for dinner," Caroline pouted.

"Cookies," Butch repeated again.

"Why don't we try something different tonight? Something exotic, like hamburgers?" she said, noticing the fresh package of ground round on the second shelf.

"Hamburgers are dead cows ground up. We don't eat dead cows," Caroline said sternly.

"How about some eggs?" Nelly offered.

"Eggs give you cholesterol," Caroline said.

"Did you ever have Surprise Eggs?" Nelly asked, surprised at herself for reverting to her mother's tricks.

"What are Surprise Eggs?" Caroline asked, her curiosity aroused.

"Well, if I told you it wouldn't be a surprise, would it?" Nelly said.

"I bet they still give you cholesterol. Don't you know anything about food?" Nelly didn't answer. She wasn't sure she did.

"My mommy says that if you leave children alone and let them eat what they want, they'll automatically eat what's good for them," Caroline said.

Maybe the kids were right. Let them choose what they wanted to eat. It wasn't going to kill them as long as they ate something. "What kind of cookies do you want, Butch?"

"Chocolate chip." Nelly searched the cupboards. There were no chocolate-chip cookies. No cookies at all. Only graham crackers. "There don't seem to be any chocolate-chip cookies, honey," Nelly said.

"You have to cook them," Butch said, salting the kitchen table with the salt shaker.

"Mommy always makes them from scratch," Caroline offered over her thumb.

"Oh," Nelly said. She had seen a bag of Nestle's chocolate chips on the shelf. Well, if Miriam could make them from scratch, then so could Nelly.

Dinner was ready. Chocolate-chip cookies from scratch. Pancakes from Pillsbury. It was past nine. She went into the den. The TV was blaring. The two younger kids were asleep on the couch. B.J. was wide awake, sitting stiffly in an overstuffed armchair.

"Kids, wake up. It's time for dinner," Nelly said. "You hungry?" she asked B.J.

"They already ate," he said. "They ate before you came. Rosa gave us our dinner." Rosa was the housekeeper.

"What about you?" Nelly asked.

"I wasn't hungry.

"Well, how about some cookies and milk?" she asked.

"Mother doesn't want us to snack between meals," B.J. said. Nelly wondered if Miriam had really left or was lurking around somewhere cueing the kids in.

"Well, it must be about your bedtime," Nelly said.

"It was our bedtime an hour ago," B.J. said. Strike two, Nelly thought. Or maybe it was already strike three. She hadn't been keeping count. B.J., with his pocket calculator, undoubtedly had.

Nelly went upstairs to tuck them in. "Do you want me to read you a story?" she said to little Butch, who was now into thumb-sucking like his sister. She hadn't noticed him doing it before. Was this a bedtime ritual, or had he just picked up the habit tonight? Maybe Brian could get a deal on two pairs of braces.

"If he wants a story, I can read it," B.J. said from the doorway. "But he doesn't want a story, do you, Butch?"

Butch shook his head. The thumb remained intact. Nelly bent down and tucked in the covers, then leaned over, her head close to his.

"Can I give you a kiss good night?" she asked him. Butch shook his head again.

"He doesn't like to kiss strangers," B.J. said. And then, backing away from the door, "Neither do I."

She went into Caroline's room. She was already fast asleep. Nelly tucked in her blankets.

"She doesn't like to sleep with her covers tucked in," ever-watchful B.J. said. "It gives her claustrophobia."

"Oh, sorry," Nelly said, pulling the covers back out again. She turned to B.J. "Well, good night, B.J.."

"What's good about it?" he retorted, and turning in his tracks, he went into his room and slammed the door.

Not exactly an auspicious beginning, Nelly thought.

Brian called at 4 A.M. that morning.

"What's wrong?" he asked without even saying hello.

"What do you mean, what's wrong?" Nelly said, trying to shake herself awake.

"You sound funny. Is something wrong with one of the kids?"

"Brian, I just woke up. Nothing's wrong."

"Nelly, don't try and keep anything from me." He sounded slightly hysterical. "I'm their father."

"They're all asleep in bed. Everything's fine. I promise."

There was silence at the other end. Clearly this was not the late-news bulletin he was expecting.

"Did Butch wet his bed?"

"Not that I know of. I didn't hear anything," Nelly said, wondering if, in fact, you could hear someone wetting a bed.

"Go check."

"Right now?"

"Please," Brian said between tight teeth.

Nelly went into Butch's room. He was sprawled across his bed with his head hanging off the wrong end. One foot was propped up on the wall. She gently rearranged his little body so that his head was back on the bed. Then she took the pillow off the floor where it had been kicked and placed it under his head. Finally, she felt around on the sheet underneath him. It was dry. She went back to the phone.

"Nope," she said.

"That's funny," Brian said worriedly, "he usually wets his bed."

"Every night?"

"No, I mean he usually wets his bed when he's upset."

"Maybe he's not upset," Nelly said helpfully.

"Of course he's upset," Brian snapped. "I'm away. His mother's gone." There was another long pause. "He's holding it in. I don't like that. He could rupture a kidney or something. You better wake him up, Nelly."

"To wet his bed?"

"No, no, to take him to the bathroom."

"Okay," Nelly yawned, "I will." Brian's hysteria was having the opposite effect on her.

"No, I mean now. I'll hold on."

Nelly went back to Butch's room and gently shook him awake.

"Time to go to the bathroom," she said, hoping he wouldn't think she was crazy. He didn't say a word but sleepwalked with Nelly's assistance into the bathroom. She lifted the toilet seat and he took out his little penis. Nelly waited. Butch just stood there holding his penis. Nothing. Dry as a bone. Nelly looked at his face. He was fast asleep, standing over the toilet. She guided him back to his bed.

"Mission accomplished," she said to Brian.

"Is Caroline sucking her thumb?"

"Do you want me to check on that, too?"

"See, the thing is that when she's sleeping, she sucks her thumb on one side of her mouth and the corner of her pillow on the other and I worry about her suffocating."

"Has she ever suffocated before?" Nelly asked, starting to worry herself.

"No, but it's something to keep your eye on."

"Okay," Nelly said tiredly, "hold on."

Caroline was curled up in a tight little ball. Her long hair was flung upward on the pillow. Her cheeks were shadowed by the long, silky, dark lashes. She was holding her thumb in place in her mouth with the other hand. What a beautiful child, Nelly thought as she took the coverlet and placed it up over her shoulders.

"She's fine," she said to Brian, getting ready to hang up.

"Did B.J. have diarrhea?"

"I don't know," Nelly said. "He didn't say anything."

"He's not going to tell you. It's something you have to sense for yourself. What did he finally eat for dinner?" Nelly was tempted to lie. She decided to face the music. "Well, actually he didn't."

"Didn't what?"

"He didn't eat dinner."

"Oh, Jesus," Brian groaned. "Let me talk to him."

"Brian honey, it's after four in the morning here. The kid is fast asleep. He can eat tomorrow. I'll make sure he gets a good breakfast."

"You don't understand. It's not the eating, it's the eliminating I'm worried about. I don't care what time it is, when a kid is upset he needs to talk to his father."

"You're right," Nelly said, beginning to wish Brian would take up thumb sucking like his daughter. It might help. She went in and woke up B.J.

"B.J., it's your father. He wants to talk to you."

"I'm sleeping," B.J. said groggily, hiding his head under the pillow.

"I know you are, sweetheart. But he needs to talk to you. Please."

B.J. stumbled out of bed and slowly zigzagged down the hallway to the phone. He looked as though he was walking with his eyes shut.

He nodded his head into the phone. "Mmmmmmph," he said a few times, then: "Yep. Yep. Nope. Nope, I wasn't hungry. I had a sandwich in the afternoon. Tuna fish. Aw, Dad," he groaned, "I don't remember. I think so, but I don't remember." He listened a minute more, handed the phone to Nelly, shook his head slowly, and then shuffled off to bed.

"Here's the thing about B.J.," Brian said, his voice high with tension. "He's extremely erratic with his bowel movements. He'll have diarrhea for days and then he won't move his bowels for weeks at a time. It's very important to keep a close watch on his b.m.s. The diarrhea is one thing. That we can deal with. But when he goes through his retentive stage, it's impossible. You know when he's going to shift over from diarrhea to constipation when he starts skipping meals, saying he isn't hungry. He says he had a bowel movement today. But I don't always think he's being truthful with me. So watch out for that, will you, Nelly?"

"Of course, Brian."

There was a deep sigh on the other end. Brian was obviously making an effort to pull himself together. "So how's it going with you?" he asked.

"Oh, I had a bowel movement this morning," Nelly said, trying to lighten him up. He didn't laugh.

"Listen, I meant to tell you, if Miriam calls, don't answer the phone."

"How will I know if it's Miriam?"

He thought that over for a minute.

"Well, if she does call, don't let her talk to the kids. No, that's not fair. You can let her talk to the kids, but keep it to a minimum. And don't give her any information. Don't tell her where I am, who you are, or say anything about B.J.'s bowel movements. Okay?"

"Okay, if you say so."

"Give the kids a big hug and a kiss from me."

"Right now?" She was getting annoyed.

186

"No, it can wait till morning. I miss you."

"Miss you, too."

"Talk to you tomorrow." Nelly was seriously considering yanking the phone out of the wall, but instead she gently replaced the receiver. She wondered if he had put Miriam through the same kind of second degree. Probably not. Things were different now. He was a man with a mother's work. And she was discovering, as the old saying goes, a mother's work is never done.

She looked in on B.J. before she went back to bed. His eyes were closed, but they popped open the minute she leaned over his bed.

"Sometimes I think my father is crazy," he said.

"He's just concerned about you. He loves you," Nelly said.

"What he loves is my b.m.s," B.J. said, turning his back to her.

"Well, sleep tight, B.J."

"Fat chance," he said to the wall.

Poor kid, Nelly thought. It was hard being the oldest. He's got a lot on his mind. And only eight years old. It's funny. That was the same age as Anjelica. Somehow she had pictured Anjelica younger at eight. She still missed her. She missed the sense of closeness she had conjured up about her. If only she could recreate that closeness with B.J. She knew that she was capable of relating to eight-year-olds. She had been eight years old herself once. How different could it be? And she certainly knew what it was to be the oldest child. It was a drag.

Nelly didn't wake up until almost eight. She showered, dressed, and hurried downstairs. Caroline and Butch were sitting at the breakfast table eating cereal with their fingers, one flake at a time. A heavy Puerto Rican woman was unloading the dishwasher.

"*Buenos días, Señorita*," the woman said.

"*Buenos días—Rosa?*" Nelly asked. That was the extent of her Spanish.

"Yes, Rosa," Rosa said, smiling and nodding her head. Apparently that was the extent of Rosa's English.

Nelly poured herself a cup of coffee and sat down at the table. Caroline got up from her chair and came over to Nelly. She lowered herself into Nelly's lap and looked up at her adoringly. Something must have happened during the night.

"You're so pretty," Caroline said. "I wish my hair were golden like yours."

"You have beautiful hair, Caroline," Nelly said, fingering a few strands. "It's like silk."

"I use Wella Balsam creme rinse," Caroline explained, flinging her hair from side to side, obviously pleased with the compliment.

Butch left his cereal bowl and tried to occupy the other half of Nelly's lap. Nelly felt an almost sexual warmth run through her body. She hugged them both, patting their respective fannies.

"So, did you have a nice sleep?" she asked.

"I had a dream," Caroline said.

"What did you dream?"

"I dreamt you took me to Bloomingdale's and you bought me so many things that you used up your whole charge account. You bought me a hundred dresses and shoes to match and a running suit and roller skates and a skating skirt and you didn't buy anything for B.J. or Butch and they were mad," she said happily.

"Where is B.J.?" Nelly asked.

"He's still in bed. He's going to be late for school."

Nelly went upstairs. B.J. was lying in bed reading the *New York Times*. It was turned to the financial section.

"So what time do you have to be at school today?" she asked brightly.

"I'm not going to school today."

"Are you sick?"

"Nope, I'm dropping out."

"You mean you're never going to school again?"

"Nope."

"Not even college?"

"It'll be pretty hard for me to get into college if I don't even finish grammar school," he said with a sneer.

"Well, I can't make you go," Nelly said, trying to reason with him like one eight-year-old to another. "I know when I was a kid, I hated school. I did everything I could to stay home. It's just that I don't want to worry your father or get him upset."

"He wouldn't be upset."

"Well, you think about it. If you think it'll be okay for you to stay home, then I'll stay home with you and we'll both read all day." She almost hoped that B.J. would decide to stay home. It would be a good opportunity for them to get to know each other.

"If B.J. gets to stay home, then can I?" Caroline asked from the doorway.

"No," B.J. said, "you have to go to school, you're a girl." Caroline seemed to accept this.

She drove Caroline and Butch to a quaint red brick schoolhouse in a quiet section of Mamaroneck, about a half-hour away. The plaque on the front of the building read: The Mamaroneck/Montessori Advancement School. Nelly watched until they were safely inside.

As she drove back, she thought about what to do to make the day special for B.J. A very special eight-year-old kind of day. There was nothing more fun in Nelly's mind than having permission to play hookey from school.

Maybe she and B.J. would go to a movie. Or even better, what about Coney Island? She hadn't been to an amusement park since she was twelve and Sarah had been knocked unconscious after careening off the whirling disk in the fun house. Her mother had pronounced the amusement park a death trap and they were never allowed to go back. But Nelly loved amusement parks. What kid didn't? Coney Island would be just the thing to loosen up B.J. They would stuff themselves on hot dogs and pizza and cotton candy and ride the roller coaster and have fun in the fun house. And there wouldn't be any little sisters to worry about or mothers to cramp their style.

She pulled up the long driveway, got out of the car and ran up the steps to the house.

"B.J.!" she called from the hallway. "B.J., I've got a great idea." No answer. She went into the kitchen.

Rosa was down on her hands and knees scrubbing the floor with an old wooden brush. Hadn't she heard of sponge mops? She looked up, her round brown face aglow with exertion.

"*Ou esta* B.J.?" Nelly asked in broken French.

Rosa shook her head.

Nelly went upstairs and checked B.J.'s room. The *New York Times* was strewn all over the floor. But no B.J. She checked all the kids' bedrooms and the three bathrooms, then went into the master bedroom and looked out the window which overlooked the front of the house.

Her car was slowly backing down the driveway. Had she forgotten to put on the hand brake? Suddenly she saw the top of a dark curly head. It was B.J. "Oh, my God," she gasped and ran down the stairs two at a time.

By the time she got to the front door, the car had maneuvered a wide rear turn. He must have released the hand brake, Nelly thought. She ran down the driveway to the car. She reached for the door handle just as the car pulled away with a lurch. Nelly almost fell to her knees, but caught herself just in time.

The car screeched to a halt twenty feet down the street. Nelly ran for it. Just as she got there, it took off again and continued slowly down the street. Not that fast, but fast enough so that, even running, Nelly couldn't quite catch up with it.

Nelly was huffing and puffing. B.J. didn't seem to have any control over the steering. He could just barely see over the dashboard. He was now a half-block ahead of her.

Her heart was pounding both from the running and the sheer terror of watching an eight-year-old trying to maneuver a car down a curving street.

"B.J., B.J., put on the brakes," she screamed. "Turn into the curb. Turn into the curb." It was then she heard the engine and realized that he hadn't just released the hand brake, he had started the car.

He was driving, not coasting. He was going to crack up and kill himself. How was she going to explain that to Brian?

"No, Brian, he didn't have a bowel movement today. In fact, he had no movement at all."

She was still running. She felt as though she were exhaling every cigarette that she had ever inhaled.

She watched in horror as the car swerved to the right up onto the sidewalk and across a well-kept lawn. It flattened a rather elaborate sprinkler and mowed down a bed of birds of paradise before pulling back onto the road.

It was one of those old New Rochelle streets that curved gently around the big houses. Beautiful to look at, but impossible to maneuver in a car when your vision was obscured by a dashboard.

B.J. was still driving under twenty miles an hour. Nelly knew that the street curved into Post Road a hundred yards further on. It was a fast-moving thoroughfare with no stop light, just a stop sign for those entering into the heavily trafficked avenue. Not that it mattered. B.J. obviously wasn't following the standard rules of the road.

The car was zigzagging wildly down the street now. A woman was walking her small, hairy Yorkshire terrier. She didn't notice the car. She had her eyes on Nelly, who was running toward her waving her arms.

"Stop that car. There's a kid in it," Nelly yelled.

The woman glanced over to the car. It careened up the sidewalk toward her and she jumped out of the way. The little terrier didn't. He crouched shivering on the sidewalk as B.J. drove over him.

"Oh, no!" Nelly cried. The car continued on the sidewalk a few feet and then veered back toward the street. The dog was still crouching in the same spot, apparently unharmed. He yelped and jumped into his mistress's arms. Nelly apologized as she ran past. The woman stood, holding her dog, her mouth open and her face white with shock.

B.J. was now fast approaching the intersection.

Nelly's breath was coming in ragged, painful gasps. She was almost blinded by the sweat that was pouring off her forehead into her eyes. Her lungs screamed out in outrage. The muscles of her calves turned inward in agony.

B.J. had reached the corner.

"Stop!" she screamed with what little breath she had left in her.

The car slowed down and turned leisurely onto Post Road. Nelly heard the sounds of horns blasting and tires screeching to a halt. She stumbled to the corner in time to see the car making its way shakily up the wrong side of the road. Oncoming traffic swerved to avoid it. Her heart was about to go into total arrest. She ran, dodging the confused drivers.

The car picked up speed, moving directly in front of an oncoming Pepsi truck. Nelly stopped and covered her eyes with her hands.

When she took her hands away the car was gone. Vanished. Then she spotted the tail end of it just as it turned off onto the next small side street.

Traffic had already resumed its normal pattern, going on as if nothing had happened. As if an eight-year-old driving blind down the wrong side of a busy avenue was an everyday occurrence. Where were the traffic cops?

Nelly was sobbing now. She hobbled to the corner, where she had seen B.J. turn. Halfway down the street she saw the car parked neatly on the sidewalk.

She limped over, opened the door on the driver's side, and looked in.

B.J. sat there still clutching the wheel. He stared straight ahead, his face ashen. Beads of perspiration popped out on his chalk-white forehead. His upper lip quivered. The radio was softly playing some disco tune.

"B.J., what in the hell do you think you're doing? You could've been killed!" She had trouble getting the words out. There wasn't enough breath in her lungs.

"I just felt like taking a drive," he said, his voice quaking. He didn't look at her.

"You felt like taking a drive?" she yelled. She pulled him out of the car. He came out easily, like an overdone chicken leg. She sat down on the grass and pulled him over her knees. Her words were punctuated by her hand coming down hard on his denim-covered bottom:

"You bad, bad boy. That was a stupid, stupid thing to do. You could've been killed. You could've killed other people. You scared me to death. Don't you ever, ever, ever, ever do anything like that again. Do you hear me?"

She picked him up by the shoulders and looked at him. He was crying. Bawling like a baby. She caught her breath and lowered her voice.

"Do you hear me?"

"Ye-e-e-e-s," he sobbed.

"Do you understand that that was a dangerous and reckless thing and that you could've been hurt?" she said.

"Ye-e-e-e-s," he burst into a fresh storm of tears. Long, deep sobs that sprang from some source that went deeper than fear, deeper than apologies. Some buried well of sorrow had been tapped. They had hit a real gusher. He just cried and cried. Nelly began crying, too.

"I'm sorry I had to hit you, but you really scared me. I've never been so scared in my life."

"Me neither. I'm sorry," he sobbed, throwing his arms around her, pressing his hot, wet face into her neck. "I'm really sorry."

"Okay, okay, sweetheart. I know you are." She rocked and patted him, her voice choking and tears streaming down her face. "What a trip, what a trip," she said to herself.

They stayed that way for several minutes until her tears stopped and his sobbing had subsided to sniffles. The little smart-aleck tough guy had had the fright of his life. Nelly guessed he had needed it, had needed to do something so terrible, so frightening that he would scare himself into letting loose all the tears that had been sitting there for so long. How long? Since his mother left? Maybe even before that. The little man of the family needed to feel like a baby again.

"Well, I guess we've had enough excitement for one day," she said, giving him a squeeze.

Part of her wanted to say, okay, all is forgiven, let's you and me take in a nice quiet air conditioned movie with a lot of popcorn. A double feature and don't spare the butter. But her instincts now told her that a little grounding, a little discipline was called for. She understood that he needed to know that she was there to take care of him, not just to be a pal. He had to know she would watch out for him, save him from certain death, and then dish out the appropriate punishment. She realized she had made the mistake of trying to relate to him as a person and a peer. Someone his own age. He didn't want that. He wanted an adult to mother him, discipline him, place limits on his rather shaky universe. While B.J. had had his first driving lesson, Nelly had learned her first lesson in motherhood.

"I think you and me had better go home and you had better spend the rest of the day in your room doing something nice and constructive like hitting the old schoolbooks."

"Okay," he nodded, wiping his nose with the back of his hand. Then he looked up at her and smiled for the first time. It was a dazzling, wet-eyed, snot-faced grin. She put her arm around him and steered him toward the car.

"Do you want me to drive home?" he asked, his eyes twinkling mischievously.

"The only way you're going to get to drive home is right over my dead body," she said, taking his slender neck in both her hands and strangling him with comic exaggeration.

By the end of the day, they were friends. Not friends like two kids, but friends of two very different generations. He liked and trusted her because he knew that she liked, but didn't necessarily trust, him. It was a beginning.

The kids settled into a sort of routine. Nelly realized that routine was exactly what they needed at this time in their lives. Part of the routine involved each child taking a turn at being impossible for a day. First it had been B.J., then it was Caroline. Sensing Nelly's newly formed relationship with B.J., she started in. From all sweetness and cuddles she turned, overnight, into a vindictive little bitch.

"Mommy doesn't fold napkins that way. She makes triangles," Caroline said, watching Nelly set the table for dinner that night.

"Well, each to his own napkin," Nelly said, unbothered.

"My mommy doesn't smoke cigarettes," she said to Nelly, who was just lighting up her first afterdinner cigarette.

"Your mommy's very smart," Nelly said. Cigarettes were a lot more of a touchy subject to her than napkin folding.

Caroline must have sensed this. "Mommy says cigarettes give you cancer. Are you going to get cancer?" she asked hopefully.

"Not at the dinner table," Nelly said, stubbing out the cigarette. Caroline stared at her for a long moment.

"Do you have children of your own?"

"No, I'm sorry to say I don't," Nelly said.

"How come?"

"I guess I just never got around to it."

"How come you never got around to it?"

"I was doing other things. I was too busy working," Nelly said, wanting desperately to change the subject.

"My mommy says her children are the best things she's got. She says we're her most priceless possession."

Then how come she left you like a stack of last year's magazines? Nelly thought.

"What's your most priceless possession?" Caroline asked.

"Well, I don't know. I'd have to think about that."

With Caroline there were always sudden changes of mood and affection that kept Nelly totally off balance.

"Do you wish I was your child?" she asked, climbing into Nelly's lap.

"I do. I certainly do. I think you make a very priceless possession."

"I wish you were my mommy," she said, hugging Nelly. "Except you're not a very good cook."

"I could learn," Nelly said, unthreatened.

"No, you couldn't," Caroline said, climbing off her lap. "You smoke too much."

Butch went through his bad day on schedule, right after Caroline's. They were sitting at breakfast when Nelly felt a spattering against her bare leg. She looked down. Butch was holding his little dick and aiming a fine thin stream of pee right at her feet.

"Butch," she shrieked, "what are you doing?"

"I'm making wee-wee."

"Not on my foot. Use the bathroom."

"That's because he likes you," Caroline explained. She was going through one of her good days.

"No it isn't," argued B.J. "It's because he thinks he's a dog."

A little while later Nelly was putting on her makeup in the bathroom. Butch came up behind her, grabbed one leg and began humping it energetically.

"Butch, stop that. You made me get mascara in my eye." She actually thought it was funny. She was in mid-chuckle, reaching over for a piece of toilet paper to take the mascara out of her eye, when he bit her on the calf.

In that short time, that one week, she experienced the pains and joys of motherhood in miniature.

She had never been with children for this long a time. And it was her first experience as a mother, even though she was still operating only in a ringer capacity. She was amazed at her calmness and competence. She knew she was a reassuring presence to them. She had taken to it like the proverbial duck to water. She was in her element without ever having experienced that element before. Maybe it was because the kids made it so easy for her. They were warm, intelligent, responsive, and challenging. They were also impossible, difficult, demanding, and spoiled. Most of all, they were real. In all her dreams, all her fantasies, Nelly hadn't imagined it would be like this. The children of her fantasies had been projections of herself. These kids had a reality and individuality and a richness of spirit that went beyond what even her fertile imagination could create.

The expression They grow on you began to make a lot of sense to her. They grew on her, all right. She learned to accept their quirks, their crazy talk, their simple childish needs. Sometimes she felt bored, sometimes frustrated, many times exhausted. But mostly she felt happy, very happy just being with them. She felt as though all these many months of effort and frustrated attempts at motherhood had finally paid off in spades. No, not in spades. In triplicate.

When it came time for their second go-round of bad days, they weren't so bad at all. There was relative peace and intermittent harmony. They were one small, happy family. Until Brian came home.

24 The Marriage

At three in the morning Nelly was awakened by the sound of an alarm. It was a high-pitched electronic buzz, which she immediately identified as a smoke alarm. The word *fire* blazed through her brain, and she acted immediately without even having to think.

She ran into B.J.'s room and shook him awake.

"Get up, B.J., we have to go outside." He looked at her groggily, not understanding, but getting out of bed nonetheless. She went into Caroline's room and woke her. The little girl looked frightened, and Nelly made an effort to keep her voice calm.

"Come on, honey, it's just a fire drill like you have in school." She couldn't get Butch awake so she picked him up in her arms and the four of them hurried downstairs.

Halfway down the stairs Nelly stopped and gasped. A man's dark figure stood at the bottom of the stairway. She clutched Butch protectively to her bosom. The other two kids ran the rest of the way down the stairs toward the dark figure.

"Kids, come back," Nelly cried out. They threw themselves at the man, holding onto his arms. Were they trying to protect her? Were they crazy? Nelly screamed. The man turned on the light switch next to him. It was Brian. He was holding a rolled-up newspaper, the end of which was scorched.

"I'm sorry," he said, looking sheepish, "that was really stupid. I was just checking the smoke alarm to see if it worked. I worried about it the whole time I was gone."

"I guess it works," Nelly said angrily. She took a deep breath.

"What's wrong with Butch?" he asked.

"Smoke inhalation?" Nelly offered.

Brian bounded up the stairs.

"Butch, Butch honey. Wake up. Are you okay?" Butch opened his eyes sleepily.

"Hi, Daddy," he yawned.

"I thought you weren't coming home until day after tomorrow," Nelly said.

"I finished early," Brian said.

Brian turned his attention to the children. He examined each one carefully as though looking for signs of neglect, ringworm, scurvy, polio, malnutrition, or psychological damage. Finally he turned to B.J.

"Did you have a b.m. today?"

"I don't remember. Did I?" he asked Nelly.

"I think you had one yesterday," she assured him.

"Yesterday!" Brian exclaimed. "But not today?"

"Today just started. It's after three in the morning of a bright new day. Maybe you want to get an early start?" she said, winking at B.J.

Brian gave her a dirty look. "Come on, kids, it's time for you to be in bed," he said, taking control of the situation.

"Will you read me a story?" Caroline asked.

"Sure I will, honey," Brian said.

"No, I mean Nelly." Brian looked for a moment as if someone had thrust a croquet mallet through his heart. Nelly felt badly.

"It's too early for a story, Caroline. Besides, I already read you one last night. It's time for bed, okay?" Nelly said.

Caroline nodded sleepily. Brian took Butch out of Nelly's arms. "I'll put him to bed," he said.

"I want Nelly to sleep with me," Butch cried.

"No, me," Caroline piped in.

"No," Brian said. "Everybody sleeps in their own room. Nelly can sleep in the guest room because she's a guest." Thanks a lot, Nelly thought.

"But I get nightmares," Caroline whined.

This gave Brian a moment's pause. "When did you start having nightmares?" he asked with concern.

"The other night," Caroline said, pleased to have his attention.

"What was your nightmare, sweetheart?" he asked, bending down to her level. Brian hadn't had six years of therapy for nothing.

"I dreamed Nelly took me to Bloomingdale's."

"Yes," Brian said, urging her on.

"And she bought me a billion trillion things and we took everything home and there wasn't enough room in my closet."

"Yes?" Brian said, as though waiting for the punch line.

"And you said I could only keep what would fit into my closet and so I pushed and pushed and I got more and more things in and Nelly helped me," she said, smiling at Nelly lovingly. "But when we finally got the door shut, the side of the house fell off." Caroline giggled. Was this actually her original Bloomingdale's dream, or had she changed the ending to suit her father's paranoia? Did she always have dreams about Bloomingdale's? And what did they all mean? Nelly wished Dr. Abrams had been bigger on dreams. She didn't have a clue as to what was going on in Caroline's mind. Brian was pursuing that very subject.

"What do you think it means, honey?" Jesus, Nelly thought, maybe Brian had about one year too many of analysis.

Caroline thought for a minute. "I don't know. I guess it means that you can't put too much things in one closet. Or maybe it means I need a bigger closet."

"She doesn't have dreams," B.J. said, "she just makes them up."

"How do you know?" Caroline snapped. "You don't sleep in my bed. I have lots of dreams and nightmares and you don't know anything about it."

"Oh yeah?"

"Yeah."

"Come on, kids, cut it out," Brian interrupted. "It's late. Let's get to bed."

Nelly watched Brian as he unpacked. "The kids seem upset," he said.

"What do you mean?"

"They just seem upset, that's all. It's only natural. They're probably angry at me for going to California."

"I don't think so," Nelly said. "I really think they were fine about it."

Brian looked at her. "Are you trying to tell me they didn't miss me?"

"No, I'm sure they missed you," she reassured him. "It's just that they're very adaptable kids. They're terrific kids, in fact. They went through a little acting out in the beginning. But I think that's only natural."

"They were probably repressing their real feelings."

"I think they're basically very healthy kids. Obviously you've done a good job raising them."

"Thank you," he said, visibly relaxing. "Of course, I told you before, it'll take time, but I think if you're patient, they'll learn to accept you."

"I hope so," Nelly said sincerely.

"The thing about the story, though, that bothered me."

"What story?"

"Caroline asking you to read her a story. That isn't like Caroline. She was trying to ingratiate herself. Obviously she doesn't feel completely at ease with you yet. You get to know how to read their signals, living with them all these years."

"I imagine so," Nelly said, stifling a yawn.

Brian formally escorted Nelly to the guest room. It was downstairs next to the kitchen He kissed her good night as if returning her home from a first date.

"I really think it's amazing how the kids seem to have taken to you," he said, still on the same theme.

"I don't think it's so amazing." Nelly was getting tired of the subject. "You took to me."

"Yeah, but still, I thought there would be a lot of resentment and hostility about your trying to take over their mother's place."

"It's funny, they barely mentioned her," Nelly said. "Do you think there's any chance that she'll come back and take the kids away?"

"Oh, she'll come back. She left her beaver coat. As for taking the kids away, she'll have to take me to court first." He said "court" as though it were the Roman arena and he the champ gladiator.

"So you think we have a case, legally?"

"I'm the lawyer, aren't I?"

"I just think it's weird. Not one phone call the whole week. I can't imagine why she hasn't tried to get in touch with you or the kids."

"She'll get in touch when she wants to get in touch. Don't worry about it. Forget about Miriam. Let's talk about us. You still want to get married, my little maternal one?"

"More than ever. I really see us as a family now. All of us."

"I am one lucky guy," Brian said, giving her a hug. "I find a lady who's not only willing to take over the old man, but his kids too. Say," he said, "what about that little girl you were going to adopt? I forgot all about her. We can adopt her too. The more the merrier."

"Oh, she got adopted by somebody else, I'm afraid."

"Well, we can always have kids of our own, if you want."

"I'm happy with what we've got, Brian. Three's plenty. Just plenty." She felt him getting hard against her. "Well," she said sadly, "I guess I have to move back to my apartment tomorrow."

"I guess so," he said. "Listen, let's celebrate our unofficial engagement tomorrow night. I'll take you someplace special. Just you and me."

"What about the kids?"

"I think it's a little soon to tell them."

"Well, we don't have to tell them. We can just all go out to dinner together, can't we?"

"But don't you want to be alone with me? We haven't been alone in a long time. I can get Rosa to stay late."

"It wouldn't seem right without the kids. What about if I come here and make a nice dinner?" she said.

"No, no. We'll go out alone. A night on the town," he said adamantly.

Nelly realized this was not the time to push. "O.K.," she smiled.

"Sleep tight, sweetheart," he said, sweeping her up in his arms.

' You too." They kissed like new lovers. When Brian turned to go upstairs, Nelly followed him.

"Where are you going?" he asked.

"Just to check on the kids. Make sure they're okay."

"I'll check on the kids," Brian said quickly. "You go to bed."

"Okay, okay," she said, turning around and going back to her room.

Nelly lay in bed. She couldn't sleep. She worried about Miriam. Where was she? Why hadn't she called? Wasn't she worried about her children? Didn't she care about some woman coming in and usurping their affection? It seemed to Nelly that they had, indeed, transferred their love directly onto Nelly. Maybe there was something wrong with them that they could so easily change mothers in midstream. It had only been five days, but Nelly felt as though the transfer had, indeed, been made. If someone tried to take those kids away from her now, she would have fought to the death. How could a mother give up her children like that?

Nelly tried to put herself in Miriam's place. She had spent the last eight years working as a mother. Maybe she did feel like changing careers. There were many cases now of women not only leaving their husbands but their entire families. They had a right to a fresh start and a new life. Certainly men had been doing it for years. Well, it was fine with Nelly. Give someone else a shot at it. Nelly was more than ready to take up the reins or apron strings or helm or whatever.

Her mind turned to Brian. He seemed so sure about being able to keep the children. She had to trust him. After all, he was the lawyer. But she was worried just the same. She had lost too many children already not to be worried.

Nelly remembered then that they needed milk. She hoped there was enough for breakfast. What else did they need? Let's see, milk, eggs, butter . . . another bag of chocolate chips . . .

She dreamed she was in a huge supermarket. It was almost closing time. She started down the aisles, filling her shopping cart with the things she needed. But every time she turned her back just for a second, the cart would disappear and she would have to start all over again. Finally she managed to get everything on her list and she wheeled the cart over to the one checkout that was still open.

"This is the excess lane," the checkout girl said. "You've got to have a minimum of six hundred items or I can't check you out. And you better hurry, the store's about to close."

Nelly began running up and down the aisles throwing food into the cart, but the cart wasn't big enough and there wasn't enough time and the kids were at home starving . . .

She woke up crying. She felt as though she had been dreaming the one dream on and off all night. A marathon nightmare. She immediately analyzed the problem. Separation anxiety. She was going to be moving out today and she was worried about losing the children. It was silly, she said, trying to calm herself. As soon as Brian got his divorce, they would all start living together happily ever after.

"Did you have a nice vacation?" Ben, the executive producer, asked. He had been waiting in her office when she arrived that morning.

"Terrific," Nelly said. "Did I miss anything exciting?"

"Oh, let's see. We had a mass murder in Queens, someone hijacked the BMT during rush hour, Cartier's was held up by two nine-year-old boys wearing ski masks, and the mayor announced at a press conference that he was going to convert."

"Convert to what?"

"He didn't say. Just that he was open to any recommendations from the city's religious leaders. Listen, Nelly, are you ready to get back to work?"

"Why else do you think I dropped in today?"

"Okay, I know you needed the vacation. But I want to see the old Nelly back there pushing the news. Your heart hasn't exactly been in your job these past months."

Nelly's stomach lurched. He was right. She had really been sloughing off. He was trying to tell her something. Well, he didn't have to worry. Now that her home life was taking shape, she was going to put all her energies back into her job.

"Don't worry, Ben, Brenda Starr is back on the beat."

Nelly was a veritable whirlwind of activity the whole day. They were extending the evening news time, and she made ten suggestions for the new format. She handed in twenty-five special news segment ideas. She had an interview with the head of network news. They were looking for people to anchor a projected "60 Minutes"–type program slotted for Sunday night. It was a big opportunity and the competition was very stiff. A lot of big names were going after it. Nelly felt like she had a chance. It would be perfect. There would be midweek taping, but she'd have more time to spend with the kids.

Nelly, wanting to impress Brian with her new-found domesticity, talked him into letting her cook dinner the next evening in her apartment.

"Did the kids get their dinner okay?" she asked over dessert.

"Listen, Nelly, I couldn't be happier that you're so fond of my children. But I feel that I have to remind you that they *are* my children. I am the father here."

"And what am I?" she asked tensely.

200

Brian was instantly sorry. "You are the bride-to-be," he said, trying to give her a hug. She pulled out of his arms.

"But Brian, if we're going to be married, I want to have an equal part in raising the kids."

"You will, you will. You'll be their stepmother, after all."

"I hate that name: stepmother. It sounds old and mean and ugly. It reminds me of poisoned apples," Nelly snapped.

"But Nelly, it's just a term. Don't get so upset. We don't have to call you stepmother. We'll call you Nelly."

"You know what your trouble is? You want those kids all to yourself. You're jealous of anybody else's involvement with them. You're afraid they'll love me more than they love you. You think just because your wife left you that your kids might leave you, too. You're so possessive, you won't give me a chance."

"Me, possessive?" Brian screamed. "I get the feeling that the only reason you said you'd marry me is because of those kids. You seem to want instant children, an instant family. You aren't even taking me into consideration."

Nelly did the only thing a person can do when accused of something that is absolutely the truth: she denied it.

"That is not true. I happen to adore your children. But I adore you too. You should be happy. A lot of men have to choose between their children and their second wives." She softened her tone. "Listen, honey, I know how much you love your children. Why would I want to interfere with that? If you think these are areas that are none of my business as far as raising them, well, then tell me. I can understand." She felt she would make any compromise, avoid any argument in order not to jeopardize her future with B.J., Caroline, and Butch. She was trying to be so rational and logical and understanding. Underneath she was filled with fear—fear of upsetting the apple cart, of losing the children. Why had Brian suddenly become her enemy? She tried another tack.

"I don't understand you. You've got everything you say you ever wanted now. The kids, me, and an imminent divorce. Why are you looking for problems?" She struck a chord there. He paused a moment to think it over.

"I'm not looking for problems, am I? Maybe I am. You could be right. Creating problems was part of my old problem. I better make an appointment with Shapiro." Shapiro was his old shrink. "I have to be on the lookout for that kind of behavior. I'm sorry, Nelly honey, I think you put your finger on it. I probably can't stand all this happiness, so I have to make a problem out of it. Don't you worry. We'll work it out. Shapiro and me. In the meantime, I think we'd better cool it for a while."

"What do you mean?"

"I mean, until I get my resentment, hostility, and need to negate happiness worked out with Shapiro, maybe we'd better not expose the kids to this."

"Why can't you work it out with me?"

"Nelly, you know Shapiro's the expert on this stuff."

"How long do you think it'll take?" Nelly said, starting to panic.

"Oh, I probably just need a booster session or two. But let's take a few days off, okay?" he said, putting his arms around her.

"Okay," she said, sighing. He moved his hands to her breasts.

"Wanna make love?" he asked huskily. "Just to patch things up?"

"What about the kids?" she said.

"They're asleep by now."

"But Brian, it's late, you should get home. Especially after your California trip." She had never refused to make love with him before. Besides, she knew down deep she was pissed at him. He was possessive. She wasn't going to take the kids away from him. She just wanted to share and share alike. And beyond that, she knew she was angry with him for being right. In the little hand-embroidered sampler in her mind, she could read "God Bless B.J., Caroline, Butch, and Nelly. God Bless This Happy Home." There was no mention of Brian.

But maybe it was only natural. They were already behaving like married folk. Along with money and sex, weren't kids one of the big three battles every couple waged? They had to fight about something, didn't they? It might as well be something important.

25 The Divorce

Nelly was sure things would work out. She was again operating on that old childhood superstition: good and bad things happen in threes. According to her calculations, she was into the good cycle. She counted up the bad things just to reassure herself. Number one: she couldn't have her own children. Number two: she had lost Anjelica and the door to adoption had all but been closed to her. Number three? Number three? She hated this approach to life. She had long since learned to determine her own cycles, whether they occur in threes or not. But she had had a number of bad breaks recently, and she had to make these misfortunes work in her favor. Consequently, the rule of three. She counted again.

Number one: she couldn't have her own baby. Number two: she was too old to have a test tube baby. And number three: she wasn't able to adopt. She breathed a sigh of relief.

Now she was into the good cycle. Number one: Brian's wife had left him with the kids and Nelly had taken care of them and they were beginning to love her as she certainly loved them, and Brian had asked her to marry him so they could all live together in perfect harmony for the rest of their lives. That was number one. At this rate, she didn't need to worry about a two or three. She could stretch out number one ad infinitum.

Her birthday was the next day. She had wanted to spend it with the kids, but she was going to stick to her agreement with Brian to cool it for a few days while he worked things out with Shapiro. She didn't like making a big deal about her birthday anyway. She was going to be thirty-six, and one did not go around handing out blowers and funny hats on the occasion of one's thirty-sixth birthday. On the contrary.

Ordinarily the addition of another year would have depressed her a little. But now that her new life with Brian and the kids was about to take off, she hardly gave it a thought. Tyler had thought about it, though. He called her the morning of her birthday.

"You been 'bout as scarce as a horsefly when the swatters are out," he said on the phone.

"I know," she said. "I've been busy."

"Not too busy to celebrate your birthday, Ah hope."

Nelly decided this was as good a time as any to clear things up with him. He had to be told about Brian and her.

"Well, I don't know about celebrating, but I would like to see you."

"You got a hankerin' for some pankerin'?"

"Oh Tyler," Nelly laughed, "cut out the cattle talk."

The longer Tyler lived in New York, the thicker his Texas accent became and the worse his figures of speech. Nelly firmly believed that when he had first come to the city he had spoken perfect English.

"How about coming over here and I'll cook you dinner?" She was really into cooking for some reason.

"No, no. Y'all come to mah place. I wanna show ya what Ah've bayn workin' on."

"Okay, pardner."

It was almost six o'clock when she went downstairs for a taxi. She wondered if the kids had had their dinner yet. She wondered if they missed her. Considering the way they had adapted to their mother's absence, they might have already forgotten her name. Once they all started living together they'd remember it all right. Mommy-Nelly? Just plain Mommy? Or was that intruding on Miriam's territory? How about Mommy-Two? Actually, just plain Nelly was fine with her.

"Seventy Wooster Street," she told the taxi driver.

"Which way do you want to go?"

Oh Christ. She didn't have the faintest idea how to get down to SoHo, which was where Tyler lived. Nobody in New York did, for that matter. That's probably what made SoHo so chic. It was like the place in *Lost Horizon;* nobody could ever find it.

"Don't you have a little book that tells you how to get to places?" she asked.

"We've got a book that gives us the addresses of all the restaurants and hotels. But even that doesn't tell you how to get there. It's like when you look up how to spell a word in the dictionary. If you don't know how to spell it in the first place, how can you find it? Say, Ma'am, don't I know you? You're on TV, right?" he said, turning around in his seat.

"Right," said Nelly, wishing he'd get going.

"Nelly Diamond and the News, that's you, right?"

"Right."

He stuck his hand through the narrow opening in the plastic partition. "This is Robert Duncan speaking," he said.

She took his hand and shook it. "Pleased to meet you, Robert."

"Call me Mr. Duncan," he said, chuckling. She chuckled too. She felt friendly and warm. She loved the world.

When they did locate Tyler's place, after being hopelessly lost for almost three-quarters of an hour, Nelly gave him a big tip. Out of remorse, he had driven most of the way with his meter off.

"Well," Robert Duncan said, "I thank you, Ma'am." Ma'am. That was the second time he'd called her that. It seemed only yesterday that taxi drivers, saleswomen, doormen, and waiters had been calling her miss. Now, suddenly, it was ma'am. Ma'am sounded so matronly, so chintz dress and orthopedic shoe-ish. She took her hand mirror out of her bag and stared into it. The street light was directly above her. It exaggerated the contours and lines of her face.

Her eyes had lines around them, no doubt about that. A network of small, fine, laugh lines at the outside corners. And the smile lines on either side of her mouth were deeper, more clearly etched than she remembered. But, hell. Smile lines, laugh lines—what was so bad about that? She drew her brows together. Oh-oh. There were frown lines, too. She raised her eyebrows. And worry lines. So what? she said to herself, shoving the mirror back into her bag. So what? She was thirty-six years old. She didn't expect to look like a spring chicken all her life, did she? Besides, looking like a spring chicken wasn't exactly great shakes anyway.

If only they wouldn't call her ma'am. That killed her. It was funny, it seemed like she had just gotten used to thinking of herself as a woman. A ms. Years of girlhood had extended way past the age of twenty-one. But then there was revelation, liberation, and womanhood. Now, suddenly, woman had turned into ma'am. Did ma'am mean middle-aged. Was thirty-six middle-aged? No, it couldn't be. She tried to figure it out as she walked up the six flights to Tyler's loft.

If the average life span was seventy (was it seventy?), then thirty-six was smack dab in the middle. That made her middle-aged, all right. Oh, Jesus, how did that happen? A middle-aged ma'am after one five-dollar taxi ride. She certainly didn't feel any older. Perhaps wiser, but definitely not older. Thank God she had a bright, shiny future with a wonderful new family. Otherwise she would feel like shit. She was glad to be spending her birthday with Tyler. If anyone made her feel young and beautiful, it was he.

"Whale, howdy, Ma'am," he said as he slid the door open. It was one of those freight doors built large enough for a truck to pass through.

"Don't call me that."

"What, howdy?"

"No, ma'am. It's my birthday. I'm thirty-six, and I don't want anyone calling me ma'am."

He whistled a deep, low whistle. "Thirty-six? I thought you were only thirty-two."

"I lied."

"Whale, you're the most beautiful thirty-six-year-old hunk a woman Ah know," he said, swinging her around in his arms. One swing and Nelly snapped out of her momentary funk. Two swings, she was smiling. Three swings and she was giggling like a four-year-old. And then he stopped. Her eye caught something in the corner of the room.

"What's that?" she gasped.

"That's mah new thing. That's what Ah've been workin' on." It was a huge, life-size, self-portrait. In the painting Tyler stood nude except for a red rose that he held languidly in one hand. His eyes had a dreamy, serene look to them. But what had grabbed Nelly's attention was his belly. It stuck out as though he were nine months pregnant.

"Here, let me show you," he said, leading her to the other end of the loft. Huge canvases were stacked painting-side against the wall. He turned them one by one. The next canvas was another nude of Tyler. This time he was sitting in a simple, straight-backed chair. He was holding a tiny little baby who was sucking greedily at one of two enormous breasts that Tyler had added to his chest. The next was Tyler holding another little baby, or the same baby six months older. The baby was dressed in a little christening dress. Tyler was dressed in a velvet ribbon around his neck. The baby was held on his lap in such a way that you couldn't tell if Tyler was a man or a woman. The only real giveaway was the hair on his shoulders.

"Whale, what do y'all think? Ah call it maternal art."

"It's really quite extraordinary," Nelly said, trying to catch her breath.

"Does it upset you some?"

"Why should it upset me? It's just a painting of a man who happens to be the mother of a child."

"Ah heard about what happened with the home study. That Miss Glass called me. She was hot for me to levitate with her again. Ah'm really sorry, Nelly honey."

"I know. Thanks, Tyler."

"'Member me tellin' you Ah wanted to have children?"

"I remember."

"Ah guess at the time Ah thought Ah wanted to hev kids like men do. You know, git married and git the woman pregnant and then be a father."

"That's the usual way."

"Then when I got into doin' these paintings, Ah realized that it wasn't a father Ah wanted to be, it was a mother. Ah really, way down deep, wanted to be pregnant and hev a baby. And there just ain't no way."

Everyone was getting into the act, Nelly thought.

"You see, not bein' able to hev one myself, Ah know how y'all feel. Course Ah guess it's got to be harder on you than it is on me."

"Who knows?" Nelly said blithely. "Maybe it isn't." She couldn't believe none of this was bothering her. She'd certainly come a long way.

"I've got something to tell you, Tyler."

"What?"

"I'm getting married."

"Yore gettin' married? To who?"

"To Brian Goodstain."

"Who's Bran Goodstein?"

"He's a man I know."

"That's a hell of a good start," Tyler said angrily.

"Okay. He's a man I know who's got three beautiful children."

"Oh." He dwelled on that for a moment and then started to get even angrier. "You're marryin' someone who's got kids just because Ah cain't have any."

"Wait a minute, Tyler. You're getting all mixed up. You can have children. All you have to do is go back to the old-fashioned way and get some woman pregnant."

"Things shore don't always work out the way we want 'em to, Ah guess," Tyler sighed unhappily.

"I can testify to that," she said.

"Whale, what kind of guy is he, this Goodstain fella?"

"He's a wonderful man and a wonderful father."

Tyler fell on his bed, groaning and holding his stomach.

"What's the matter? Are you sick?"

"Nah, Ah think Ah'm gettin' the blues," he moaned. "You know Ah never get the blues. Ah don't know if mah system kin handle it. What do y'all do for depression, anyway?"

Nelly thought a moment. "I could tell you a joke."

"Okay. Shoot."

"How many Texans does it take to change a light bulb?"

"Ah give."

Nelly didn't have the punch line. She had just started the joke hoping a punch line would come to her.

"Ah still feel depressed," Tyler said after a minute.

"Maybe we could make love?" Nelly suggested.

"Ah think I'm too blue to make love."

"Really?" Nelly asked, amazed.

"Well, maybe we could try it. Jest a little."

By the time she left Tyler's loft, he said he was feeling much better. The blues had vanished in the night.

She called Paisley the next day.

"I know why you called," Paisley said.

"I bet you don't."

"You called to apologize."

"Apologize for what?"

"For the way you attacked me that night we had dinner."

"No, as a matter of fact that's not why I called. I forgot all about that night."

"Well, Nelly, if you don't apologize," Paisley said primly, "then how can I ever forgive you for all the nasty things you said?"

"You can always let bygones be bygones," Nelly answered, trying to be helpful.

Paisley thought a minute. "I could. Yes, I could. That would be the big thing to do. Okay, *je t'éxcuse.* So, what's up?"

"I'm getting married."

"You're getting married? To who? Not the gays' answer to Annie Oakley?"

"No, it's not Tyler, if that's who you mean. I'm marrying Brian Goodstein."

"But I thought he was already married. Nelly, don't tell me you lowered your standards and went and broke up a marriage."

"No, his wife left him."

"Oh. What's wrong with him?"

"Nothing's wrong with him. He's a wonderful man with three wonderful children," Nelly realized she was repeating herself.

"You're not taking on the kids too?"

"Absolutely."

"Well, let me just repeat to you what you said so very hurtfully to me in my very own kitchen: 'One of these days your perversity is going to get you into a lot of trouble.'"

"What's your problem with me getting married? You've done it yourself four times already."

"Three," corrected Paisley. "I had my reasons, though. I had the family estate to protect. So I was wrong. So what? At least now I'm getting married with my eyes open."

"You're really marrying that cop?"

"He's not a cop anymore. He quit the force. Yes, we're getting married. He's the first man in my whole life who's ever loved me for myself. *And* for my family estate. Which happens to be very much a part of me. He may be marrying me for my money. But I'm marrying him for his lack of it. Why are you getting married?"

208

"I happen to be in love," Nelly said.

"*Quelle idée*," Paisley snorted. She was silent for a moment. "Listen, maybe we could have a double wedding. It might be fun."

"I don't think so, Paisley. I imagine we won't have a wedding at all. Just a small private ceremony."

"I suppose you'll be wanting a wedding gift," she sniffed.

"No, that isn't necessary."

"Does that mean I'm not getting one?" Paisley shot back.

"No, no. We'll exchange wedding gifts if that'll make you happy."

"How much are you going to spend on mine?"

"I don't know. Do you want to establish a limit or something?"

"Not on a wedding gift for me, I don't."

"Well, to tell you the truth. I can't think of anything you might want or need."

"Robinson's. Fifty-seventh and Madison. A set of Georgian teaspoons. Only seven hundred and fifty. Ask for Mr. Roth."

"But Paisley," Nelly moaned, "that's a fortune."

"I know," Paisley said gleefully.

Nelly wondered if she was jumping the gun a little, announcing a marriage before she had been officially engaged. But engagements were kid stuff. She didn't have to concern herself with those little formalities. They wouldn't even get engaged. Brian had been talking about marriage for as long as she'd known him. He was the kind of man who wouldn't spend more than one day unmarried if he could help it. That was fine with her.

She knew in the past she had gotten way ahead of herself as far as children were concerned. In this instance she felt secure. The children existed. Brian existed. They were not figments of her imagination. There was nothing that could go wrong. Was there?

Yet she still felt the need to spread the word. Make an official press release out of it. It was all part of revving up. She was getting geared for happiness. No more disappointments for Nelly Diamond. Happiness, marriage, and kids. What every healthy thirty-six-year-old woman should be geared for.

She saw her life now in stages. Getting through childhood and all its insecurities; that was the first stage. Then the period of total self-involvement and self-analysis; that was her coming of age. The third stage was putting all that inner knowledge to work, the self-fulfillment trip. Success: social, professional, and emotional. Now she was entering into her golden age where she could turn her attention to others. She could give and receive love freely. She was ready to share her life because her life had a future with a clear-cut curriculum.

In fifteen years Butch would be in his second year of college. Caroline would be ready to graduate. And B.J. would already be in law school.

She saw a continuum, a family history unfolding. They would grow up and graduate from college and have careers and get married and have children. Grandchildren. That's when Nelly would get her babies. She had never thought she would embrace the concept of grandmotherhood, but now she couldn't wait. Maybe she would encourage the kids to marry young so they could start having children immediately. She didn't want to interfere with their lives, but after all, she would certainly be available for baby-sitting anytime.

She saw big family dinners at Thanksgiving, with her sitting at the end of the table. She would make turkey according to her grandmother's heavenly chicken recipe. The dressing would be made separately. The drumsticks would fall off at the slightest touch and yet the meat wouldn't be overdone. It would be moist, perfect.

She would remember all their birthdays and graduations and all the special events of their lives. People would marvel at how she did it. How she could carry the names and dates of so many grandchildren in her head.

And they would love her in that special way that grandchildren love grandmothers. That generation-removed way, where there was no need for discipline or nagging, just loving and spoiling and coddling. That's what grandmothers were for.

She would learn to knit and crochet so she could make all those lovely things that grandmothers make to be handed down to their children and their children's children. Pillowcases with tatting and tea towels with the days of the week embroidered on them.

They would call her Nana or Nana Nelly. She chuckled. She could hear the little ones struggle with that one. Nanelly. Nananally. Nanell. Or maybe just plain Grandma. Thirty, forty, fifty years from now. That would make her eighty-six. Forget seventy. At this rate she would certainly live till ninety. On her ninetieth birthday there would be a huge party. And she would tell them the miraculous story of her life. Of how lucky she had been at the age of thirty-six to have become part of this wonderful family. She would tell them how she had tried to have children of her own, tried to adopt, tried until children had become the most important thing in the world to her. How she had never dreamed that she, a childless woman, could become the mother, the grandmother, the great-grandmother of a big, fertile family.

There wouldn't be any shame or sadness to the story. No one would think there was anything wrong with her because she couldn't have children. People didn't look at grandmothers that way. Look at Rose Kennedy. You just couldn't imagine her in labor with all those kids. She was just The Grandmother. And nobody ever thought of grandmothers as barren or sterile. Just the opposite. She would be the Rose Kennedy of the Goodstein family.

She dropped by Brian's office to see if he was able to handle a little light lunch with her. A woman was sitting in a chair facing the desk.

"Oh, excuse me," Nelly said, backing out of the office. "I didn't know someone was with you."

The woman turned. It was Miriam. Nelly recognized her from the picture on Brian's desk.

"Nelly, this is Miriam," Brian said tensely.

"Oh, hi," Miriam said, standing up and extending her hand. "We were just talking about you."

"How do you do," Nelly said, taking Miriam's hand. Miriam smiled. Nelly liked her immediately. Why shouldn't she? After all, she was the mother of her children. She had B.J.'s straight nose, Caroline's warm brown silky hair, and Butch's dark blue eyes.

"Nelly, I've told Miriam about our plans to get married." He seemed tense and nervous. Like a lawyer whose client has just told him he was guilty after all.

"Congratulations. I wish you and Brian the best. I really do."

"Thank you," Nelly said. She was wondering if she should invite Miriam to the wedding. She seemed so nice. Why couldn't they be friends?

"Where are you planning on living?"

"Why, I don't know. I suppose the house in New Rochelle," she said, looking at Brian for assistance. He didn't say anything.

"It's a hell of a place to keep clean," Miriam said. "But then you can always keep Rosa on. She's terrific."

"Yes, she is terrific," Nelly said. Why would she want to get rid of Rosa?

"But isn't it going to be awfully big for just the two of you?"

"There'll be five altogether," Nelly said, surprised that someone who appeared as intelligent as Miriam couldn't count. "You know, what with the kids."

"The kids? You're not talking about my kids, are you?" Miriam asked. She was no longer smiling. "The kids will be living with me, of course."

"But I thought you didn't want them."

"What in the world gave you that idea?" She turned to Brian. "You're more than welcome to my husband and my house, but I'm sorry, my children are not part of the deal. Brian, how could you let this woman think I would ever give up those kids?"

Brian shrugged helplessly. "But I thought you wanted to start a whole new life. I thought you left them because you didn't want them anymore, that they wouldn't fit in."

"I am starting a new life," Miriam said. "I'm getting the divorce I should have gotten years ago. But I'm not throwing the babies out with Brian. Brian, of course, will have generous visitation rights—weekends, holidays, you know, that sort of thing."

"Brian, she can't do this, can she?" Nelly pleaded.

"I'm surprised that our legal mind here didn't explain that the court always awards custody of the children to the mother unless the mother proves unfit. And I assure you that I am not unfit. I really don't think that Brian wants to go through a long legal battle, especially when the chips are stacked against him, do you, Bri? I would venture to say that the fact that there has been a long-term affair going on and the correspondent has spent time in the home of the estranged wife even before the separation papers have been signed constitutes a lot of chips. Wouldn't you agree, Bri?"

"But you abandoned them," Nelly cried.

"I did what? I merely went to see my mother for a week. Brian knew that. The children knew that."

"They never even mentioned you."

"That's because they knew I was coming back. I've taken trips without them before. Why should they make a fuss?"

"Brian, say something," Nelly said, choking over her words.

"I don't know what to say," he said.

"But you told me," she sobbed.

"Well then, he lied to you," Miriam interjected. "He was lying to himself. Why shouldn't he lie to you as well?"

Suddenly Nelly wanted to kill this woman. Wanted to hurt her, to make her sorry, to make her cry. Wanted to make her understand what she was doing to Nelly. She wanted to explain about the children and the time she had spent with them and what they meant to her, and she couldn't speak. There were no words. And then there was no time. Miriam had left. And Nelly hadn't even seen her go.

Brian sat at his desk, holding his head with his hands. "What are we going to do?" he said.

"You're the lawyer, Brian," Nelly said in a strange, cold voice.

"Corporate law," he said. "I'm a little rusty on everything else. She does have every legal right to the kids. But I will get visitation rights. Weekends, holidays, maybe even long vacations in the summer. She's talking about moving to California. But I'll fight that. I don't think she can take the kids out of state without my permission. I'm not sure. I'll have to call a lawyer on that . . ."

Nelly wasn't listening to him. She was looking at a picture of herself sitting at a table. She was very old, very gray, and very gnarled. There was a huge turkey in front of her and several bowls of food around it. She was dishing out helpings onto plates. The camera pulled back and revealed that she was sitting at the end of a very long table. There were twenty chairs and they were all empty. The camera kept moving back slowly as Nelly kept dishing out food. A slice of turkey, a spoonful of cranberry sauce, sweet potatoes, mashed potatoes, dressing, and peas. A slice of turkey, a spoonful of cranberry sauce, sweet potatoes, mashed potatoes, dressing, and peas. A slice of turkey, a spoonful of cranberry sauce, sweet potatoes, mashed potatoes . . .

"Nelly, Nelly, talk to me."

Nelly looked at him strangely. "If you think you're getting the drumstick, you've got another thing coming," she snarled. And then she turned and walked out of the office.

Nelly called Dr. Abrams. He was away at an advanced TM course in Switzerland. She hung up the phone and stared at her fingernails.

Had she lost count? Or was the old system not operative anymore? That had been the fourth big blow, the last straw, the final insult. She knew she shouldn't have counted her children before the divorce proceedings. She knew she shouldn't have believed Brian so quickly. He had turned out to be as big a dreamer as she was. She knew exactly what her mistakes had been. But that didn't do any good. She was wrong again. Wronged again. Again, without a future to stand on. She was still childless.

Only now she was no longer expecting.

26   Leave of Absence

Nelly was not a quitter. Not by a long shot. Never one to throw in the towel, wave the white flag, or say uncle in the fat face of adversity. But neither was she a dummy. She knew about quitting while you're ahead.

She had done it in her marriage. Jordan would have continued trying to work things out for the rest of their lives. He had enjoyed working things out. Like he had gotten a kick out of fixing things around the house.

"I don't think it's going to work," Nelly had said.

She shouldn't have used the word *work*. To Jordan that was like yelling *charge!*

"Of course it's going to work," he had enthused. "We'll make it work," he said, as if he were about to attack a 1950 Bendix washer.

But Nelly knew better, and she got out while the getting was good.

Maybe she couldn't quit while she was ahead now, but at least she could cut her losses. She didn't even bother to add them up: the months of planning, preparing, plotting, scheming, pushing, pushing, pushing to be a mother. No, it was no good to look back. In fact it was impossible to look back.

It was too excruciatingly, unbearably, impossibly painful.

She could have easily stayed home and cried for a week, but she refused to give in to that.

As things turned out, it might have been better if she had given herself at least a couple of days.

214

But she shut the door firmly and forever on the nursery of her dreams.

Like any other normal human being, she had in the past been forced to give up certain unrealistic dreams, abandon impossible expectations. But there were always new ones to take their place. This time she was swearing off a dream, but she was doing it cold turkey.

And, unfortunately, there was no such thing as a methadone program for mother addicts.

So she turned her back on all the children she never had and never would have and faced what was now the black-and-white small-screen world of her reality.

First, she coldly calculated her assets. She was, after all, the woman Abby once said had everything. She had a lovely apartment, tastefully furnished, with an enviable view of the park. She had a closet full of very expensive, mostly designer clothes. She had her weight under control. She had a car with very little mileage on it, a checking account with free checking, in addition to some sixty thousand dollars in certificates of deposit. She had investments in a cable TV company, municipal bonds, and a share in a dairy farm which was a terrific tax shelter. She had her health, her good looks, and all her teeth, although the spirit of four molars had long since departed through root canal. She had a ladies' Rolex watch and half of her grandmother's antique jewelry. She had a set of loving, thank God still living parents; a group of good and interesting friends; and a terrific, challenging job, a job for which many women would give their right arms. What more could she ask for? For once she didn't even bother answering her own question.

For the first time in a long time, Nelly was using her head exclusively. Just as well. Her heart was temporarily out of commission. It was as though she had sent it out for repairs and told them that she was in no rush to get it back.

She assured herself that she was back on track, back in the driver's seat, back in full control of her own destiny. Or so she thought.

She had forgotten how feelings had a way of sneaking up behind you when your back was turned . . .

It was the first of November, the day they finalized the news features for the upcoming month. Ben asked her to wait after the meeting.

"Brooks Abernathy called me," Ben said. Abernathy was head of network news. "It seems they have their eye on you for that news magazine show."

"Really?" Nelly said.

"Well, let me put it this way. They're narrowing down the candidates. They've probably got the list down to a manageable six hundred. Anyway, he wanted to know about you—how you were to work with, what I thought about your abilities, whether or not I thought you'd be willing to cut your hair and wear glasses. You know, important stuff like that."

"What did you tell him?"

"I told him you wouldn't cut your hair, you look terrible in glasses, and that you were an impossible prima donna."

"You didn't."

"No, I didn't. I, in my considerate, unselfish way, ever-mindful of your career, gave you a terrific recommendation."

"I will remember you long after I'm rich and famous," Nelly promised.

"You know, Nelly, they're going to do a lot of soft news."

"I understood that there would be some very exciting investigative stuff," Nelly said.

"I really think you ought to think twice about taking it if they offer it to you."

"Think twice about making three times as much money and having national exposure?"

"It's taking a big chance. The show may not go. They may decide after six weeks that you're not right for it. Look at what happened to Sally Jameson."

"Who? I never heard of her."

"Exactly my point. Anyway, I would think it over if I were you. I would hate like hell to lose you."

"Ah-ha!" Nelly said.

"Remember, they haven't made up their minds yet. They'll be keeping their eye on you for the next few months. Just don't get your hopes up."

"Oh, don't worry about that," Nelly assured him. "I'm not counting any chickens."

"See you tonight," Ben said as she was leaving.

"Tonight? What's tonight?"

"The annual affiliates dinner. Did you forget?"

"No. Why should I forget?"

It had been exactly a year ago. Just another drunken sales meeting. Except this one had started her off on her unholy pilgrimage to motherhood. It was the night of the man from KWRZ, Albuquerque. Funny how she still recalled his call letters. She wondered if they had some special significance. It was an evening she would like to forget. But then she didn't remember that much of it anyway. Just a lot of champagne.

Well, she would stay away from the champagne tonight. And she would stay away from good old KWRZ. She had bigger fish to fry. Tonight was a good evening to make friends and influence the network biggies who were involved in putting together the new show.

Things were going great. Despite herself Nelly was excited about the new job possibility. But she wasn't going to get carried away. It was a big deal even to be considered for the position. She knew that even if she didn't get it, her value had been greatly increased in Ben's eyes. She could look forward to more and better assignments, maybe eventually an anchor position on the evening news. No question about it, big things were happening. She could hardly be blamed for not noticing the little things. The strange little things.

She took special care in dressing for the evening. She wore a full-length black velvet dress with long sleeves, a high neck, and a side slit that went up almost to her hipbone, with nothing underneath but Christian Dior dotted sheer pantyhose and very sexy, very high sling-back Charles Jourdan shoes. Her hair was swept up on top of her head in a loose French knot, with a few ends artfully falling free. She spent an hour on her makeup, painstakingly applying it so that it looked like she wasn't wearing any at all: the softest gray shadow with the thinnest gray pencil line to accentuate the blue of her eyes. She knew she looked smashing.

In order to avoid KWRZ, she arrived after the cocktail party in time for the big sit-down dinner. It was difficult to avoid someone when you didn't remember what he looked like. As it turned out, Nelly didn't have to worry about recognizing the man from Albuquerque. She was seated right next to him. His place card clearly identified him: Pat Tiernan, KWRZ, Albuquerque.

She had chalked up that evening a year ago to too much champagne and an unexpected attack of hot pants. Seeing him again made her realize that it had been something more. A lot more. First of all, he was probably the best-looking man she had ever laid eyes on. He had thick, prematurely gun-metal-gray hair that was cut short and stuck out in cowlicks in three different places. As light as his hair was, his dense brows and absurdly long lashes were a dark sable brown. They served to bring unneccessary attention to the warmest green eyes Nelly had ever seen. She had never thought of green eyes as being warm, but his had soft gold flecks in them. They literally shone. He had a straight, strong nose, a soft wide mouth with an upper lip that protruded slightly over the lower one à la Paul Newman. He was a big man with big hands and sturdy, square fingers.

When he smiled, his eyes crinkled up and a dimple appeared out of nowhere on his right cheek. His teeth were so flawless they appeared capped, but on closer inspection Nelly could see that they weren't. He was dressed in a tuxedo that must have been in fashion the night Buddy Holly died. The sleeves stopped three inches short of his wrists as though he were still growing.

Best of all, he was horribly, awkwardly shy. He actually blushed when Nelly sat down next to him. He kept smiling and clearing his throat and turning his dinner fork over and over as if he had never seen an eating utensil before. He had a very snappy opening, too:

"Hi, remember me?" he asked, almost as if he expected her not to. The evening of a year ago came back to her now in bits and pieces. He was married, very happily married, and the father, very much the father of nine, count

217

them, nine children. Clearly, hopping into bed with Nelly that night had been a highly unusual experience for him.

He was Catholic to the core and Nelly had found him charming beyond belief. Totally unobtainable, unpolished, inexperienced, and irresistible. She remembered now when they made love he had asked her if he was hurting her, as if she were a thirteen-year-old virgin with a back problem. She remembered his body: strong and long but not overly muscled, with dark silky hair that fanned out beautifully across his chest and stomach.

She even remembered his penis: a veritable pillar in a community of cocks.

"I was sort of hoping I'd see you again this year," he said, knocking his drink over on the table. Nelly handed him her napkin to soak up the spill. She was mesmerized. "I, uh, really enjoyed myself at last year's meeting." She realized that this was as close as the man probably ever got to an innuendo.

"Me too," Nelly said. She was sitting sideways in her chair, facing him. He was getting noticeably more uncomfortable. He picked up his fork again, examined the tongs, turned it over and placed it back on the table. It fell on the floor. He picked it up, leaned back in his chair, crossed his legs and accidentally kicked her foot.

"Oh, 'scuse me," he said.

"That's okay," Nelly smiled. He uncrossed his leg to get it out of the way of her foot and, in doing so, he kicked her again.

"Jesus," he muttered to himself. If he had had a handkerchief in his pocket, he probably would have mopped his forehead at that moment. He looked around the room. He was thinking, carefully forming his next remark.

"Sure are a lot of people this year," he said finally.

"Sure are," Nelly agreed.

She was throbbing. She literally felt her vagina opening and closing as if it were trying to speak, trying to get in on the conversation.

"Hi Nelly, how are you doing?" A man passed behind her chair and touched her shoulder.

Nelly looked back. "Oh, hi," she said absentmindedly to the tall, distinguished-looking gentleman in the superbly cut tuxedo. He looked familiar but she couldn't for the life of her place him. She turned her attention back to Pat Tiernan. There was some kind of incredible magnetic current that was being transmitted back and forth between their two chairs.

"That was Brooks Abernathy, wasn't it?" Tiernan asked.

"Was it?" Nelly asked, not taking her eyes off his.

"You look very pretty," he said.

"I have to go home now," Nelly said. His face fell.

"Oh no. Really? Can't you stay?" He had a look of utter disappointment on his face.

218

"No, I can't stay. I have to go home," she repeated. "And you have to go home with me." His mouth fell open.

"I do?" He was confused.

"Yes," she said, taking one of his huge hands in hers. It must have weighed at least ten pounds. "Yes, you do," she said, squeezing his hand.

"Oh! Okay," he grinned, finally getting it. "I guess I do. I guess that's what I have to do, all right. Yep." He got up to help Nelly out of her chair. His feet got caught up in his napkin, which had dropped to the floor.

Nelly took him by the hand and, looking straight ahead, led him out of the ballroom just as the president of the network was getting to the hot part of his "How We Won The Ratings War" speech.

She had no idea of what she was doing with this man or why she was doing it. It was like the red salmon swimming upstream. It defied logic. It was purely instinctual.

They went to bed without a word. He was sweet, kind, and considerate. The sex was warm, wholesome, and uncomplicated.

Before either of them realized, it was almost dawn. They had just finished making love for the fourth time. Nelly rubbed her chin across the silky hair on his chest and whispered in his ear: "Again."

"Again?" he asked with amazement.

"Yes, please," Nelly begged, "just once more."

"Okay," he said, giving her shoulder a friendly squeeze. "Just one more time and that's it." It seemed extremely odd to him but it seemed to make her happy, so he took a deep breath and plunged ahead.

"Okay, there's Shannon—she's the oldest, she's twelve. Then there's Carey she's ten. Then there's Ryan, age nine. Kelly, he's eight. Catherine, she's seven. Joseph is six. The twins, Stacey and Steven—they're five. And the baby, Patrick, is two. That's the nine of them."

He'd already gone through the list several times during the night. She even had him whisper the names in her ear as they made love. In fact, they had talked about nothing else. Not about her, not about him, not even about television. Just his children. How old they were, their names what they looked like, what they liked to do. how they got along with each other. He really didn't mind talking about them. It just seemed odd.

"One more time, please," Nelly coaxed, "and then we'll go to sleep."

"It's silly," he protested.

"No, it's not. I just like hearing the names."

"Okay," he yawned and started at the other end. "There's Patrick, he's the baby, he's two. Then come the twins, Stacey and Steven . . ."

"That's a boy and a girl, right?" Nelly asked.

"Right. Stacey and Steven are five. Then there's Joseph who is six . . ."

Nelly was mouthing the names along with him. She had them memorized by now. Her eyes closed and she fell into a deep, dreamless sleep.

By the time she woke late in the morning, he was gone. A lovely man, she thought. A real family man.

She gave no more thought to him or to the evening or even to the names of his children. She just put the whole thing out of ther head and went on about her work. She was, after all, a professional. She knew how to focus her attention and energies. She covered the news.

Being in front of the camera all the time, Nelly was not that well versed in the behind-the-scenes technical aspects of her profession. If she had been, she might have understood what was happening to her.

Nelly's head had been tuned in for far too long to one channel, to one continuous program called "The Mother-Child Show." She had, indeed, recently switched channels, but she had no way of knowing how strong the transmission was from the previous program.

In the business they call it TVI, television frequency interference, when one station overlaps or leaks into another. It's a common problem, easily remedied by the filter that is found in most television sets. So most television viewers never even experience TVI. Nelly wasn't a television set. She didn't have a filter.

The weeks went by fairly uneventfully. She heard they had narrowed down even further on the number of candidates for the news magazine show. She heard she was still in the running. It was the day before Thanksgiving and Molly Daniels, the show's home economist, was doing a short piece on turkeys: the difference between butterball, self-basting, injected, and fresh. She finished up and the anchorman gave Nelly's cue.

"And now, to talk turkey about the proposed federal tax cut, is Nelly Diamond."

Nelly wasn't listening. She was thinking about turkeys.

It was only a matter of fifteen seconds. But fifteen seconds is a long time on a half-hour news show. The anchorman had to repeat his cue. And the stage manager waved his arms wildly above his head, trying to get her attention. She snapped out of it and managed, by rushing, to finish her tax story in time.

A week later Joe Williams was doing a story about a man in New Jersey who had killed his wife and three kids and then shot himself.

"The bastard," Nelly whispered. Her mike was off but she said it loud enough so that it was picked up on Joe's.

They were just little things. Things that happened when you weren't concentrating or you were concentrating too hard on something else. Little slips like when she quoted a statement made by the First Lady:

"I think my husband has had a very good pregnancy," Nelly read, "not perfect, but certainly free from the kinds of problems that plagued the previous pregnancy."

The news team laughed. That should have clued Nelly in to her slip. But she looked up startled, not knowing what they were laughing at. A harmless mistake. Good for a laugh. Nothing to make a big issue of.

The big issue came the afternoon of the bank robbery.

Nelly was sent out with the mobile crew to cover it. It was still in progress. The bank robber was holding twenty-five people hostage. It was a big story.

First Nelly talked to the detective captain in charge to get background while the guys hooked up the cable.

"The perpetrator's a real jerk-off," the detective said. "He doesn't go for one of the tellers, mind you, like a normal bank robber. Oh, no. He goes for the cash machine. And this is while the bank is still open. The guard sees him trying to pry open the cash cylinder with a crowbar. Of course he can't make a dent on it. It's solid steel. So he goes into a real frenzy, breaking windows and stuff. Naturally by this time the guard has walked over with his gun out to make an arrest. That's when the guy opens his jacket, shows he's got dynamite taped all around him with wires, the whole schmere. Says he'll blow the place up and everyone in it." The captain sighed as though this were a boring story he was tired of telling. "So now he's got twenty-five people in there and he's been holding 'em hostage for four hours. Says he'll push the plunger if we don't give him what he wants."

"What does he want?"

"Ready for this? He wants to talk to Golda Meir."

"But Golda Meir is dead."

"That's not my fault," the captain said. "Anyway, he says he'll only talk to her. Naturally he's given us a deadline." The captain looked at his watch. "We've got two hours to go. Meanwhile, we've got the wife here. She's been trying to talk some sense into him. But how do you talk sense into a squirrel?"

Nelly went over to her crew. "Guys, can you get a shot of the inside of the bank?"

"No way," Jack, the cameraman, explained. "We can't get that close."

"Okay, do me this then: give me a long establishing shot of the exterior of the bank with the crowd and cops over there, and then I want you to cut into a two-shot of me and the wife."

"You think you can get her to talk to you?" Jack asked.

"Does a bear . . ."

"Okay, okay," Jack said. "I got it. Pro-ceed."

The bank robber's wife was surrounded by six or seven police officers. She was a sweet-looking woman in her late twenties. She was wearing a man's leather jacket that was miles too big for her over some sort of housedress and a pair of worn-down bedroom slippers. Her hair was extremely long. She wore it tied back but still it almost came down to her waist. She had a strange, lost look on her face, as though she had just landed at the wrong airport in the wrong country.

Nelly pushed her way through.

"Excuse me, ma'am, I'm Nelly Diamond, WABC News. Can I talk to you for a few minutes?"

The bank robber's wife turned to Nelly and smiled in relief as though Nelly was a long-lost friend or a ground hostess who had come to tell her how to get the next plane home.

"Oh sure. Hi, howaya?" the woman said. This was going to be easy, Nelly thought. And if she could get some air time with the woman, it would be a real coup.

"I'd like to get you on the air, Mrs. . . . ?"

"Mrs. Schnabel. Moishe Schnabel. That's the thing, see. We're Jewish. Have you ever heard of a Jewish bank robber?" she asked, rolling her eyes toward the heavens. "My mother's gonna die. Of course, she's in Detroit. Does Detroit get you?"

"No," Nelly answered, "this is only for the New York—New Jersey area."

"Oh." The woman was eyeing Jack, who stood ready with his camera. She was obviously tempted to talk.

"See, Mrs. Schnabel, it might help if people could understand your husband's motives. There have been so many bank robberies lately. And it could actually be very good for the Jews," Nelly threw in, not knowing exactly what she meant by that.

"Well, I don't know. My hair," she said, reaching almost absentmindedly to her head as if to make sure she was still wearing it.

"I could lend you my brush," Nelly said, reaching into her shoulder bag.

"That's very nice of you. I just washed it, it's clean," she assured Nelly. She took the brush and, undoing the barrette that held her hair together, she leaned down and began furiously back-brushing her hair in the manner prescribed by beauty magazines. She counted each stroke softly.

Nelly leaned down to continue the conversation through Mrs. Schnabel's thick curtain of hair.

"Fourteen, fifteen, sixteen," Mrs. Schnabel was counting.

"The kind of questions I'll ask you, Mrs. Schnabel, are these: Why your husband wanted to rob a bank? Does he really have explosives on him? Does he really intend using them? Why does he want to talk to Golda Meir? What sort of person he is, in general."

Mrs. Schnabel peered through her hair. "Gotcha," she said, and went back to her hundred strokes. "Twenty-seven, twenty-eight, twenty-nine, thirty, thirty-one, thirty-two, thirty-three . . ."

Nelly signaled for Jack to get ready for the two-shot. Her earphones told her that the station was ready anytime she was.

222

This was real. This was live. This was news. This was what Nelly Diamond excelled at.

She leaned down again. "Okay, Mrs. Schnabel?"

Mrs. Schnabel threw her hair back, almost unbalancing herself by the thrust and weight of it.

She pulled her hair back and refastened the barrette. Out of the corner of her eye Nelly saw a SWAT team moving carefully along the side of the bank. Things could start getting crazy.

"Ready, Mrs. Schnabel?"

"Just let me get rid of this old jacket," the woman said. She turned away and Nelly saw that it was a jacket that must have belonged to her husband. It had the words *Hell's Hebes* embroidered in sequins on the back.

She was cued in from the station. The lights were on. The sound man gave her the signal. Nelly faced the camera.

"This is Nelly Diamond, outside the Citibank at Seventy-second and Broadway, where alleged bank robber Moishe Schnabel is holding twenty-five people hostage inside. At about one-thirty this afternoon, Schnabel was caught trying to break into one of the automatic cash machines. At that time he revealed the fact that he has explosives taped to his body and threatened to blow up the bank and everyone in it if his demands aren't met. So far his only demand is a personal interview with Israeli ex-Premier Golda Meir, who passed away some time ago. With me here now is Mr. Schnabel's wife. We're hoping she can shed some light on her husband's rather bizarre behavior." Nelly turned with the mike toward Mrs. Schnabel, who, having removed her leather jacket, stood hands clasped behind her back, smiling like a schoolgirl.

For the first time Nelly noticed the belly. The big, wide-screen belly. Mrs. Schnabel looked as if she was not eight, not nine, but ten months pregnant.

As Jack moved the camera in for an even tighter close-up of the two women, something clicked in Nelly's head and her mind drifted off to another channel.

"Let me ask you this, Mrs. Schnabel, how many months along are you?" Nelly said, passing the mike closer to the other woman.

The bank robber's wife looked confused. She glanced down at her belly and then back up at Nelly.

"Uh, oh, I'm due next week is what the doctor says."

"Is this your first baby?"

"Yes, it is. My first," Mrs. Schnabel said, obviously warming up to the subject. This was a lot easier than talking about her *meshuggener* husband.

"Are you having natural childbirth?"

"Well, I didn't take any of the lessons, ya see. And I guess it's kinda late to sign up."

The questions Nelly asked were perfectly normal questions, the kind one would ask of any expectant mother. But not normal of an expectant mother whose husband was holding twenty-five people hostage inside a bank, threatening to blow them to smithereens.

The station control was stymied. They had no idea where this line of questioning was going. Perhaps that was why they didn't cut her off immediately.

"Are you hoping for a boy or a girl?" Nelly asked.

"I don't care," Mrs. Schnabel said, "just so long as it ain't no bank robber." The mention of bank robber should have cued Nelly in, but it didn't.

The cameraman, not getting a signal to cut off, had no other choice than to continue filming. The sound man couldn't believe his earphones. Back at the station they finally made the decision to terminate the broadcast when Nelly and the woman got into a discussion about the benefits of cloth diapers vs. Pampers.

Pampers was one of the show's sponsors.

"Nelly," Ben screamed shortly afterward, back at the station, "what in the hell is going on with you? That was the first time in all my years as a producer that I had to cut off a live braodcast! A fucking bank robber's wife, and you're discussing diapers! What in God's name were you thinking of? What do you think, this is "Saturday Night Live" or something? Are you trying to commit professional suicide? Answer me!"

But Nelly had no answers. How could she explain to him that she had just experienced technical difficulties due to circumstances beyond her control? She stood there shaking her head.

"Listen, I can't begin to understand what's going on in that lovely head of yours," Ben said finally. "But I do know one thing. You're about to screw up what until now has been a very promising career. And I, for one, am not about to let you do it. Here's what I want you to do: I want you to take some time off, see a shrink, take a trip, do whatever it is you have to do to get your head together. I've already notified management that you're taking a leave of absence."

"Oh, no!" Nelly cried. "I can't leave now. I need to work."

Ben ignored her, making notes on a schedule. "Take however much time you need. A month, two months. But I don't want to see you back here before the first of the year, minimum." He glanced at Nelly. There was a look of sheer horror on her face. He got up and put his arm around her shoulders.

"Come on, Nelly-girl, this isn't the end of the world. I'm not firing you. I can't fire you. You've got too damn many fans. I happen to be one of them."

A leave of absence. Just when she needed, desperately needed, to work. Needed something to pour herself into. But Ben was right. She had screwed up, screwed up terribly. She was lucky he hadn't fired her. She didn't know what was the matter with her, but she was going to find out and fix it.

She called Dr. Abrams for an appointment. He had just returned from TM camp in Switzerland and sounded happy to hear from her. He had a free hour first thing the next morning.

"I hate to resort to terminology," Dr. Abrams said after Nelly had brought him up to date, "but that's what I would call your typical obsessive-compulsive behavior." Nelly couldn't understand what Abrams had against using terminology. Just giving a label to what she had been going through made her feel so much better. She wondered if there were a pill for obsessive-compulsive behavior.

"What do I do for it?" she asked.

"Well, my first suggestion would be TM just as a calming influence. But before you get into meditating, you've got to get yourself into a tranquil, sensitized, receptive state."

"How do I do that?" she asked.

"You just do it, that's all."

"But I don't . . ." Nelly started to cry.

"Stop that," Dr. Abrams ordered. "Give me your hand." Nelly extended her hand. Abrams took it in his and then brought his other hand down hard on the back of hers.

"Ouch!" Nelly yelped. "Why'd you do that?"

"You're acting like a child. So I'm treating you like a child. A spoiled child. You can't get something you want and you just won't accept it like an adult. You try and get pregnant, you throw yourself into adoption, you get involved with another woman's children, and God knows what else. Then you mess up with your job. Now that's what I call stupid, childish behavior. Just because you can't be a mother doesn't entitle you to behave this way. There are a lot of people who aren't mothers. Worthwhile, effective people."

"Name six," Nelly snapped.

"I'm not going to engage in your immature games. I want you to snap out of this. Stop feeling sorry for yourself. Get involved with other things. Start thinking about other people for a change. Your friends, your family. Get yourself a hobby . . ."

"I liked it better when we were talking terminology," Nelly interrupted. "Is that part of your assertiveness training?" she asked, remembering what he had been into the last time she saw him almost a year ago.

"No, it's good, sound advice," he said. "It's the kind of advice my mother gave me when I was a child."

For the first time, Nelly didn't feel a hell of a lot better after a session with Dr. Abrams. She thought about trying another shrink, but decided against it. The idea of starting from scratch with someone totally new just exhausted her.

Besides, she liked Dr. Abrams. She trusted him. He had to know what was best for her, didn't he?

Ben had said she couldn't come back to work until after the first of the year. What was she going to do until then? It was only the tenth of December. Well, she would try to take Abrams's advice. Get involved with her friends, her family, do things, see people. Anything to get herself together and certainly anything to avoid having to take up, of all things, a hobby.

No, she would get a good, strong, solid, Nelly Diamond grip on herself.

If only she didn't feel so tired. So very tired.

27 Friends and Family

In her early years in New York, Nelly had collected friends like a squirrel collects nuts, as protection against the legendary loneliness of the big city. She had a million of them, it seemed.

Close friends, casual friends, professional friends, passing through-town friends, neighbor friends, summer friends, women friends, men friends. She knew so many people that she had to rotate them, and by the time she got back to seeing someone, so much time had elapsed that they had to start getting acquainted all over again. Many times she had to see them in groups in order to see them at all. She found that she had so many friends she had no one to talk to. So she narrowed down the number of friends and fattened up the relationships of those that remained.

She realized now, as she hadn't realized with her job, that these past several months had been very hard on her friendships. She had been thinking only of herself, of herself as a prospective mother. She had spent very little real time and given very little attention to her friends and their problems. She hadn't bothered to try to understand Paisley's sudden need to marry the vice cop, or Abby's involvement with Clark, or Clark's involvement with himself or Tyler's need to be a mother. Nelly made a vow to make amends and make strong again the special friendships that she had nurtured and maintained over the years.

She called Paisley for lunch.

"Let's go someplace extravagantly expensive. Someplace so chic even you haven't been there."

"*D'accord*," said Paisley, obviously pleased by Nelly's suggestion. It never occurred to Nelly to say, just you and me. She had assumed Paisley would know that this was to be just the two of them, just the girls, just like in the old days.

Nelly realized she should have suspected something when Paisley suggested Al's Steak House. It didn't sound that expensive and certainly not that chic. She met Paisley in the foyer. Nelly looked around the restaurant. There were carcasses of dead steer hanging in the window, pictures of beaten-up boxers hanging on the walls and there was sawdust on the floor. Definitely not Paisley's kind of place. So Nelly wasn't surprised when Joe walked in a few minutes later.

She waited patiently while they kissed hello. They continued the kiss. Nelly continued to wait. She began to feel silly so she turned her back to give them privacy, which seemed a little ridiculous, considering they were standing in the middle of a restaurant foyer.

Finally, after having given them what she assumed was ample time to break their clench, she turned back again. They were still kissing. Was this the same kiss or had they started a new one while her back was turned? Joe was running his hands slowly up and down Paisley's arched spine. Nelly leaned close to Joe's ear and whispered:

"Hey, kids. It's soup. Got to keep up the old strength."

They broke apart, smiling and gasping for air. Nelly wondered if she should ask the waiter to screen their table. Could they get through lunch without being arrested for *in flagrante delicto*? She would just have to rely on Joe's discretion. After all, he was the vice expert.

"Let's have lamb chops," Paisley said, "Joe loves lamb chops."

The lamb chops were served blood rare on a bed of congealed fat. Nelly gagged. She tried to eat her salad, but the big lumps of Roquefort got stuck in her throat. No one seemed that interested in the food. Paisley chattered on and on except for long lapses of silence, when Joe took to stroking her wrist. (Oh, no. Not the wrist, Nelly thought. Not here.)

Joe said hardly a word. He just sat and smiled in admiration and adoration at everything that came out of Paisley's mouth. She described their forthcoming wedding (the Pierre), their china and silver patterns (Tiffany's), the house they were moving to in Darien (for the school system), and the place they were going to buy in Palm Springs (Joe loves the beach). It was basically a blow-by-blow description of the rest of their lives, including how many kids they were having (two, possibly three) and the color of Cadillac (Joe believes in the American Car) they were going to get.

"He's doing his best to spend all my money," she said, beaming at Joe proudly, "but he just doesn't know where to begin, do you, sweetheart?"

Joe grinned and shook his head. To his credit, he seemed genuinely embarrassed. And Paisley seemed genuinely happy. Happier than Nelly had ever seen her before.

228

"How's the boyfriend?" Joe said, finally able to pull his eyes away from Paisley.

"What boyfriend?" Nelly asked.

"The guy with the three kids. Paisley told me you were gonna take the big plunge. Congratulations."

"Oh, that's off," Nelly said quickly.

"Nelly, I'm so sorry," Paisley said sympathetically.

"Don't be sorry."

Joe took Nelly's hand in both of his big paws and squeezed it softly. "I got a couple of buddies on the loose. Howdja like me to fix you up?" he asked.

"No, thanks. Thanks, no," Nelly said.

"I'm really, truly sorry Nelly," Paisley said again. There was a look of real concern on her face. Who did she think she was, Nelly thought, sitting there so sanctimoniously, as though she were the better half of the couple of the year. She who had gone through more men, more marriages, and more abortions than anybody Nelly knew. She, of all people, was feeling sorry for Nelly, because Nelly didn't have a big strapping man in her life. She wasn't getting married. She didn't have a china pattern, or a house picked out in the suburbs, or a Cadillac on the way.

Nelly couldn't get out of there fast enough. The lunch had not only physically nauseated her but had put her into a terrible funk. She felt like taking herself to a movie, but she was too tired. Why was she so tired all the time?

Brian called her in the late afternoon.

"I tried to get you at the studio," he said, "but they told me you were on a leave of absence. Are you sick?"

"No, I'm not sick. I just need to take a little rest," she said.

"He cleared his throat. "Nelly, I wanted to call you and explain."

"Explain what?" Nelly sighed. How you managed to pass the law boards with a moron's grasp of basic domestic law? she thought. She wanted very much to ask about the kids. But she wanted just as much to avoid the whole subject.

"I've been to Shapiro three times this week already," Brian was saying.

"And . . ." Nelly prodded.

"And this hasn't been easy for me. In fact, this has probably been the worst week of my life." He waited for that to sink in. Nelly had no comment. "First of all, I feel as though I let you down terribly." He said it as though saying it would make it all better.

Again, Nelly had no comment. Letting her down was not exactly how she herself would have phrased it. Fucked her over was more like it, she thought. Brian continued on to point number two.

"Second of all, I've realized some very important things about myself." Again, he paused. He seemed to be waiting for her to say: "Really! How fascinating! Do tell all." She didn't say a word. She knew she was making it difficult for him. She knew she was being cold and cruel. She couldn't help it. She felt cold and cruel.

"I discovered, number one, that I am a family man."

Nelly wondered if Brian realized that he was starting a new list without finishing the old one. According to her count, he should be at number two-A.

"Number two," Brian was saying.

"That's B," Nelly interjected.

"What?"

"B. You were on two when you started subcategorizing about all the things you learned about yourself. Two-A would have been, you're a family man. That makes this two-B."

"Nelly, if you're gong to take that tone with me, it will make it impossible for me to go on."

"Sorry," Nelly said, "go on."

Annoyed as he was with her interruption, Brian fell into her count.

"B: I am a family man whose family whose children are more important to me than anything else in the world. C: My feelings for Miriam go much deeper than I ever knew. When I found out that she was leaving me, that she really wanted a divorce, I realized that I didn't want to lose her. I can't throw away ten years of marriage just like that. And she is, after all, the mother of my children. And D," Brian said, taking a deep breath, "she's pregnant again."

Nelly didn't bother asking how that happened.

"Okay," was all she could think of to say.

"Okay? What do you mean, okay?" Brian demanded. "How do you feel about all this? You must feel something. You must have something to say."

"Who wants to know, you or Shapiro?" she asked.

"I do."

"Let me think. No," she said after a minute. "I don't feel anything." This was a man she had carried on an affair with through two years of the worst restaurants anyone had ever had the misfortune to eat at. This was a man that she had once cared for. She had cared for his children. But she felt nothing. Nothing at all. Except that she wanted desperately to get off the phone and take a nice long nap. Brian was still talking. Already onto point number three-A when Nelly hung up the phone.

She felt much better after her nap and, adhering to her resolve to get in touch with old friends, she called Abby.

It was difficult to hear her. Jane and Jill were shrieking and giggling in the background and in the foreground Nelly could hear Jada, the new baby, crying.

"Do you have to feed the baby?" Nelly asked. "I can call back later."

"No, I fed her. She's just expressing her dissatisfaction with the menu. She's on the bottle now and she doesn't love it. Just a second, Nelly. Jill, Jane," Abby roared, "I told you: no Crayolas on the floor. Now take that stuff up to your room."

Nelly was always amazed at how such a big voice could come from such a small woman.

"Hi, sorry. What were you saying?" Abby asked.

"I'd gotten as far as hello, I think."

Abby was roaring again. "Jane, get that Crayola out of your nose. You'll hurt yourself. Sorry, Nelly."

"Why don't you take some time off and come to the city? We'll have lunch or something."

"I can't, Nelly. I'm trying to get ready for our trip. We're leaving the day after tomorrow."

"What trip? Where are you going?"

"Jeff and I are going to Puerto Rico for a week. That's why I had to get Jada used to the bottle so quick. Hold on a sec." Her voice took on a menacing tone. "Jill, I don't listen to your conversations when you're talking to your friends. I don't think it's fair that you should listen to mine. That's not respecting a person's privacy. Now, do me a huge favor and take your sister upstairs." Abby came back to the phone and lowered her voice. "You-know-what is kaput between you-know-who and ours-yay uly-tray."

Nelly didn't have the decipher for Abby's code.

"Abby, I'm not understanding you. Could you be a little more specific? Like, English?"

"Little pitchers," Abby said.

"Well, that really clears it up."

"Wait, don't say anything. Just listen a minute." There was a long silence. Nelly could hear herself breathing. Then she could hear Abby breathing. And then she could hear the loud adenoidal breathing of two young noses.

"Jane, Jill. Hang up the phone this minute," Abby screamed upstairs. There was another long silence, broken only by the four noses breathing.

"I'm warning you," Abby shrieked. There was a muffled giggling and then a click.

"Anyway," Abby continued in a calm voice, "Clark and I are finished. It's over. Finito."

"What happened?"

"I'd say basically it was a sexual problem. Remember I told you how crazy he was about my belly when I was carrying Jada?"

"Right."

"Well, when I lost my belly, he lost his lust. Anyway, it made me see what a terrific, sexually mature person I had in Jeff. It's not that I regret the affair, mind you. I'm just sorry I had it with a big baby. So anyway, we're having sort of a second honeymoon, Jeff and I."

"Who's going to stay with the kids?"

"I've got a programmer coming in."

"A what?"

"A Pro-Gramma. Professional Grandma. You must have read about them. It's a big business. They do baby-sitting, knitting, baking from scratch, that sort of thing."

"Well, have a terrific time," Nelly said, "and I'll talk to you when you get back." When Nelly hung up, she had the feeling she had forgotten something. Then she remembered what it was. She had forgotten to talk about herself. And Abby had forgotten to ask.

It wasn't that late and she was restless. She had a sudden urge to see Tyler. When he slid open the door to his loft, he was wearing nothing but cowboy boots. Nelly thought she had interrupted him at his work. She hadn't.

"I'm taking your advice," he said softly.

"What's that?" she asked.

"Doing it the traditional way."

She still thought he was talking about art. "Doing what the traditional way?"

"You know, gettin' pregnant."

"Oh," Nelly looked beyond him. She could see the feet of the potential mother-to-be draped over the edge of Tyler's platform bed.

"Well, good luck," she said.

She was running low on friends. She called Clark the next morning. His answering machine left a number where Clark could be reached. She called the number.

"Hi, you're just in time for visitng hours," Clark said. "Come on over."

"Where are you?"

"Payne Whitney, Bellevue for the Beautiful People."

"I'll be right over."

Clark's room looked more like a class-A hotel instead of a place in a nut house. There was a desk, a typewriter, two matching overstuffed chairs, a coffee table, a floor lamp, and a console TV. Clark was sitting on the bed, dressed in a maroon silk dressing gown with black satin lapels that looked as if it had come right off George Brent's back. He was working on his bottle-cap collection.

"How are you feeling?" Nelly asked with concern.

"Never better. Never better," Clark boomed.

"Then why are you here?"

"I got smart. Booked way in advance. This is peak season at Payne Whitney, what with the Christmas holidays coming up. If I'd waited till the last minute, I would never have gotten a room. Let alone a corner room," he said, making a grand gesture with his arm.

"Are you having a breakdown or something?"

"I don't have breakdowns per se. I have phases. This happens to be my manic, as in manic-depressive, phase. Now most manic-depressives make the mistake of checking in during their depressed cycle. But then they get no pleasure out of the benefits of hospital life: round-the-clock room service, the newest medications, concerned doctors, caring nurses, peace, quiet—what more could I ask for? I'd be a fool to waste all this on depression. And it certainly beats going to Puerto Rico."

"Speaking of Puerto Rico," they both said at once.

"Go on. Speak of Puerto Rico," they both said at once.

"Go on. Speak of Puerto Rico," Clark said. "Talk to me of plantains, suntans, and San Juans." Nelly had never seen Clark cheerier.

"Well actually, I was speaking of Abby. She and Jeff are going to Puerto Rico for a week. I thought maybe your affair being over had something to do with you being in the hospital."

"Not in the slightest. What's over is over. What's done is done. 'We shall not pass this way again.' She *was* my ultimate mother figure," he sighed. He eyed Nelly. "As long as you're here," he said, "how does a little therapeutic sex strike you?"

"I'll pass," said Nelly. "But speaking of sex, I understand your attraction to Abby. But what I don't understand is what you ever saw in me, given your thing for mothers."

"Oh, don't you know? You don't need to be a mother to be a mother figure. I always found that you possessed a multitude of maternal qualities. You probably weren't even aware of them."

"Probably not; not at the time," Nelly said. She absentmindedly picked up a shirt of Clark's that had fallen to the floor and carefully folded it up.

"See what I mean?" he said, indicating the folded shirt in her hand. "You were always doing little things like that. You used to straighten my collar and pick lint off my coat. Oh," he groaned, closing his eyes and holding his groin, "what a turn-on." He opened his eyes and looked at her.

"Would you mind if I sat on your lap for a while?" he asked, getting out of bed.

"I'm really not in the mood, Clark," Nelly warned, backing away.

"Then tell me a story," he pouted.

"Stop it!" Nelly screamed. "Just stop it. Quit acting like a baby."

"You like me better depressed, don't you?" he said accusingly.

"Maybe I do," she said.

"As long as we're on the subject, you seem to be suffering from a smidgen of the old Woe-Is-Me yourself," he said, fixing her with a cold, clinical eye.

"No. It's an obsessive-compulsive thing I've been going through," she said, quoting Dr. Abrams.

"Ah," Clark said, savoring the words like a fine French wine, "obsessive-compulsive. Well, you can't get a room here, not with just that. Not unless your doctor has a real in. Who is your doctor, by the way?

"I have no desire to check into Payne Whitney," Nelly snapped. "I just came to make a sick call. And getting as much of a kick as you do out of being shut away in a hospital really is sick, if you ask me."

"It is, isn't it?" Clark said, flattered by her observation.

Nelly laughed despite herself. She left the hospital with what almost had the makings of a good mood. Yes, she was running low on friends and lovers. She must widen her circle of friends, tap the second string, those people she had been so fond of over the years but never had the time to see. Completing her relationships with her old crazy pals left her free to make new ones. She felt optimistic. She could handle her life, she knew she could. She was never going to end up as a perennial Payne Whitney house guest like Clark. Not Nelly Diamond.

She was prepared to work hard at new friendships, put more energy into her job. She was prepared to do whatever was necessary to regain the happy, friend-and-lover-filled professionally satisfying life she had enjoyed only months before.

What she wasn't prepared for was the phone call from her parents. How could she have been? She would have had to be as crazy as Clark to anticipate their news. And she would have had to be a little saner than she was at that moment to handle it.

"Nellikins!" Ma and Pa Bell, in unison.

'Mommikins! Daddikins!" Nelly mimicked with affection. She was glad to hear from them.

"Guess what," her father said.

"What?" Nelly asked.

"Go on, guess," her mother urged.

"I give up," Nelly said, following what she thought was the routine formula.

"No, come on, guess," her father begged, his voice rising with excitement. "Just take a guess."

"Can you give me a category? Maybe a clue?" Nelly asked.

"Should we give her a category?" her father asked her mother. It was a new game, obviously. And so complicated that they had to consult each other on the rules.

"Sure, give her a category."

"A letter. What if I gave her the letter the category starts with and then she could guess the category?"

"That's good," her mother said, matching her father's enthusiasm.

"Okay," he said carefully, "the category starts with the letter s."

"No, honey," her mother corrected, "I think it starts with a p."

"A p? Why a p?" her father asked, perplexed.

"You know," her mother said meaningfully, "a p."

Her father thought that over.

"Well yes, you're right. Actually, we're both right," he told Nelly. "It's both an s and a p."

Nelly's mind had been wandering during all of this. She was brought back to attention again by her father saying:

"Okay, now guess. It's a big surprise and it has to do with something that starts with the letters s and p."

Nelly sighed. "Couldn't you just tell me?"

"We'll tell you this much," her mother said. "This is something you'd never guess in a million years." Her mother must have thought that this was a real giveaway clue.

"Okay, I'll play. An s and a p. Let's see. Does it have to do with slippers-pink?"

"No," her mother chortled, "guess again."

"Surprise party?"

"Nope."

"Silly Putty?" Nelly said, giggling. Maybe it wasn't such a bad game after all.

"Nope."

"Salt and pepper?"

"No."

"Standard procedure? Sausage pie? Skin peeling? Sales promotion? Signpost? Stereophonic?"

"Nope. Nope. Nope. Nope."

"Do you give up?" her father asked her.

"I wanted to give up twenty minutes ago," Nelly reminded him.

"Okay, here it is," he said.

"Oh, let me tell her," her mother pleaded.

"No, I want to tell."

"But you got to give the category letters," her mother complained. Nelly wondered if Payne Whitney had family plans.

"Okay," her father, always the gentleman, said. "Go on, tell her."

Her mother took a deep breath. "Remember Sarah?"

"My sister, right?" Nelly guessed. So far so good.

"Well," her mother said, slowly and distinctly, caressing each word with her mouth, "Your. Sister. Sarah. Is. Pregnant."

28   Leave of Senses

Nelly thought she was catching on. Now it was her turn to say something like, "The Pope is Jewish." Sarah pregnant? It wasn't that funny. She could do better than that. Wait. Maybe that wasn't the punch line. She pursued it further.

"What do you mean, Sarah is pregnant?" she asked.

"Sarah is pregnant," her mother repeated.

"We're going to be grandparents," her father said.

"And you're going to be an auntie," her mother shrieked.

Oh Jesus, Nelly thought, this is serious. The together couple has gone bonkers, simultaneously. I'm going to fly home and deal with this. I wonder if I'll have any problem getting a reservation. No, it's still early enough. The Christmas holidays haven't officially started. Maybe she could get them to come to grips with this on the phone. It was worth a try.

"Could you please explain how my sister Sarah, who is living with and having a relationship—and when I say relationship, you *know* what I mean by relationship—with another woman, could possibly be pregnant? Just because they're living in a foreign country and speaking a different language doesn't mean the laws of nature are different too. So could you kindly explain how this is possible?"

And her parents explained how. How Sarah and Schottzy, living in same-sex bliss, deeply in love, totally committed to each other, felt something was missing from their lives. So they arranged with Schottzy's brother, who happened not only to be a doctor but the honored donor, to have Sarah receive artificial insemination. And she did. And it took. And now she was pregnant and expecting the baby in the spring. And they were going to be grandparents and Nelly an aunt and wasn't it all so exciting?

Furthermore, her parents had come to accept their daughter's strange union. All was forgiven. For any union that could produce a grandchild was a union worth not only accepting but blessing. They were even flying to Dusseldorf for the holidays.

The numbness that Nelly had been feeling for the past week suddenly vanished. It was pushed aside by a sharp sudden knot, a deep, hard core of pain that settled in the center of her sternum and made it difficult for her to breathe.

Sarah, her sister, the one who used to put both legs in one hole of her underpants, who fed ducks blindfolded, who couldn't get the right shoes on the right feet, who couldn't remember a little detail like removing her arm before slamming a car door, who never ever seemed capable of taking care of herself, had managed, living in a lesbian relationship, to get herself pregnant. She was going to be the mother of a child.

Her parents were still talking. It was responsive reading. He first, then she.

Dad: You ought to write her.

Mom: She thinks you're mad at her.

Dad: Why don't you write her and tell her how happy you are for her? She'd appreciate that.

Mom: I've got a record that teaches knitting. I've already made a little sweater.

Dad: Isn't that a kick in the head, though? What do you think, Nelly?

Nelly wasn't thinking anything. She was screaming at the top of her lungs. Not her! Not her! It's not fair. It's just not fair! Except there was no sound. And there was no picture either. Something had been switched off, some little tube or transistor that controlled the thinking, feeling, responding portion of Nelly Diamond's program had been disconnected.

The audio returned long enough for her to mumble something apparently appropriate to her parents, she wasn't even sure what it was. She was just aware of her lips moving, and then she hung up.

This is not to say that Nelly had lost her marbles. She hadn't totally flipped out. She wasn't what Clark would call certifiable. She was aware of exactly what she was doing. She was monitoring her actions. She just wasn't analyzing them.

Dr. Abrams had once told her that the most important piece of advice he could give her was always to trust her instincts. She should follow her intuition and learn to act spontaneously and intuitively.

"One of your problems is you think too much, Nelly my dear. Act first. Think later."

237

"I think that's the opposite of what my mother always told me," Nelly had said.

"Ah, your mother," Dr. Abrams had said with great import.

But Nelly was not thinking about Dr. Abrams now. She was thinking how hungry she was. There was a hollow, forgotten feeling in her stomach. She felt as if she hadn't eaten in days and days. She was absolutely famished. It was not an unspecified hunger, either. She knew exactly what she wanted to eat. Not wanted, but craved. It was one of Abby's turkey-and-cranberry sandwiches on thick white bread with lots of mayonnaise and lettuce.

It never occurred to her that there was anything strange about driving out to Abby's house for a sandwich. Especially since she knew Abby had just left for Puerto Rico. Nor was she bothered by the fact that, once she arrived there, her hunger disappeared. Instead, she remembered there was something she had to pick up. And she knew exactly what it was.

A woman in her late sixties answered the door. She was wearing a black sweatshirt with white letters that said "Gray Power" over a pair of tight black vinyl pants. Her hair was done and sprayed into a high bouffant, as hard and white as the north face of Mt. Everest. What must once have been a strong jawline now melted into her neck in soft pleats. Her eyes had the same color and all the warmth of twin ball bearings.

"What is it?" she demanded. "Mrs. Cunningham isn't home."

"I know that," Nelly said. "I'm a friend of hers, Nelly Diamond. I came to pick up the baby."

"You're supposed to pick up the baby?" the glacial grandma asked. "She never told me about it. You know, we get paid by the head. And the company doesn't allow for reductions in pay after the job has been contracted for," she growled.

"Oh, I'm sure Mrs. Cunningham understands that," Nelly said.

Jill and Jane stuck their heads around the formidable figure of the baby-sitter.

"Hi Nelly," they shrieked, throwing themselves at her, perhaps thinking that she had come to rescue them from the clutches of the Pro-Gramma.

"Are you going to stay with us?" Jill asked hopefully.

"No honey, I just came to pick up the baby."

"Take me, take me," Jane pleaded. "I'm lots more fun."

"You've got to stay here, sweetheart. I just came for the baby." No further explanations were necessary.

Jill and Jane were delighted to get rid of their little sister, and once the Pro-Gramma had been convinced that she wasn't going to have to take a cut in pay, she went and packed a bag for the baby.

Nelly looked down at the crib. Jada was wide awake and staring up at her. Nelly hadn't seen her since she was born. She was now over four months old. She had astonishingly thick, dark hair. It framed her fat face in silky curls. Her eyes were total blue. Royal blue pupils surrounded by pale blue whites and outlined in dark, almost black lashes. She was a fat baby with folds, rather than bends, in her elbows and knees. Her feet and hands were large for her size. Her mouth was a tiny, delicate line of cherry red.

"Hi, Jada," Nelly said, touching Jada's fat little foot.

Suddenly the most amazing thing happened to Jada's mouth. From the tiny red line it opened and enlarged into a huge, gaping chasm, a fun-house door, a toothless, goofy grin that took up almost the whole lower half of her face. Nelly nearly swooned from that one smile.

"Isn't she ugly?" Jill said, leaning over the crib to poke her baby sister in the arm.

"Oh no," Nelly breathed. "She's beautiful. Just beautiful."

"She isn't either," argued four-year-old Jane. "She's ugly and she makes poo-poo in her pants."

"Well, she's just a little baby," Nelly reasoned. "Like you were once."

"I never did that," Jane said, insulted. "I always used the potty."

"You did not," Jill said, giving her sister a hefty push. "You made big grunts in your diapers."

"I did not."

"You did too."

The Pro-Gramma handed Nelly a bag with all the essentials and a car seat for Jada to ride in.

"Bye-bye, poo-poo pants," Jane called from the front door.

"Dirty drawers," Jill yelled. The girls giggled and pushed at each other. The Pro-Gramma turned and gave them a laser-beam look and they shut up immediately.

Nelly strapped Jada securely into her car seat. The baby pulled at the end of the strap with her pudgy, awkward hands. Her mouth was slightly open and a drop of drool was edging off her lower lip.

"Poo-poo pants," Nelly said, looking at her. "The very idea." She put the car in gear. "Okay, sweet puss, we're on our way to big times in the big city."

It never occurred to Nelly that she was doing something rash, let alone illegal. Her mind was working on a very basic level. When you're hungry, you pick up a sandwich. When you're sleepy, you grab a little shut-eye. And when you're feeling as Nelly was, you simply snatch a baby. Just like that. She was only satisfying a basic need in the most immediate way possible.

From the moment Nelly and Jada were alone, Nelly didn't stop talking to her. It was as though she had been waiting for someone to talk to all her life. She hadn't realized how lonely she had been. But it didn't matter. She didn't feel lonely any more. On the contrary, the one baby, the four-month-old soft, round little body made her feel like she was surrounded by friends, filled to the brim with family.

It was, by necessity, a one-sided conversation. Yet Nelly found it a strangely satisfying form of communication.

"Do you like your milk warm, Jada, or do you like it cold?" she said when they got to the apartment. "You like it just right? Well, I don't blame you. I think that's how people should drink their milk. Not too hot, not too cold, but absolutely just right."

She had no crib for Jada. So she pushed her bed into the corner of the room, then took all the extra pillows and bolsters and built a little three-sided fort.

"Are you wet? You are? You want some nice, new, clean diapers, do you? Well, I think we can arrange that. Nice new clean diapers for the most beautiful baby girl in the whole wide world. Yes, that's just the ticket."

Nelly took off the dirty diapers, washed Jada's beautiful baby-pink bottom, dried her, and sprinkled her with talcum powder. Jada cooed and blew spit bubbles from between her tiny red lips.

Then Nelly changed into her nightgown and, taking one of the baby books she had bought when she had thought she was going to be pregnant, she got into bed next to Jada. The baby grabbed hold of the silk ribbon from Nelly's nightgown and stuffed the end of it into her mouth.

"Is the baby sleepy? Yes, she is. She's very sleepy. She had a big trip. Well, we'll just read a little bit, then we'll go to bed."

Nelly couldn't keep her eyes open. She picked up Jada and laid her down against her breasts. Jada sighed and put her silky dark head on Nelly's neck. Nelly could feel her strong little hands playing with the skin on her throat, pulling and pinching without really hurting. The warm, live weight of her made Nelly almost groan aloud with pleasure. She felt an incredible feeling of contentment, an almost postsexual warmth and satisfaction. She closed her eyes. It was only seven o-clock, but she fell asleep.

She was woken up four hours later by the ringing of the phone. Nelly gently lifted Jada off her chest and reached for the phone on the bedside table.

"What, I mean what, in the world has gotten into you?" It was Abby. They had a bad, staticky connection and Nelly could tell only by the pitch, not the volume, that Abby was screaming. Other conversations in another language were getting crossed with theirs.

"Muchos la plada," a man was saying.

"Abby, is that you?" Nelly asked.

"Un momento, por favor," an operator was saying.

"Did you ever hear of a little thing called kidnapping? Do you know what they do to kidnappers? Do you remember what they did to the Rosenbergs?" Abby, in her hysteria, was confusing her executions.

"I didn't kidnap her," Nelly said.

Spanish.

"I don't know what else you call it when you take a child from her home without the mother's permission and/or knowledge," Abby seethed. "That's what Jeff would certainly call it. Lucky for you I haven't told him. He would want to fly back immediately. Now I want you to . . ."

More Spanish.

"What?" Nelly said.

"I said, I want you to take Jada back home right now."

"But Abby, she's fine. She's fast asleep." Nelly glanced over at the baby. She had half of her fist stuffed into that wonderful, ever-expandable mouth. She was making eating noises as she slept. "Oh, let her stay with me, just till you get back," Nelly pleaded. "I'll take good care of her, I promise."

"You could've asked me before I left. I would've said yes. But no. You had to sneak behind my back and get me in trouble with my Pro-Gramma."

"I'm really sorry, Abby. I had this sudden impulse. I guess I just felt like having company."

"Why don't you pick on someone your own size?" Abby said sternly. "You know, a baby, especially my baby, isn't going to bring you happiness."

"I'm not looking for happiness," Nelly said, her voice breaking for some reason. "I happen to be a very happy person. I just felt like baby-sitting."

There was a silence. "Maybe this will cure you once and for all," Abby said after a minute. "A week with a screaming baby might just do the trick. Okay. Fine. Be my guest. Keep her."

"Oh thanks, Abby. Don't worry, she'll be fine."

"But you better have her back at my house next Saturday morning by ten o'clock or Jeff is going to kill you. And best friend or no best friend, I'll call the CIA."

"Right you are," Nelly piped in.

"Your mommy sure has a temper," Nelly said, covering the sleeping baby with a blanket. She wedged a pillow in between her and Jada so she wouldn't roll over on her in her sleep.

Nelly gave no further thought to Abby's Saturday morning deadline. In fact, she was not thinking ahead at all. Her only concern was Jada: keeping her fed, keeping her safe, keeping her healthy, and keeping those smiles coming. She was living as babies do and as mothers are forced to, in the diaper-changing, milk-warming, back-patting, bubble-blowing present.

Had Abby's prediction of a crying baby come true, things might have turned out differently. Had Jada been one of those fussy, fretty babies, Nelly might have experienced all the frustrations, difficulties, and sheer boredom of taking care of a young infant. But, as luck would have it (or not have it), Jada was a wonderful baby—responsive, intelligent, interested. And she never cried.

At first Nelly worried about this. She had certainly traveled on enough airplanes, been to enough movies, attended enough weddings to know that babies did, in fact, cry. Was there something wrong with Jada?

But Jada was in that blissful in-between stage: she had accepted the bottle and was yet to be bothered by teeth painfully breaking their way through her soft pink gums. And, aside from all that, she just seemed to prefer smiling.

She and Jada were never separated for a moment. Included in the bag of stuff the Pro-Gramma had packed was something called a Snuggli. It was a complicated strap-zipper-bag affair made out of pillow-ticking material. It took Nelly awhile to figure it out. It went over the shoulders, tied in the back, and then the baby got zipped into the kangaroolike pouch in front. And that's how they went everywhere. The fabulous feeling of heavy, but not too heavy, warmth right against her belly made Nelly feel like she could walk forever.

She took Jada grocery shopping. At the time Jada was still on just formula, juice, and a terrible gluelike baby cereal. But, in anticipation of her changing diet, Nelly walked Jada by the shelves stacked high with baby food. She read the labels aloud to see if anything struck Jada's fancy.

Food shopping left a lot to be desired. But there was other shopping for the girls to do. Nelly bought Jada Tubby, an inflatable baby bathtub. She ordered an American traditional crib which wouldn't come for two weeks. It had four posters and a little ruffled canopy. It was a ridiculous thing to put a baby in, but Nelly loved it. She bought an imported English crib cover with something called Mr. Squirrel embroidered on it. Nelly didn't think it would go too well with the American traditional but what the hell, she thought, we can be eclectic. She purchased little shirts with hand-embroidered flowers, birds, and bees, a tiny hand-made quilt, two dozen baby-duck diaper pins. Abby used Luvs diapers. Nelly contacted a diaper service. She also bought baby shampoo, baby soap, an adorable baby brush and comb in the shape of a fish, and baby scissors in the shape of a stork. She took Jada to a children's store on Seventy-second Street called Sprouts, where everything was hand-made and incredibly expensive. By the time they left, Jada had a wardrobe that would make her the best-dressed baby on the West Side.

She also bought a baby scale, a baby bracelet with Jada's name on it, and a digital fever detector. She was still debating between a stroller or one of those wonderful English prams. She bought herself a diaper-tote travel baby bag that carried bottles, diapers, powder, ointment, and a change of baby's clothes.

Nelly and Jada followed the same simple schedule each day. Jada's breakfast, Jada's morning nap, play time, lunchtime, nap time, walk-in-the-park time, bottle time, shopping time, song time, dinnertime, bath time, hugging time, bedtime.

Each little thing she did with the baby gave Nelly incredible pleasure. She loved just watching her. Jada's mouth was always working, forever moving, sucking, drooling, opening, closing. She would take Nelly's finger and stick it in her mouth and suck on it. Those powerful, toothless gums and the wet, warm sucking set a tingle up Nelly's spine. She loved bathing her. Jada adored the water. The skin on the bottoms of her wide, flat feet was so brand new it was as soft as the skin on Nelly's hands. Her little fingernails were just beginning. There weren't even any half-moons showing yet.

She was amazingly strong. She liked to pull on things: Nelly's hair, the skin on Nelly's cheek. She would take Nelly's chin in her tiny fat fingers and pull and pinch until Nelly yelled ouch.

Only once did she start to cry. Nelly had gone into the kitchen to get her bottle. Just the beginning of a whimper and Nelly had come running back. But it had only been a try-out for crying. Seeing Nelly, Jada screeched with delight. She was all-powerful. She controlled, by invisible strings, Nelly's coming and going.

"Were you actually thinking about crying? I don't believe it. I just don't believe it." She lifted Jada high above her head and then brought her down again so that their two noses touched. She could feel Jada's cool drool dripping on her face and she laughed.

She concocted a whole bagful of names for the baby. Baby names, silly names, love names. Names she conjured up out of nowhere. Names that made no sense at all. Names that just seemed to fit.

Jadalah. Mootchky-Pootchky, BooBoo, Petunia Pie, Jelly Bean, Lumpkin, Baby Puss, Fishey, Love Bunny. She addressed her by a different name each time as though they were in a Russian novel. And without even realizing it, she stopped calling herself Nelly. She had a new name, too. She now referred to herself as simply Mommy.

"Is Mommy's BooBoo hungry? Yes, she is. She's very hungry and she wants to have her bottle and Mommy's going to heat it right up for her."

"Did Mootchky-Pootchky make a poo-poo in her diapers? I think she did, and now Mommy's going to change them so she'll be a nice sweet-smelling lumpky pumpkin."

It was silly; it was absurd; it was baby talk and she just couldn't stop herself.

Nelly dressed Jada for the cold winter day in a new quilted, down-filled baby bag and a soft knitted cashmere hat.

"Mommy's going to take Bunny Breath to the park and we'll look at the snow. Isn't that a wonderful idea?"

The doorbell rang. Who could that be? Nelly wondered.

"Mommy better go and see," she said to Jada, hefting her comfortably onto the shelf of her hip, where she seemed to fit as though Nelly's body had been designed for her.

She opened the door and a suntanned Abby rushed in.

"Jeff is fit to be tied. He's double-parked downstairs, and if I'm not down in two minutes I think he's going to storm the place." Without waiting for a response, she pulled Jada out of Nelly's arms.

"You promised you'd have her back this morning," Abby yelled. "We had to make a special trip all the way into the city."

Nelly didn't say anything. She just stared at Jada. Something terrible was happening to the baby's face. It was turning from pink to red to crimson. Jada's eyes were scrunched shut and her little mouth had opened to its widest possible position. But no laugh came out. Instead, there was a strange, high-pitched sound that Nelly hadn't heard before.

She was crying! She reached out her fat, sausage-link arms toward Nelly. Nelly stood frozen in place. She wanted to cover her ears to block out the appalling sound.

Even through the closed door, she could hear Jada's cries from all the way down the hall. She felt her own lungs filling, felt herself gasping for air. Her face turned red, as red as Jada's, and then the tears burst forth. But there was no sound. Only that of Jada's angry screams as Abby waited for the elevator.

It was like one of those vaudeville acts, where one person does the arms and voice while standing behind the other person, who does all the facial expressions and lip movements.

Jada was doing the crying and Nelly was doing the tears.

The elevator must have come, because then it was quiet. Only then did Nelly put a sound track to her tears, her sobs taking up where Jada's had left off.

She collapsed on the couch, holding one of Jada's new cloth diapers to her face to muffle the sound and absorb the wetness.

29 No Room at the Inn

Like most New York shrinks, Dr. Abrams had no receptionist. Just a small waiting area with the usual collection of periodicals: *Art News, Opera News,* and *Down East Magazine.* No one ever read them. But then no one ever waited in the waiting room, either. It was a matter of courtesy. Even though the inner office was sound-proofed, you never knew what might leak out, especially during a highly emotional session. And hearing someone else's session could be even more traumatic than having someone hear yours.

Nelly was not into waiting that day. It hadn't even occurred to her that Dr. Abrams might be busy with someone else. She had not bothered to make an appointment. How can you make an appointment for an emergency? She just went right on in.

Dr. Abrams looked up, startled. He was sitting, as usual, in his brown Barcalounger. There was a tiny, birdlike woman sitting in the chair opposite him. She was holding herself tightly with one arm as though her bones would fall out of their sockets if she didn't. The other arm was bent up and her thumb was in her mouth.

"Nelly!" Dr. Abrams exclaimed, "what is this?"

The woman let out a small cry as though Nelly had just confirmed her worst fear: that someone, someday, would burst into the middle of one of her sessions.

"Excuse me, but I have to talk to you," she said firmly.

"I'm sorry," the woman squeaked over her thumb. "I'll go." She started to get up. Her eyes were red. The mascara was smudged darkly beneath them, giving her face a bruised, beaten-up look.

"Sit down, Mrs. Kimmelman." Mrs. Kimmelman sat down and hunched over her thumb again. "Can't it wait?" Dr. Abrams said angrily.

"No, it can't. If it could wait, I would've waited, wouldn't I? I have to talk to you now," she said, just as angrily.

"I'm sorry, I'm really sorry," Mrs. Kimmelman said, starting to get up again.

"Sit down," Dr. Abrams commanded.

"Sorry to interrupt you," Nelly said, turning to the woman. "I'll be happy to pay for your hour."

"Mrs. Kimmelman was right in the middle of something very important, Nelly. I believe she would like to finish," he said, looking at the folded-up woman.

"Oh no, no, that's okay. I'm really sorry."

"I'll make it quick," Nelly said. "I need to be committed."

"Ohmygod," Mrs. Kimmelman cried. "Ohmygod! Oh, I'm so sorry." She stuffed her hanky in her mouth along with her thumb and gagged.

"Don't do that," Nelly warned the woman, "you're going to spoil your mouth." She turned back to Dr. Abrams. "I kidnapped my best friend's baby."

"You did?" Dr. Abrams asked, showing the first signs of concern or mild interest. It was difficult to tell which. "Do you still have the baby?"

"No, she took her back. But you have to admit that it was a crazy thing to do and I really should be put away. I'm simply not responsible for my actions," Nelly said, remembering what she thought were the buzz words for the criminally insane. "Could you please call Payne Whitney and arrange a room for me as soon as possible?"

"No, I can't. First of all, I'm not affiliated with Payne Whitney. Second, I don't believe in having people committed spur-of-the-moment. Third, being committed isn't going to help you work out your problems. It's merely a delaying tactic."

"Oh, I'm so terribly sorry," Mrs. Kimmelman was saying again. She twisted the wet hanky around her thumb and chewed on the corner of it.

"Stop saying that, Mrs. Kimmelman. This isn't your fault. And take your thumb out of your mouth. You're too old to wear braces," Dr. Abrams snapped.

Mrs. Kimmelman removed her thumb and smiled weakly at the doctor. Nelly could see that the woman was, indeed, wearing braces. With rubber bands. Dr. Abrams swiveled his chair to address Nelly.

"You are most certainly responsible for your actions," he said. "Who else would be? Certainly not me. Assuredly not Payne Whitney. Obviously not Mrs. Kimmelman here." Mrs. Kimmelman shook her head. Under cover of her hanky she was sneaking her thumb back toward her mouth.

246

"That leaves you, Nelly girl. You have to take responsibility for your life, for your actions, even for your bizarre behavior. Tell you what I'll do," he said, taking his prescription pad from the desk and writing on it. "Here's a prescription. Get it filled and take two every morning with juice."

"What is it, a tranquilizer?"

"No, it's a multivitamin. You know I don't believe in tranquilizers. Now I want you to pull yourself together and call me after the holidays. It's going to be a tough pull, Nelly. This is a bad time of year. As I told you before, get involved with other things. Your friends, your family. Take a trip. Do some Christmas shopping. Buy yourself something nice. Even better, buy me something nice." He chuckled at this last. "And keep in touch, in constant touch with your feelings."

"A multivitamin," Nelly mumbled. She stared at the prescription and shook her head slowly. Then she turned and started out the door.

"Wait a minute," Dr. Abrams called after her. He was writing on his prescription pad again. "This is against the rules and I don't like doing it, but if there's really an emergency, then use this." He tore the sheet off the pad, folded it into fours, and handed it to her.

"What's this?" Nelly asked, looking at the square of paper.

"It's my mantra," Dr. Abrams said. "Don't look at it unless you absolutely have to."

The Muzak in the elevator at Payne Whitney was playing "Joy to the World." Clark was decorating his room with red and green pine tree branches made of aluminum.

"Hey-hey-whaddya-say. Long time no see. Slip me five, now slip me ten." Clark was even more into his manic stage than before.

Nelly ignored his outstretched palms, walked over to the bed, took off her coat, scarf, and shoes, pulled back the covers, and got in. She sighed and then pulled the sheet up over her head.

Clark stared at her for a second. Then a strange gleam came into his eye. Making a running jump, he landed on top of the bed with such force he nearly knocked her off.

"Want Santa to stuff your stocking?" he asked, bouncing up and down on top of her sheet-covered body.

"Leave me alone," Nelly said, her voice muffled.

Clark stopped bouncing and looked down at her.

"Wait a schecond, schweetheart," Clark said, slipping into his horrible Humphrey Bogart imitation. "Can't exchpect a fella like me to control hishself around a looker like you."

"Please, just leave me alone," Nelly pleaded in a tiny, trembly voice.

Clark leaned back, studying her curiously.

"Hold on just one little minute. You're not planning on staying here, are you?" There was no answer. He was getting agitated now. "Nelly, you can't stay here. This is my room. My commitment. It's my nervous breakdown," he yelled.

Nelly lowered the sheet off her face. "Just for a few days," she pleaded. "Just until I get my self together."

"You're crazy," Clark said disgustedly.

"I know," Nelly sighed. "But all I need is just a few days. Just till after Christmas."

"Nelly, they aren't going to let you stay here, I'm telling you." He tried to pull the sheet away from her but she held it firmly to her chest.

"I'll hide in the closet," she said, yanking the sheet out of his hands.

"And *I'm* not going to let you stay here. If I wanted to entertain people for the holidays, I could've stayed home and had eggnog parties." He got her shoes and shoved them under the sheets. "Come on, get up. A manic-depressive is not somebody to toy with." Nelly turned her back to him. "I'm warning you," Clark said, clenching his fists, "I'll get violent."

"Go ahead and get violent. You don't scare me. Nothing scares me."

"If nothing scares you then go back out there," he said, indicating the Manhattan skyline, "and give them hell."

"I can't right now. Believe me. I just can't."

He looked at the skyline again, walked over to the window, and closed the curtains. "I know what you mean," he sighed, sitting down on the bed. He thought a minute. "Well, okay, maybe just for a few days. But don't think you're getting any of my medication," he warned.

He pulled back the sheet on his side of the bed and got under the covers with her.

"Uh-oh," he said, "I think I'm slipping into my depressed stage. Don't try to talk to me."

"Don't worry. I won't."

The nurse found them curled up like twin fetuses. It took a second nurse, two orderlies, and finally a doctor to talk her out of bed, get her shoes and coat on, and get her back out on the street. They were gentle with her. But firm; very firm.

It was December twenty-third and the streets were crowded with people. Christmas shopping, Nelly remembered from somewhere in the not-too-distant past. Christmas shopping.

She was carried along by the mass of people to Fifth Avenue and then into Rockefeller Center, where the huge Christmas tree stood, its lights made even more colorful by the dark, cloudy day. There was a chorus from a Catholic girls' high school. They were all dressed like the Virgin Mary and they were singing a song of the same name.

Nelly's mind had emptied itself. She was operating on automatic. Her eye picked up isolated scenes like a videotape receiver. She had no control over what was being shot. All she could do was register it. The pictures she was receiving were all part of a colossal "Christmas Family Special."

Cut to: a good-looking couple in their late twenties. The man is tall and dark, the woman is almost as tall and blonde. Strung out between the man and the woman are four children, ages five on down. They are all (including the mother and father) wearing identical Chesterfield coats and red scarves. The man is playing daddy to the hilt. He thinks he's Ted Kennedy. He roars instructions jauntily to his small band of Chesterfield coats.

"Come on, kids. Everyone hold hands now and we'll cross the street. Hut-two-three-four. Right, left, right, left."

They knock smaller, less-organized families out of their way.

Cut to: another family, very large. Only four of them, but together they must weigh almost six hundred pounds. They are all very dark and all have mustaches varying in density according to their age and sex. The father carries the little girl in his arms. She alone must weigh ninety pounds. The kids' cheeks are red and round as though their mouths are stuffed with pomegranates. The mother is angry at the big little boy.

"You're a person," she says, shaking his soft shoulder so hard that his cheeks jiggle, "now act like a person. Stop acting like a child." The boy's round red face turns even redder and his mouth opens in preparation for the tears. The mother takes a huge soft pretzel out of her bag and shoves it in his mouth. He smiles around it. The mother notices Nelly's stare. She winks at her as if to say: Kids! Aren't they something?

Pan across: families forming happy little huddles. Posing for pictures. Posing, Nelly feels, for her.

"Okay kids, get closer together now." The father has red hair and a red lumber jacket and a lot of expensive-looking camera equipment strung around his neck like Hawaiian leis. "Sally, look at Daddy. Mother, wipe Jeffrey's face. He's got chocolate all over it. Sally, look this way. Look at me. Look at the camera. Mother, can you put down your shopping bag just for a second? Okay, everybody, look at me and smile. Wait a second. Excuse me, miss," he says to Nelly, "would you mind taking a picture of the family?"

Nelly takes the camera without a word. The man runs over to the rest of the group. Nelly looks through the viewer. Amazing; they all have the same noses. Even the wife. Big, parrotlike noses. That's how they find each other in crowds, Nelly thinks, by their noses. She takes the picture and hands the camera back to the man.

The families all seem to be clearly identified by some characteristic marking. Like birds. Some have the same noses, some the same clothes. Sometimes it's the height or weight. Sometimes the hair color or curl. Or teeth or freckles or the way the feet turn in or out or just the sound of their voices.

The voices. Nelly was picking up a cacophony of dialogue.

"Stop a second, Jimmy, and tie your shoe before you trip."

"Barbara, you are not to cross the street without us. How many times do I have to tell you? Do you want to be a traffic accident?"

"Why didn't you say you had to go while we were in the restaurant?"

"Sweetheart, you can't just take things off the counter like that. Mommy has to pay for them first."

"Tamara, watch the fuck where you're walking."

Parents fussing in that loud, proud, important parental way. Why were they talking so loud? Raising their voices. Not for the kids. The kids could hear. They had ears, all right. No. It was an announcement to the rest of the world. Like station identification.

"This is Walter Schmidt, father of three."

"This is Mrs. Brenda Falk, mother of two, with one on the way."

"This is Earl and Nancy Greenfield of Teaneck, New Jersey, parents of six."

They were all announcers. Mom and Dad voice-overs: See this kid here? He's my kid. I made him. I grow him. He's my creation. The fruit of my womb. The issue of my loins. The delight of my eye, flesh of my flesh, my hope eternal, my reason for being, my footprint in the sand, my notch in the tree. Proof positive that I was here. I mattered. I had my say. I left my mark. I paid my taxes. He may not look like much to you, snot-nosed, scrape-kneed as he is. But this is no inconsequential kid. This kid is my corporate logo. He's my goddamn peacock, is what he is.

Everyone around her is attached, connected, touching. Kleenex to bloody knees, hands to shoulders, mittens to gloves. Everyone is holding onto someone. Holding onto thick, down-filled arms, holding onto tops of heads, steering bodies. Holding onto purse straps. Grabbing onto trouser legs. Holding onto carriage handles. Touching, connected. Holding. Fixing. Fussing. Scarves being wound round and round again. Hats replaced. Shoelaces tied and retied. Noses wiped. Faces slapped. Tears dried. Hands held.

She felt like an alien. Like someone from another world. The streets, the city, perhaps the entire planet was inhabited by strange multiheaded, six-, eight-, sometimes ten-legged creatures. They moved around her in their stumbling, many-footed way and she felt as if she were the only two-legged being on earth. All the rest were families.

She is in Korvette's. She feels tired and sick to her stomach. What is she doing here? she wonders. Christmas shopping? There is an announcement on the loudspeaker:

"Will the mother of a three-year-old boy wearing a red parka and blue corduroys who answers to the name of Ronnie please come to the security office on the sixth floor."

250

Little Ronnie is crying to beat the band. A security guard is crouched down next to him, trying to get him interested in a green lollipop that is shaped like a Christmas tree. Ronnie wants no part of it. The guard smiles up at Nelly and stands back from the little boy. Nelly bends down and sweeps him up in her arms.

"Okay, Ronnie honey. Stop crying. It's okay. Everything's going to be just fine," she says.

"That's the tenth one today," the guard is saying. "We've really had a run on them."

Ronnie is still crying, though not as hard now. He is clutching Nelly's neck. His face is hidden in her scarf. Nelly pats his fanny and makes shooshing noises as she carries him out of the office and down the escalator to the first floor.

"Look, Ronnie, look at the pretty angels," she says, pointing up to the ceiling where sparkly silver and white angels blowing long golden trumpets are suspended by invisible wires.

Ronnie stops crying and looks up.

"Everything's going to be okay," she says, not knowing quite what she means. "You want to see Santa Claus?" she asks him. He is still looking up at the angels and still holding onto her neck with one small, tight-fingered hand. His mittens are tacked onto the sleeves of his parka.

A flush-faced woman with wild curly hair, dressed in an identical red parka, runs up to Nelly and grabs the boy out of her arms. She squeezes the little boy and smiles at Nelly.

"Oh, thank you so much," she says. "Thank you for taking care of him. Ronnie, you scared Mommy. I thought I'd lost you. That's what happens when you let go of Mommy's hand." She smiled again at Nelly. "Now thank the nice lady." Ronnie stares at Nelly and then bursts into a fresh batch of tears.

"Well," the mother shrugs, "I guess we're a little upset." She walks away, still talking to the boy.

Nelly walks out of the store. Outside there is a man roasting chestnuts and soft pretzels. The smell hits her and she feels like she is going to get sick all over the sidewalk. She has no control over her stomach. It is turning against her. She hates being sick. The very idea of vomiting is enough to nauseate her. For some reason losing her lunch here on the sidewalk, in front of all these people, is more appalling to her than losing her marbles in the middle of Korvette's.

There are no taxis to be had. She walks home through the fields of families, fighting the need to puke every step of the way. The cold fresh air makes her feel better. By the time she arrives home, she doesn't feel sick anymore. She is just tired. Tired beyond belief.

I must have the flu, she thinks, falling on the bed. She reaches for the thermometer in the drawer of her bedside table. It is the same thermometer she used to keep track of her ovulation when she was trying to get pregnant. Even the chart is still there. She stares at the thermometer. She can't remember when she had her last period. It was way before Thanksgiving. But she can't remember.

A cold spasm of fear grips her stomach. A terrible thought flashes across the screen: something is wrong with her. Something is really, physically wrong. Except when she had the pelvic inflammation, she has never missed a period. Never.

The sheer terror she is now feeling brings all the fuzzy edges of her mind into sharp, frightening focus.

She got up off the bed and started pacing the room. She felt her stomach. She couldn't feel anything. But people say you can't always feel cancer. Maybe it's a hysterical pregnancy. That would be just my speed, she thought.

But she knew with a dreadful certainty that she had been through too much. Her mind was too well versed in the principles of pregnancy to fall for that.

Something was definitely wrong. And for once it was not in her head. There was bile in her mouth, a weariness that went all the way through to her bones. And there was the horror of not being able to see what was going on inside of her.

It could be tumors. Malignant? Benign? She couldn't remember which was the good kind and which was the bad.

Her tubes had been the first to go, scar up, shrivel away. Now it must be the ovaries, or the cervix, or the uterus. Tumors thriving on her inoperative flesh. I'll have to have a hysterectomy and my breasts will shrink up and slip sideways off my chest and I'll grow a beard. And if the cancer spreads, then I'll have to die.

I don't want to die. She said it aloud.

She was starting to feel hysterical. She took one of her old tranquilizers and got into bed. I don't want to die, she whispered again. Then she was angry. Goddamn it. It's not fair. Then she had another thought: maybe it all makes sense then: a doomed woman was not destined to have children.

She fell asleep, her fists tightly clenched, her teeth gritted, awaiting a nightmare. She had a dream. But it wasn't a nightmare. It wasn't entirely sane. But it was a pleasant sort of dream, nonetheless.

It was something about her grandmother, in the kitchen, trying to stuff a very large grapefruit into a very small chicken.

It struck her as funny and she woke up in the morning smiling. She got out of bed slowly. She felt much better. She fixed herself a good breakfast: poached eggs, whole-wheat toast and honey, juice, and coffee. She sat down at the kitchen table, picked up her fork, and broke the egg so that the golden yolk ran thickly over the white. She dipped a corner of the crisp toast into the egg and ate it. It tasted delicious.

The next thing she knew she was holding onto both sides of the toilet bowl, retching her guts out. Oh Jesus, she said, I am really sick. I'm in terrible trouble. It all came back to her: she was dying. Hurry, she thought, before it's too late.

She had to see a doctor. It was Christmas Eve. The only doctor who was familiar with her insides was Dr. Hoffman. She called him.

She got an appointment and immediately felt better. Maybe it's just a flare-up of my pelvic inflammation, she thought. Just a matter of taking a bunch of antibiotics. No big deal. There's no more harm that can be done at this point. Did he say that she could have a recurrence? She didn't remember. But she did remember that she hadn't felt like this the last time. This was definitely something different.

Nothing had changed in Dr. Hoffman's office. The same magazines, different issues. It seemed the same women were waiting, only the shoe styles had changed. And the same stern nurse.

"Take the bathroom on your left, empty your bladder, and save me some urine in this," she commanded, handing Nelly the same yellow, flowered cup.

Same Dr. Hoffman.

"Lie back; put your feet in the stirrups, please."

Nelly was too tense to lie back. "I think it's something serious," she said, forewarning him, her voice quaking. "See, I haven't had my period and I've been feeling terribly sick and . . ."

He didn't want to talk to her. He wanted to talk to her snatch. It was too bad women didn't have microphones in their vaginas, Nelly thought.

"Just lie back," he said, "feet in the stirrups." Nelly lay back. "Now relax. This will feel a little cold at first."

What's a little cold in the face of eternal winter? Nelly thought. Her feet were shaking in the stirrups. She stared up at the ceiling. The crack that was once there was gone. He had had the office painted.

"Hmmmmm. Hmmmmm. When did you have your last period?" he asked.

He was talking to her in the examination room! It must be serious!

"Uh, sometime in October, I think. I haven't exactly been keeping track."

"All right, Mrs. Diamond, get dressed and we'll talk about it in my office."

It. The unnameable, unthinkable It. What was It?

Dr. Hoffman stuck his head back in the room as Nelly was getting off the examining table. Another first.

"By the way, did you give my nurse your urine specimen?"

"Could I have gotten in without it?" Nelly snapped, clutching the paper cover to her chest.

There were three other women in the waiting room when she went back to take a seat. It was only minutes later when the nurse signaled to Nelly.

"Who, me?" Nelly said. "I don't think it's my turn."

"That's all right, the doctor wants to see you now."

Oh, it's true, Nelly thought. It's deadly serious. He wants to get me to the hospital as fast as possible. They're going to cut me open. The longer she stalled, the longer she wouldn't have to face the truth.

"Oh no, I'll wait my turn," Nelly said sanctimoniously.

"It's your turn now," the nurse said impatiently.

Nelly glanced at the other women, hoping for a last-minute reprieve. Wasn't anyone going to complain? Why didn't they say anything? What happened to their New York sense of fair play? She sighed and got up shakily.

Dr. Hoffman was making notes in a chart. Her chart?

"I think you'll find this very interesting," Dr. Hoffman said. Is cancer interesting? Are hysterectomies interesting? Is death interesting? Perhaps to a doctor, Nelly thought.

"At least I find it very interesting," he was saying.

Nelly gathered up what scraps of courage she had left and forced herself to be brave. "What is it?" she asked.

Dr. Hoffman looked up from the chart and smiled.

"You're pregnant," he said.

30 A Shot in the Dark

She felt like she had had this conversation before. It must be everybody's idea of the sick joke of the year.

"Pregnant? How can that be?" Nelly said, leaning forward in her chair. She knew what it was. He had the wrong chart.

Dr. Hoffman opened a desk drawer and took out the pink molded plastic form that was supposed to represent a woman's body, and then, pointing with his silver pencil, he said:

"You see, the sperm swims upstream here, through the cervix . . ."

"No! I know how it's done!" Nelly shouted. "I don't mean that. Dr. Hoffman, are you looking at the right chart? My name's Nelly Diamond."

"I know what your name is. And this is your chart."

"Well, if you'll examine it more closely, you'll see that my tubes were scarred due to a pelvic inflammation and that I can't get pregnant. You told me so yourself after I had that thing in the hospital."

"The culdoscopy. I know what I told you. But I also said that there was a chance that the procedure could open up the tubes. I said it was a chance in a million. I was exaggerating the odds a little, because I didn't want you to get your hopes up. But it is rare, very rare. You see, the pressure of the liquid being forced through the tubes can cause the adhesions to open. It can clear the way. Now, when did you say you had your last period?"

"I don't believe it," Nelly said. She was in a daze.

"Your last period. When was it?"

"I don't believe it," Nelly repeated. She snapped to attention. "Let me see my chart." He handed her the chart. The notes were indecipherable. "Where does it say that I'm pregnant?"

"Here," he said, taking the chart back from her and writing on it. He held up the chart so she could see the big letters he had scrawled across the bottom: PREGNANT, they said.

"Now, when was your last period?"

"I don't know," Nelly said. She could barely talk.

"It doesn't matter," he said, turning to a fresh page in the chart. "It would help to pinpoint the exact delivery date, but I would say from my examination that conception must have taken place around the first of November. It looks to me like you're about seven weeks pregnant. So, if I were you, I wouldn't make any plans to go backpacking next August."

A chance in a million, impossible odds, a shot in the dark. But this sperm didn't need light. One in a million. One, in fact, out of 787,000,000. An Olympic swimming champ, making his way tirelessly through the thickening mucus of the cervix, through the perilous expanse of the uterine walls, swimming, swimming, propelling himself upward against the strong current, upward, ever upward to the junction of the tubes, where he hung a left, or maybe a right, continuing through the impossibly narrow channel, through the scarred battlefield of her fallopian tube.

Up and up, gasping for breath, fighting every inch of the way. Tapping energy from some unknown source. Straining with every drop of protoplasm. Seeing now, at last, the end in sight. Invisible to the human eye, but not his: a star on the horizon, a tiny round pearl, Nelly's egg.

Now, swimming in slow, graceful motions, covering the last few inches or miles—for each centimeter was a marathon mile—tail vibrating in anticipation, arms ourstretched (no, no arms), tail quivering with passion, moving toward the object of his desire, slowly, gracefully, as a lover runs across a field of flowers toward the girl of his dreams.

Nelly's egg awaits him, heart thumping, passions soaring, hopeful in spite of the odds, waiting, wanting, expecting, praying, knowing.

And they meet and embrace and kiss and whisper sweet nothings, and then, his tail draped lovingly around and, perhaps, already into her erogenous roundness, they set out together into the sunset (what sunset?) to find a home in the warm, cozy, rose-tinted womb below. To be together for always and ever, to whither-thou-goest, to love and to cherish. To start a new life.

And so Nelly was with child. Was expecting. Had one in the oven. Was knocked up. Was preggers. Was pregnant. Was walking on air.

Good old KWRZ, Albuquerque. Had to be him. Who else? That special hardy desert breed, able to withstand extremes in weather, able to travel long distances over rugged terrain. A veritable pioneer. A Daniel Boone of spermatozoa.

The first of November, the night of the affiliates meeting. Nelly had picked right after all. Number one for Nelly. Number ten for the tiger.

If Nelly had been the tears-of-happiness type, she would have cried for joy. But joy caused a different reaction in her: a gleeful, girlish, foolish, almost uncontrollable giggling.

She stood on the corner near Dr. Hoffman's office trying to hail a taxi and control her giggles at the same time. No one was about to pick up a woman who was giggling to herself in the middle of Park Avenue.

Finally a taxi stopped. She leaned back in the seat and roared. It was like one of those marijuana-induced fits of laughter. She would simmer down for a second, almost stop, sniff once, then sniff again, trying to catch her breath in short little intakes of air. And then the sniffling would strike her as funny, and off she went again on another run of the giggles.

She felt as if she had just heard the ultimate punch line to the world's longest, most tedious joke, the capper that made it worth sitting through the whole horrible story in the first place.

She should never have doubted that there would be a delivery. She had been right to expect it all along. All those months of anticipation, frustration, failure, and despair. How else could it have ended but like this? How could she have ever doubted the outcome?

She let herself into her apartment, dropped her bag, untwirled her scarf, and threw off her coat. She pirouetted into the bedroom, stretched her arms straight out and fell backward on the bed. Then she sat up abruptly and jumped off the bed. She couldn't stop moving.

She went into the bathroom and looked at her reflection in the mirror. Her eyes sparkled, her cheeks glowed, her whole face was doing the radiant mother bit. She kissed her reflection. Would the baby look like her? Of course it would. With a set of extrafull lashes and a pair of warm green eyes, courtesy of the father. It would be the most beautiful baby girl in the world.

A girl was what she wanted, what she expected, and by God, what she would get. She would never, never again doubt her ability to get exactly what she wanted.

Her pregnancy would be the most peaceful, the most problem-free, grand finale'd by the most natural of natural childbirths. She would talk Ben into doing it as a special. Not just any two-minute slot, but a full hour. Live. She would have the Le Boyer method where they played music and used soft lights. The music wouldn't be taped, either. She'd hire the Juilliard String Quartet. The whole thing would be lit by one of the big-name Broadway lighting designers. And she would do the commentary herself:

"This is Nelly Diamond, WABC News, in the delivery room. Birth is scheduled for later on in the second half of the show. Pains are now coming every minute and a half. With me here tonight is Dr. Eric Hoffman, noted OB/GYN. Other guests include nurses Juanita Sanchez and Pearle Urbach, plus assorted friends, family, and crew members. Dr. Hoffman, do you have any comments?"

"Well, everything is proceeding according to schedule. Dilation is up to six centimeters. Baby is in position. I think we're going to have a fine delivery tonight."

"Nurse Sanchez? How many deliveries have you assisted at?"

"This is my three-hundredth. But I think it's the most exciting. It's just a thrill to be here tonight."

"We'll be back with more, right after this message. This is Nelly Diamond, in labor, at Lenox Hill Hospital, New York."

The baby would have a beautiful birth, a healthy babyhood, and a glorious growing-up. She would go to the best schools, have the prettiest clothes, take piano, ballet, and tap, have millions of friends, lots of boyfriends, and grow up to be the most famous woman in the history of the world.

What would she be? The first female president of the United States? No. That was too trite. Not to mention too trying. The first woman secretary of state? Too much traveling. Too much exposure to bad water and long-incubating parasites. The first female head of the Supreme Court? No. That was too somber. All those black robes and old men. The first female chief of staff of the armed forces? Too regimented. Too dikey.

Well, it didn't have to be a steady job. It could be an unheard-of feat. First woman to sail around the world solo? No, some woman had already done that. First woman to break the speed of sound? That's been done, too. In fact, by the time she came of age, women will probably already have done everything. Pushy broads. Couldn't they give a kid a chance?

What about the first woman pope? Of course, that would mean Nelly would have to convert. It was a nice place to live, beautiful jeweled vestments, but no sex. No way for a gorgeous young thing to spend the rest of her life. Wait a minute. What about the first female messiah? A fun-loving, easygoing, all-forgiving, down-to earth, sexy messiah. And not one of your martyred messiahs, either. No crucifixions, no cross to bear for our girl. Nelly wondered if you had to be related to God to be the mother of a messiah. Mary certainly wasn't. That was another thing. She'd be the first maternal messiah. Nelly's daughter would be the mother of many, many children.

She looked around the room. The stuff she had bought for Jada was piled on a chair. She would make a reconciliation gift of it to Abby and then start all over from scratch. Her baby girl would have everything a baby girl ever wanted.

Something occurred to her then. Something essential to little girls. What was it? Ah, yes: a daddy. How could a girl grow up without one? Her baby was not going to be a fatherless child.

In fact, her baby would have to have the best of all possible fathers. But who would it be? KWRZ, Albuquerque, was out. Ditto Clark and Brian. What about Tyler? No, Nelly thought, he was too unsettled, too unsure about whether he wanted to be a mother or a father.

She realized she had been involved with this baby business for so long that she had neglected her love life. She didn't know any men. Well, she would get right onto that. The perfect father. He would have to be kind, intelligent, brave, loyal, and true. He would have to possess good comon sense, a sense of proportion, a sense of fair play, and a sense of humor. It would also be nice if he was nice-looking. And rich wouldn't hurt, either. But Nelly would settle for a steady annual income. She made enough. He should also know how to carve a turkey.

How would Nelly know if a man was good father material? A lot of men made good lovers, even terrific husbands, but this guy would have to excel at fatherhood. Maybe she should look for a man who was a father already. It would be nice for the baby to have other brothers and sisters to grow up with.

She could check the obituary columns, keeping an eye out for young widowers with small children. She might join Parents Without Partners. Whatever she did, she had better get started before her belly got in the way. Or maybe that didn't matter. Maybe that was a good way to screen them out.

Well, she certainly had her work cut out for her.

What about a nationwide TV search? A test. Like the National Health Test. Only this could be the National Father Test. Would the network go for it? It was worth a try. Certainly Ben would at least allow her a brief spot on the evening news . . .

"Hi, this is Nelly Diamond, WABC News. Tired of living alone? Looking for a place to hang your hat? A child to call your own? A lovely, devoted wife who earns her own living? Well . . ."